SONATA
OF
ELSIE LENORE

SONATA of Elsie Lenore

Copyright © 2020 Ann Christine Fell

Cover image by Onalee Nicklin / onaleenicklin@hotmail.com

Interior format by Debora Lewis / deboraklewis@yahoo.com

ISBN-13: 9781658168069

A Novel of Suspense

SONATA
OF
ELSIE LENORE

Ann Christine Fell

~ For Donté ~

*May you, like Stefano, find the inner strength
to meet all of life's challenges.*

sonata (so-NAH-ta) noun
A musical composition, often for solo piano,
in three or four extended movements
contrasted in theme, tempo and mood.

PART I: ALLEGRO TEMPESTOSO

1

LENA VALDEZ CRINGED when her husband hammered the Steinway piano lid with his fist.

His rage growing, Enrique's knuckle bones threatened to burst through his skin. "I told you," he said, "no more of this Lecuona crap. Do the jazz. Tonight we want the best Cuban jazz." The youngest of the three Diaz brothers punctuated every other syllable with his fist until the piano's heavy bass strings vibrated with a rising cacophony.

She shrank from every blow.

"Understand?" he yelled.

"*Sí*, Enrique," she said.

"Get to the jazz. I'm counting on you tonight. *¿Comprendes?*"

She looked down, her fingers rubbing the familiar ivory ridges of the piano keys.

"*¿Lena?*" he said.

She felt rather than saw his arm rise and spoke with haste. "Please, Enrique. Don't hit the piano."

"Jazz then. Hear me?"

She nodded. Yes, she heard him. How could she not? She could hardly recall a time he spoke to her without yelling. "*Sí*, I will play jazz."

"One hour. Then we dress for the show. No more Lecuona."

She flexed her fingers, took a deep breath, and leaned into the keys. A recent island melody by Jorge Marin swelled from the piano. Swinging with the beat, Enrique danced out the door of the Caribbean Breeze, a nightclub in New Orleans.

Her hands flew over the keys as she coaxed melodious rhythms from the worn Steinway. It wasn't that she hated jazz. After all, jazz expressed Cuba's heart and soul. It sang of the courage and beauty of her countrymen. She loved jazz, but she loved classics more and she needed Lecuona right now. Their mother raised her and her brother on Lecuona, embracing classical Cuban tradition.

Lena completed the Marin number and stifled a sob.

"You okay *Señorita?*" Roberto, the bartender and manager of the nightclub, peeked in from a back room.

She nodded. "I will be fine."

"I heard some yelling," he said and cocked his head, inviting her to say more.

She forced a laugh. "Enrique. He's always yelling," she explained away the outburst. "It will be fine."

"If you're sure."

She nodded and met his gaze with a grateful nod.

He turned back into the storage room. She waited a moment, gathering her nerve, her fingers silent on the piano keys. In a timid voice, she said, "Roberto?"

When he didn't respond, she tried again, louder. "Roberto?"

He stuck his head through the swinging door again. "You say something?"

"I just wondered if you would tell me where I could mail a postal card." She fished a postcard from her handbag.

"Sending greetings from good old New Orleans?" he said with a smile.

"*Sí.* I want to contact my brother."

"Stefano? How is he anyway? I heard he'd tied the knot with a beauty from up north somewhere."

She nodded. "I just want to let him know I am here. Where could I mail the card?"

He extended his hand. "Leave it with me. I'll make sure it goes out tomorrow."

"*Gracias*, Roberto."

The bartender disappeared into the back room with her card. Lena took a deep breath before she continued her rehearsal. If only Stefano would meet her here. Would he even get the postcard in time? He didn't know she was booked at the Caribbean Breeze, their old favorite nightclub. Maybe he wouldn't even believe she was here, set to perform on Mama's piano, "Elsie Lenore." He sure didn't know she'd married into a family of drug smugglers or that she was miserable.

He didn't know.

She launched into another Marin number. At its close, she whispered into the keys, "Elsie—Elsie, what will I do?"

Unexpectedly, her mother's voice whispered in her mind. "We do what we must."

In a flash of recollection she visualized the lewd sneer of her former stepfather as he appraised her youthful body and her mother stepping between them— "Not my daughter, you bastard!" Her mother had split up with that man before the next week passed.

A year later a new gentle suitor presented her mother with the same Steinway she'd lost after the Revolution. A gift from her father when she was young, she had fondly dubbed the piano Elsie Lenore. It was offered as a wedding gift for the woman he'd loved all his life and Lena's mother could not refuse his proposal. Lena and Stefano had grown to love that piano as much as their mother did.

Her mother's voice whispered again. *We do what we must.*

"Yes, we do." Lena's hands teased the keys as she pondered her limited options. Elsie Lenore and her brother Stefano offered one thin thread of hope. Surely he would understand. He had to.

Her fingers caressed the keys and cajoled an Afro-Cuban piece from the belly of the piano. The melody grew, and then waned. She dropped her left hand and allowed her right hand to sketch a rhythmic melody up the keys as she diverted her left hand to the piano case.

Following the melodic sequence, she ran her fingertips to the treble end of the mahogany trim at her waist and pried upward. With a full-keyboard glissando, she moved to the bass end and inched up the trim until the keyslip was free of its mounting screws. She placed it across the music desk without the slightest click.

The music soared again when her left hand joined in. She strummed repeated staccato chords, lifted her hands at the finale, and froze, listening.

Silencio.

Roberto must have gone out for a few moments. Nobody remained inside the club.

She retrieved a set of dining utensils and a paper napkin from the nearest table and spread the napkin beneath the bass keys. Slipping the knife tip underneath a key, she scraped against the key frame, teasing a fine white dust to the edge. She repeated the process under four keys, and scraped the powder onto the napkin. Tossing the knife to the floor, she lifted the napkin's corners, cradled the powder into its middle, and with a sigh folded it into a tiny envelope. Her brother would have been proud to know she'd learned some intricacies of piano construction. She, for her part, was grateful for his fascination with the technical side of the instrument.

"*Gracias*, Stefano," she whispered.

She tucked the parcel securely into her cleavage, replaced the trim, and lost herself in the music.

2

"WAKE UP, STEFANO," a woman's voice reached through the haze in his dream world. A gentle hand tugged on his left foot. "Wake up, son."

Confused, Stefano Valdez asked himself a silent question. *¿Despiértate?*

"Are you sleeping under my piano again?" Isabel Woods chuckled as she tapped his knee.

He pushed against the concrete floor and rose onto his elbows, bumping his head on the heavy beams underneath a grand piano. Rolling to his knees, he backed out from under a parlor-sized Vose grand piano and grinned at his mother-in-law. He rotated his shoulder blades and winced.

"What are you doing under there anyway?"

"I was checking the soundboard ribs. Guess I dozed off."

Izzy offered a hand and pulled him to his feet. "You better wrap things up here. Mel will be worried if you're late."

He snapped to attention, shooting a glance at the wall clock. "Six-fifteen—she will flog me."

Izzy shook her head. "You had a nice long nap, evidently. Though I don't know how on that hard floor."

"Gotta go," he said and bounded through the open shop door.

≈≈≈

Stefano tiptoed into the kitchen of the duplex apartment in Arkansas City, Kansas, where he and Melody lived. He stepped behind her and wrapped his arms around her eight-months-and-counting pregnant form. She twisted to face him and their lips met in a passionate kiss.

She melted in his arms for a moment before jabbing his chest with her forefinger. A teasing smile lit her face. "Bit late tonight, aren't you?" she said.

"Sorry, Mel. I nodded off under the Vose."

She attempted a scowl before her face crinkled and she laughed. "Do I have to get you a piano to lull you to sleep?"

He sighed, wagging his head in mock defeat. "*Sí... sí.* You found me out. I can't sleep without a soundboard over my head."

"You certainly haven't been sleeping in our bed at night," she said, tapping his chest with a serving spoon.

"Better than you, I'm sure." He patted her pregnant belly and turned, sniffing the air.

"Shrimp gumbo?"

Melody nodded.

He savored the aroma and twirled a spoon in the gumbo. "My favorite."

"What happened to good old black beans and rice?"

"Anything you cook is my favorite. You sit down. I've got this, *mi enamorada.*" He ushered Mel to their crowded living room and settled her into a recliner squeezed between the front door and an upholstered loveseat. He handed her the day's mail and returned to the kitchen to set the table. "Dinner for two, coming right up. Soon to be three," he said with a smile.

"Can't be soon enough for me. I'm more than ready."

"Ten more days, right?" He returned to the kitchen and busied himself at the stove.

"Ten years in my calendar," she said. A moment later she raised her voice. "Did you hear the news?"

"Guess I slept through it. What news?"

"It's all over the TV. Sounds like geologists are anticipating a really big earthquake somewhere in the Pacific." She shuffled the mail.

"They can predict an earthquake?" he asked.

"New technology, you suppose? Look here, real mail—a picture postcard. And..."

"What is it?"

Her tone changed to puzzlement. There was a long pause before she said. "It's for you."

Stefano stepped into the arched doorway, a pitcher in his hands. She raised the card to display the lavish hotel lobby pictured on the front. He set the pitcher on the kitchen table and took the card. On the back side, a small caption identified the photo as Embassy Suites in New Orleans. His shoulders dropped as he read the penned message.

"You're pale. What's up?" she said. "Stefano?"

"It's Lena," he said in a piercing whisper. "She's in New Orleans."

"That's impossible. After Hurricane Francine when I found you under the church piano, we looked everywhere. We put the entire resources of Global Relief Service behind the search. But she'd vanished. It's been what—almost twelve years?"

"I know. We gave up."

"And it's not the policy of Global Relief to give up until there's no hope left."

"You'd know all about that, as many disasters as you've worked. When I went to Havana, I couldn't find a trace of her, but maybe she did find a way home." Stefano's voice trailed into his reverie. "And now she's back."

"The card can't possibly be from her. If she was still alive, why didn't she contact you sooner? Or at least acknowledge your search? This has to be a scam."

"I might think so too, but this is her mark. It was something she dreamed up when we were kids and nobody outside the family would know about it."

"Why wait until now to contact you? It makes no sense."

"I agree. It doesn't make sense, but here it is. Lena is in New Orleans." He ran his fingers through the black curls on his head. "And she wants me to go there too."

"No way, Stefano. Look at me."

He patted her belly. "I know. Bun's 'bout done." He shoved the postcard into her hand. "But read this."

"It's in Spanish. Read it to me," Mel said, "And translate, please."

He swallowed hard. "Lena says, *'Dearest Brother, I'm playing The Caribbean Breeze. Elsie Lenore is here too. Please come when you get this note. Urgent. We need you.'* Then, her trademark signature. At the bottom she scrawled, *'Remember we loved Ernesto Lecuona's "Vals Arabesque." It's all in the melody.'*"

3

THE ROOM GREW so quiet Stefano could hear the gumbo simmering on the stove. He rubbed his fingertips over the card, and wilted onto a chair across the room from Mel, his brows drawn together. He felt as ragged as the worn carpet between them.

"Stefano—what does it mean?" Mel asked.

He shook his head and met her gaze. "I'm not sure—I can't think. There's a deeper message here, but I can't say what it is."

"Why did she wait all these years to contact you?"

He shook his head.

"Stefano, we looked and looked after that storm. Where was she then? How did she survive?"

"I can't answer you, *mi flor.* She wants me to understand something but why not just say it? Is she being watched? Does she want to avoid suspicion?"

"Suspicion of what?"

He shook his head. "Out of the blue, she sends me a card. I had given her up for dead.... Yet here she is. Something changed. I don't know what."

"Let's take it at face value. Maybe she escaped to Havana after the storm and had no way to contact you. Maybe she thought you were dead and gave up on you. Now she's back in the states and somehow she found out you were here. She invited you down for a visit. Simple and sweet." Mel's waving hand dropped to her belly. "Lousy timing."

Stefano shook his head. "No. It's more than that. I feel it."

"What do you mean?"

"The Caribbean Breeze is the club in New Orleans where we played our last gig together."

"So?"

"Why would she go there again? Why wouldn't she just call me? She obviously knows where I am, even if I knew nothing about her."

"You think it's a coded message or something?"

"I can't think. But, I dreamed about her this afternoon for the first time since our wedding. Her eyes were beseeching me, begging me for something."

"Give me a break. It was just a dream."

He shrugged. "Here's the card."

"A dream, Stefano. You can't put any credence in a dream."

"My grandmother always did. She could interpret dreams."

Mel raised her voice. "Now you're going to set out a glass of water to appease the spirits?"

Stefano waved away her derision. "Dreams hold your future if you understand them."

"Lena wants you to drop everything and go down to New Orleans and she told you so in a dream?"

He nodded, narrowing his eyes, willing her to understand. "A dream and a card."

"How long will she be there?"

"Doesn't say."

"She could be gone already."

He rubbed his thumb across the inked postmark. "Or not. Postmarked two days ago."

"Who's that other girl anyway? Someone she wants to hook you up with?" Mel's voice rose a notch.

Stefano looked at her, a bemused expression on his face. "You mean Elsie Lenore?"

"Yes. Who is she?"

"I already have a relationship with Elsie Lenore."

"Stefano." She spat out his name. "Don't mess with me. I am not in the mood." Her eyebrows scrunched together as she glared at him.

"It's not who, it's what," he explained. "Mother called her Steinway Elsie Lenore."

"A piano. THE piano? Don't tell me Lena shipped your mother's piano over here so she could play a nightclub in New Orleans. Are there no pianos in Louisiana?"

"I know. It just doesn't make sense."

"Not just. Stefano, it's nuts. Who would do that?"

"My question is why? She wants me down there for an urgent reason that has to do with our mother's Steinway."

"Oh, no. No, you don't. You can't be thinking you'll actually go to New Orleans—you can't."

"Mel, I don't know."

"Stefano—"

"You heard her—it's urgent. She needs me. Elsie Lenore needs me too, though I can't imagine what that means."

Mel struggled to rise from the sofa. "Stefano. Look at me." Her heaving breaths shook her pregnant belly. "I. Need. You. Too."

"*Sí*, I know." He sighed. The piercing look from his wife shot daggers through his heart.

"Come, my love. Let's dine on that gumbo." He stood and gripped her elbow with tenderness, guiding her to the table in the kitchen. He pulled out her chair and helped her into it. He stirred the gumbo once more before he turned off the burner and transferred the pan to the table. "May I?" He asked in a gentle voice, his words coated with tenderness.

She relented and allowed a tiny smile to curve her mouth upward.

"One dipper or two?" he asked with a bow.

"One for now."

Stefano spooned the steaming concoction into her bowl. He shook out a napkin with a flair no professional waiter could best, tucked it into her collar, and tweaked her chin as he backed toward his chair.

After dinner they cleaned up the dishes together. "You know we have to talk about it, Stefano," she said as she washed a plate. "The big fat elephant in the room. And I don't mean me. I know you've got that card on your mind. It's looming like that pending earthquake. What will you do?"

He toweled a glass and polished its rim. "What will we do, you mean?"

"No. I mean what will you do? I can't do a damn thing right now. I'm kind of stuck."

"I don't know what to think, let alone do."

"I know what you need to do. Help me bring your child into this crazy mixed-up world."

He closed his eyes and ran his fingers through his dark curls. "What if her life is in danger, Mel? What if it's do or die? I'd never forgive myself if something happened to Lena because I ignored her cry for help. And then there's the Lecuona *Vals*. What in the world did that mean? I can't think."

"Do or die, huh? What peril could she possibly be in?"

"Who knows? Cuban history is rife with murder, deceit, corruption."

"Sounds pretty normal for any country."

"Shush," he said. "Let me sleep on it. I need to figure it out." He turned to face her, arms raised.

After a moment's hesitation, Mel walked into his embrace. "I'm sorry. I know you're worried about your sister. It's just—I can't do this without you."

4

STEFANO FLIPPED OFF the light as Melody crawled into bed. He drew the blanket up to her chin, patting her belly as his hand passed over. "*Buenas noches, mi enamorada,*" he whispered and kissed her tenderly.

"G'night," Mel murmured.

He lay in the dark, eyes wide open, staring at the blackness. Though Mel's breathing eased into the regular pattern of sleep, his mind remained active. She twisted in the bed, turned to her side, and released an unconscious moan at the effort. He closed his eyes and tried to relax. Every few minutes he was jostled into wakefulness when Mel rolled or twisted in her perpetual discomfort.

When his mind drifted toward slumber, Mel's jostling morphed into the nudges of the terrified crowd in New Orleans years ago as Francine swept across the city, the first hurricane to surpass Katrina in sheer destruction. He threw his arm over Mel's shoulders, and they became Lena's in his half-wakefulness. The vision of their last moments together haunted his dreams. They had raced to the lobby of the New Orleans hotel that fateful afternoon with other hotel guests, employees, and terrified pedestrians from the street where they awaited evacuation. The crowd's contagious panic drowned his rational thought. The roar of their frantic voices escalated as the wind battered the windows three stories above them in the open atrium.

He clung to Lena's shoulders, his arm draped tightly around her. Without warning, the upper level windows shattered. Rain water driven by 120 mile-per-hour winds pelted the crowd. People screamed as glass shards knifed through the throng. Bodies pressed against him from all directions until a current of humanity flowed toward the exits, surging like a river whipped with torrential rains. The human tides split and coursed toward doorways on opposite sides of the lobby.

He clung to her rigid fingers, but the tide was too strong and her fingers inched from his grasp, her nails, gouging his palms as they were forced apart and the crowd separated brother from sister. He twisted his head, reaching backward, determined to remain connected. Her arm stretched toward him and her gaze clung to his with twin desperation. As they locked eyes, a wall of water surged through the front doors, driven by hurricane winds into the submerging city. He was tossed away from her with half the crowd, a piece of living flotsam on the storm tide. He swam for his life, fighting against the current, searching with every breath for his sister's terrified face. She clung to a column in the lobby, her mouth open in a scream he couldn't hear above the storm.

That last vision of Lena had haunted him ever since. It directed his desperate search through the ruins after the water receded. It drove his tireless laps through thousands of refugees that landed in the stadium. He chased her vision through mountains of debris left by the storm and was the last thing he saw before his exhausted body dropped into a deep slumber under a piano in a small parish cathedral.

When he woke, Melody Woods was looking at him, as beautiful as an angel. Through the following days, this experienced Global Relief worker guided him through all the avenues for locating a missing person. Weeks turned into months. And during their fruitless search, a love blossomed between them. When at last, in tears, he exhausted every tip and resource Global Relief Services offered, he resigned himself to the reality he'd never see Lena again. Mel brought him home to Kansas where they were married and he began the arduous task of creating a future devoid of his past.

Beside him now, she stirred in their bed. He massaged her back tenderly and smiled as she murmured her gratitude. She remained his angel, the one thing that had pulled him from suicidal despair. And therein lay the problem.

He couldn't possibly choose between his new family and Lena. But he now believed his sister had somehow survived that hellish storm. She was alive and had asked for his help. He couldn't ignore that. Why did life always present such impossible conundrums?

Stefano tossed, unable to sleep. What did Lena want him to glean from her note? Why would she transport Elsie Lenore to the Caribbean Breeze? Why wouldn't she give him advance notice of her tour? Did she think he could drop his own life and run to see her? That wasn't Lena. She had always been the planner and scheduler in their duet act. How did she find out where he was? And find the correct address? Did she know he was married? The Lena he knew would have asked them both to come months ago—if she'd been able to do so. Deep down, he knew she would never have asked him to come if she'd known about Mel's condition.

He rolled over and wrapped his arms around her—around his whole family. He rested a palm on her distended belly and smiled when the little one moved, a ripple crossing her abdomen. Mel stirred. With a sigh, she returned to a deep slumber. He pushed away and tiptoed from the room, resigned to his sleepless night.

In a few days, they would welcome a child to their family. They raced toward the finish line like cars at a drag race. For Mel, it would drag by. Ready for the event, she had long ago packed a bag for the hospital, including a tiny outfit for their newborn son and clothing for herself. He felt prepared to be there and support her through the labor and birth. The day they'd anticipated was almost upon them.

But then Lena sent him a card.

He didn't blame Mel for being upset. How could he even think about leaving, heading to the Breeze to meet his sister?

Stefano couldn't shake the feeling that Lena's note meant volumes more than she'd penned. The words sounded desperate and mysterious. What if he'd never have another chance to see her? He longed to see her face light up when their eyes met, to hold her in his arms. To play that Lecuona *Vals* with her once again. To tell her about his expected child.

In the ten days before the due date, he could fly there, check things out, discover what Lena wanted, and bring her back here. What would that take, a couple days? He'd be back with days to spare.

Unless the baby made an early appearance.

No. He banked on the accuracy of the doctor's prediction. The baby wouldn't arrive late since the doctor would induce Mel's labor if need be. But early? That would be bad for him if he was in New Orleans.

What other options did he have? He supposed he could call. He'd look up the phone numbers for the hotel and call them. He'd call the Caribbean Breeze for that matter. He had maintained contact with its proprietor, Roberto. A couple phone calls would tell him all he needed to know and appease Melody's anxiety, not to mention his own.

He brewed a pot of coffee and settled into recliner, ready to greet the dawn. His eyes fluttered closed. When he opened them again, Mel was gazing at him. He remained lost in her eyes while she caressed his cheeks with her fingertips.

"Rough night?" she said.

Stefano nodded. "Lots to think about."

"Thought you were going to sleep on it?" She flashed him a teasing grin.

He shrugged.

"What did you decide?"

"I'm going to call that hotel and the nightclub. See what they can tell me over the phone."

Mel smiled. "That sounds reasonable."

He lowered the recliner's footrest and struggled to stand. Mel offered her slender hand and he rose to her embrace.

"Oh, my God," she said, wincing. "I ache all over."

"We're on the last lap, my dear," he said in commiseration. "Just a few more days."

5

EVERY TIME SHE drove across the cattle guard at the Double M Ranch, Izzy shivered. Though she'd accomplished years of routine service work here, the harrowing events of the previous decade proved impossible to shake. She expected to be past the memories and the sense of foreboding the place instilled in her, but not so. Though Brett Lander had long since removed the remotely controlled gate and its tracks, she still felt apprehensive when her car rumbled over the steel bars of the cattle guard. She paused on the driveway, closed her eyes and took a deep breath.

Adagio, Isabel. Calm down.

She managed to drive into the pasture and wound along the dusty track. Mounted on Star, his favorite quarter horse, Brett cantered straight toward the spot in the road where their paths would intersect. His eyes met hers and he tipped his hat. She stopped the car on the circle drive and got out to face the rancher.

"Isabel Woods. Right on time," he said, swinging his leg over the saddle and dropping to the ground.

She followed him inside the ranch house with her piano service bag. She set her tool bag down and rummaged inside. He was silent, gawking at her face. She flushed and ducked her head. Formerly employed as a federal agent, he'd helped her out of an intense situation a few years back and never failed to fluster her with his magnetic personality and direct approach. She looked up into a teasing twinkle in his eyes and shook her head. "Maddi coming home this weekend?

"As a matter of fact, she should be here today. Maybe even before you finish."

"I'd love to see her." Izzy raised the lid on the grand piano and laid her felt mute strips along the keys.

"How's Mel these days? Isn't that baby due about now?" Brett asked.

"A few more days."

They each stared silently into the other's eyes before he nodded conclusively. "I've got to round up some cows, so I'll leave you to the piano." He strode briskly from the house.

An hour later, Izzy completed the routine tuning and ran a micro-fiber dust cloth over the cabinet. Tool case in hand, she headed to her Prius where Brett waited astride Star. He grinned at her and nodded toward a thin wisp of dust rising from the pasture lane.

"Maddi?" she asked.

"In the flesh."

Izzy greeted Maddi with a smile as the girl parked her blue Focus beside the Prius. "Izzy," she called as she threw open the car door and dashed into the older woman's embrace. "G-g-great to see you."

"Easy, girl," Brett said. "Breathe."

"How are you?" Izzy said.

Maddi pouted. "My classes are s-s-so demanding. I don't have time to get down here as often as I want." She turned to Brett. "You working cattle today?"

"Got a couple of heifers to bring in," Brett said.

"Can I go with you? I'll change right now."

"I'll go saddle Lady." He turned toward the corral.

"Izzy, come with me. We have to c-c-catch up. How's Mel? Has she had her baby yet?"

"Not yet." Izzy returned to the house, answering questions about Mel while Maddi shed her school clothes and donned a plaid shirt, jeans, and cowboy boots.

Outside again, Maddi swung into her saddle and took Lady's reins from Brett. He mounted Star and turned his mount toward a distant bawling heifer. With a click of his tongue, he urged the quarter horse to an easy trot and headed toward the distress call. Maddi followed on her mount.

As Izzy headed to her car, another wisp of dust spewed into the air along the lane. She called to the riders and waved toward the column of dust. He turned his mount and trotted to the hitching post.

"Wonder who that is?" Brett said.

Maddi had turned her horse in a wide circle and cantered easily along the edge of the yard.

"You expecting a friend this weekend?" he asked her.

She reined in her mount and shook her head. She hung to the rear as the car stopped and a sandy-haired young man hopped out. He bounded toward them, an expectant smile on his face.

After an awkward silence, the stranger scratched his head. "Is this the Double M ranch?"

Brett nodded, his demeanor blank. "May I help you?" He dismounted and sauntered toward the young man who grinned again, as if they all should know who he was.

After a moment's hesitation, the stranger extended a hand toward the older man. He raised a taunting eyebrow and said, "Hi, Dad."

6

BY ELEVEN THAT morning Stefano had completed the preparation work on the Vose piano in Izzy's shop. He slid the piano's action, complete with polished keys and reshaped hammers, into its cavity, ran a lightning chromatic run on all 88 keys, and pulled up a bench. Flexing his fingers in preparation, he struck a chord and dove into a passionate melody.

His father-in-law, Kurt Woods, stepped into *the* shop. Stefano nodded at him and played another phrase.

"I thought that sounded like you," Kurt said. "Beautiful song."

Stefano nodded in agreement. "A love song I wrote for *mi enamorada*. Our song—Melody loves that tune."

"I thought I recognized it. It was played at your wedding, wasn't it?"

"*Sí.* She needs it now, I think." Stefano grew pensive. "Anyway, I'm glad you're here. I could use your help to crate this piano."

While he knelt and reached under the keybed to remove the pedal lyre, Kurt rolled the long, rectangular skid board beside the waiting piano. They removed the leg beneath the bass keys and lowered the piano onto the carpeted board. Together they tipped the lidless piano onto its side.

"Thanks, Dad," Stefano said. "I can take it from here."

"Is this the last piano for your Cuban shipment?"

Stefano nodded. "This makes four decent instruments headed to the Institute for the Arts in Havana."

"I bet you'll be relieved to get this done before my grandbaby arrives. You'll be plenty busy after that. Changing diapers. Midnight feedings. Pampering your wife."

Stefano ribbed him back. "The voice of experience, no doubt."

"How's Mel? No baby yet?"

"Naw. Nine more days. You know that."

"Could come early."

"So I hear. But Mel's fine."

"Got your cigars ready?"

"Cigars?"

"Haven't I mentioned that? Old tradition. A new father will hand out cigars to announce his child's arrival."

"I better get some pronto."

"Cuban cigars, right?"

"Think I can find any here?"

Kurt grinned. "If anybody can, you can."

"I will add it to my list."

"I'm going to grub up some lunch before I skedaddle back to campus. Want a sandwich?"

Stefano shook his head. "I'll finish here and head in to eat with Mel."

Kurt waved as he headed to the kitchen. Stefano fit the extra case pieces into slots designed for their safe transportation and sealed the shipping crate shut with a row of long screws. He left the shop and headed around the building toward his small truck. On the south side, he leaned against an antique hitching post, soaked up the warmth of the sun, and checked the time. Even after a late night, Lena was sure to be awake by now. He withdrew his phone from a hip pocket. After slipping her postcard from his shirt pocket, he entered the phone number listed for the hotel and double-checked the sequence of numerals before he clicked the green call button.

The phone rang twice. A hotel desk clerk answered the call.

"I wonder if you'd connect me to one of your guests. Lena Valdez?"

"What room?"

"I don't know the room number. Can you look her up?"

"Sorry sir. Against our policy. We respect the privacy of our guests."

"Could you at least tell me if she's still there?"

"Sorry sir. Against our policy."

"Look," Stefano said, struggling to control the exasperation creeping into his voice. "I know you don't know if I'm a kook or a stalker. But I'm her brother. I'm only calling because she mailed me a card—your hotel's card—and asked me to see her. I'd like to talk to her please."

"Sorry sir—"

"Against your policy. I know. Thanks for nothing." He disconnected the call. What now?

❧ ☙

Izzy met Brett's astonished gaze, her eyebrows raised. She snapped her open mouth closed and stepped back, watching intently.

After a moment of stunned silence, Brett said, "You're mistaken. I have no son." He twisted his hand from the younger man's grip.

The stranger grinned, his eyes steely. "No mistake," he said. "You're Brett Lander, aren't you?"

"Yes."

"I'm Dirk. Dirk Lander."

Brett stared at him, speechless.

"Surprised?" Dirk said.

"You could say that," Brett answered. "Tell me why you think I may be your father."

"Because my mother told me so."

"Who might your mother be?"

"Remember Dee? Deanna Martin?"

"Dee." Brett's whisper hissed in the stillness of the air. The heifer bawled in the distance. "Why didn't she tell me?"

"I think she's been sort of mad at you for a long time."

"Sort of mad?"

"Okay. Really mad. She didn't want to share me. But after my rebellious teen career, she said I was too much like you and we deserved each other."

"You were a handful."

"Damn right."

"What are you, about twenty-five?"

"Turned twenty-six the fourteenth of last month."

Izzy said, "I can definitely see a family resemblance."

Brett and Dirk studied each other. They stood the same height and looked at each other with sky blue eyes. Dirk's hair, however, was a sandy brown contrasting with the silver-lined black waves under Brett's hat.

"Twenty-six. I had no idea." He turned to Izzy, his mouth open, eyes wide. "My son?"

Izzy nodded but said nothing.

The young man cleared his throat. "Like I said, Hi, Dad."

Brett took a step backward, removed his hat and rubbed his hair. He shook his head. "I don't know what to say."

"How about, 'Hi, Dirk?'" Izzy said.

Brett looked at her. "My son." He repeated the thought, his brow wrinkled with confusion. His gaze bored into Dirk's eyes as he gripped the hitching post and leaned heavily against it. He looked at Izzy. "I have a son," he said, his voice uncertain.

She smiled and nodded. "Apparently so."

Brett beckoned Maddi over. She dismounted without a word and led her horse to the hitching post.

Brett turned back to Dirk and pulled his son into an embrace. "I have a son. My God—I have a son. I don't know what to say."

Maddi slipped beside Brett, her gaze aimed downward at the artist's pallet of brown-tinted dormant grass. She blinked rapidly as she avoided looking into the visitor's piercing blue eyes.

"It's okay, gorgeous," Dirk said. "I won't bite." He grinned, accenting the dimples in his cheeks and stepped toward Maddi. "How about introducing me to this pretty young thing. My sister perhaps?" He nodded at Izzy. "Her mother?"

"No such luck," Brett said draping an arm across Izzy's shoulders. "This is my piano tuner and friend, Isabel Woods. He gathered Maddi into his free arm. "And this young lady is Maddi Campbell, one of the M's in the Double M ranch. She's actually my boss and a very good friend."

"That's even better," Dirk said. "No relation." Dirk stepped close to Maddi. "I hope we might get better acquainted."

Maddi flushed. Her mouth dropped open and she took two steps backward.

"Watch it, Dirk," Brett said. "You harm one hair on her head and you'll answer to me."

"Calm down, Dad," Dirk said, an element of sarcasm evident as he addressed Brett. "I appreciate a beautiful woman when I see one. Just like you." He winked at Maddi.

"Exactly what I'm afraid of," Brett said under his breath.

Maddi leaned close to Izzy and whispered. "He's chocolate."

"Chocolate?" Izzy whispered back.

"Yes. Ch-chocolate. Smooth, creamy, luscious chocolate. Oceans of sweetness. Melting. I'm melting in ch-chocolate oceans. I-I-I've never sensed this in my life."

"Ah. Chocolate." Izzy understood. The girl who had always experienced emotions through strong fragrances had just discovered a new emotion. Her heart was aflutter and she smelled chocolate. Given her previous repertoire of scents— lavender, fecal material, lemon, cinnamon, turpentine— chocolate was a first. This could be serious.

Maddi stepped toward Dirk. "Hi," she said and laughed. "D-d-dirk. Pleased... pleased to meet you." She dropped her eyes and gave a little curtsy.

Izzy said, "Folks, I've got to go." She drove out the pasture lane, watching the three of them in her mirror engaged in animated conversation, with no interest whatsoever in her departure.

They hadn't even noticed she was gone. High time to head home.

7

THE BREEZE.

Stefano would call the Caribbean Breeze. Roberto might know Lena's schedule.

He consulted his phone's contact list, found the Caribbean Breeze and hit the call button. Relieved when he actually recognized the voice that answered, he said, "Roberto? This is Stefano Valdez."

The surprise in Roberto's voice was genuine. "Valdez—hey man, how are you doing? I can't believe it. Your sister was just in here for a gig. She got hold of you then?"

"Yeah," Stefano said. "She sent me a card. You told her I moved to Kansas?"

"First thing she asked, if I had seen or heard from you. It was a bit strange, though. She asked real quiet, like she didn't want her husband to hear."

"Husband? She's married?"

"Some bad dude from Havana."

"She sounded strange in the card, a little desperate. I want to find out what's going on."

"You and me both, man."

"*¿Qué tal?*"

"If I was you, I'd be worried."

"Lena—tell me she was all right."

"Lena?"

"*¿Sí?*

"She played as awesome as ever, but she looked tired and kind of stressed out. End of her rope, you could say."

"Stressed out."

"And then, the strangest thing, the three of them just disappear and leave the piano here."

"Piano?"

"Yeah, man. They insisted on bringing their own piano. I said, not necessary. I got the best. They insisted. Like they weren't having it any other way. I said okay. It sure was good to hear Lena's music again. Then they just go off and leave the piano here."

"Elsie Lenore."

"What?"

"That's the piano. Our mother's piano. Lena's note said Elsie Lenore was there and they both needed me. It's still there?"

"For now."

"What's that mean? Do you expect them to return?"

"No. I don't think I'll be seeing them again. Hey—I don't know that there's anything you can do for either your sister or this here piano. Lena disappeared. And some nut broke in here the night after her gig and smashed up the piano."

"Smashed?"

"Yeah, man. Like took an axe to it or something."

Stefano sucked in his breath, air whistling through his teeth. "You still have the piano?"

"Yeah. But I'm gonna have it hauled to the dump."

"Save it for me, would you? I'll be there tomorrow."

Stefano re-pocketed Lena's card and his phone and jogged toward his truck as Izzy returned from the Double M ranch. He waved.

Her Prius rolled to a stop beside him. "How's the prep work?" she asked.

"Done," he said. "Got all the pianos crated and ready to ship. Do me a favor?"

"If I can."

"Would you be able to meet the trucker day after tomorrow?"

She consulted her phone's calendar. "Looks like it. I've got that day scheduled for shop and office work. Why? You planning on an early baby?"

"Hope not. I gotta make a quick run to New Orleans." He backed toward his truck. "Thanks, Mom. Love you for it."

"Wait a minute—New Orleans?" Izzy repeated, yelling after him. "What?"

But he was already driving toward the county road.

8

THE UNSEASONABLY HOT afternoon sun blazed against the roof on the two-bedroom duplex apartment. Stefano braked to a stop, stirring a layer of dust on the pavement to dance in the still air. Having spent his childhood in the tropics, the heat didn't bother him. He burst through the front door. Mel sprawled on the loveseat, arms and legs spread across both cushions. Cheeks flushed, and forehead glistening with perspiration, she squinted at him when he opened the door. The air had been dry enough since the rains stopped last June that dust gave him a continual urge to clear his scratchy throat, but she could hardly catch her breath at times.

He paused to squeeze her hand. "Where are the snowflakes when you need them?"

"This is February, isn't it?" She moaned.

"Last time I checked."

"Doesn't seem like it. I'd give anything right now to lay in a fresh snow blanket and sweep a couple dozen snow angels in the front yard."

"It's been so long. I hardly remember what snow looks like," he said.

She chuckled. "I remember the look on your face the first time you saw a snowflake. You were so excited." Her face contorted with a grimace of discomfort.

"I don't think we've seen snow since... when?"

"It's been a while. I think about a year and a half, when we got that weird October dusting."

"Global weirding, for sure."

"Snow may be a thing of the past."

"Lost in my memories."

She closed her eyes and her nostrils flared with a long, slow breath.

He caressed her damp tresses. "You rest. I need to find something."

Her eyes flickered open and she watched him hustle down the short hallway to their bedroom. He threw a small bag onto the bed.

"What's going on?" she asked.

He returned to the living room, an apologetic smile plastered on his face. "I'm packing for a couple days in New Orleans."

Melody stiffened, but said nothing.

He knelt beside her and reached for her hand but she yanked it away. "Giving me the silent treatment?" he said.

She took a deep breath and responded with anger-filled words. "I can't believe you're leaving. I know where we fit on your priority list."

"Don't be that way. Baby's not due for—"

"Nine days."

He nodded. "I'll be back in two. I promise—"

"Don't make promises you don't intend to keep."

"I've already got my boarding passes. Two days. And I've got these." With a sweeping motion, he presented a fancy box of cigars. "For the birth. I wouldn't miss it for the world."

Melody scowled. "Right. Thought you were just going to phone the hotel."

"I did, Mel. They would tell me nothing. Roberto at the Breeze confirmed Lena had played there, but he hadn't seen her since. He did say she left Elsie Lenore—the Steinway. It's in bad shape and he wants it gone. I've got to go get it before he hauls it to the dump."

She choked on a cough and eyes swam with tears. "There's nothing to say, Stefano. Get out. Right now. I don't care whether you come back."

He stared at her, lines etched across his forehead. "I'll call Mom," he said.

"You do that. Explain to her why you're chasing off to New Orleans when your wife—her daughter—is nine months pregnant. See if she will understand."

"Mel. I have to try. Two days. That's all I need—at least grant me that."

"It wouldn't matter since I have no choice."

"Look, I'm going to run to the store but I'll be back before I have to leave."

"How will you get to the airport? I might need the truck."

"I've already thought of that. I bummed a ride from Juan when I got the cigars. He has to run to Wichita anyway." He caressed her cheek at arm's length.

She wouldn't meet his gaze. Her shoulders tensed and nostrils flared at his touch.

With a sigh, he dropped his hand and left the house. An hour later he returned, a crimson Mustang following. His mother-in-law's Prius sat at the curb. He dashed past her car and burst inside to face two angry women, glaring at him. His hopeful grin disappeared.

Mel's eyelids drooped low over her bloodshot eyes. She struggled to a stand and clamped her jaw shut, glaring at him. The rebuke in her eyes pierced him like poisoned darts. Izzy stood at Mel's elbow, her gaze reflecting Mel's sour mood, although Stefano caught a flicker of a smile at one corner of her mouth before it disappeared.

"Hi, Mom." He forced himself to smile as he searched her face for some glimmer of acknowledgment for his tough situation, a hint of sympathy but there was nothing. Izzy shook her head and reached for Mel's fisted hand.

"I guess Mel told you I have an emergency," he said.

"Is that what you call this?" Izzy said. "I don't get it, Stefano. Neither one of us can understand why you think you have to leave now."

He grinned and winked. "Better today than tomorrow?" he said in a futile attempt to lighten the mood. The driver of the Mustang appeared behind him in the doorway. At Juan's appearance, Stefano borrowed brashness, his words barely tempered with a weak apology. "I know," Stefano said. "The timing is lousy. But, hey. I'll be back in just a couple days. See?" He pulled up his flight information on his cell phone. The round trip ticket was confirmed, with the return flight two days after the original departure.

"Stefano," Izzy said, "What was it about the postcard that makes you think this is an emergency?"

"I'll show you," he said, reaching into his coat pocket for the postcard. He handed it to Izzy.

She took the card and studied it for a moment. "Sorry. My Spanish isn't that good. What does it say?"

Stefano retrieved the card and translated the message.

"That's it? That's all? This short message after a decade of silence has you convinced you cannot wait another minute to look for your sister. Sorry. I still don't understand." Izzy shook her head.

"It's not just this card. I tried to call. The hotel clerk was mum when I asked for information. The bartender at the Breeze described Lena, her performance, and the vandalized piano left in his club. I don't know what it's all about, but I intend to find out. And the sooner the better. I need to go now or I'll miss my flight. Izzy, will you meet the transport tomorrow for the crated pianos?"

Her mouth fell agape and she gave a slight nod.

Stefano rushed past the two women and returned with his packed shoulder bag. "I'm hardly packing for more than a day." He grabbed Melody's hand and planted a farewell kiss on her fist. "Mel, I will be back, day after tomorrow. I love you more than life itself. I promise. I'll be back."

He bounded out the door and sped down the street with Juan.

9

A FOREBODING OF pending disaster gnawed inside Izzy as she watched Stefano leave. It was so unlike him to rush things, to shorten any steps in his projects. True to his word, he'd crated the Vose this morning. Before coming to town, she had noticed it standing ready for pickup with the other donated pianos. He was one person who did what he said, and said what he did, a rare kind of integrity in today's world. If he decided to leave before the truck arrived, he had to sense some dire circumstance. Stefano would never have left the wife he adored for anything less than a crisis.

Izzy closed her eyes, desperately wishing for his mission to conclude with the results he wanted.

"Mom," Melody wailed. She raised her arms and burst into tears.

Izzy pulled her into a maternal embrace, whispering murmurs of sympathy.

"Stefano," Mel sobbed. "He... I can't... Mom, what am I going to do?" Unable to say more, she wailed miserably.

Izzy pulled her tighter, rubbing her heaving back.

"Why now, Mom? Of all times—why now?" She stopped speaking and choked on another sob.

Izzy shook her head, continuing the backrub.

"So his sister needs him," Mel said. "As if I don't need him right now too." She pushed out of the embrace. "Look at me. I'm about to pop."

Izzy searched for words that would reassure her daughter. "I know. I can't understand it either. Couldn't be worse timing." She took Mel's face between her palms and tipped her chin, looking deep into her eyes. "Listen, sweetheart. If there's one thing I know, it's that Stefano cherishes you and Little One here. I have no doubt he was torn by this. He knows your due date."

Mel hesitated a moment before she nodded.

"And he will be back in two days, right?"

"But what if the baby is early? Or what if he can't get back? What if he misses his flight?"

"You can worry yourself sick over things that might happen, even when they are just remote possibilities. Or you can trust your husband. Is there a smidge of trust in there somewhere?" She tapped a silent piano scale on Mel's chest.

"Of course," she said, shaking her head. Then she wailed again. "But I don't want him to go."

"Why don't you sit down?" Izzy grasped Mel's hand and led her to the recliner by the front door. "Can I get you a glass of water?"

Wilting into the chair, Mel closed her eyes. She nodded.

Izzy retreated to the kitchen and poured a glass of filtered water from a pitcher inside the refrigerator. "I'll clean up the dishes while you get a little rest," she said when she handed the glass to Mel.

A moment later, Mel's eyes fluttered closed. Izzy washed the breakfast dishes and checked on Mel. Her chest rose and fell in regular, deep breaths. Izzy gathered used towels in the bathroom and a few scattered clothes in the bedroom and moved them to the laundry room. She found a dusting cloth and bustled around, cleaning the spare living room furnishings, the hutch in the kitchen, and the dresser in the bedroom.

"Mom?" Mel called, her eyes still closed.

"Hmm?" Izzy appeared in the hall doorway.

"Could I come out to the house for a few days? I don't want to stay here alone."

"That's a great idea. Can I pack a few things for you? We could take your laundry and I'll help get it done out at the house." As she pulled a satchel from the closet shelf, she chattered to help relieve Mel's anxiety. "Guess where I was working this morning?"

"No idea."

"Double M."

"Regular tuning day for Brett?"

"Yes. And guess who showed up while I was there? Maddi. Down from K-State. She asked about you. I think she'd like to visit. I'll let her know you'll be at my place."

"Okay."

"And guess what else—you'll never believe this one."

"What?" Ice edged Mel's voice and her eyelids remained closed.

"Brett's son showed up."

"Didn't know he had one."

"Oddly, he didn't seem to know it either."

"What do you mean?"

"He'd never met this young man before. Dirk Lander is a few years younger than you. Brett never knew."

≈≫

His bag slung over one shoulder, Stefano burst from the Uber car in New Orleans. In two strides, he entered the Embassy Suites hotel. He glanced around the lobby and joined the short line at the check-in desk, fidgeting, stepping from one foot to the other, twice every second. When at last he faced the clerk, he blurted, "I need a room tonight."

"Reservation?"

"No."

"Sorry, sir. We're booked solid."

"I'd take anything."

"Sorry. It's the season. Mardi Gras, you know." The clerk offered a worn smile in a weak apology.

"I know..." He sighed and half turned away but fumbled in his bag to find the postcard. "I'm looking for my sister. She sent this a couple days ago." He shoved the card across the desk, hotel photo facing up.

The clerk acknowledged the lobby scene.

"Could you tell me if Lena Valdez is still here?"

"Sorry. I can't share that information."

"Can you confirm that she registered here last Friday?" He flipped the card over, checking the post mark. "No. Saturday."

"Lena Valdez, you say?" The clerk clicked a few keys on his computer. "No Valdez registrations in the last few days."

Stefano slipped his wallet from his hip pocket and offered a worn photo from years before, his only photo of his sister. "This is Lena. Please. Did you see her?"

His irritation barely contained, the clerk waved him away. "I can't help you. Please move on."

He slid the photo across the counter. "Look—have you seen her?"

The desk clerk pushed his hand away, but glanced at the worn photograph for a split second. He froze, staring at Lena's smiling face. "This is your sister?"

"Yes," he whispered. Something about the clerk's sudden interest made trepidation gnaw at his belly.

The hotel clerk pushed a button on his desk phone. "There's a guy here claiming to be the brother of that Cuban woman." He listened to the response and returned the phone to its cradle. "If you please, wait inside this office. The manager would like to speak to you."

10

STEFANO ROUNDED THE end of the counter and entered the office. The door closed behind him. He sank into a padded office chair, but couldn't relax. The clerk had recognized Lena's photo. He was sure of it. Why had her image changed everything? Something was wrong. Lena was in trouble. What kind of trouble?

Where is she?

The unrest in his gut threatened to spill his stomach contents onto the office floor. He stood, restless and confused. He paced the length of the short office, studied scraps of paper left on the desk and the computer screen that glowed with a screen saver image cycling across it. He glanced at the wall clock.

7:24.

He sat again, leaned back in the chair and crossed his legs. A moment later, he threw his arms up and bounded from the chair. How long would they keep him waiting here? And for what? Damn it, he didn't have all night.

He crossed the room and lifted the corner of a window blind to look out on the street, lit now by bright lights. Crowds of people wandered toward the business district, laughing and pointing at the quaint Mardi Gras decorations. He turned back and stared at the clock again.

7:27.

Three minutes. He couldn't stand it.

The door opened, admitting a man in a disheveled suit. The manager forced a smile into his tense grimace, introduced himself, and extended his hand. Stefano shook the outstretched hand and studied the man's face.

"You are Cuban?" the hotel manager asked. His voice sounded weary.

"*Sí.* I was born there but I now live in Kansas."

The manager grunted, assessing the information in silence.

Stefano broke the silence. "Please. I am here looking for my sister. She was lost after the hurricane years ago, and I just now got word from her. Here." He pulled the hotel's postcard from his pocket. "She begged for me to come."

"You have a photograph of your sister?"

Stefano fumbled with his wallet and produced the worn image from long ago. The hotel manager studied the smiling face in the photo. He nodded. "This is the same woman."

"She was here?"

"Yes."

"But not here now?"

"There was an incident."

Stefano closed his eyes, breathing heavily.

The manager paused a moment before he added, "She and her companion abandoned the room leaving an unpaid bill."

Stefano coughed. "She's gone."

"Vanished."

Stefano sank into the padded office chair, his eyes squeezed shut. He didn't want to hear this. Vessels rose on the backs of his hands as he gripped the chair arms.

The hotel manager's voice softened. "Perhaps you could assist if you'd come with me and look through the items left in the room. It might help with positive identification. Would you help?"

Exhausted, his shoulders drooped. Stefano stared at the manager like a forlorn puppy and bit his lower lip before nodding quickly. The manager ushered him into the hotel lobby. They wound through small groups of gaily dressed visitors to the elevator bay. Inside the first one, the hotel manager raised his hand to stop a couple from joining them, shut the elevator doors, and clicked the fifth floor button. When they stepped into the carpeted hallway, the entire corridor was lined with ribbons of yellow crime scene tape, warning casual visitors to stay away. Heart pounding, he followed his guide to a room halfway down the hall. The manager nodded at the police guard, unlocked the door, and they peered into chaos.

"Do you recognize any of the items left by our unnamed guests?" the manager prodded.

Stefano glanced over the room, his cheeks growing heated as panic defined itself in his heart. He scanned the open bathroom, turned back to the sleeping quarters, and exhaled in shock at the disarray. "I don't know. I haven't seen her for years. I don't think I can—"

He noticed an ornate brooch lying upside down beneath a lamp on a table beneath the draped window beside the door. "That brooch." Stefano sucked in his breath. He'd never forget his mother's favorite brooch, the intricate silver vines and the gemstones they cradled. Lena had worn it in every performance when they were young.

He reached toward the tabletop but the New Orleans officer grasped his wrist before he could touch the family heirloom. "I can't allow you to disturb evidence."

"But, this was my mother's. Lena wore it when she performed."

"You might be able to identify the patrons who rented this room?" the hotel manager asked.

"I would know my sister."

The manager became distracted when his mobile phone rattled in his left hand. He accepted a call, spoke in monosyllabic replies, and abruptly disconnected. He ushered Stefano brusquely to the elevator. At the door Stefano pulled back. "The brooch?"

"Sorry. It's evidence. Come. We have company downstairs."

II

TWO UNIFORMED NEW Orleans cops waited in the elevator bay. "You the Cuban?" the taller of the two threw a question at him when they stepped from the elevator.

Startled, he protested. "I am American. I'm from Kansas."

"I see. Yet you have a photo of a Cuban hotel guest."

"My sister."

"Then you are Cuban."

"I was born there. I'm now an American." He pulled his driver's license from his wallet.

The officer studied it critically. "Kansas. You know the Cuban woman who fled?"

"I know my sister, if that's what you mean."

"And the men she traveled with?"

He hesitated. The pause prompted further questions.

"Would you recognize the men she traveled with?"

"I don't know. We've been out of touch for years."

"Please come with us."

He backed away, hands raised in objection.

The officer repeated his request. "I insist you come with us."

"I've done nothing wrong."

"Noted. But if you know these people, we need you to come with us."

"Why?"

"One of those Cuban visitors left here in a body bag."

Damn. He was too late. He coughed and emitted a low moan. "*¿Muerto?* The woman?"

"No, one of the men. Your alleged sister disappeared with the second man. They left no identification with the body, and registered here under fictitious names."

"How did he die?"

"It's not known yet. We're investigating this as a likely homicide."

He struggled to control churning panic. "Why do you need me? I didn't kill him."

"We need a positive ID. If you know these people, we'd be obliged if you'd come have a look. It could help us locate those who fled."

"Murder suspects?"

"Top of our list."

Lena! What has happened?

At the downtown morgue, Stefano followed the officers to a windowless room in the building's interior. They nodded to a woman in a lab coat who led them past three steel tables with draped and motionless human forms on them. They stopped at the fourth table. The lab technician pulled down the sheet covering the body. All three turned to look at him. He met each set of eyes before directing his unsteady gaze to the pale body on the table.

He stared into the lifeless eyes of the man and covered his mouth, gagged, and squeezed his eyes shut, tormented by the look of agony frozen forever into the gray features of the dead man. The lifeless face resembled someone he had seen before, but he couldn't be sure. He recalled a bully in Havana, a contemporary who lived a privileged life compared to most Cubans, including Stefano's family, but the name eluded him. It had been too long.

"Do you recognize him?" the tall officer prodded.

"I couldn't tell you his name. He looks kind of familiar, but I can't recall his name."

"Think back. Sometimes it helps to clear your mind and think of details from a day in your past life."

Stefano took a deep breath. He closed his eyes. The effort to set aside all that had happened since he'd received Lena's postcard proved too much. He couldn't shut out her words, her face, the panic in her eyes as she clung to the hotel pillar. He couldn't shutter the vision of Melody, couldn't ignore Mel's look as he left for the airport, full of loathing. It was too much.

He opened his eyes, once again admitting the probing glances of the New Orleans professionals in the city morgue. The lifeless face on the table resembled somebody from his past. Actually it resembled everybody from his past. It was a typical Cuban visage overcome with the pallor of death. How could he offer a name?

This man was someone his sister knew, and she knew him intimately. The thought struck him like a blow placed squarely into his solar plexus.

Who is this man, Lena? What did he do to you?

"Anything?" the officer asked.

Stefano shook his head. "I'm sorry. I really wish I knew who he was, but I can't think right now."

They dropped him off in front of Embassy Suites Hotel twenty minutes later. Stefano slid out of the police cruiser, his shoulders drooping. As the patrol car disappeared, he eyed the revolving doors of the hotel.

Booked solid.

At least they were this afternoon and that was not likely to have changed. What would he do now? Chances were slim to none that he'd find an available room anywhere, given the presence of all the Mardi Gras guests. He swung his bag over his shoulder and dragged up the street, the bag thumping his ribs with every step. A block and a half later, he decided to head to the Caribbean Breeze. The nightclub would undoubtedly still be open. He could crash there in a dark corner and figure out what to do about Lena. About the time the bright neon of the Breeze's beckoning sign showed up in the distance, a name crept into his mind until it became an overwhelming silent roar.

Diaz.

The body of the man in the morgue was one of the Diaz brothers. A memory flickered, and then burned into his cerebral cortex. He recalled a bully in Havana, Julio Diaz. Julio was one of three brothers. The youngest brother, Enrique, was in Lena's school class. There was an older brother also, by several years. Stefano had few specific recollections of the eldest brother. But he recalled the Diaz family name, notorious for seizing power through heartless means. An angry memory from his youth re-established the burning rage—the impotence and helplessness—he had felt when Julio Diaz jeered at him from a passing car. It was a common thing back then. He uttered a low growl.

And Lena had checked into a New Orleans hotel with Diaz brothers?

The unrest in his heart soared. He sensed the peril his sister faced if she was in Diaz family company. He had no remaining doubts. She had summoned him out of desperation.

God help us.

∾

The tap on his office door in the family's Havana headquarters was barely audible. Teofilo Diaz diverted his gaze from the computer screen and tilted his head, listening. There it was again. A tentative knock. If someone wanted to interrupt his morning work, they should be bold about it. He slammed the desktop with his palm. The impact resonated around the room. That was more like it. Why couldn't people be firm? Decisive? Secure in their intentions. Did they desire his audience or not?

Tap. Tap. Tap. Again. It was irritating, like a mosquito buzzing at his ear. He'd like to squash it.

"What?" His voice bellowed. The office door opened a crack.

"Excuse me, *Señor Diaz.*" It was Felipe's nanny.

"What is it?" he said, anger lacing his voice.

"Apologies, sir. Felipe has outgrown his boots. We need a larger pair."

"Get them, then," he said. "Don't bother me with trivial stuff. That's what your expense account is for."

"Excuse me, sir. There is no money in Felipe's expense account. We've been waiting for the monthly allowance, but have not seen it."

"It will be there when Julio returns today. The account will be replenished."

"What shoes should he wear until then?"

"Put him in sandals if you must. Don't bother me."

"*Sí, Señor Diaz.*" She backed out of the office, shutting the door behind her.

12

STEFANO SLIPPED INSIDE the open door of the Caribbean Breeze and wormed his way through the scattered tables and random chairs, oblivious to the hoots and cheers from the drunken crowd as they applauded the night's featured music ensemble. He found an empty chair in the farthest corner, scooted it until the chair back was against the wall, and sank onto the seat. His eyes stared at the duo beneath the lights, but he saw nothing beyond his own haunting memories. A waitress sauntered by to take his order. When she left, he leaned back and closed his eyes. The background roar mesmerized him and he dozed off until the order arrived.

The waitress prodded his shoulder. "You okay?" she asked with genuine concern.

He nodded. "It's been a helluva day. Thanks." He pulled the hamburger and Cajun fries in front of him and tipped the beer glass up for a long sip. As he ate, his gaze roamed the dark room. The tables and chairs had been replaced after the big storm. A new and upgraded bar with swiveling stools had replaced the old one he remembered. There was still a small stage opposite the bar with the evening's jazz combo swinging in synchronized beat, still a wall of mirrors behind the counter, and Roberto, himself, still filled mugs for his guests, laughing as he volleyed jokes with a couple of the patrons.

Behind the string bass player, an oddly shaped heap covered in flamboyant serapes drew his attention. One curved edge faintly resembled the tail end of a baby grand piano, but it was tilted precariously. Stefano could have sworn the whole mound rocked with the musical beat. This couldn't be the chosen backdrop for the musicians. On the other hand, what else could the dubious mound under the vivid hues of homespun serapes be? No way was it Elsie Lenore. Not in this condition. Was it possible that Roberto allowed it here in front, on stage with the jazz duo, still taking up precious floor space during Mardi Gras? No wonder Roberto wanted it hauled off. That he had delayed this long testified to the bartender's respect for Lena and her music.

As the night progressed, guests left and were replaced by others. Stefano remained in his chair. He dozed lightly a couple times, had the waitress refill his drink a couple times, and visited the men's room a couple times. When the musicians left at two in the morning, he stayed put until the friendly waitress approached him with a smile. "We're closing in fifteen."

He nodded. As she turned to leave, he said, "I'd like to speak with Roberto, if he has a moment."

"You know Roberto?"

"Old friends."

She nodded in understanding. "I'll send him over."

Roberto sidled over ten minutes later. "Hey, *amigo*. Gotta ask you to leave now."

Stefano met Roberto's gaze and stood, extending his hand in a friendly invitation.

"Well, I'll be damned," Roberto said when he recognized his lingering guest. He gripped Stefano's hand and pulled him into a brotherly hug. "You did come. I 'bout gave up on you."

"Yeah. Hey, all the hotels are booked. Mind if I hang here tonight? I won't be any trouble. I could even help mop up the place."

"You can stay. Sure. As long as you get this piece of crap out of here tomorrow." Roberto headed toward the serape-covered mound and with the flourish of a stage magician he swept the drape from the bones of what once was a piano. Stefano gasped. Shaking his head, he surveyed the damage: two legs cracked, multiple keytops mangled, lid split into three pieces. He searched beneath the keys for a special landmark he and Lena had carved together. Found it. This was Elsie Lenore without a doubt.

Stefano gasped. "Why would anyone do this?" He reached unsteady fingers to a long splinter in the rim and touched it fondly. His mother—rest her soul—would have been devastated.

"Beats me," Roberto said. "What I want to know is what you're going to do about it?"

Stefano stared at the piano, mouth agape. Lena had asked him to assist with Elsie Lenore. What had she expected from him? He shook his head slightly. "I don't know."

"Want me to just call the city refuse department? Have it hauled off?"

Stefano considered that option. He pulled Lena's card from his shirt pocket and read her words again. *Please come for us.... Urgent. We need you.*

Still baffled by the implications, he shook his head. "She said both of them needed me. I doubt I can help this old gal now. But I'd really like to have a chance for a closer examination. Maybe there was something." He spoke softly, talking as much to himself as to Roberto, trying to ease his doubts.

"You don't have a lot of time. I really need this gone," Roberto said, emphasizing his stance with staccato words. "Tomorrow. You have the rest of the night, and then I'm calling the city."

"I know, man," Stefano agreed. "I don't blame you. How about I crate it up and ship it to a place where I could take all the time in the world to perform some kind of autopsy?"

"What d'you mean?"

"Could we order some lumber first thing in the morning? With a few hand tools, I could build a shipping crate and have her crated up by noon."

"Lumber yard half a mile west of here," Roberto said.

"You got any portable shop tools?"

"Just the basics for repairing this place when needed.

"Tape measure, square, power saw, screw driver?"

"I could come up with those."

"She'll be ready to go before noon. I give you my word."

13

THE MORNING SUN blazed through the window over his shoulders as Teofilo Diaz studied the computer screen. He slammed his palm on the desk. *Curse them both.* The family finances had plummeted. Though Enrique and Julio had wired money from their sales the last two months, it hadn't been as much as he expected. He suspected one or both of his brothers had skimmed the top off their sales.

Julio. Had to be Julio. Enrique was never alert enough, nor bright enough, to cross him. A socialite, the youngest Diaz knew how to entertain their clients in style, but to skim the sales money? Never. Besides, the kid brother was dead, likely murdered in his New Orleans bed.

A bold knock interrupted his thoughts. He answered gruffly. "What is it for crissakes?"

The door swung open, admitting his majordomo and a suited man who chewed on a cigar stub. "Your nine o'clock, *Señor.* Rolph Mateo." The servant nodded his head, ushering in the guest before retreating.

Teo nodded to an upholstered chair across the desk. They chatted briefly about trivia before Mateo said, "You mentioned you'd have samples."

"I do indeed." Without breaking eye contact, Teo reached under his desk and retrieved a bamboo cigar box embossed with gold trim and the logo "Diaz Cigars."

He opened the lid and handed one to Mateo. His guest tossed the stub of his own cigar into a trash bin and reached for the offered cigar, studying the plain appearance of the product before asking for a light.

He passed a lighter across the desk, leaned back in his chair, and watched, smug confidence lighting his face. Mateo puffed on the cigar, drawing air through it into his mouth until the cigar's tip glowed.

The new client waited a few seconds, and blew it into the room in tiny wisps. A smile spread his face. "How do you manage this?"

"As I said, only the best. With regular shipments of the finest Colombian products, my people have designed fusion methods. This is the result. A smoke so smooth and so pleasing, you'll never get enough of it."

The office door burst open and Julio Diaz rushed inside, breathing heavily, his face a mask of apprehension. Teo glared at his intruding brother, his eyes shooting arrows of displeasure, but his rebuke was silent.

"Pardon," Julio apologized in haste. "I didn't know you had a guest."

Teo offered introductions, his forced smile unwavering. "Rolph Mateo. My brother, Julio, in charge of our farm management. Though he is an excellent manager, he has much to learn in the way of business protocol. Please forgive his tactless interruption."

Mateo nodded and took another draw from the sample cigar. "This is good, Diaz. I'd take a crate just like this one. But if you ever skimp on the product—"

"Not to worry, my fine man. The Diaz family is good to its word. We depend on repeat business." Teo nodded cordially.

"When could you have the crate delivered to the dock?" Mateo asked.

"When do you want it?"

"Tomorrow. Noon."

"Consider it done."

"I'll see myself out." Mateo offered his hand again and left the room.

For a moment that lasted an eternity, Teo stared through the large window across the palms on the hillside below the Diaz mansion. He turned slowly to Julio. "You ever interrupt a business meeting again, you will regret it."

Julio hastily apologized. "We just got in. Thought you'd want to know."

"It could have waited five minutes. If your clumsiness reflects on the deal, there will be hell to pay."

✌❧

Through the rest of the night, Stefano removed pieces of the damaged piano, measured them, and recorded notes on a scrap of napkin from his corner table. At 8:00 a.m., he called the lumber yard and ordered several two by four lengths of pine lumber, two full sheets of half-inch plywood, and a box of screws. When the supplies were delivered, he started marking his measurements and cutting pieces to specified sizes. True to his word, by noon the remains of Elsie Lenore had been crated inside its plywood coffin. All that remained was to arrange for shipping, and attach a shipping label.

"You going to rent a truck to haul this north?" Roberto asked.

"I'm going to contact a trucking company. I've dealt with a good one to transport donated pianos to the Miami shipyard. They'll have this old gal delivered before I get back."

"Back. Back where?"

"That's the hot button question. I'm supposed to return home tomorrow. But I have to find out what happened to Lena. Time's running out. She's somehow involved with pricks from Havana and I'm worried about her."

"Those two she was with?"

Stefano nodded. "The Diaz "Bad News" brothers. One of them ended up dead at the hotel. Lena and the other brother disappeared."

"Dead? How do you know?"

"They dragged me down to the morgue last night to identify the body."

"No joke?"

"God's honest truth. It's being investigated as a homicide. I have to find out if Lena is all right. Mel's going to kill me," he said, wincing at the thought of the coming storm at home.

"Mel?"

"My wife."

"Hope you know what you're doing, man."

"I really have no clue. But I've got to find my sister, or at least try."

"And your wife?"

"I'll call her and tell her what I know. Which is nothing, except that there was a murder—or at least a death—in the hotel. And Lena is involved somehow but she's disappeared again. And this piano is a disaster."

"What do you plan to do?"

Stefano met Roberto's intense gaze. "What would you do if you were traveling and one of your party died mysteriously? Where would you go?"

"I probably would call the police."

"Yeah, but if you knew the murderer? Or you were involved yourself somehow?"

"I don't know, man."

"If I wanted to disappear I think I'd head home as fast as I could get there."

"You think they flew to Havana?"

"That would be my guess. And I think I better follow them. Mel is going to have my hide. But what else can I do?" Stefano's voice faded as he considered his options. If he had any chance to help his sister, he had to move now. The clock was ticking and its echoes sounded more like screams for help every minute he delayed.

14

"I'M GOING TO need papers," Stefano mumbled. "Know where I could get a passport really fast?"

Roberto had connections. He summoned a ride to take Stefano to an office building in central New Orleans. During the ride Stefano tried to call Mel. He hesitated before hitting the green call button on his phone, anticipating the fury of the woman he loved, and feeling trapped in a hole with no way out. When he finally did place the call, it rang until her recorded voice asked for a message. He disconnected.

Three hours later, he returned to the Breeze with forged papers that would allow him to travel to Havana and back, no questions asked. At least he hoped that would be the case. He called Mel again. Still no answer.

She was mad enough she refused to answer his calls. He tried his mother-in-law and got the same response. Nothing. They were both ignoring him. Unless... unless they were at the hospital delivering a baby.

He discarded that notion. Surely they would have notified him if labor had started. How could he let them know what he planned if they weren't answering his calls? He begged a blank sheet of paper from Roberto and sat down at the bar to pen a letter to Melody. He owed it to her and to her parents to explain the arrival of the damaged piano to Izzy's shop in Kansas. He could almost hear Mel yelling at his change of plan.

What am I doing? Enfocate, Valdez.

This whole plan was insane, the choice of a desperate man. He visualized Mel's cherry-red face, her eyes blazing, vessels raised in her delicate neck and on the backs of her clenched fists. What kind of man would knowingly anger the one woman he loved most in the world? He hated himself with a vengeance that he hoped surpassed Mel's loathing. But he was trapped between Lena's desperation and Mel's fury. How could he explain to his beloved the quandary he faced? What words could he pen that would explain his decision in a way she would understand? Such words did not exist. But he had to try.

My Dearest Melody, he wrote,

You are the song that gives my heart wings. I am in agony to think how deeply you will hurt with a boundless rage. I am the cause of your heartache and I hate myself for it. There is no way to explain that you will understand. I hardly understand myself.

I am going to Havana. I have to go. I still hope to return to you before the birth of our child. I still dream of our future life, raising our beautiful children. I cling to this vision as I descend into the personal hell of my past.

Someday I think your generous heart will open a place for my sister Lena. She needs rescuing far more than I did when you found me under that piano so long ago. I wish for her to find the same kind of joy you brought me when I was alone. Mel, you are the beauty I worship in life, but you are also my strength. I love you for your resolute determination when it comes to helping people and braving all kinds of dangers to find lost souls. Someday I believe you will come to understand that is why I must follow my sister to Cuba, because I love you and admire you so much.

Lena is alone. She has nobody to turn to. And thus she summoned me. I know this as surely as I have ever known anything. I have wrestled with the reprehensible choices I face. Neither is without a steep price.

Mel, I wanted to talk, to tell you what I have discovered here in New Orleans. I tried to call, but you would not answer. I can only surmise you chose to give me the silent treatment I deserve, that you meant what you said. Perhaps you really don't ever want to hear from me again. My heart is heavy with that possibility.

I have crossed a line, broken a trust. And the deed can never be undone, nor adequately compensated.

Perhaps someday you'll reconsider. You may want to know what I was thinking and feeling when I took this course of action, if not now then perhaps someday you'll read these words and know how much I love you and realize my agony.

Here's what I wanted to tell you. There has been a murder. One of the men Lena was with is dead and she herself has disappeared. I believe she fled to Havana with her other companion. Mel—they hauled me to the morgue to identify the body, I didn't recognize him at first, but then it came to me. He was Enrique Diaz, a scourge to my friends in Havana as a youth. He is bad news, and the thought that Lena was with him puts great fear into my bones. The Diaz family is power-hungry and they will take any means necessary to achieve their deceitful goals. Even murder, apparently. If Lena disappeared with the other man, I have to believe it was against her will.

Thus my quandary. On the one hand I have you, mi enamorada, *already angry at my absence on the eve of our child's birth. I long to be in your arms and share your bed. There is nothing I wish for more.*

On the other hand is my sister, sweet Lena, the only member left of my Cuban family, the duet partner we gave up as dead, killed in that horrible storm. Yet she lives.

My precious Melody, when I consider these things, I have to think you will be all right. You are strong. And you are not alone. Even without my presence, you still have devoted family who will be by your side to help you through this darkest of moments. Lena, however, has nobody. Just me. And I find it impossible to ignore the difference. I must answer her summons.

In my perfect world, I will find Lena soon after I land in Havana. I will extricate her from the evil clutch-

es of whatever hold the Diaz clan has over her. And together she and I will return to you, in time to celebrate the birth of our child.

Pray that this is so and until then, God speed my love to you.

Forever yours,
Stefano

Stefano laid down the pen and folded the paper with tenderness. He closed his eyes and lifted it to his lips, pressing them into the page until it wrinkled with moisture. He slipped it into the envelope. With a sudden inspiration he pulled Lena's card from his pocket and added it to the correspondence before he sealed it shut and wrote "Melody Valdez" in bold lettering on the front. He slid it into the plastic shipping envelope behind the delivery instructions. He pulled his return flight confirmation from his wallet and balanced it in his open hand as he weighed the impact of his decision in his mind. His jaws set in determination, he ripped the flight confirmation into small pieces. They fluttered into a waste can at the end of Roberto's bar.

He closed his eyes, trying to imagine Mel's face when she read his letter. Would she even read it? She would likely resist. It might take a nudge from Izzy to even get her to read his words... "No, no, no, no, no." Stefano's voice swelled in a crescendo that punctuated his mood. He pulled his letter to Mel out of the shipping envelope, turned over the parcel addressed to her and wrote a declaration of his love on the back side.

"Melody, I love you forever. I WILL BE BACK!"

15

IZZY TIPTOED INTO the darkened room where Melody slept and kissed her daughter's forehead. She tiptoed out and clicked the door shut, breathing deeply to help clear her mind for the day's work. It would be hard to focus on the morning's tunings, but she'd try her best.

About mid-morning, Mel called. Izzy answered her phone on the third ring, trying to sound cheerful. "Good morning!"

"Hi, Mom. Want to meet me for an early lunch at Steamy Joe's?"

"What time you thinking?"

"Eleven."

"Perfect. I'll see you there."

When Izzy joined her in a quiet upstairs dining room a few minutes after eleven, Mel stared at her vibrating phone, nostrils flaring.

"Aren't you going to answer your phone?" Izzy said.

"Nope. It's Stefano. I don't want to talk to him."

"Tone it down. You want people to hear?"

Mel snorted. "Who's around to hear? In case you haven't noticed, we're alone in this room."

Izzy sighed. "Maybe you should see what he wants. He could have run into a problem."

Mel pushed to her feet and pounded the table. "He'll encounter a problem here if he ever gets—ooh!" She stopped mid-sentence, grabbed her belly and lifted forcibly with all the upper arm strength she possessed.

"Are you having contractions?"

Mel nodded and burst into tears. "I think so."

❧

In spite of the day's warmth, goose bumps raised on Stefano's forearms as he sealed the shipping envelope with his love letter to Mel inside. He stapled it to the outside of the piano crate and reviewed the trucking company's instructions with Roberto. They would arrive for the piano by three that afternoon. Elsie Lenore should be delivered to Izzy's piano repair shop before a week had passed. He wondered how long his detour would delay his arrival. With any kind of luck at all, he might even beat the old gal home. But he wasn't going to count on that. His luck to this point had exceeded nobody's expectations and seemed to be in a downhill spiral.

He bade farewell to Roberto and made his way to an automatic teller machine in a nearby bank's parking lot. After withdrawing significant cash to fund his impromptu voyage, he strode east on an old highway, energized by the hope of finding Lena and removing her from harm's way. He walked purposefully, his thumb extended to hitch a ride, Miami his destination. With a little luck, he'd make the shipyards before his donated pianos shipped out. Maybe he could bribe the ship's captain to let him tag along by offering technical support for the shipment. He had all the papers he needed. Now he needed a smidge of good luck.

◈◈◈

"When did the contractions start?" Izzy asked.

"I don't know. Maybe an hour ago." Mel sucked in her breath, digging her fingernails into her abdomen, her face contorted. "That was a good one. I need to use the bathroom." She took two steps toward the doorway before a flood of water saturated her jeans. She turned toward Izzy and wailed.

"It's okay, sweetheart," Izzy said. "Your water broke."

Legato, Isabel. No frizzy Izzy today.

Melody sobbed. "Am I in labor, Mom?"

"I think so. I've only done this once, you know, and it was years ago." She offered a nervous grin to her daughter. "It's going to be okay."

"It's a week early."

"That can happen. Let's get you to the hospital."

On the table, Mel's phone vibrated. Izzy glanced at the screen. "It's Stefano. I think you should answer. Want me to give you the phone?"

"No."

"Shall I answer then?"

"Don't you dare!"

"Mel. He should know."

"Don't touch my phone, Mom." The threat was unmistakable. The phone went silent.

"Has he called often?"

"A few times."

"And you won't talk to him?"

"No." She grimaced, clutched her abdomen, and suppressed a scream as she wilted to the floor. With an agonized look, she stared into her mother's eyes. "I hate him. Mom, I can't do this alone."

"You're not alone," Izzy said. "I'm here. And I'm not going anywhere. Let's get you to my car."

❧❧

Standing at the bow of the freight liner, Stefano scanned the horizon. A late afternoon tropical sun warmed his forearms as he leaned on the steel railing. When the captain reluctantly agreed he could accompany the piano shipment, he'd indicated their arrival in Havana was expected before dusk. Tense with apprehension, and aggravated that he hadn't yet identified the dark line on the horizon which would define the island nation of Cuba, he leaned over the deck rail, gripping it with an iron grasp.

When he did see Cuba, he couldn't take his eyes off it. The freighter plowed through the waves bringing him closer to home. He recognized landmarks. La Cabana guarded the mouth of the bay. A huge statue of Christ towered above the hillside. Stefano scanned the beloved icons of his homeland as one-by-one they came into view.

His eyes brimmed with moisture and bumps rose on his arms in spite of the heat. He hadn't expected this sentimentality. In the haste to arrange passage and his overwhelming concern for Lena, he had not once considered he'd be returning to his homeland for the first time in years. The Capitol building, the cherished figure of poet Jose Marti mounted on a horse, the *Malecón* peppered with strolling Cubans, and the assortment of forgotten but familiar structures lining the bay tugged at his heart. With a feeling close to awe, he watched the sun descend behind the city of his birth, sky flaming from gold to crimson. By the time the ship had docked, the city lights twinkled across the bay like diamonds in a mermaid's tantalizing hair.

Stefano followed the crew across a ramp and stepped onto the dock. He passed through a warehouse to a street crowded with slow-moving traffic. A motorcycle wove through stalled traffic complete with classic antique autos in fresh vivid pink and blue paint jobs, fancy Chinese manufactured tour busses, expensive European late model cars, and horse-drawn taxis. Most horses looked malnourished, every rib showing through their hides. One wagon carried a full-grown hog to its slaughter. Bicyclists laden with guitar cases, and numerous pedestrians milled along the edges of the street.

He flexed his knees and ground his toes into crumbling pavement and smiled. He was home.

16

THE CAPTAIN SHATTERED Stefano's reverie, clapping a hand on his shoulder. "Will you head to the conservatory now?"

Stefano nodded.

"Let their acquisitions office know they need to have the crates picked up tomorrow. They will be off-loaded during the night."

"*Sí, Capitan.*" Stefano set off across the shipyard toward the avenue he recalled so well. As he walked, he checked his mobile phone, useless in Cuba without international service. He ambled along the *Malecón* a good three kilometers before he got serious about flagging a motorcycle taxi. They headed first toward the *Hotel de Nacional*, where he intended to change his dollars into Cuban currency. From there they wound through city streets toward the Arts University de Havana and detoured through the *Siboney* housing neighborhood, with fancy houses at the ends of gated driveways, expensive autos parked on the paved drives. One driveway included armed guards in a small stone guard house.

Stefano swung his hand at the guard house. "What is this place?"

The driver grinned over his shoulder. "That's the drive to Castle Diaz. They lock out us commoners."

"Diaz?"

"*Sí.* The brothers Teofilo, Julio, and Enrique. The family became big in Cuba after the revolution."

"I remember." Stefano studied the gate and the lush vegetation along the driveway that concealed the dwelling.

"Stay out of their way if you value your life. There's nothing good to come from meeting these brothers," the driver said.

At Stefano's request, the cyclist dropped him off in front of a neighborhood *paladar* close to the university. A sharply dressed waiter ushered him to a table and he ordered a large helping of traditional island poultry, fruit, rice and beans. Halfway through the meal, a familiar voice yelled his name across the room and he waved to Carlos Gutierrez. His classmate from university days shared the latest neighborhood news as he prepared for the evening's live music. "I heard you were out of the country," he said, tweaking the tuning pegs on his string bass.

"I live in the states now," Stefano said.

"When'd you get back?"

"Just arrived. You wouldn't know where I could find a room for a few nights, would you?"

"Check with Maria Lopez. She's opened a hostel in her family's home near Cathedral Square."

"My Tia Maria?"

Carlos nodded. "She's your aunt?"

"Not really. We adopted her years ago."

Delighted to see him, Tia Maria offered Stefano a room, gratis. He and the aging woman reminisced long into the night about the challenges of the *period especial* of the 1990's, when resources were so scarce many of his compatriots starved.

The following morning, Stefano rose early and headed to the university. He accompanied his former professor to the shipyard to claim the crate of piano donations, helped unload the instruments, tore off their packing boxes, and set up the four grand pianos in the shop area for instrument maintenance.

"Nice," the shop manager said, surveying the acquisitions.

"I made sure they'd be worth sending. Still need some tweaks in regulation, and climate control."

"A never-ending process. I'm surprised you took the time to bring them down."

"I have other business too. Just worked out very conveniently."

Mid-afternoon, Stefano summoned another driver for a return to *Siboney*. He requested a drop-off around the corner from the Diaz gate. The 1955 Chevy rattled to a stop and Stefano scrambled out. He reached across the worn upholstery and handed the fare to the driver, with the proper gratitude and commendation. *"Gracias, Amigo."*

The young man beamed and waved as Stefano heaved against the Chevy's door. Its hinges creaked as he forced it closed. The driver worked with the stick shift until it groaned into first gear. It backfired twice, spewed oily smoke into the air, and rolled forward.

Stefano watched the car jerk forward, sputtering smoke until the engine smoothed and the car roared down the hill. He turned the opposite direction, to find a place he could wait and watch the house and driveway. He scrambled into a hollow in the midst of azalea bushes beneath a palm tree across from the guard house and leaned against a crumbling masonry wall topped off with a lattice of arrow-shaped ironwork. With his hat cocked low over his eyes he hoped any casual observer would assume he slept. But he watched from below his hat with an intensity that he hadn't mustered since his last public piano performance.

Evening approached before a chocolate brown Audi rolled past, pulled into the gated drive and stopped. The driver's window opened. A gruff male voice addressed the gate attendant before issuing instructions to an occupant inside the car. A child responded from the back seat. The driver turned, upbraided the child, and in a voice devoid of sparkle, the child responded, *"Sí."* The driver chastised the child again. This time, the child responded emphatically, but with no enthusiasm, *"Sí, Señor."*

The gate opened, the car entered the grounds, and the gate rolled shut again. The Audi disappeared up the winding driveway, working its way through lush vegetation to the expansive residence at the top. An hour later, a second car arrived, this one an electric blue Ferrari. The driver blared the horn until the gate attendant opened the gate. Stefano remained concealed in his leafy nook until sunset but there was no further activity before he dragged himself to Tía Maria's comfortable hostel.

At dawn, he walked to a *paladar* in the square, joined the roomful of tourists waiting for breakfast, and returned to his post at the base of a palm tree refreshed. The hours dragged by and his attention wavered. There was no activity all day. By evening, he felt exhausted. He stood, stretched his legs, shouldered his bag, and hobbled away, wincing as feeling returned to his numb extremities. He had learned nothing beyond the facts that the family arrived at different times in different expensive cars. And there was a child involved. A new generation of Diaz outlaws.

Splendid. Just splendid.

17

NICOLAS STEFANO VALDEZ gurgled. Tiny bubbles appeared around his delicate lips. Izzy dabbed the corners of his mouth with a burp cloth rocked him in the living room of their earth-sheltered home. Cradling her grandson she swayed slowly, humming a little tune that popped into mind the first time she saw him in the hospital. Mel dozed in Kurt's recliner.

So peaceful. At the moment anyway.

She blinked back tears. Stefano had sent no news since before Nico's birth. Izzy had surreptitiously tried calling him, to no avail. She dared not try again, lest Mel's wrath descend on her. But there had been no further calls from him after that lunch at Steamy Joe's.

Nothing. Not a word.

Nico gurgled again. She shifted the little bundle to allow his tiny eyes to see Mel. "There's Mama, Nico. Isn't she beautiful?"

She tiptoed away, showing him things in the house for the fiftieth time. They toured the kitchen, the music room, Kurt's office, and the bedroom where his tiny crib sat an arm's length from Melody's bed.

As she turned toward the back door, Melody called, "Mom?"

Izzy hurried back to the living room. The recliner was upright, and the new mother moved stiffly toward them. "Good morning," she said, injecting cheer into her voice.

Mel settled into a morose mood. "What's good about it? And anyway, it's not morning."

Nicolas squirmed. Izzy bounced him. "Sh-sh-sh. Hush little baby. Don't cry. Grandma loves you." She hummed a lullaby and transferred the wiggly bundle to his mother. "Did you have a nice nap?"

"I don't think that's possible."

"You looked peaceful."

"Hardly," Melody said. "Stefano should be back by now. I guess he didn't make the plane. What am I going to do?"

"Call him."

"I tried. Over and over. He won't answer. He left me, Mom. He's gone."

"I can't believe that. There must be some logical explanation."

"What could it possibly be?"

"I don't know about you but I have nightmares that Stefano is lying in some back alley, bleeding to death."

"I picture some Cuban beauty taking his hand and cajoling him away from me." Mel coughed and cleared her throat. "Mom, what am I going to do? He's gone."

"I'm not sure there's anything you can do but wait. It's kind of like finding out you're pregnant, but you have to wait those forty weeks before welcoming a baby. We need to be patient. He'll call as soon as he can. If you want, I could call the sheriff."

"What could he do? Stefano's a grown man, and an immigrant. Would anybody even care? They'd assume he went back to Cuba. If anything, they'd just notify New Orleans. I'm sure the people there have lots to worry about. It's Mardi Gras season, isn't it?"

"Yes, I think it is. What else can we do?"

"If you are so worried, why don't you go to New Orleans and look for him?"

"Me?"

"Obviously I can't with a newborn, but you..." She left the sentence unfinished.

Izzy nodded. "Do you want me to go?"

"If you think it's worth the trip, find out what happened to him."

❧❧

Stefano settled in for another day, broiling in his hideaway in the tropical sunlight. His thoughts turned to Mel. With no lack of chagrin, he wondered how she was. How had she dealt with his change of plan? Had she received the letter? He counted the days of his absence on his fingers and lost track, but he was sure the birth of their child was imminent. Maybe today. Had the baby come early? When would he be able to see and hold the child?

Will I ever?

He cursed the angular stones in the wall behind him which bruised his ribs the longer he leaned against it. Shifting sideways, he kicked a pile of leaves and trash and hunched down, searching in vain for a comfortable position. A wandering dog, searching for a few edible scraps, discovered his hideaway and wriggled in beside him. Stefano scratched the dog's ears, and the mutt stretched out along his legs. He began to itch. The longer he sat with no activity, the more he itched. By mid-morning he was insane with discomfort. He stood to pace and stretch.

"Damn fool, Valdez," he muttered to himself. It was becoming clear his mission was senseless, the task of an irrational man. He cursed himself for following the fading call of a sister he'd not seen for years. "If you haven't already done so, Melody, you should file papers against me. Dissolve this sham of a marriage." He didn't deserve her.

A limousine with dark windows drove up the avenue and stopped at the Diaz gate. Activated by the guard on duty, the gate rolled open and the vehicle rolled through. It rounded a tree-lined curve and disappeared on the hillside. Moments later, a second car, shrouded against curious onlookers, followed the limousine. Before it had disappeared another vehicle arrived.

Stefano shrank against the weathered stones. He pulled his hat low over his eyes. From his concealment, he watched three additional vehicles arrive. He settled in to wait. It was late in the afternoon before activity picked up on the hillside again. One by one, each of the six vehicles exited the Diaz estate. They dispersed in different directions. None paid him any heed.

Action over, he was preparing to take his leave when another engine roared to life on the concealed drive. The blue Ferrari from the previous day raced down the curves and stopped with squealing tires at the closed gate. Stefano froze, lowering his head. The Diaz car purred. When the gate opened, the car catapulted across the street straight toward him. The mongrel dog yelped and ran. Stefano scrambled to his feet and leapt to grab the iron work mortared into the top of the weathered stones. The Ferrari screeched to a halt inches from the palm tree. The driver's door swung open and Julio Diaz jeered at him over the hood of the idling car.

18

"GET LOST, BUM." Julio Diaz spat on the stones beside Stefano. "We don't allow beggars on this street."

Stefano stared with unmasked loathing at the driver of the Ferrari.

"You look familiar," Julio said, drawing out his words, searching for a name. "Do I know you?"

Stefano narrowed his gaze and clenched his teeth. "I don't think so."

Diaz shrugged once to dismiss the vagrant and reiterated the threat. "You scum are all the same to me. Get lost. Hear me?" He returned to the driver seat, backed the Ferrari into the avenue and spun the tires as he drove away.

The following morning Stefano tagged behind a small group of tourists as they made their way up the avenue of fancy homes. As soon as he was out of sight of the Diaz guard house, he turned to pass by again. Continual walking past the driveway would be beneficial in more than one way. He'd hardly be able to fall asleep and he could remain watchful from a distance without drawing the ire of the brothers. Admittedly, it would be more difficult to discern details about any of the people entering or leaving, but he was ready to try something different.

On his third pass, the owner of a *paladar* across from the Diaz driveway emerged from the front door to enjoy a smoke in the morning sunshine. Stefano accosted him with a friendly greeting. *"Buenos dias, amigo."*

The brown Audi exited the driveway through the Diaz gate. Stefano commented casually about its appearance. The neighbor man scoffed at the display of opulence. "They are not Cubans at heart, or they could never stand to watch others go hungry while they drive such monsters around Havana."

"I never saw anyone enter or leave who wasn't a man," Stefano said. "Don't they have any women up there?"

"*Sí.* One brother took a wife. Lovely little thing, but you hardly ever see her. They don't allow her to roam on her own."

"Pity. Wonder what kind of woman would take up with such braggarts."

"Either one who has no choice in the matter, or one who craves the fancy life they offer. From what I saw of this one, she fits in the first category. Fine features, sad eyes. I caught her glance once or twice. They say she is an accomplished musician. Grew up between here and La Boca. Sometimes she takes a holiday there and I wave as she rides past."

La Boca.

Stefano knew exactly where it was. He excused himself, hoping against hope that Lena might be there. He needed to find out. He turned to face oncoming traffic and extended his arm. A few minutes later, a young man on a motorcycle pulled over. "Need a ride?"

"Heading to La Boca. Going that way? I'll make it worth your time."

With a nod from the cyclist, Stefano swung a leg over the seat behind the young man. They wound through the narrow streets toward the outskirts of Havana. As they approached the neighborhood of his youth, he was again overcome with sentimentality. At the main crossroads, his driver turned for further directions. Unable to speak, Stefano simply nodded and disembarked, handing the driver generous fare for the ride. He stared into the familiar face of the revolution's hero Che Guevara on a weathered billboard and turned onto the old familiar street.

Delicious aromas wafted from open doorways as he strolled up the hill and he remembered the delicacies his mother crafted in her kitchen. At the end of the winding street stood the two-story apartment his mother had shared with two other families, the original home of her father's people. Memories floated through his mind like seeds on a fresh breeze and he stared, unable to look away. The trim palms which had delighted Lena were unkempt. Blue water tanks dotting other nearby roofs were absent from the roof of his childhood home. Tropical vegetation tangled in disarray around the front windows. Laughter from the surrounding tenements floated on the evening breeze and he stepped gingerly toward the familiar apartment. Though the windows were dark, he knocked anyway. Nobody answered.

He pounded again. As he waited he rattled the doorknob. It was locked.

A boy rode past on a bicycle. "*Hola, Señor,*" the cyclist called to him.

Stefano looked over his shoulder. "*¿Qué?*"

"Nobody there."

"*Gracias.*"

The boy pedaled past. Stefano felt overwhelmed by an urge to get inside, to walk through the familiar rooms again and see if anything remained of his mother's prized furnishings. He stepped off the front porch, rounded the corner, and slipped into the back yard they had shared with the other residents. Overgrown with weeds, it had become a tangled mess. Piles of windblown trash filled every corner of the yard, trapped by a broken fence and the knotted weeds. A padlock secured the back door of his mother's apartment.

He glanced up toward the bedroom windows on the second level and worked into the matted center of an overgrown azalea bush which surrounded the base of a palm. With a little luck, as well as the coordination of his youthful self, he hoped to gain entrance to his childhood home. He used to do this often, slipping out to meet his friends after the women of the house slept, and returning like a ghost before they awoke. He straddled the palm and shimmied upwards until he was level with the balcony railing. He slung an arm over the weathered railing and stepped onto the precipice. After transferring his weight to the balcony, he threw his leg over the rail and stepped to the window. He lifted the window frame but it was firmly fixed in its tracks. As he remembered doing in his youth, he pressed into the window's bottom edge, and pushed upward again. It resisted but he renewed his efforts, and pressed upward with more vigor. With a snap, the window broke free and Stefano pushed it upward, the pane creaking in its tracks.

When the opening was large enough to admit his adult frame, he stretched into the darkened space, hands groping for the floor. His feet dropped through the window and he scrambled to a stand. He groped his way along the wall and flicked a light switch. Dim light filtered from a dusty, bug-filled fixture above the narrow stairway. Holding his breath, he descended the stairs into the dining room. His mother's hand embroidered napery scrunched in disarray on the table. He stepped into the front room and reached for the light switch. Though it clicked, no light appeared. He groped forward, straining to see the front room, imagining its arrangement from the last time he'd seen it. He bumped into something and stopped. Things weren't the same.

On impulse, he pulled his mobile phone from the side pocket of his shoulder bag and activated its flashlight function. He'd stumbled against a dining chair, tipped over and lying on its side. He shone the light into the front room. His mother's old easy chair filled the honored space Elsie Lenore once occupied.

A chill shot through his entire body. Someone slumped in his mother's old easy chair.

19

STEFANO RUSHED THROUGH eerie shadows cast by the kitchen lamp, knelt beside the figure in the chair, and tipped the head up.

Lena.

He jerked backward and her head dropped forward until her chin rested on her collar bone, her ghostly gaze resting on an open book in her lap. His chest heaving, he reached toward her with trembling hands and shook her shoulders, but they were held tight against the chair by loops of hemp rope. He cradled her face in his palms and wept.

Too late—I'm too late.

His head spun. He needed fresh air. Stumbling to the front door, he opened it, and sobbed his anguish into the twilight. A fresh ocean breeze filled his lungs and he turned back into the dark room. With a clearer head, he knelt before Lena and fingered the rope binding her to the chair. He crawled behind and worked the knot until it loosened and the coils fell into her lap. As he lifted the rough coils, Stefano noted the poem on the open book in her lap. The last thing she'd seen on earth was her favorite poem, "My Mother's Piano."

He set the book on a small table beside the chair and cradled Lena in his arms. Why didn't he arrive a little sooner? He lifted her slender limp body and circled the room, tears running down his face. What could he do now?

A voice inside his mind provided an answer. *Get her out of here.*

But how?

Call for help.

A flash erupted through a crack in the closed blinds. Cradling Lena in his arms, he elbowed the blinds aside. Headlights wound along the narrow street and the roar of an engine announced the arrival of Julio Diaz in his Ferrari.

There was no time to think things through. He heaved Lena back into the chair and caressed her silky hair with a tender farewell touch. On impulse, he grabbed the book of poetry and stuffed it inside his shirt as he passed through the dining room in its telltale disarray. The light filtering from the stairwell caught a wrinkled piece of paper on the tabletop, partially covered by his mother's hand-crafted tablecloth. In a quick glance as he passed, he read the last typewritten sentence, "I can't take it any longer." It was signed by his sister's hand, "Lenabelle Valdez," a nickname she hadn't used since childhood.

It was a sign. And he had no time to figure out what she might have wanted to say.

The Ferrari stopped on the neglected yard and stripes of light splayed across the front room until the engine died. He stole one last look at her body before the driver doused the headlights. The room returned to darkness. He lunged up the stairway, two steps at a time.

A key rattled in the front door lock. *Damn.*

He'd overlooked the lock. Having already unlocked the door, it opened all too readily. Julio Diaz entered, yelling expletives, confused.

Stefano rushed to the window and dove through it onto the balcony. He rolled to the railing and hauled himself erect. Diaz shouted from the living room. He'd discovered the unlashed rope. Light blazed on the stairway and footsteps thundered up the stairs. No time. He'd have to leave the window open.

He crouched and catapulted into the palm fronds. With thighs wrapped loosely around the palm trunk he shimmied down, dropping into the dense foliage of the azalea bush. He tore through it, blindly fighting the scratching twigs. Fury filled his whole being as fresh air filled his lungs. He ran from the back yard, vaulted the low garden fence at its boundary, and plowed through the unkempt weeds of a neighboring tenement, yanking his pant legs against brambles. At the narrow paved street, he raced down the hill, never once looking back.

He passed through the small shopping district, its cobblestone walkways lined with park benches, empty in the darkness of night. He ran past the historic buildings, now decaying after years of neglect. He thundered through an *Artesania* district, devoid of any displays at this hour. At last he could run no further. He hobbled under the cover of a gazebo, near a statue of Jose Marti. There was no movement anywhere.

He bent over, bracing his hands against his quaking knees. Clearing his throat, he spat on the ground, closed his eyes, and struggled to control the frantic inhalations. The poetry book slid from his shirt and fell open on the ground. Lena's favorite poem, stared back at him in the moonlight. Tears in his eyes, he read.

My Mother's Piano by Julia Dagenais

Huddled beneath that keyboard
I peered out through Corinthian columns—
A priestess surveying with pity
The silent world outside my singing sanctuary.
Above my head sounds rippled and crashed
From her fingers.
Beside me the firm feet pressed a pattern
From the worn-bright brass.

Long after the music stopped
I, a weeping votary,
Washed the cracked and yellowed keys
And polished the rosewood varnish.
Still smooth and shiny in protected places,
It was mostly rough and crazed by time.

Before I could quite name the notes
She summoned with such mastery,
The song was over and a stillness struck
That muffled all melody.

What did I learn then from the flashing hands
And the doomed figure swaying on the claw-foot stool?
That a woman should sing;
That joy should flow in beauty
From her fingers and her feet;
That the rising chord re-echoes
When the hands and lips are stilled.

Lena was gone, her hands and lips silenced forever. He saw her again, lifeless in his arms, another vision of his beloved sister that would haunt him forever.

20

LITTLE BY LITTLE, distant night sounds invaded Stefano's awareness. Human voices murmured nearby and he crouched low in the center gazebo, staring in the direction of approaching footsteps. They belonged to a man and a woman who walked along slowly, each gazing intently into the other's face in the moonlight. The woman spoke a few words and the man responded with a gentle laugh. They stopped walking when they reached the open square, faced each other, and drew together for a passionate kiss.

A solitary sob escaped Stefano's throat. The couple on the bridge stirred, looking his direction. Could they see him? He didn't want that. He wanted to be alone, but the woman raised her arm to point. He had to get out of there.

He sprinted down the gazebo steps, away from the couple. His legs pounded pavement, then gravel, then the weeds alongside a farm road. He ran as if the rhythm of his footfalls would numb the pain in his mind. Lena was dead.

Murdered.

Julio Diaz murdered his sister and the cur had the audacity to return to the scene. Why? To make sure she had died? When had she been taken there? Was it during one of the intervals when he dozed off across from the Diaz drive? Had he missed his last chance to help his sister while pacing up and down the street, determined not to draw attention to himself?

In the moonlight he ran, blinded by remorse and unquenchable rage, oblivious to everything but the heavy ache in his heart. Turning on a side road, he plummeted down an incline and arrived on a strip of sandy beach. He charged across the sand into the waves, splashing deeper until the water dragged against him and he could no longer run. He sank to his knees and plunged his hands into the fluid sand. An incoming wave washed over him. Sputtering, he blew salt water from his face, shaking his head. Water streamed from his black curls and he howled.

His cry blew away on the wind, lost in splashing surf. He sat back on his heels and wept, long and hard. He wept for his mother, who had watched her dreams evaporate during the *period especial* years until she met an early grave. He wept for Lena, murdered by a tyrant. And he wept for Melody, his own jilted wife, left alone by a husband driven to a mission of futility.

He had failed. As a son, he'd failed. As a musician, he didn't measure up. As a brother, he fell far short. As a husband and father, ditto. Sinking into despair, Stefano felt more hopeless and inept than he'd felt in his entire life.

As a man, he had failed.

Let the sea take him. What did it matter? He let his head droop forward, his lips kissing the Atlantic. The breeze died. Moments later, it renewed itself, coming from the opposite direction.

Tia Maria's wise voice echoed in his mind. *Life is the wind, always there until it isn't, and never long from the same direction.*

The breeze gained velocity and he heard it whistle through a structure on the shore. In his grief, the whistle became Lena's voice, singing a lamentation. Stefano opened his eyes. She was calling to him on the breeze. He strained to hear her voice with clarity and grew agitated when he could not. Shaking his head to clear his mind, he turned his head toward the shore and he heard it again. A cry, a woman's voice—Lena's dying song. She sang two words, "Elsie Lenore..."

Our mother's piano.

And it hit him. He had to get back to Kansas, to Mel and the baby. He'd make it up to her and she'd surely forgive him. He'd rebuild the destroyed Steinway, make it as good as new or die trying. For Lena. For their mother. He would do it. And then...

Then he didn't know what he'd do.

One step at a time.

First, he needed to deal with Julio Diaz. The man deserved the same fate Lena suffered. After justice was done,
he'd leave Cuba and never return. He rose to his feet. With an
unsteady gait, he splashed toward shore. His resolve to exact
vengeance on Julio Diaz grew with each step.

And the wind wailed, "El-sie-e-e-e Le-no-o-o-ore."

❧ ❧

Three thousand miles away, sirens blared in every coastal
town along the Pacific coast of North America, as the Juan de
Fuca tectonic plate grated beneath North America to produce
an earthquake that surpassed all geological predictions. The
fault line bounced, releasing billions of tons of pent-up force.
After centuries of relative peace with the crustal plates creeping along at the rate of two inches every year, the section beneath the Pacific Ocean had amassed incredible amounts of
energy on its journey toward the mantle of the earth and the
resistance provided by Earth's colliding crustal plates could
not hold it back any longer. Juan de Fuca surged seventy feet
at once beneath North America along the fault line boundary,
rumbling the crust above in a mega-earthquake, magnitude of
9.2 at the fault line.

Coastal highway 101 crumbled into fragments. Sections of
it dropped fifty feet below the previous level. Poorly designed
buildings tottered and crumbled on Vancouver Island, British
Columbia, and south to Cape Mendocino, California. Hundreds of schools numbered among the devastated buildings.
Local crises escalated due to the mid-day timing of the quake
with schools in session up and down the coast. Children by
the thousands and their teachers were either trapped in
classrooms, or crushed by teetering walls as they collapsed
inward. Aftershocks arrived that brought the massive global
forces into a new equilibrium, and ill-prepared cities faced
Earth's natural and ancient forces.

Sirens screamed and warned of a separate devastating
event. For communities that had offered tsunami drills, in-
habitants knew what was coming. Those who could still walk

or ride bicycles had mere minutes to climb to safety. The streets and highways were useless. Crippled by infrastructure damage during the earthquake, public emergency systems were unable to answer the volume of emergency calls. Beyond the warning sirens, there was no help available for millions who desperately needed it.

A tsunami generated by the megaquake wave raced shoreward. Within twenty minutes, a wall of water 125 feet high smashed the crumbling coastal towns. Cars, whole houses, earthquake rubble, panicked pets, and screaming children were swept out to sea. Hours later, waves generated by this Cascadian Subduction Zone earthquake would slam across Hawaii, on their way to Japan and other eastern Asian countries.

As the tectonic plates settled into a relative equilibrium, the disruption beneath the zone disturbed magma vents and woke two sleeping volcanoes in the upper Cascade Mountain Range. Sirens shrieked yet again to warn inland residents to flee before the anticipated volcanic eruptions.

The telephone on the desk of Harvey Blackstone, CEO of Global Relief Services headquartered in Dallas, rang constantly for three hours following the earthquake in the Pacific Northwest. Once alerted to the developing situation, he issued orders for office staff to contact every one of their trained relief workers. Melody Valdez topped his list. Though she had requested a lengthy maternity leave, he needed every single one of his trained rescue staff.

21

WITH FATALISTIC DETERMINATION, Stefano purchased minutes of the island internet usage. He needed to contact Mel. Even if she had ceased to care for him, she deserved to know what was happening in Cuba. He sent multiple emails and attempted voice connections through internet applications but his repeated efforts to contact his wife or her parents in Kansas were fruitless. He hoped to talk through his plans, to polish ideas, and to come up with something that would work, maybe even to find a rational voice that would talk him out of it. Mel continued to ignore him. His funds dwindled along with his options. He needed a plan, a job, and a weapon to act against Julio Diaz.

"Piensa, Valdez," he said aloud. *"One step at a time."* He first had to find a job of some kind.

He returned to the music conservatory and offered his assistance with the repair and regulation of his donated pianos. The staff technician hired him on the spot.

Each evening he returned to the room offered by Tía Maria. She took to him like a mother hen, supplementing her food rations to prepare delicious meals. When she could, she shared the local news.

One evening, the weekly newspaper *Granma* was filled with photos from the Pacific coast of North America. An offshore earthquake had generated a devastating tsunami that hit the west coast of Oregon and California with the ferocity of a hydrogen bomb. Tia Maria clicked her tongue, gazing over the photos of splintered buildings. She shoved the paper across the table to Stefano and he read with intensity, remembering the aftermath of the hurricane.

"Casualties?" he asked.

"They say thousands died." Tía Maria shook her head. "Just glad that was in the Pacific."

Stefano nodded absently.

A week later, he rubbed an oil polish over the case on each donated piano and helped move each of the four instruments to its designated studio. When the last one was placed, he nodded his approval. "Know where I might find other employment?" he asked the staff technician.

"Depends on what you are willing to do."

"At the moment, anything."

The conservatory technician thought for a moment. "My wife's brother started a new cab company two months ago. It's a booming business. You might try there."

"Sounds perfect." Stefano shook his mentor's hand and departed.

With the taxi job, he had a level of mobility he'd not previously enjoyed. The next step was to secure a rifle, and learn to use it. With firearms strictly forbidden in Cuba, the acquisition of a weapon presented a serious obstacle. After a Facebook message to Roberto in New Orleans, he soon connected with an arms dealer in Miami.

Waves lapped onto the beach twenty meters off the left side of his small boat. Grateful for the bright moonlight, Stefano squinted along the coast, searching for the area of breakers the email instructions described. He adjusted the rudder, moving closer to shore. Beyond any sign of Havana, he glanced over his shoulder, scrutinizing the surface of the Atlantic.

Nothing amiss. Nothing notable either.

He detected no floating objects anywhere in the moonlight, nor was there any telltale motion along the shoreline. How far was it to that rocky point? He revved up the engine and rounded a small spit. Whitecaps topped gentle swells in the distance as his destination came into view. He closed the distance to the breakers and slowed the propeller to maneuver toward a sheltered spot between two boulders. He looped a tie-down around a knee-high stone and clambered onto a rock, surveying the surrounding area.

Nothing. This was the date, was it not? He was sure of it. Hard to know the time, though. Had he missed the rendez-vous?

Patience, Valdez.

He sat on the rock, knees drawn up with his arms wrapped around them. Mist from the splashing waves coated his face and hands. He shivered against the chill.

What if something was wrong? He could easily be fingered in this ruse, with hell to pay. But for Lena, he steeled himself, resolute to see it to the end.

At least he'd come this far in his plan of vengeance. He had a regular job with decent pay, for a Cuban. He had a place to stay as long as necessary. And he had Roberto's con-nections to supply the needed merchandise. Given the illegal status of firearms on the island, there was no other way but to meet this stranger at midnight in the moonlight. He hoped Roberto knew the supplier well.

He stood, stretching his shoulders. He swung his arms to increase circulation, and hopped a few dance steps on the boulder. A spot in the distance caught his eye. Something on the ocean gleamed in the moonlight. He crouched while a small motor boat pulled beside his craft.

A dark figure rose in the boat. "Valdez?" the stranger said.

"*Sí.*"

The man leapt to a stone and reached into the boat for a long, narrow case. "You have the cash?"

"*Sí.* In US dollars. May I see it?"

The man opened the case and Stefano fingered the rifle inside.

"Remington 700, as you ordered, with a modified stock to accept magazines." The delivery man pulled the case away and held out his open hand.

Stefano reached inside his jacket for an envelope of cash. "Can you show me how to use this?"

With a nod, the stranger removed the Remington and handed it to Stefano. "Best to use this when you are prone. It gives a good kick. But you can use the retracting bipod." He clicked down two short legs. "Rest the buttstock on a shooting sock. A bag of rice or sand will do. Holds it steady. Here's the safety. I'd keep it on until you're good and ready to fire. All too easy to lose a foot."

Stefano nodded. He fingered the safety and the trigger. "Ammunition?"

The stranger pried a box from the transport case. "You ever used something like this?"

"No," Stefano said, his nostrils flaring in the darkness. "How do you load it?"

"Easy enough." The man pulled a magazine from the box and snapped it into the magazine well. "I suggest you practice before you..." His voice trailed off.

"I get it," Stefano said.

22

TWO MORNINGS LATER, Stefano dropped his first fare in front of a *paladar* in Old Havana. He found a parking spot in the shade of a banyan tree near the art museum and settled in to wait. He unrolled the local *Granma* newspaper. He tried to send Mel a message from his phone. There was no response.

Of course not.

The minutes on his internet card ticked away until the minutes expired. He shrugged, defeated. Purchasing another card would be futile. He'd just have to wait to make amends in person.

Julio Diaz raced past revving the engine of his Ferrari and Stefano flicked off his cab light, started his engine, and pulled onto the street a few cars behind Diaz. The Ferrari wound through traffic toward the dock warehouses. Diaz found a parking spot beside a long warehouse and dashed inside. Stefano passed the warehouse and rolled into a parking area for taxis around the next corner. He secured his cab and strolled back to the shipping street in time to see Diaz sprint through the traffic to a cigar factory and disappear inside.

Stefano paced the walk in front of the factory until Diaz exited and ducked onto a side street. Stefano tailed him to the *Plaza Vieja*, where they wove around outdoor tables set up to serve passing tourists and Diaz entered a *paladar*. As Stefano passed the open entrance, the voice of Julio Diaz roared as he demanded a drink and a meal.

Stefano returned to his cab and patrolled the harbor street, keeping an eye on the Ferrari. A family group beckoned as he swung through the shipyard, but Stefano directed them to another cab with a nod. He was out-of-service until further notice. Diaz returned to his car ninety minutes later. Trapped in stalled traffic a block away as the Ferrari darted away,

Stefano blared the auto's horn until he managed to extricate his cab from the snarled traffic. The blue car wove toward the thoroughfare that ran from the harbor to the hills above the *Siboney* housing district. Stefano stepped on the accelerator and closed the gap.

Julio braked suddenly and swung across the boulevard into the front entrance of Colon Cemetery. He parked behind the chocolate brown Audi Stefano recognized from the Diaz mansion and hustled to join a crowd of mourners processing along a narrow walkway between the opulent granite monuments. One of the largest cemeteries on the planet, Colon Cemetery honored Cuba's European discoverer, Christopher Columbus. It was every Cuban's right to be interred there, though only important families owned their own vaults. Mourning processions occurred multiple times daily. This one, though, gave Stefano a start.

¿Qué tal?

He parked his taxi behind other waiting cars along the boulevard, slipped into the cemetery gate, and walked casually along the road, parallel to the line of mourners. At the front of the procession, Julio walked with his head bowed, two strides behind another Cuban in an expensive-looking suit. Between the two men, a boy of about ten or twelve years stumbled along the path. The whole family was there, two brothers and the heir of the next generation.

Stefano kept to the shadows of neighboring monuments and worked near enough to study facial details on the Diaz brothers as they proceeded to a waiting vault. They appeared to be following two caskets.

Stefano felt confused. *Dos?*

But, of course. Enrique's remains must have arrived home. He wondered what results the autopsy had shown. How had the third brother met his demise?

The procession halted and the crowd gathered close to the Diaz vault. A priest raised his arms to begin funeral rites. With a clear view of the surviving brothers' faces, Stefano noted the family resemblance. Julio and his older brother stood the same height, with the same tan complexion and narrow facial shape. Definitely, they were cut from the same mold. Stefano couldn't recall ever meeting the oldest brother.

Teofilo.

The jaws of this oldest brother ground together, muscles flexing, and his nostrils flared. He obviously was the family patriarch, given the space everyone around him allowed. Even the priest deferred to Teofilo.

The boy between Enrique's brothers never looked up. He stayed behind the men and disappeared from view when the arriving crowd pressed close. Stefano caught a few words of the soliloquy, which left no doubt that he was viewing Lena's burial rites. "Grieving widow..." the priest mentioned. Stefano sighed. She had married the brother who died, then.

"Could no longer face life without her loving husband..."

Right.

Lena's plea on the postcard screamed in his mind. "We need you." His arms felt the weight of a ton of unanswered questions with the lifeless body that he had freed from bondage to a chair.

Suicides don't tie themselves up.

Tears welled in his eyes. He backed away from the farce of a ceremony and when he was beyond sight, he turned and ran.

23

NINETY MINUTES LATER, Julio's Ferrari lurched onto the boulevard. Stefano turned into traffic and tailed the speeding car. He stopped the meter on his taxi and concentrated on keeping Julio in sight. The Ferrari left the city and purred into the countryside. Houses thinned out, and businesses disappeared altogether. Stefano varied his speed but stayed close enough to watch his quarry.

The radio on his dashboard crackled with scratchy fragments of his employer's angry voice, demanding an explanation for his lengthy break from service. He picked up the speaker and spoke with careful enunciation. "Sorry. Can't hear you."

He flicked off the radio. He'd just lost this job, but after today he wouldn't need it.

As he followed Julio into the countryside, he met a few oxcarts laden with produce for the city markets. He passed scattered thatched-roof cottages nestled among palm copses and shrubs along the roadside. Farmers worked fields on both sides of the narrow blacktop track, closely following their beasts of labor on foot. Cotton puffs of cumulus clouds floated across the idyllic scene.

The road ascended a slight incline. At the crest, a valley stretched ahead lined with lush green tobacco. Mountains encircled the pastoral landscape with random steep dome-shaped rock formations jutting from the valley floor, the legendary *mogotes* of Cuba's *Valle de Viñales*. Clusters of palm trees marked the location of fresh water pools, collecting above ground in the karst landscape. This was the place where fine Cuban tobacco was grown for cigars exported to world markets. Fortunes were made here, and sometimes lost.

He thought of the cigars he'd proudly bought and presented to Mel for the birth.

Which I missed.

Intense remorse seared his mind. With concentrated effort he refocused on the day's unfolding mission. Soon enough, he'd be home again.

The road stretched across the valley and disappeared in the distance at the base of a line of *mogotes.* Blue flashed in the sunlight as the Ferrari rounded the base of a limestone crag, its nearly vertical sides covered by dense vegetation clinging to life in rugged crevasses on the dome. Tobacco fields increased in number and size, their rectangular outlines appearing alien among the random hillocks scattered on the plain, as if they'd been abandoned after a frenetic soccer game among the gods.

The road passed a plantation mansion, its columned two-story residence set off by resplendent fenced courtyards and patios. Julio drove past the plantation headquarters, but as he rolled past, the brake lights on the Ferrari blazed. It swerved onto a path through a tobacco field. Stefano slowed as he approached the field, staring intently at the cobalt car working through the ripening plants toward a slatted tobacco-drying shed, thatched roof draped over the cornice and eaves. Two stories high, its white-washed walls peeled under the assault of uncounted seasons in the tropical sunshine. A sea-blue door adorned the otherwise unbroken drabness of the shed. Smoking a fresh cigar and nonchalantly watching Julio approach, a man leaned against the slats beside the door.

Stefano drove on, rounding the dome-shaped hillock that towered over the tobacco shed. When he was out of sight, he pulled off the road and entered a thicket of palms and dense shrubbery. He killed the engine of his car, fished a set of field glasses from beneath his seat, and removed the rifle and extra rounds from the trunk. He stood tall beside the cab, closed his eyes and drew a deep lungful of air.

Now or never. Enfocate, Valdez.

⋙⋘

Her arms loaded with luggage, Izzy pushed open the door and entered her kitchen. With a nudge from her foot, she swung the door closed and stumbled to the living room. Afternoon light filtered through the leafless trees on the circle drive, throwing stripes of warm sunlight across the parquet flooring. Mel sat in the upholstered chair by the south window, eyes closed, the infant Nico asleep at her breast. Izzy set her bags under the curve of her parlor Steinway across the room.

Mel's eyes fluttered open. "Mom?" she asked. Her voice quivered with confusion.

Or was it incredulity? Maybe even anger?

"Hi," Izzy said gently.

"What—why are you here? Where's Stefano?"

Definitely anger.

It wasn't enough that her husband absconded on the eve of Nico's birth. Now her own mother had let her down.

Frizzy Izzy. Can't do anything right.

Izzy silently scolded herself for her clumsy entrance. She sighed. "Mel, honey. I looked everywhere. He wasn't to be found."

"Why didn't you keep looking then?"

"That bartender, Roberto. He told me Stefano had been there. Evidently your husband followed Lena to Havana."

"Cuba!" Mel's jaw dropped open. "Son of a—two days. He said two days."

"There was an incident, Roberto said. It had to be serious. Stefano would not have gone further without a good reason. We have to believe that."

"You believe it if you want. I'm so fed up."

"You said he tried to call."

"Several times."

"But you didn't answer."

"I didn't feel like talking to him. Why didn't you keep looking? Drag him back from Cuba? Wait till I see him again."

"Mel, you are making no sense. In one breath you won't even talk to him. Then you're mad at me for not chasing him to Havana."

Mel closed her eyes, her chest heaving.

"Mel, sweetie—"

"Stop, Mom! I know it's crazy. I can't even explain it. I am furious. But then I'm worried sick about him."

"It's because you love him. If it helps, I did check into traveling to Cuba myself."

Mel stared at her mother, lips trembling.

Izzy answered the unspoken question. "It's complicated. First, I left my passport here. Then, it takes weeks to get a travel VISA approved, if at all. And you know travel to Cuba is extremely limited lately."

"How could he go then? He's probably still in New Orleans."

"No. He's a Cuban native. That's a different story altogether. Roberto told me that Stefano had crated up the Valdez family piano and shipped it to the shop. He's planning to return." She took Mel's hand and gave a little squeeze. "We need to be patient."

"The family piano?" Mel narrowed her eyes, staring at her mother.

Izzy nodded. "Haven't had any shipments arrive, have we?"

With a barely perceptible nod, Mel said, "Yesterday. I thought it was something you ordered."

"In the shop?"

Nico stirred and woke. He began to cry and his mother checked his diaper. "He needs a change."

"I'll check that shipment while you take care of my grandson." Izzy headed to the shop.

24

CLINGING TO THE shadows, Stefano crept around a jagged outcrop. On the far side, a jumble of vines hid the mouth of a small cave. He stepped inside, parted the vegetation with one hand, and peered intently at the weathered shed through his binoculars. It was the same as he had left it. The Ferrari was parked, its nose a meter from the turquoise doorway, no sign of any people around. Julio and the tobacco farmer must have entered the shed. He'd wait.

He eyed the rugged stalactite rock outcrops that framed the cave opening. Similar jagged surfaces appeared on the rocks visible through the leaves. It was as if the cave had turned inside out. At any rate, scrambling over the bare rock would present hazards he'd not anticipated. He reached for a mid-sized tree limb extending from a small tree anchored in the rugged crevasse between two open air stalactites. A tug on the limb assured him it would hold his weight. He clasped an overhead limb, locked his fingers together, and swung up until his thighs draped over the limb. The rifle strapped to his back, he reached for another and pulled himself higher. The process made him recall the nights of his youth when he'd sneaked out and back into his upper level room using the backyard trees.

He climbed into a nest of vines woven through another tree's limbs. Ten meters above the valley floor, he straddled a forked branch and re-checked the scene across the tops of the tobacco plants. From this height the view was much clearer. Nothing had changed. He leaned forward, reclined on the maze of interwoven vines and branches, and set himself up for a target shoot. This time, the target would be real.

Every few minutes he scanned the area with the field glasses. Minutes ballooned into hours. Perspiration beaded on his forehead. He checked the safety on the Remington and took practice aim. He'd only get one shot. It must count.

Steady. Stay calm.

Fluffy clouds floated lazily across the azure sky, barely intercepting any of the sun rays. Distant fields wavered as heat lifted from them. Not a breath of air stirred around his perch. The branches beneath him displayed no more signs of life than the still shed in the distance. No leaves rustled. He swatted a lone fly that buzzed his forehead, but other than that, no wildlife murmured on the dome. A few birds chattered in the neighboring trees. Blood rushed through the veins in his ears. High overhead, an airplane droned over and disappeared in the distance.

He looked through the field glasses again. No sign of Julio Diaz.

The afternoon passed and heat built in the greenery. At one point, a slight updraft wafted the scent of an orchid toward him. It passed and did not return, leaving only the putrid stench of his own perspiration. A droplet of sweat coursed from his hairline across his forehead, stinging the inside of his right eye. He blinked, clearing his vision, and swiped his forehead with the back of his hand. His thirst grew until his tongue felt like sandpaper. He swallowed. Saliva poured across his tongue and he licked saltiness from his perspiring upper lip.

He shifted on the bed of vines and leaned across the gun barrel. It seared his cheek and he recoiled. Shifting again, he brought the steel barrel into the shade. Again he checked the shed through the field glasses.

Still no Julio.

The afternoon heat lulled him into a stupor and his head drooped. He snapped to attention, squinting toward the shed. He felt his head nod again, shook himself to regain alertness, and checked the shed again. Everything was the same—a vacant scene at the door of the drying shed.

How long had he been balancing in the trees? He had no clear notion other than the lowering arc of the sun, halfway to the horizon now. How long would this meeting continue, he wondered. Had Diaz left through another door? He considered climbing down.

The blue door swung open. Instantly alert, he adjusted the shooting sock to steady his aim, and leaned into the scope. The tobacco farmer followed Julio Diaz out of the building. The expression on both men's faces was tense, as if they'd argued for hours. With a dismissive wave, Julio turned his back on the other man.

Stefano took a deep breath and flicked off the safety on his gun. He took careful aim at Julio's chest. The farmer lifted his hand and gestured obscenely at Julio's retreating back before he disappeared inside the shed, slamming the door behind him. Stefano's aim followed Julio as the man rounded the Ferrari.

Easy now. Easy. Enfocate, Valdez.

He inhaled again, and let the breath escape. He blinked to clear his vision and fingered the trigger. Before he squeezed, a ripe cherry erupted on Julio's forehead. The man's face registered an instant of shock and he crumpled to the ground.

¿Qué tal?

Stefano checked his gun. It was primed and ready, but it had not been fired.

❧❧

When Izzy returned to the kitchen, Mel stood in front of the open refrigerator, studying the items on the shelves. Nico draped over her arm, drooling onto a white cloth under his chin. Mel pulled a pitcher of fruit tea from the shelf, then shook her head and pushed it back.

"What d'ya need?" Izzy asked.

"Nothing. Nothing looks good."

"Want me to brew some fresh tea?"

Mel shrugged and returned to the living room chair.

Izzy followed her, pulling an envelope from her shirt pocket. "Look what I found in the shipping envelope."

Mel closed her eyes.

"It's for you, honey."

The new mother leaned back in the chair. Her eyes remaining closed against the world.

"Melody?" Izzy whispered. When her daughter made no reply, she said. "That crate came from New Orleans, the piano Stefano sent."

"So?"

"This letter was on the crate." She placed the envelope on her daughter's knees and tapped it gently.

Mel opened her eyes a slit and stared at the penmanship. "Take it away. I don't want it."

"Sweetheart. Don't you want to see what he wrote?"

She snorted. "Sure. You think I need to see it with my own eyes? *'Dear Mel. The last six years have been wonderful for me. However, I must find Lena. I will never forget you. Take care of our child and have a good life.'* He's not coming back, Mom. I don't need to read it."

"Why would he send his mother's piano here if he didn't plan to return?" Izzy said.

"His mother's piano?"

"I think it must be. It's a Steinway. It must mean something to him because it's in really bad shape. I think you should read the letter. Please."

"Later." With a resigned grimace, Mel glared at the sealed envelope. She stood and the letter slid onto the floor, unwanted and unread. "I can't do this, Mom. I can't." She stomped to the bedroom and slammed the door. A wail rose from the startled infant.

Izzy knelt to pick up the letter, for the first time seeing the note on the back. *"Melody, I love you forever. I WILL BE BACK!"* She set it gently at the base of a lamp on the walnut end table beside Mel's favorite chair. As she turned toward the piano shop, a ringtone jangled inside the bedroom with an incoming call for Melody. "Please, let that be Stefano," she whispered to herself.

25

IZZY LINGERED IN the hallway, loathe to intrude on Mel's private phone conversation, but too concerned to leave. The snippets of conversation she overheard convinced her that Mel was not chatting with the absent Stefano.

"I heard," Mel said, her voice firm. "Yes, it's terrible."

What's terrible?

Mel continued the one-sided conversation. "I understand, but you have to realize I have a newborn here. I don't see how..." her voice trailed away. "Okay. I'll think about it. That's all I will promise right now. Day after tomorrow? Yes. I'll call you back then."

There was silence after the call ended. Izzy waited a few minutes before she tapped lightly on the bedroom door.

"What, Mom." The tone of her daughter's voice hinted at unrest.

"I overheard a bit of your call," she said through the closed door. "Was it Stefano?" She had to defuse suspicion. Mel would surely not object to her curiosity about a call from Stefano.

"No." Mel's voice sounded tired. "It was Global Relief."

"Oh?"

"You know that big earthquake on the west coast?"

"Yes. Terrible destruction."

"They need help to organize relief and reconstruction."

"You told them you were unavailable. You've got Nico."

"I did, Mom. I told them."

"Well, that's that."

"Maybe. It's really bad and they need everyone. I told them I'd give it some thought."

"Mel..."

"Stop. Just leave me alone okay?"

❦

Stefano gasped. He'd heard nothing, no shot, no shouts, no rustling movement anywhere in the surrounding plantation. There was nothing different about the scene other than Julio, now dead on the ground.

How could that be? He checked the rifle again. It definitely had not been fired. His cheeks burned and he grew acutely aware of every detail around him, the chatter of birds, a whine of mosquitoes, the crackling of leaves as a larger animal moved in the early evening near the base of the dome.

Somebody else shot Julio Diaz.

Damn.

He'd wanted to serve justice to this arrogant scumbag. But he had not fired.

Somebody else wanted the man dead.

That person was highly skilled, and possessed equipment he did not. Who was it? And why did he kill Julio? The tobacco farmer? But the shot came from the wrong direction.

In all the advance preparations, Stefano had not once considered this possibility. The Diaz family was too powerful. Only a madman would take a chance like this. A madman like Lena's grieving brother. Yet somebody did the job for him.

He felt exposed and vulnerable. There were things about the Diaz family he had not learned, forces at work he couldn't imagine, let alone control.

He lowered his eye to the rifle scope, and studied the scene at the Ferrari. A tall man sauntered into view from the field to his right, a rifle slung over his shoulder. It was the older Diaz brother—he was sure of it. The man still wore the expensive suit he'd worn at the morning's funeral ceremony. Teofilo Diaz strolled to Julio's body and nudged him with the toe of his boot. There was no sign of distress in his actions. He knelt over Julio and twisted his brother's head one way, then the other. Standing again, he pulled a mobile phone from his shirt pocket and took a photo of the dead man.

This man's brother had just been murdered, yet Teofilo Diaz seemed strangely unconcerned.

¿Qué tal?

This made no sense whatsoever, unless... unless it was Teofilo Diaz who had pulled the trigger. Teofilo Diaz murdered his own brother?

The turquoise door swung open and the tobacco farm manager erupted, gesturing wildly, shouting a torrent of panicked words. The man pointed to Julio's body, then to himself, madly shaking his head. Teofilo calmly stepped back a pace, slipped the rifle from his shoulder and shot the frantic farm manager. The hapless man dropped to the ground, clutching a crimson flood spurting from his chest.

Stefano reared back. In his haste, he forgot all about the safety on his weapon. It was already disengaged, the rifle ready to fire. And it did. The shot rang across the tobacco field, echoing and re-echoing against the randomly spaced mounds jutting from the valley floor, in stark contrast to the suppressed weapon of the eldest Diaz brother. Teofilo turned toward him in slow motion, raised his rifle and peered through the scope above its barrel, swinging it in an arc toward the random *mogotes*. He zeroed in on the branch Stefano had claimed.

Caramba!

For a fraction of a second that seemed to echo eternity, the two gunmen gazed at each other through opposing scopes. Teofilo spread his feet, braced his stance, and aimed his weapon directly at Stefano.

You're screwed, Valdez. Run!

26

STEFANO PUSHED UPWARD from where he lay on the branch and his knee broke through the vines. Swearing, he reared backwards and tumbled head first along the limbs. He released his hold on the weapon and grabbed for anything that would break his fall. The Remington dove through the vines and landed in a thicket of thorny shrubs. He clutched the vines, scraping flesh from his palms. Digging his heels into the maze of leaves, he was able to check his fall, breaking through the vines as he continued toward the valley floor.

He landed on his back at the edge of the tobacco field, rolled into the plants, crouched, and froze, listening.

Piensa, Valdez.

There were no telltale sounds of pursuit through the tobacco fields. He crashed through the tobacco toward the base of the dome. At the thorn bushes beneath his afternoon blind, he plunged in up to his shoulders. Swearing under his breath as the needles ripped tiny rivulets of blood along his forearms, he stretched as far as the thorns would allow. The rifle was half a meter beyond his reach. There was no way to retrieve the weapon, without shredding the skin on every inch of his body.

Leave it.

Retracting his arms in another round of vicious scratches, he stood with his back against the dome and stared along the empty roadway. He retraced his steps to the shallow cave, now illuminated in the late afternoon sunlight. For a moment, he slipped into the cavern and knelt. Rubbing the scratches along his arms vigorously, he masked the pinpoints of pain. He froze stock still, and listened again. Still there were no sounds to alert him to danger.

The car.

He had to get to the car. He patted his front pocket to assure himself the keys remained where he'd put them, and stepped from the cave mouth. He rounded the dome, clinging as close to it as he could, jogged through the brush to the copse of palms where he'd left the car, and pawed through his pockets for the ignition key. He yanked the driver's door open and fell into the seat, stabbing the key clumsily into position. When it roared to life, he bounced over the matted tufts of roadside grass to the rough highway.

Stefano wound his way along unlighted dirt paths toward the city. Only once did he find himself on a dead end road, having to back track. He moved slowly, windows open to allow aural surveillance of the surrounding area. He was not so naïve to think that the remaining Diaz brother would be satisfied to leave him alone. Not if he was a witness to two murders. Unless he could avoid a confrontation with Teofilo Diaz, his days were undoubtedly numbered.

He left the taxi at its garage after midnight. Keeping to the shadows on the residential side streets, he made his way to Tia Maria's and dropped into bed. Though exhausted, he couldn't sleep. The day's events replayed in his mind until thoughts of Mel and the baby replaced them. He had the best chance of eluding Diaz in the states. Come to think of it, going home to Kansas offered the best chance at everything. He had no idea how he would get there. He simply knew he had to get home.

He rose before dawn and packed his bag. He kissed Tia Maria and left before the sun peeked over the eastern horizon.

He would have to leave as inconspicuously as he had arrived, but there were no piano shipments heading in the opposite direction. He caught a ride with a motorcyclist to Old Havana, ordered breakfast and contemplated his options as he ate. He found himself staring at a garden shop across the plaza which offered produce, including potted flowers and cut arrangements as well as caged tropical birds. He thought of Lena wistfully. She deserved a bouquet of the most beautiful tropical flowers on her resting place.

The conversation at a table behind him caught his attention. Two men who worked on a freight ship that traversed the Gulf waters each week indicated their vessel was due to disembark for Houston that same night. Stefano turned to them, offering a smile. "Need any help on that ship?" he asked.

He was directed to the captain, who arrived a few minutes later. The captain, however, turned him away. They were fully staffed.

Breakfast done, Stefano followed the seamen toward the dock and watched until he identified the ship they boarded. He paced the dock, studying the exterior of the ship as unobtrusively as he could. When he had memorized every porthole, every handhold on the hull, every service ladder extending to the water's surface, he returned to the garden shop and purchased a bouquet of orchids. He bummed a ride to Colon Cemetery on a horse-drawn taxi by offering half the bouquet to the driver. At the main gate, he headed to the vault where he'd watched the funeral a day earlier.

Alone at Lena's gravesite, he placed the flowers at the stone marker sealing her vault. He hung his head and closed his eyes and spoke to her, visualizing her face. "Lena, it's done. Your murder is avenged. I am sorry I didn't get to you soon enough to save your life. I wanted to avenge your murder for you, for me, for Mama. But somebody beat me to it. I watched it happen, and Julio Diaz is now dead and gone. There is only one brother left. This is good-bye, my sister. I will never return to Cuba. I hope your spirit can find me in Kansas. I return now to my own wife, and our brand new baby. I wish you could have met them."

He paused and wiped a tear from his cheek. "Good-bye, Lena." Without looking back, he left the cemetery.

As the sun set in the western sky, Stefano slipped onto the shipyard dock. He made his way toward the freighter, pacing the pier where it was moored. When the bridge to the deck was withdrawn he stopped at a post along the pier. With a casual glance around, he sat on the edge, slipped into the water, and swam for the ladder on the freighter, grasping the submerged rung just as the ship thrust backwards into the harbor. Like a barnacle, he flattened himself against the hull. When they had cleared the harbor, he climbed to the rail above and peeked over the top. With no crew member in sight, he swung over the rail and dropped between the railing and a canvas covered lifeboat. He was going home. Relaxing at last, he fell into an exhausted sleep.

27

ROUSED BY A violent shaking three hours into the journey, Stefano struggled awake. He opened his eyes to flashes of lightning that erupted into a bright beam that shone straight into his face.

Caramba!

For a moment he couldn't remember where he was. A deep voice boomed above him, "Here he is, Captain, the stowaway."

The ship.

He'd been discovered. He struggled to stand, blinking against the beam of light, shielding his eyes with his arm.

"You look familiar," another voice said derisively. "Oh, yes. I remember. You wanted a job this morning."

Stefano pasted a smile on his face and spoke toward the voice hidden behind the beam of light. "Still do," he offered a weak explanation. "I'd do anything—wash dishes, scrub decks, clean toilets."

"Don't need a flunky. I've already got too many of them," the captain said with finality. "Unfortunately for you, we don't take kindly to stowaways. Juan, prepare the old lifeboat."

"You're going to put me off?"

"You understand me now."

"Here?"

"Yes. That was your choice."

"Where are we?"

"Somewhere between Havana and Houston."

Stefano said, "How can I find my way in the dark?"

"That's what stars are for."

Stefano looked up into the night sky but saw no stars. There was nothing to scribe a line between the sea and the sky. Far to the east, a flicker of lightning lit a distant cloud bank, but there were no stars.

"What stars?" he said, but his voice was unheard, carried away on a gust wind. He raised his voice. "Evidently there's a storm coming. You can't set me off in a storm."

"And you can't tell me what to do. Juan, prepare the old lifeboat."

The man holding the beam of light pressed for further information. "The one with oars?"

"No. Leave the oars here. This jerk will go where the wind wants to take him."

"Wait," Stefano objected. "You can't do that. Please. I just need to get home to my family."

"That's what they all say," the captain said and walked away.

❦

Stefano hunkered down in the bow of the old lifeboat, staring into the black void. He could see nothing besides flickering lightning shafts that danced across the blackness, breaking its density with occasional flares. Blackness behind him swallowed everything. The boat bucked through invisible waves, each one drenching him with sea water. With his raiment soaked, he was unaware when the rain started. At some point, it dawned on him that there was a downpour beating on the open boat.

The waves intensified. He tightened his fingers until his hands were numb. Rain pelted his face and bare forearms, stinging his skin. The boat mounted wave after wave. "Lord, help me," he mouthed into the wind, bowing his head to protect his face from the driving rain. He was determined not to lose his grip and clamped his fingers tighter until they ached. The night's chill numbed him until he could no longer feel his hands. He pried his freezing fingers from the rim of the boat, working them until circulation was restored.

Open-close-open-close.

Dropping his hand to his knees against the hull of the boat, he felt rough coils of a thick rope. Exploring further with his fingers, he discovered it was fastened to a ring bolted to the rim of boat. He uncoiled the rope and wrapped it around his chest beneath his arms, knotting it securely. At least if he was tossed into the waves, he would be able to return to the fragile craft. He turned back to the bow and renewed his grip.

The lifeboat crested wave after wave but aside from flashes of light that seared the clouds he could see nothing. He surely must be heading westward. But with the way his luck had run lately, he would likely find himself back in Cuba by morning. Blackness surrounded him. Under the lightning, rain pelted the water and sizzled on the waves. Each burst of light flickered brighter than the previous one, illuminating the voracious black hole of the angry sea. Mountainous waves billowed around him.

After one harrowing descent into a wave trough, he reared back, riding the wave like it was a desperate bronco determined to unseat the rider. A second later, the boat plunged over the crest of the next wave. Stefano lost his balance and flew from the boat. The rope tightened around his chest as he crashed into the black sea.

Sea water flooded his mouth. Chilled to his bones, he swept the area with his arms but they dragged in slow motion, impeded by the churning sea. He kicked and his legs met the solid hull of the lifeboat above him. The realization that he would drown filled his mind and he relaxed. No more worries. No more problems.

With a jolt, he regained wary wakefulness.

The boat. Enfocate, despreciable hombre.

He reached the rope and pulled it to his chest. Hand over hand, he pulled himself up, inch by agonizing inch, his lungs on fire with the urge to draw breath.

Do this or die.... Do or die.... Sink... or swim.... Swim, fool!

As his head broke the surface he coughed gasped for air. With a gargantuan effort, he slithered over the rim into a pool of seawater on the boat's floor and convulsed into violent shivers.

Gritting his teeth, he dragged himself to the bow and rose to his knees. He stared into the blackness of the storm. A solitary shaft of light blinked across the wave tops.

¿Qué?

Was he almost home? Or had he blown back to Havana? Lightning bursts illuminated a ship, its beacon dancing above the waves. He hadn't come far from that freighter, then. Evidently he had dragged himself to the stern and was looking backward. Or was the wind pushing him back? In an instant, everything intensified. The water on his lips tasted more salty. The rain against his face became thousands of tiny knife blades. A needle of warmth seeped into his heart. He was alive. And he could feel it.

Lightning blazed across the sky. Thunder rent the air with each cloud-searing bolt. Then a gargantuan crackle, and Stefano's whole body went rigid. The wind pushed him further from the ship with each wave. A surge of wind whipped a pail that had been tied to the crossbar. It flew through the air and struck Stefano on his left temple. Fireworks exploded along his optic nerve and a dull pain spread through his head to his neck. As the fireworks dimmed, his thoughts grew muddy. He struggled to focus on something, but he faded fast.

He tried to scream. "Mel—". His voice died on the wind and he slumped to the bottom of the small boat, unconscious.

28

STEPPING INTO MEL'S room, Izzy swept her arm over the bed, open luggage spread across it. "What's all this?"

"I'm packing."

"Are you going home?"

"No. I'm heading to Oregon."

Izzy clicked her tongue and twisted a silver curl behind her ear. "I don't understand, Mel."

"I told you Global Relief asked for my help. They really need me."

"What about Stefano?"

"I'm not going to wait. I don't want to see him."

"But—"

"Try to understand, Mom. He abandoned me in my hour of greatest need."

"You don't know what he was thinking."

"I do know that he chose his sister over me. How can I get over that?"

"But," Izzy said, "you can't possibly know that."

"I read his letter, Mom. He spelled it out with no doubts. See for yourself." Mel swept pages of handwritten notes from her pillow and threw them at her mother. They drifted one-by-one to the floor.

Izzy collected the wrinkled pages, sorted them, and sank into the chair by the bed. Her mouth fell open as she read Stefano's intimate and passionate words written in a private message to his wife.

"Mel, I don't think I should be reading this."

"Why not? You are his family too."

"But it's so personal."

"If you want to know why I decided to accept the call for help, you need to read this, Mom." Mel folded a shirt and laid it on a pile of shirts in the corner of her bag.

Izzy read to the end. She folded the letter in half and held it gently, her eyes closed.

"You have to admit he's right. We were here for you. Can you imagine his quandary, the agony he must have gone through to arrive at his decision?"

"At this point, I don't care, Mom. I simply don't care. He abandoned me."

"Mel, you are not yourself. I know how hard it is to adjust after a baby is born. Lots of women get depressed. Their personalities change. I think you should consult a doctor before you go rushing off. Stefano's letter is perfectly rational. His was not an easy decision. He clearly had to answer his sister's cry for help."

"That means she was more important to him than Nico and I put together."

"No, I don't think so. He thought he could be there for all of you. He had no clear idea what he'd face in Cuba."

"What, Mom? What was he facing? Why couldn't it have waited a couple weeks?"

"Because it was urgent."

"My needs were pretty pressing also. He missed Nico's birth. That will never change. It's done. Why didn't he just wait?"

"What would you have done in his place? He'd not seen his sister since before you two met. Of course he had to find her."

An infant's wail wafted from across the hallway. "Not now, Mom. I need space."

Izzy followed her across the hall. "You have to consider your son, also. Please see your doctor. How can you manage his needs if you are out combing the rubble for people or valuables? How can you take care of him if you are distraught over all this?"

"They know I have a baby. I will help organize the efforts from the tent headquarters. Nico won't be neglected."

"But he's just days old."

"He's two weeks, Mom. And I'm answering a call for help."

"That tsunami? It's no place to take a newborn baby."

"They need me, Mom. Harvey Blackstone called me personally. And this is what I do, remember?"

"Stefano needs you too."

"Just like I needed him, right? He'll have to wait. I've made my decision. I'm leaving at first light tomorrow morning. Dad said I could stay in the cabin on the coast."

"Is it sound after that earthquake?"

"I hope it's not too badly damaged. If it is, we'll just camp at headquarters."

Izzy tried again. "Mel, you can't just leave."

"Stefano did."

"But you can't. What if he comes back hurt?"

"Let him feel as unwanted as I felt."

Izzy reached for her grandchild and Mel placed him in her arms. She grinned and made faces, bouncing the baby while they talked. "You want Stefano to suffer?" Izzy asked.

"Why not? I did."

"I'm sure he already has."

"Not enough. Not nearly enough."

"Mel—" Izzy gave the child a squeeze. She couldn't wrap her mind around the idea that her grandchild would leave tomorrow also. "You sent me down there to find him. I can't believe you'd abandon him now."

"This is different."

"I don't see how. And I'll miss you and Nico so much. I'll worry constantly. He's my only grandchild, you know. Won't you reconsider?"

"No, Mom. Arguing won't change my mind. I'm packed. I'm ready to go. And I'm leaving. End of discussion."

29

BIT BY BIT Stefano grew cognizant of a rhythmic rocking. Water lapped gently somewhere near his left ear. He struggled to wake and fought to raise his eyelids, confused by a mixture of oven heat searing his face and chest, opposed to the sticky cool wetness below him. Something poked between two ribs along his spine. He forced his eyes open, blinking against a bright morning sun. He had no recollection where he was or why he would be jostling in the bottom of a crude boat. The floor tilted precariously as waves lapped against the boat.

He struggled to sit up. Using the trim along the side, he pulled himself up and immediately fell back, screaming as pain shot along his spine toward his feet. A few deep breaths eased the waking nerves. With shaking hands, he massaged his legs to restore circulation and rubbed each arm. He sat up a second time, slowly, his re-wakened consciousness warding off the electric pain with slow, purposeful breaths.

Peering over the edge of the boat, he felt astonished to discover he was surrounded by water as far as he could see. The inclination of the boat belied the fact that he was adrift. He must have washed up on something. A closer look revealed a gash in the bottom of the boat. It had impaled on a submerged object. Stefano sat taller, and dared to rise onto his feet, hands extended to assure balance. At this height he glimpsed a line of green, clearly outlining the boundary of a land mass half a mile distant.

It was coming back to him.

The boat... the ship... set adrift with no oars. The storm... Lena.

Lena was gone. For a moment he longed for oblivion. But here he was, still alive. How much time had passed since... since what? What had happened? Reaching to his forehead he found a tender knot. He remembered. Something hit him on the head. And then? He remembered nothing after that.

Somehow he'd managed to survive the storm. And now here he was, close enough to land he should be able to paddle there.

If I only had a paddle.

And if the boat didn't sink, given that rip in the bow. He should be able to swim it then. His mother hadn't brought him on beach vacations for nothing. He would swim to the land.

What land is it though? Where am I?

The only way to find out was to get over there and investigate. Lying prone under the sun, the front of his clothing had dried with crusty salt coating it. The backs remained soggy where he'd lain in seawater on the floor of the boat. His shoulder bag was crammed beneath the splintered seat in the bottom of the boat. He stripped to his underwear and wrung the water from his clothing. He pulled his wallet out of his pants pocket and checked its contents. Kansas ID, check. Credit card, check. A few Cuban pesos, check. Soggy American bills in different denominations, check. It would have to do. At least the wallet wasn't lost.

He tucked the wallet deep inside his satchel, rolled his clothing, and stuffed it inside with his shoes. After fastening the clasp, he wrapped it all with the shoelaces tied together, and adjusted the shoulder strap to lace under each arm. With his bag secured on his back, he peered at the line of green again and slipped into the water.

Stroke after stroke, kick after kick, he swam for land.

The beach was deserted when he waded ashore. He spread his clothing across scrubby bushes and let it drip. As the sun crested its zenith and descended towards the horizon, he dressed for a hike through dunes. He had no idea where he was, but he had only one goal now. He had to get home and make things right with Mel.

He slogged through a marsh, angled toward a tree line, and at dusk found a two-lane blacktop road. In the distance to his left he could make out a road sign. He jogged toward it down the middle of the deserted road. When he was close enough to read it in the dimming light, his heart fluttered. With a burst of speed, he sprinted to the sign. It was in English. "Pensacola 15 miles."

He whooped. He'd made it home.

Before the yell died on the breeze a feeling of remorse shrouded his elation. He had no right to feel ecstatic when Lena was dead and Mel, in all probability, had given him up as the scoundrel he was.

Headlights of an isolated Ford pickup threw beams on the sign. He stepped aside to let it pass. The truck stopped, its window down.

"Need a ride?" a congenial voice asked.

"Going to Pensacola?" Stefano replied.

"Hop in."

∽❧∼

Twenty-four hours later, a 727 landed at Eisenhower National in Wichita and passengers disembarked. Stefano dragged behind the rest. He wiped sweat from his forehead. Strange to be perspiring in the winter air. It was his nerves. He was anxious to greet Mel, to sweep her into his arms in the kind of passion you reserved for your wife. But how would she react? Would she be glad to see him?

In the lobby, he glanced from one end to the other, searching in vain for the one person he wanted to see. He saw a wildly waving hand, and glowered at his mother-in-law. Mel hadn't seen fit to meet him, then. He descended the escalator and Izzy dashed to him and wrapped her arm around his shoulders. He shrugged her off.

How could he have dared to hope Mel would come? He'd made such a mess of their lives, he'd be lucky if he ever saw her again. The postcard from New Orleans had turned his life into shambles.

PART II: ANDANTE MYSTERIOSO

30

IZZY CRANED HER neck to watch the passengers descend the exit stairs at Eisenhower National. There he was, but what a sight. He limped along, staring at the crowd around her, his fingers clutching the railing as if he was unsteady. His shoulders slumped and the luster was gone from his eyes. She hustled to meet him at the foot of the stairs.

"Hey, you okay?" Izzy asked in a voice laced with concern. "Did you find your sister?"

He swallowed hard. "Yes," he said in a gruff voice.

She waited for more.

At last he said, "She was dead, murdered."

"Oh God," she whispered.

"I was too late. I held her in my arms, but it was too late." His voice broke on a sob. He shrugged his shoulders, clamped his jaw, and refused to say more.

"I'm sorry, Stefano." Her words sounded lame.

He'd have to live with his sister's death forever. Moreover, he'd missed Nico's birth and nobody could turn back the clock. She did not want to tell him that Mel had hurried to Oregon to avoid him. The urgency in the northwest was understandable, but Izzy failed to see why Mel couldn't at least have waited another day.

Drat. Mel—one measly day.

Stefano needed reassurance and compassion. The mother in Izzy ached to ease the pain she witnessed in his slumped shoulders, but anything she offered would not be enough.

At last she said, "Let's get you home."

The question morphed into how to move forward from here. She vowed to do everything in her power to make it up to him and help him mend things with Mel.

Like air above the prairie before a storm, tension seasoned the agonizing ride home. In a futile effort to mask her unease, Izzy chatted nonstop. She told him about Nico's birth, how Mel had stayed in her childhood home the last few days. She paused every few minutes to glance toward Stefano, an invitation for him to speak. But he remained silent. He wouldn't even meet her eyes. She prattled on but sensed his despair deepen. On the outskirts of their hometown, she quit talking.

"Little Nicolas?" he finally said, his voice emotionless.

She bit her tongue. What could she tell this new father that would ease his despair? There were no words equal to the task.

Stefano choked on a sob. "Mel?"

Izzy shook her head.

"Did she get my letter?"

"She did. She was pretty upset."

"She didn't understand."

"Give her time."

At the duplex in Ark City, Izzy tiptoed behind Stefano as he moped through one room after another in the silent house. He stopped to stare at the empty nursery a moment before he stumbled on to the master bedroom. The bed in the master bedroom was tidily made up. A plain white envelope with "Stefano" written across the front in Mel's handwriting was propped prominently on the cover quilt. He snatched the envelope and held it a moment before he tore it open and unfolded a single sheet of paper. He read the note through tear-filled eyes, crumpled it into a ball and tossed it to the corner.

"What did she say?" Izzy asked, her voice filled with compassion.

"Read it yourself," Stefano mumbled as he left the room, agony in his voice.

As Izzy picked up the papers, a wallet-sized photograph of Nicolas slipped from the envelope. She ran her fingers over Nico's face and glanced quickly at the empty doorway, but shook her head. It would add no comfort to call him back. Images offered no substitute for what he needed, a chance to cuddle his son in his own arms. She lined up the letter's torn edges and smoothed it on the bed quilt.

Stefano—I'm glad that you are safe and on your way home. I won't be here when you arrive. Please understand how abandoned I felt when you left and didn't come back, even though you promised to do so. My heart aches with the knowledge that your own wife and your own son were not your first priority as his birth approached. You chose to leave me at the worst possible time. I need time to sort this all out. I'm glad you're safe, but I can't face you now. Not yet.

You may have heard about the tidal wave disaster in Oregon. I've agreed to help with the relief efforts. Global Relief is desperate for trained help and I have to go. Of course Nicolas is going with me. We'll return after relief efforts calm down. In the meantime, search your heart. We both need time to consider options for our future.

Melody

A crash alerted Izzy to Stefano's moribund mood. She found him in the kitchen, flinging glassware against the refrigerator door. He kicked the shards aside and yanked open the wall cabinets, one by one, smashing the doors against the wall. At the corner cupboard, he turned to her, a bottle of rum in his hands. He twisted the lid off and raised it to his lips.

"Stefano—stop. You're not even going to mix a *mojito*?"

In answer, he took a swig and closed his eyes as it trickled down his throat.

She reproached him, maternal concern infused in her voice. "Listen, son—"

"I'm not your son!" he shouted and raised the bottle again.

Legato, Isabel. She told herself. *Take it easy.*

She gave up. She raised her hand and patted the air to diminish his frustration. "When you cool off, give me a call," she said. As she turned to go, he tipped up the rum for another long swig.

31

TEOFILO DIAZ SETTLED into his captain's chair and stared out the window in Havana. Lush vegetation in the valley hid the road to the family's hilltop mansion and business headquarters. Beyond a crossroads teaming with aged vehicles, bicycles, and pedestrians, the Atlantic Ocean sparkled in the afternoon sunshine. Teo's grandfather, a general in the Castro's rebel army, had been awarded the mansion for his steadfast loyalty during the Cuban revolution.

Since the triumph of the revolution, life had not always been easy. The Diaz family patriarchs, though outwardly loyal to Castro's regime, made many a shady deal in order to retain their new status. Military to the core, Teo's grandfather passed his rigorous discipline and thirst for power to his son and grandson.

After Fidel's death, trade in Cuba expanded for the first time in decades. Now head of the family, Teo made a business decision to expand their investments into the big money of illicit drug trade. He'd be damned if he would ever let the Diaz family sink into second-class status again. Julio and Enrique acquired valuable business contacts along the US Gulf coast, from Miami to Houston and every port between. But they'd lost a significant investment when Enrique died in New Orleans and Julio fled, leaving that damn piano behind.

He needed to get it back. The wares hidden in its recesses were indispensable. With Julio now gone, it would be up to him. He could enlist Felipe's assistance, he supposed. It was time to augment the boy's intense training. His brothers had missed the same rigorous instruction he'd faced. As the eldest, he'd shouldered his father's temper without fail. And if not his father's, then his grandfather's. His brothers missed all that and sometimes he hated them. They were soft. They never had the backbone for discipline in the first place. More than likely his father favored the woman who bore him Julio and Enrique over Teo's own mother and went easy on them because of it.

Whatever had happened, he could not afford to let the boy slip. The family business was at stake and it was vital to train Felipe right. The boy would be raised to honor his destiny. He reached a handset on his desk and pushed a button.

Felipe's governess answered. "*¿Señor?*

"Send Felipe to my office."

"*Sí, Señor.*"

Moments later the boy tapped on his office door. Teofilo swung the chair around. "Enter."

Felipe Diaz, the first and only son of the next generation, pushed open the door.

Teo stood, his mouth a straight line, eyes piercing Felipe's gaze. The boy looked down.

"Stand at attention in my presence," Teo said, his voice a growl.

Felipe tipped his chin up, but did not meet Teo's scrutiny.

"Look at me, boy," Teo said.

The boy looked up, eyes wide.

"You know why I summoned you?"

Felipe shook his head, a short sideways twitch, as if he was shooing a fly.

"You know about your uncle Julio?"

"*Sí, Señor.*"

"You know I witnessed his murder?"

Felipe nodded.

"I went after the killer that night. Do you know that?"

"*Sí, Señor.*"

"Aren't you going to ask me what happened?"

Felipe hesitated before he spoke. "Did you find the shooter?"

Teo took a deep breath and relaxed his shoulders. "Thank you for asking. No, I did not."

"I heard you had a helicopter."

"Yes. My trusted pilot accompanied me to the ship we heard he was on."

"But... you didn't find him?"

"The helicopter was disabled in the storm. We bailed out and crewmen from the ship rescued us."

"Was the shooter on the ship?"

"He had been, but he was no longer there. He escaped on a lifeboat. It's doubtful he survived the storm, given its severity."

"Did he drown?"

"I hope so. But he might also have met a bigger, faster ship, or drifted ashore somewhere."

"If he killed my Uncle Julio, he should die. I wish he would die."

"*Sí.*" Teo smiled. The child was honest. Everything was simple to him. Right or wrong. Black or white. Live or die. When had life ever been simple? It was better that Felipe never know the truth. "We should find out, don't you think? I want to take you on a trip. We'll have a holiday. And we'll look for this killer in the US. If we can't find him, we'll look for his family. One way or another, he will pay for his crimes. How does that sound?"

Felipe stared at Teofilo with a somber expression and shuffled his feet.

He's impatient, Teo thought, *like I once was.*

When his grandfather trained him, he'd been anxious to please, yet fearful he'd disappoint. Teo saw that same conflict in the boy's flickering gaze, jumping from one thing to another, never meeting his scrutiny longer than a second.

He laid his hand on the boy's shoulder. "One more thing."

Felipe stood straight, and stared at Teo.

"Julio and Enrique left valuable merchandise in New Orleans. I want to retrieve it and you will assist."

The boy's jaw dropped. He stopped fidgeting.

"You're my second-in-command and it's time you learned the business. You first learn to follow orders without question. While we are away, you will follow my orders. *¿Comprendes?*"

Felipe drew himself up straighter and taller. *"Sí, Señor."*

"Go talk to your governess, Felipe. Tell her to pack a bag for your journey. We leave tomorrow. *Adiós.*" Teo dropped his hand and stepped toward the desk.

"What if she won't listen?"

"Send her to me. I'll make her listen."

32

IZZY LUNGED FOR her cell phone when it jingled with her daughter's ringtone. Melody had arrived at the family's summer cabin. Travel with an infant slowed her down and it took an extra two days to cover the distance between Kansas and Kurt's Oregon art studio. She described the damages she'd seen along the coast. Located high enough along the bluffs, the studio escaped major damage from the earthquake and tsunami. A few shingles were gone, and two windows broken. There was minor water damage inside, but the cabin remained secure. Mel nailed plywood over broken window panes and reported to the Global Relief headquarters forty-eight hours after she arrived, with Nico wrapped at her breast in a cozy baby sling.

Days passed with no word from Stefano. Hoping to interest him, Izzy uncrated the dilapidated piano from New Orleans, but he still did not answer her phone calls, nor would he come to the door when she knocked. He did answer Kurt, though. Through Kurt's reports Izzy knew Stefano was still alive—incessantly drunk, but alive. Each day that passed with no improvement increased her concern. She didn't know how to help.

Mel grew concerned too. Her worry showed in her eyes during video calls and her voice wavered when Stefano was the focus of conversation but she refused to discuss coming home.

One Friday in April Izzy took her morning jog around the pasture, showered, and sat at the kitchen table. She shuffled through the papers stacked at one end until she found the weekend entertainment section. Grabbing a pencil, she spread the Sudoku puzzle on the table.

One-two-three-four-five-six-seven—

Any other day, the number puzzle calmed her anxiety. But not today. She couldn't concentrate. The grandfather clock in the living room chimed a quarter hour. She clicked her phone's calendar, and scolded herself. She had an appointment in fifteen minutes.

Accelerando, Isabel.

She threw her technician tool bag in the car and headed to town. After the day's appointments she headed to the repair shop. She squeezed past Lena's broken piano in the shop. "Excuse me," she said, patting the old gal on her cracked lid. "What did they call you? Elsie? Elsie Lenore. I bet you miss making music. Bet you miss your family. I promise I'll work on Stefano. You'll see him someday—good grief—now I'm talking to a piano."

Pianissimo. If anyone hears me, they'll suppose I'm nuts.

But Elsie seemed to beckon to Izzy, even in her dilapidated condition.

When they met for that day's video chat, Izzy confessed to Melody. "I catch myself talking to that poor excuse for a piano every time I slide by it. I need a conspirator to help reach Stefano. Maybe Elsie will."

"He won't come to the shop?"

"Not yet. He doesn't even talk to me. At least the piano listens."

"Mom," Mel said, "why don't you take it apart yourself?"

Two days later, Izzy headed to the shop after lunch. She photographed the Steinway from every conceivable angle, zoomed in on the damage and shot dozens more photos. She removed cabinet parts, and photographed each piece as it was freed from the instrument. With a fractured stretcher bar, the tuning pin block sagged. There wasn't adequate clearance for the small drop screws when she attempted to slide the action from its recessed cavity.

She set up two sturdy stands and clamped a two-by-six bar across the piano. With ratchet straps, she straightened the misshapen bar enough to move the action assembly out of the piano and onto a work bench. Several piano keys were cracked. Some were warped. A dozen or more didn't move at all. Many hammer shanks were cracked or broken. Izzy removed the piano's hammer stack to get a closer look at the key damage.

When she lifted one key from its balance pin, she discovered two alphabet letters written on the underneath side, E and M.

Ritardando. What's this?

She found more letters underneath other keys. In fact, letters appeared beneath most of the keys. She fingered a miniature computer SD card lodged into a chiseled-out groove beneath the highest key, C88. "Would you look at that?" she spoke aloud, her voice echoing off the cabinets and concrete shop floor.

She clamped the keys into a key clamp and headed out the door, circling the building with them to Kurt's kiln room. "Look here." she said, holding the tiny data card in her open palm.

"Where'd you find it?"

"Underneath this key." She turned the key clamp to expose the key bottoms. "Here, in this groove. Someone carved the key to fit the data card."

Kurt scrutinized the key. "I see what you mean."

"What could it be?"

"Something someone hid? A mysterious message?" He waved his hand over the piano keys. "What's with all the letters below the keys?"

She shook her head. "I can't see any logical sequence to it."

"Another hidden message," Kurt said.

"You think?"

"That seems plausible doesn't it? Why don't you ask Stefano."

"He's beyond caring right now," Izzy said.

"Would this interest him?"

"He has yet to answer anytime I call."

"Be more obnoxious about it. He can't ignore that," Kurt said.

"So you say."

"Worth a try, isn't it?"

"I'll run by the duplex tomorrow. Could we check out this device tonight?"

"You stole my thoughts. Better take a picture of the card in the key, and all the letters too. Stefano might respond to pictures better than words."

Izzy snapped a few more photos while Kurt held the key clamp. In the house, he booted up the computer and slipped the disc into a mini-card reader. It opened to a page which prompted a password in Spanish.

"This could be a problem," Kurt said. "*Habla Español?*"

"Is it like the Italian musical terminology? I'm afraid I don't speak Spanish well. Try something," she suggested.

"I wouldn't know where to start."

"Stefano would, if he was sober. I'll let him know we need him. How could he refuse?"

33

TEO STOOD AT the hotel room door, hand on the knob. "Lay low, Felipe. I'll be back before the night's over. Don't open the door for anyone. Hear me?" He turned to go.

"Where are you going?" the boy asked.

Teo's voice rumbled, ominous with unspoken disfavor. "Not your business."

Felipe stifled a grimace and ventured a personal request. "May I watch movies?"

Teo agreed. "Until midnight. Go to bed when this clock reads twelve. Understand?"

Felipe gave a weak nod, and Teo clicked the door behind him and hung the "Do Not Disturb" sign on the exterior handle. He hurried to the street bustling with people. The Caribbean Breeze was his destination, four easy blocks away.

He entered the night club, wormed through a throng at the bar and found a corner table. He settled in for a long night to observe patrons, bartender, and wait staff. At 2:30 in the morning, two encores beyond the featured jazz quartet's planned finale, people filtered from the room and spilled onto the street. Teo remained seated until the other customers left. A waitress, "Gina" on her nametag, approached him, as she cleaned tables. "Sir, we close in ten minutes," she said.

"I will talk to the manager."

"Now, sir? Morning would be more—"

"Now." He left no room for argument.

Gina bowed her head and took a step back. She gestured toward the bar, where the manager mopped the countertop, nodded, and said, "See Roberto."

The chair's legs grated against the floor as Teo stood. He sauntered to the bar but the bartender ignored him until he slapped the counter.

"Sorry, sir. Bar is closed for the night," the bartender said without looking up.

"I don't need a drink," Teo said in a voice as menacing as thunder over the Gulf. "I need information. You manage this place?"

The bartender met his gaze. He side-stepped along the counter and ran his fingers along under the cleaning rag.

Teo whipped a .40 caliber Glock from inside his jacket. "Push the button. It will be the last thing you do."

Across the room Gina shrieked. Roberto pulled his hands away from the counter and held them up, palms facing Teo. "Let's not get excited," he said. "What do you want?"

"I need information."

"About what?"

"Last month there was a Cuban pianist here."

Roberto nodded. "Lena Valdez. Gorgeous. Talented."

"She brought her own piano."

"Yes. She did indeed. Too bad it didn't leave with her—somebody broke in and took an axe to it after her performance."

"An axe? I see. Where is that piano now?"

"I don't know. It's not here. I had to get it off the stage area."

"I repeat. Where is it now?"

Roberto lifted his palms to the ceiling, empty. He shook his head.

"Don't make me ask again." Teo raised the Glock.

"Okay. Relax. Her brother came by a few days later and shipped it out. That's all I know."

"Where to?"

"How would I know? I just wanted it gone."

Teo tipped the barrel up, perfecting an aim at Roberto's heart. "Where?"

"Hey, man. Take it easy. I believe he shipped it north, to a piano shop."

Teo drew his lips into a tight line and inhaled a slow, deep breath. He lowered his weapon. "Location?"

"Oklahoma, maybe? Missouri? Maybe Kansas. Or Colorado. I'm guessing since I really have no idea."

Teo waved the gun barrel in an arc across the bartender's chest. He raised his eyebrows in an unspoken question.

Roberto spoke in haste. "Believe me, I'd tell you if I could."

"What truck company?"

Robert considered for a moment before he shook his head. "Something like Overland Express."

Teo scrutinized the bartender for a moment before he returned the gun to its holster. "All right. Appreciate your help."

"Right."

Teo sauntered toward the exit with the bartender at his heels. The shades fell on the door's glass pane and the deadbolt clicked into place as he strode down the street.

34

"GO AWAY," STEFANO mumbled when Izzy pounded on his door the next morning. He sounded half asleep.

Or half drunk.

"Stefano, open the door." She pounded again, and put muscle into her words.

"Go away," he said again, his voice quivering.

She punctuated her next request with urgency. "Stefano, I need to talk to you. Please open the door."

"Wha' d'ya want?"

"It's about Melody and Nico."

Stefano mumbled an expletive, then silence. Was he unconscious? Was he ignoring her? Could he even stand without falling?

The door knob rattled and the door swung into his chest. He clutched the edge, swinging on his feet as it swung on the hinges. Stefano raised his gaze and looked into eyes that sparked flames.

"My God, man, look at you." She spat out the words.

"That what y'wanted to say?" Stefano slurred his speech. "That what y'came for? Jus' go home, then."

"You've got to get a grip, Stefano. Don't you want to see Mel again? Don't you want to meet your son?"

"They're gone, Izzy. They're not comin' back."

"Why would anyone want to come back to you when you're drunk? I haven't given up on Mel. You shouldn't either. But give her a husband worth returning to. They need you, but they need you alert and whole."

"Nobody needsh me."

"Some of us need you very much but you choose to be unavailable. You drown yourself in booze."

He was silent for a moment before he repeated, "Nobody needsh me."

"Stefano, stop. You're killing yourself with self-pity."

Stefano shook his head. "I can't stop. I'm worthless."

"As long as you're intoxicated, you're right. Pull yourself together because Melody needs you. Nico needs you. I need you. Even Lena needs you."

"Lenash... dead."

"I know. But she brought you to her piano and you sent it to me. That piano sits in my shop, waiting for your attention. Lena may still have a message for you in that piano. Help me find it."

"It'sh too late."

"Look." She clicked into the stored photos on her phone and offered the images. "I found all this in that piano she wrote you about. Help me figure out what it means."

"It doesn't matter now. She's gone."

"You don't know that. Come on, Stefano. If there's one thing I know, it's that Melody didn't fall in love with the man you've become. Find your old self and come back to her."

"I don't know how."

"There are ways. Get grief counseling. Join AA. I'll do what I can to help you but you have to start yourself."

Stefano brought his hands to his head, squeezed his temples, and muttered, "My head."

Her voice softened. "Why don't you clean up? Shower. Get into fresh clothes. Let me take the rum. Make a pot of coffee."

He stood aside and allowed her to enter. As she passed, she wrapped her arms around him and his trembling subsided a bit. "I miss them all—my mom, Lena, Melody," he mumbled.

As the morning passed, Izzy lugged dirty laundry to her car. She searched the kitchen shelves, collected all the liquor bottles she could find, and loaded them also. Before she left, she gave him a fond squeeze. "Why don't you come out for dinner? After that we can take a look at Elsie Lenore."

Stefano startled a bit when she mentioned the piano's nickname, but he shook his head.

"I'll come get you."

"No. I remember the way."

"Got fuel in Mel's little car?"

He nodded.

"Okay then. See you later."

She waved to him as she got behind the steering wheel. He stood in the doorway, his face somber and eyes lusterless. Would he show up in the afternoon? Deep down, she harbored doubts.

35

BY MID-APRIL MONEY from around the world poured into Global Relief headquarters. After a short lunch break, Melody collected the day's mail and returned to their onsite offices. She parked beside the tent headquarters, grabbed Nico from his car seat and hung him over her left arm, while she balanced a stack of envelopes from the make-shift post office in her right. She kicked at the flap that sufficed as a door and wormed her way under the canvas. She piled the mail on her cluttered desk, woke the computer with a finger click, and settled Nico into a wind-up swing while she got to work.

She clicked open a donor list and opened the first envelope. The door flap lifted and two men entered, one balancing a deluxe video camera on his shoulder. The other man approached her, his hand extended and a ridiculous grin on his face.

Melody sighed. Two more ambulance chasers, no doubt. "May I help you?" she asked. With forced courtesy, she clasped the offered hand and dropped it after a brief acknowledgement.

"Jepson Bogart, ma'am, Coastal News Sleuths, the internet source for people who value truth in reporting."

She raised her eyebrows. Her dad relied on the CNS site, insisting that normal news sources had been bought by corporations and would tell you no more than what they were allowed to tell.

Jepson Bogart droned on, in his practiced introduction. "No Fake News at CNS." His forced grin broadened. "We'd like to get your take on the cleanup process here after that killer quake. May I talk to you for a few minutes?"

Mel stepped backwards toward the chair at her desk. She glanced at Nico asleep in the swing.

"Your baby?" Jepson Bogart asked.

She nodded.

"Hard to work while caring for an infant, isn't it?"

She glared at him a second. "That's why I've got office duty. But I couldn't ignore the need. We're all over-worked here and I don't have time for your interview."

"Five minutes, tops. I promise."

"Five minutes is all I can allow. I have too much work, as you can see." She waved a hand over the pile of mail.

"I'll take five. May I ask your name?"

"Melody Valdez."

Jepson Bogart nodded to his cameraman. He faced the camera lens and said, "Good morning, folks, Jep Bogart here in Reedsport at the makeshift headquarters for Global Relief talking to Melody Valdez, a volunteer in the office. Melody, you are here with a young baby. Are you from around here? Were your friends and family impacted by the disaster?"

"No, I'm not from here. I was called in to help. It's my job to organize, train, and supervise crews to help search for victims. Later we will assist in the long road to clean-up and recovery."

"Can you give me the current casualty count for the earthquake and subsequent tsunami?"

"Not with 100% accuracy. I believe it stands at over 1500 deaths now. Many are children who were trapped in their schools. The list of missing people is ten times longer."

"How many injured?"

"Thousands."

"Where are the injured taken?"

"To emergency clinics in nearby cities. Severely injured people are taken to the few hospitals still operating. The worst cases are flown out of state."

❧❦

Halfway across the continent, Kurt Woods dashed from his office to the kitchen where Izzy peeled potatoes for the evening meal. She held onto the hope that Stefano would join them, but as the afternoon aged, it seemed doubtful.

Kurt blurted out, "Mel's on the web. CNS is interviewing her."

Izzy dropped the knife and the potato and followed him to the office, wiping her fingers on a towel as she walked. She leaned over Kurt's shoulder to watch the interview. "Mel looks agitated," she said as the interview continued on the computer screen.

"Sh-sh." Kurt hushed her.

"How many field offices has Global Relief established?" Bogart was asking.

"There are stations like this one in every city and town along the coast, from British Columbia to northern California."

Bet she's wondering why he picked her, Izzy thought.

"How many volunteer groups have found their way to Reedsport?"

"I couldn't say. Hundreds. We manage thousands of people."

"And what do the volunteers do?"

"We divided the ruins into grids and the teams sweep through them to search for anything that might lead to injured survivors or valuables for families whose homes crumbled."

"How long will that go on?"

"We're beyond the date where we have any chance to locate survivors. They're searching for bodies now. Clean-up and re-building come next."

"You said you have done relief work before?"

"Yes. This is what I do. I helped after Sandy—and Francine, the super storm that left more destruction in its wake than even Katrina did—many other crises. Anytime a natural disaster displaces people, Global Relief moves in to help."

"How would you classify this event in comparison to those others?"

"This is much worse. I've never seen anything like it before."

"Massive devastation?"

Mel offered a grim nod but said nothing.

The reporter concluded with a tribute to her dedication. "Melody Valdez, a young mother with a big heart, far from home because helping disaster victims is her life's calling." The camera panned the tent's interior, zeroing in on the infant who stirred and cooed as the swing wound down. "Jep Bogart on the road in Reedsport, Oregon." The camera zoned out to an advertisement.

"Can we run it back? I want to see the whole thing," Izzy said.

36

STEFANO WOKE TO an insistent pounding and it was not due to the throb in his head. He stumbled to the door, opened it, and squinted into the morning sun. Izzy glared back at him. Her lips trembled, but she didn't speak. He ran his fingers through his dark curls, scratched the stubble on his cheeks, and rubbed his eyes.

"You look like you've been run over by a truck—about eight times. Did I miss a rum bottle?" she said.

Stefano stared at her, red veins rimming his brown eye pupils. "Tha's what you come to say? Go 'way." He pushed the door to close it.

She stepped into the doorway. "Enough is enough, Stefano. I did not drop everything to go look for you so you could come back here and drown your misery in alcohol."

He straightened to support himself on the door frame and retorted, "Jus' wait a minute. What gives you th' right t' come here an'—"

"Damn it, Stefano," she said. "I have been waiting. Kurt has waited. Mel too. How long will you make us wait before you decide you're worth saving yourself? Because in the end, it doesn't matter who believes in you if you have no faith in yourself."

Stefano winced and swiped at his eyes with the back of his hand. He didn't have the energy for a fight. His shoulders slumped.

Her voice softened. "I know you're miserable. You blame yourself for your sister's death. You miss her. You always will. That will never change." She hugged him. "Grief happens, Stefano. You've got to find a way to work through it. Come back to work and help me find what Lena hid in that piano."

Despiértate, Valdez, he said to himself. "Lena." Stefano's whisper rasped like sandpaper across wood. "Mama's El-she L'nore," Stefano said.

The phone on Stefano's kitchen counter rang. He dismissed it with a wave, and let it ring. After half a dozen rings, it quit, but rang again a moment later.

"Shut up," he yelled at the phone.

Izzy turned toward the kitchen to shut it off. Caller ID identified a New Orleans number. "Stefano," she said, "you should take this call."

"Mel?" he said, his face a shade paler.

"No. Unless she moved from Oregon to New Orleans. This says 'C. Breeze, New Orleans' on the caller ID."

"Th' Breeze." Stefano froze.

Another ring echoed through the dismal house and he dove to answer the phone.

"*Hola,*" he said, half lucid in his greeting. He listened a few moments and turned to Izzy with panic in his eyes. "*Momento, momento,*" he said into the phone and beckoned her closer. "You have to hear this," he whispered.

"*Por favor,* Roberto, say that again, in English." He waved his hand over the phone controls and punched the speaker option.

"Who's there?" Roberto's voice echoed around the small kitchen.

"Izzy Woods here," she said. "Stefano's mother-in-law."

"*Sí,*" he said. "As I mentioned to Stefano, last night I had an unpleasant visit from a tall well-dressed Cuban. He came in during the local jazz gig and before he left, he demanded information about Lena's piano. My waitress Gina, she was creeped out by him, the way he sized her up."

"What did he look like?" Stefano asked.

"Tall, six-foot-two. Trim. Athletic. Packing a piece. Never once cracked a smile."

"Any idea what name he used?" Izzy said.

"Nope. Never introduced himself. At closing time, this guy stayed. Gina wanted to get rid of him, and told him we'd close in ten minutes but he insisted he'd talk to me. No mincing words. No beating around the bush. He was adamant."

"Did you talk to him?" Stefano said in a rush.

"I had no choice. Guy pulls out a gun and holds it to my chest."

Stefano gasped.

"What did he want?" Izzy asked.

"He needed information. I say, about what? He names Stefano's sister and the piano she brought. I tell him that somebody took an axe to it after her performance. And he says, 'Where's that piano now?'"

"He asked about the piano?" Stefano said, his voice tight. "What'd you tell him?"

"I told him I didn't know where it went, that it wasn't here, but he demanded more details."

Stefano could not stand still. He bounced from one foot to the other, running his hand through his matted curls. "Roberto—"

"Relax, man. I told him Lena's brother came by a few days later."

"Me?"

"You did, you know."

"Why'd you tell him that?"

"I was at gunpoint, remember? It's not like I gave him your name."

"Oh, man—oh man—oh man—oh man."

"I told him you shipped it out. He says, to a dump? I say, no, I believe it shipped to a piano shop in Missouri or Kansas. Then he wants to know where to find the piano shop."

"Did you tell him?" Stefano's voice cracked.

"No way. I told him I didn't memorize the shipping address. Guy waves the gun across my chest. I say, Believe me, I'd tell you if I could. I needed the junk gone and it didn't matter where."

"So he doesn't know?"

"Nothing specific. But he's looking for you, or the piano, or both, *mi amigo.*"

"Oh man—oh man—oh man," Stefano said.

"The guy is after you and he's bad news. As soon as he left, I clicked the security button, but the beat cop couldn't find him."

"*Gracias*, Roberto," Stefano whispered. He swallowed hard and coughed as he disconnected the call. "What should I do, Mom?"

"Was this the Diaz person you ran from in Havana?"

"What if it was?"

"If he's crazy enough to follow you to the states, he'd be remorseless. You can't afford to be wasted all the time."

"What about you? Are you in danger?"

"I suppose anyone you know is at risk."

"Mel?" Stefano said, closing his eyes.

"At least she's safe, tucked away in Oregon." She grabbed his forearm. "Stefano—Mel was on web news last evening," Izzy said. "That's what I came to tell you about. We saw her live on national news."

"Holy Jesus, what do we do?" Stefano said.

"You need to sober up. You can't afford to slip, not even once."

"All right. Do I stay here? Go to Oregon?"

"If he followed you there, you'd be exposed and vulnerable. Resources are spread paper thin up there right now. You need to stay here. Come back to work. Check out that piano—Elsie Lenore. Figure out if your sister encoded messages in its bones that this Diaz fellow needs to intercept."

Stefano wiped perspiration from his brow. "Okay. I'll do it. I don't want anything to happen to Mel on account of me."

37

EIGHT HUNDRED MILES south, Teofilo Diaz stared at his computer screen.

He had entered all the key words he could generate to track down the piano, to no avail. When Enrique suggested using it as a conduit on their business tour, with Lena's skills as a cover, he'd had reservations. But with Julio's enthusiasm, he'd given in to their plan.

Damn it.

He should never have capitulated to such a ludicrous whim. Not only did half their merchandise samples disappear, his reluctant agreement had given Julio the improper idea that he and Enrique possessed more clout with the family dealings than they would ever be allowed. They both paid for their impertinence. Good riddance, as far as Teo was concerned. But he was screwed if he couldn't retrieve those samples—and shower a little Diaz justice on Lena's brother while he was at it.

He searched the entire mid-west for piano shops and found the national piano technician's guild in Kansas City. The website hosted by that group listed five hundred names in the states the bartender rattled off. He needed something to narrow down the search.

A hundred rebuilding shops appeared on the webpage he opened and each advertised expert services, with a specialty for each shop. Which one would Valdez patronize?

He shifted focus for a few minutes, searched for the name Stefano Valdez, and found a dozen men—or boys—spread around the globe. Which one might play piano? If he could believe Enrique, Lena and her brother once played as duet partners in concert venues but none of the names linked to music in any way. Either his target had changed professions, or he shunned the web's social media options.

140 | Ann Christine Fell

How would he locate his quarry?

He searched truck companies. What had the bartender said? Overland Express. He entered that name into the search engine and came up with a company that ran lines across northern US, but none in Louisiana.

Teo cursed. He watched the screen blink into an energy-saving mode and turned to stare at Felipe sprawled across the hotel bed, watching the television on the dresser. Felipe's gaze flickered to Teo and the boy squirmed. He sat upright, legs hanging over the end of the bed, his gaze riveted on a hexagon in the carpet pattern.

Teo grunted. "Oh, go ahead. Watch your damn TV."

Felipe returned to his show.

Teo turned back to the computer. With a click on the power button, he re-woke the screen. A series of small windows cycled through the larger screen. Games, music, advertisements, weather, and news flickered in icons across the screen. Activity in the news window drew his attention and he opened the screen to reports from the recent earthquake devastation on the western coast.

A natural disaster.

This resonated with him, but he wasn't sure why. Something Julio mentioned? He vaguely recalled Julio's report that Lena tried to contact her brother who remained in the states after being rescued by a disaster relief organization. Hurricane Francine marked the last time she had seen him and it also marked her entry into the Diaz family.

It seemed a long shot, but might be worth checking out. This brother of Lena's could have volunteered to work the latest crisis, payback for his own rescue. He clicked the news icon and it blinked to life across the entire screen.

"Jep Bogart here in Reedsport, at the makeshift headquarters for Global Relief talking to Melody Valdez, a volunteer in the office."

Teo sat bolt upright and absorbed the entire five-minute news segment. He re-ran the CNS clip and scrutinized the young woman on camera. Could he be this lucky? Could this woman be his wife? Name Valdez. Professional relief worker at Francine and now Oregon. Working mother with a black-haired brat. She surely wouldn't take a baby too far from home. This had to be the same Valdez family. His luck had just turned.

He cursed under his breath. The damn bartender fed him a line. Missouri or Oklahoma? Not unless you spelled it "O-r-e-g-o-n." He slammed his fist on the desk and subdued an urge to pound the manager of the Caribbean Breeze. It wouldn't be worth the delay.

He swung his chair around, reached across the gap separating the desk from the bed, and smacked Felipe's dangling leg. "Pack the bags. We're going to Oregon."

38

IZZY STUMBLED TO her kitchen in early morning darkness and settled at the table to wake up with the day's Sudoku puzzle, lulled into tranquility by the percolating coffee maker. By the time the eastern sky bloomed with shades of her favorite peace rosebush, she felt ready to face the day. A commotion at the back door jarred her from reverie. The door rattled with insistent knocks. She jumped up, banged her elbow on the table, and peeked through the diamond-shaped window. Outside Stefano ran a hand through the black curls on his head, still damp from his morning shower. He shifted his weight from one foot to the other repeatedly. Izzy flung open the door and pulled him into the kitchen. She wrapped her arms around him. "I can't believe it—you're here."

He offered a sheepish grin. "Got any work for me today?"

"Do I ever." She filled two coffee mugs, handed him one, and slipped on the work shoes at the back door. "Let's go have a look at your mom's piano."

In the shop, she pulled an old quilt off the damaged Steinway. Stefano circled the piano, his eyes brimming with tears. Izzy stepped back to allow him space as he wrestled with his jumbled emotions.

He reached a shaking hand forward, fingers splayed, but could not bring himself to touch the sorry instrument. Elsie Lenore throbbed with ethereal vitality under his scrutiny, and memories flooded his mind, parading images one after another—his mother ushering in a teacher for his first lesson—Lena teasing him to best her performance as a complex musical phrase flowed with ease from her fingers—their mother's sitting room with piano parts strewn across the floor as he struggled to make imperfect repairs. His entire life had been a dance with this broken piano, a ballet with two graceful partners twisting, leaping, and whirling against each other, their fates entwined.

Elsie Lenore, though beaten and broken, pulsed with magnetism he sensed, if nobody else could. It filled him with reverence. Her wounds ran deep. But in Elsie Lenore he felt his mother, and he sensed Lena's presence in a way that defied explanation.

He didn't know how long he stood, palms absorbing the piano's aura.

"Stefano?" Izzy interrupted his trance.

He coughed, swiped a hand across his face, and stepped back. "*Caramba,* Mom. They did a number on her, didn't they?"

She sighed. "That, they did. What should we do about it?"

"I don't know. I kept her alive for years, learned as I went, and found ways to patch her up in spite of unavailable parts. But this..." He gestured with a wave over the instrument. "I don't know how to begin here."

She touched his arm and he looked at her. "Do you want to rebuild Elsie?"

He stared at the fractured lid and warped keyboard on the Steinway. "I see my past in this piano. Good times at home. Mama and her laughter, even through hard times. Lena's face. Hours and hours we practiced together. And now this. It's my own life, a broken mess." His voice trailed off. "If I can rebuild her, I can mend my own life too. But I don't have the first clue where to start on either project."

Izzy laid a gentle hand on his shoulder. "Showing up here is the first step."

"Is it even possible to repair this damage?"

"There isn't much on a piano that can't be repaired or rebuilt if you have the time and equipment."

"And," he said with a wink, "Now you're going to tell me that there isn't much about a marriage that can't be repaired if I have the time and determination."

"Took my words," Izzy said.

"I want to see those messages you told me about."

"We'd have to dismantle the piano again before you could get to the keys but Kurt left the SD card in the office. Let's go have a look."

While Izzy fixed eggs and toast, Stefano worked with the data device, but each password he tried led nowhere. With each failure, his frustration grew. By the time breakfast was ready, his patience had evaporated.

"Any luck?" Izzy asked. She refilled his mug with fresh coffee and sat across from him at the table.

"Zip."

"What did you try?"

"Everything I could think of—Lena's name, initials, Mama's name, nickname. Our hometown, her best friend in school. Nothing worked."

"Did you try your own name?"

"Yes. My name. My initials. With my luck, that card may not even be something Lena put there. And if that's the case, it's pointless to go on. I'm doomed."

39

"I'LL TAKE ANOTHER look at that piano," Stefano said. He pushed back from the table and shuffled to the back door.

In the shop, he leaned over the decrepit instrument and fingered the soundboard splinters. "Is it even possible to repair all this?" he asked Izzy.

"Like I said, if you have the will, we'll find a way."

"But the soundboard? What if the iron plate itself is cracked?"

"Soundboard repairs are routine. Some specialty shops duplicate boards on request. As for the plate, we should examine it and assess its condition. We might find a replacement at Steinway in New York, if need be."

"Look at these hammers. And the pedal lyre swings from its mounts. Nothing secure about it."

"All repairable or replaceable. Do you want to rebuild Elsie, Stefano?"

He considered the task a moment before he nodded. "For Lena. I will give it my best shot."

"I don't want to mislead you. It will take lots work, hard and dirty. Long hours in the shop."

He sighed. The words Lena penned in the card echoed in his mind. *We need you.* "I want to do it. Will you advise?"

"I'll even assist you when you need extra hands."

"How long will it take? Two, three months?"

She chuckled. "At least, my friend. Don't be surprised if it takes longer."

"What do I do first?"

She stepped back and rubbed her chin. "I've got work scheduled this morning. Why don't you get out a check sheet and do a detailed assessment of the piano? List the parts we'll need to replace. When you're done, you could organize the work carts to make room for Elsie's parts as we pull them off.

When I return I'll help pull the action out, and we'll take a look at the letters underneath the keys."

Enfocate, Valdez.

He nodded with conviction. "Consider it done, Mom."

✽✽

Izzy loaded her Prius Prime for the day's work and drove toward town, pondering the swings in Stefano's mood.

Touch and go. Delicatamente, Isabel.

At least he showed up, an important first step toward mending their family rift. At the same time, she sensed that his fresh determination could evaporate into despair. She couldn't afford to discourage him. She'd need to select every word she spoke to him and every action she took from here forward with consideration for his tenuous emotional state. Tuning a piano always cleared her mind. There was a rhythm about it, an age-worn set of tried-and-true habits that ingrained themselves as automatic motions. Prep the piano. Set up the hygrometer. Check pitch, octave, and unison tuning. Run a chromatic scale to assess the piano's action. Insert mute strips and dive in.

She slid her thighs under the first piano's keybed until the keys pressed against her waist. Reaching over the keys, she cradled the tuning lever with her right hand and played the keys with her left hand. Wrapped in her arms as she worked, she united with the instrument in an extended embrace. From one key to the next, one tuning pin to another, moving mutes to control vibrations, she fell into the familiar rhythm. Listen to beats, clean them to a crisp tone, and move to the next key. She could do this blindfolded.

Halfway through her second tuning, inspiration struck.

Elsie Lenore.

What if Lena used the piano's name as the password? She renewed her efforts, energized and excited to get back and suggest that possibility to her son-in-law.

Izzy returned to the shop late in the afternoon, and Stefano showed her his notes and supply list. "Looks great," she said.

"I'll head home and put together Mel's famous gumbo."

"You're hungry then."

"Yes, I am. First time in... I don't know how long."

"Stay for dinner?"

"No. I need time. I'll get the place cleaned up a little."

"You're going to wait to analyze the mysterious letters?"

"I'm bushed. I'll get a fresh start tomorrow." He waved as he headed to his car.

Since she expected Kurt home late after an evening class, Izzy headed to the office and called Mel. "Hey, screen star--we caught the CNS interview."

"Yeah. They were jerks."

"You handled them well."

"That's my job. As long as they don't pester the real work in progress, I can field questions."

"You ready for good news? Guess who showed up to work at the shop today."

"You can't be serious," Mel said.

"I'm dead serious. He arrived before sunup."

"Was he sober?"

"Yes—sober and ready to work."

"How did you manage that?"

Izzy sputtered in her response. Should Mel know about Roberto's phone call? She decided not to tell that news. Mel had enough to worry about, not to mention she would feel like her mother was pressuring her to come home after the news from New Orleans. "He came around. It's about time, if you ask me."

"Way past time."

"Stefano got quite a bit done today, evaluating and tearing down the old Steinway."

"That piano from New Orleans?"

"His mother's piano. I've got my fingers crossed. He asked about the letters written below the keys and we'll check them tomorrow. He did work with the data chip today, but couldn't come up with the password. I've got an idea for him to try though."

"What's that?"

"The piano's nickname, 'Elsie Lenore'."

"Try it now, Mom."

"Shouldn't I wait for him?"

After a moment of silence, Mel said, "Given how fickle he's been, you should go ahead. If it doesn't work, don't even mention it. If it does work, suggest he try it himself tomorrow morning."

"Okay. I'll do it." Izzy carried her phone to the office and booted up the computer. She drummed her fingers on the walnut desk top while it spun to life. When the password screen for the mini SD card popped up, she narrated the progress. "Typing. E-L-S-I-E-L-E-N-O-R-E."

"Did it work, Mom?"

"No. Nothing happened."

"Try all caps."

"I did."

"How about lower case?"

Izzy tried several variations. "Nothing."

Mel sighed. "Guess 'Elsie Lenore' is not the password. It's good you found that out before Stefano got his hopes up."

Izzy sighed. "Back where we started. I won't mention this one to Stefano."

40

AT A BARRICADE across the road, Teo swung the rented Caravan into a crude gravel lot and braked to a stop in a swirl of dust. Aimed in every direction, grimy cars littered the field, mirroring the chaos in every coastal town affected by the earthquake. He slid from the car, slung a backpack onto his shoulders, and sent an unspoken command to Felipe with a derogatory glance. The boy scrambled from the back seat and Teo fitted a small pack on him.

"What now?" the boy said.

Teo nodded toward volunteers raking through the rubble. "Now we walk. Try to fit in."

They wandered along paths worn through the debris, sidestepped rotting garbage, and crossed trickles of open sewage as they searched in vain for the canvas tents shown in the CNS video footage. Toward evening they joined a line outside a trailer. At dusk, the sun sank through haze in the dust-filled air and volunteers inside the trailer distributed sandwiches, fruit, and fresh water to the hungry workers.

Felipe's eyes and teeth gleamed from his dirt-darkened face. Teo scratched a line through the dust on his own forearm and grunted. They looked every bit as worn and grimy as the bona fide volunteers. They sat on a stack of bricks and bit into the sandwiches. Their teeth gritted on particles on the crusting bread and Felipe twisted his face in disgust.

"Eat it," Teo ordered.

"I am," Felipe retorted. "See?" He chewed with exaggerated gusto, disgust still evident on his grimy face.

Teo cuffed his ear. They finished the sandwiches in silence.

"Where will we sleep?" Felipe said as the sun sank through ragged pine needles across the pathway.

"In the car." His voice ominous, Teo's answer matched his short temper. He'd not expected their mission to last this long. How hard could it be to find the relief headquarters? But the rubble resulting from the earthquake and tsunami had erased all signs of city planning. A methodical sweep through the ruins proved impossible with the rubbish heaps scattered at random.

They dragged to the volunteer parking area. Teo couldn't recognize the Caravan. After an afternoon in Reedsport, the dusty rental car was indistinguishable from other vehicles. He clicked the key fob and a remote horn guided them to their car. Felipe crawled into the back seat and fell asleep. Teo leaned the front seat back and flopped from side to side in search of comfort. His body ached and his mind grumbled with foul thoughts. He needed to find that piano, a crucial step to recover the samples his inept brothers lost. Why couldn't he locate that woman? Reedsport resembled decrepit Cuban villages that struggled to eke out a life for people after decades of deprivations. Litter cluttered grimy pathways, and open streams of raw waste ran down the hillsides.

It should have been easy. But it was not.

✍✍

Stefano arrived early again the next morning. He tapped on the kitchen door. When Izzy invited him in, he declined. "I want to get started."

"I'll be out in a few minutes." She waved him to the shop.

He reviewed the previous day's notes, rolled a storage rack adjacent to the treble end of Elsie's keys, and removed cabinet parts. With the key frame exposed, he tugged on it, but it wouldn't move. He bent lower to peer into the space beneath the tuning pins. Izzy slipped inside the shop, Kurt behind her.

"How's it going?" Kurt asked.

"I can't move the piano's action."

Izzy said, "We need to lift the stretcher bar for clearance."

Kurt helped Stefano and Izzy roll Elsie Lenore under the hoist frame. They each took a leg and nudged the piano over the concrete floor. The old gal creaked and wobbled, but did not collapse.

"You have your work cut out for you," Kurt said, rubbing his knuckles. "I'm off to class." He touched his brow in a mock salute and headed to the door.

Izzy attached straps to the stretcher bar and hoisted it up to straighten the fracture, allowing enough space for Stefano to wiggle the action out. He slid the frame onto a wheeled cart.

Enfocate, Valdez. Easy does it. Elsie needs no more rough treatment.

He handed his supply list to her and rolled the action assembly toward a workbench.

She studied his assessments. "It's a thorough job, Stefano. Looks like you'll replace almost everything. Hammers, dampers, wippens. Anything with felt in it, all the stressed wood parts."

"Can you order new keys?" he asked.

"Could. But it may suffice to repair these and replace the felt. Do you want to replace the ivories?"

"With plastic? I'd rather honor the elephant and keep the ivory."

Stefano removed the hammer rail from the key frame and exposed the keys on their pins. He played each one to test their fit on the guide pins. Izzy helped place the keys into a felt-lined clamp and they inverted the keys on the cart. He ran his fingers across the hand written letters on the smooth wood. "Here's what I've been waiting for. Clue *Numero Uno.*" The letters glared at him with a silent challenge. *Read me,* they taunted.

"You figured it out yet?" she asked.

"From your photo? I've no idea."

"You knew Lena better than anyone. What would she say here?"

"If she said anything. I don't know. I didn't even know she could pull the action from a piano."

"Had she ever seen you do that?"

"She walked through the living room when I tinkered on the old gal in our mother's music room. She paid no attention to piano parts, though. She wanted to make music."

"Maybe she watched closer than you knew and she figured this was the best way to get a clandestine message to you alone. She knew you could dissect a piano."

"Clandestine... huh?" He gazed at her, eyebrows raised.

"That's my suspicious mind at work."

He grinned. "You? A suspicious mind? No way."

She chuckled. "More than you'll ever know. If there's a secret message here, I'm sure you'll figure it out."

41

TEO AND FELIPE searched through the crumbling town two more days and Teo's anger escalated by the hour. Mid-morning on the third day, he hoisted Felipe into a splintered fir tree to look from a higher vantage point. Felipe shimmied along a rough branch and looked out over above the rubble.

"See anything?" Teo shouted from below.

The boy squinted to look over the ruined town. He pointed up the slope. "I see them."

"Come on then. Let's go."

❧

"I'm off to my day's appointments now," Izzy said. "Need anything before I go?"

Stefano waved her away. "I've got this now."

He loosened damper screws, pulled the dampers off the strings, and stored the old ones in a small wooden stand drilled with holes for that purpose. He measured the rusty string gauges to record the original engineering scale, turned each tuning pin until no tension remained on the wires, and pried the piano strings from their pins. After discarding the corroded treble strings, he hung the bass strings in order on an insulated wire for future reference.

With a drill motor, he removed all the tuning pins and tossed them in a scrap box. With the iron plate exposed, he sketched its perimeter on a large piece of corrugated cardboard and punched holes for each plate screw. The resulting map provided orderly storage for the large bolts until they could be re-installed. By the time Izzy showed up that afternoon, he'd organized the dismantled parts on the wheeled cart.

She surveyed his progress and rubbed his shoulders to massage a few kinks from his muscles. "Let's call it a day. Come in and eat. First thing in the morning, I'll help you pull the plate."

As the next morning's sunlight filtered through the blooming redbud trees, Izzy helped Stefano arrange the hoist straps through holes in the iron plate and he lifted the cast iron plate from the piano shell. They mounted the plate on two large hooks protruding from the wall behind the frame and examined every inch of the cast iron. There were no obvious compression fractures. Kurt studied the century-old iron using his sculptor's knowledge of metallurgy and pronounced it sound.

"That's a relief," Izzy said. "At least we won't need to replace the plate."

He leaned over the piano's rim and sighed. "I'm beat."

"Why don't you call it a day and relax this evening."

"I wish I could talk to Melody."

"Give her a call and see what happens."

"You think?"

Izzy shrugged a shoulder. "Would it hurt to try?"

"Could make her madder."

"I disagree. Many women experience post-partum depression after childbirth. I'm sure Mel suffered this depression, and it was compounded by your absence. She may be glad to hear from you now."

He studied her face with an intensity that chiseled a few more lines in his forehead. "I couldn't handle it if she hung up on me again."

"Try a text message. Say you'd like to hear from her when she's got a chance. Then it's her move. What about that?"

He nodded. "I'll consider it."

Teo may have located the Global Relief headquarters, but it was another matter to be able to identify the regular staff among the volunteers. The CNS interview helped him peg Melody Valdez, but as a Global Relief staff member, she was allowed access to the area in a pickup truck. He was denied admittance except on foot. He couldn't get to the Caravan fast enough to follow when she drove out each evening. After several days, he established her basic schedule, and the direction she headed at dusk. He found an empty driveway up the rough blacktop highway and settled in to wait and watch.

Felipe claimed a discarded bicycle and rolled it along the road to the rented Caravan. Teo reset the chain, and Felipe had wheels. The boy amused himself riding along the empty streets and side roads.

That evening Teo spotted the dusty Ford pickup driven by Melody Valdez bumping along the cracked pavement. He whistled for Felipe. The boy pedaled up and swirled the dust in Teo's face as he braked to a stop.

Teo swore and coughed. "Climb in. We're going for a ride."

ھھ

Melody's regular video call became the day's highlight and Izzy anticipated it with excitement. She could not sit still when watching her grandson, drool dripping off his chin, a big toothless grin on his chubby face. She couldn't stand it. "Hey, little one," she cooed to the baby. "He sure is growing fast."

"No kidding there," Mel laughed. "He's a chunk."

"When will I get to hold my grandson again?"

"Still lots to do here, Mom. Hard to say how long Global Relief will remain in active status."

"Stefano wants to talk to you."

Mel did not respond.

"I told him he should call you, but he's scared you'd hang up on him. You wouldn't, would you?"

"I don't know, Mom. Depends on his mood when he calls."

"Not to mention your mood. How do you feel?"

"I'm fine. You were right about that depression thing but I haven't got time to be depressed here."

"Would you answer a text if Stefano sent one?"

"I might. He wants to talk?"

"In the worst way."

"Sometimes I wish I'd stayed home. Every time Nico smiles, my heart cries that Stefano can't see it too. But then, I remember how awful I felt. You don't understand what it's like to be abandoned."

"I'm glad you feel tenderness for him. He's had it rough, in many ways."

"But you think he's sober and ready to talk?"

"Yes. He's dedicated—works every day."

"Mom, that's the best news."

"Did you have a bad day?"

"No. But I got a strange feeling that someone was watching me."

Fortissimo. What's up? Izzy struggled to suppress her suspicion. "Really? Those CNS guys?"

"Hard to say. I never did spot anyone but it felt creepy."

Chills raced along Izzy's arms. "Is this new?"

"Yeah, I guess."

"Please take care. You're on your own out there."

"I know, Mom. It's nothing. I'm imagining things and it kept me on edge all day."

"Don't take any chances with my grandbaby."

"I'm sure it's nothing."

42

FELIPE ROLLED BY on his bicycle for the third time. Teo stepped from the brush and beckoned him over. The boy skidded to a stop, panting with exertion.

"Did you see any sign of a man in that cabin?" Teo asked.

Felipe shook his head.

"No men?"

"No."

"When it's dark enough, sneak in there for a closer look. Let me know what you see."

The sun sank below the distant horizon and seawater gleamed brilliant orange while Felipe rode laps by the driveway where the Global Relief mom drove her truck. Nothing moved outside the cabin. He hid the bicycle behind a bush and sneaked along the driveway to peep into the windows. He found a crack in the front room blinds and watched the young woman tend a stove. The baby sat in a high chair beside a small table set for a solitary adult. There were no men in the cabin.

He hustled his report to Teo.

৵৶

Hidden behind low clouds, the rising sun brightened the morning. Teo smeared an oily make-up over his face and bare arms before he sprinted up the hill and through the trees. He crouched low in the brush and surveyed the rustic cabin from a distance. The front door opened and the young woman carried her infant to the dusty pickup truck. She secured the child in an infant seat, swung the door shut, and flung a long braid over her shoulder. Returning to the cabin, she inserted a key and locked the door.

She settled behind the driver's wheel, started the car, and drove away. As she passed Teo's concealment, she stared into the brush. He froze. The car rolled by and disappeared along the tree-lined drive. He heard her accelerate along the paved road and checked his watch. Ten quiet minutes later he stepped from his hiding place and stole to the front door. In a calculated movement, he reached down, picked up a fist-sized stone from the driveway, and smashed it through a small glass pane on the door. He reached through the jagged glass, unlocked the cabin, and stepped inside.

Teo's gaze swept the front room. Literature stacked on a small table by the easy chair included baby magazines, pamphlets describing rescue procedures for disaster victims, and newspapers. He shoved it all onto the floor and entered the kitchen. He flung open drawers and cabinets but found nothing he wouldn't expect to find in a kitchen.

He swept refrigerator shelves bare with his forearm and followed suit in the freezer compartment. Sticky fluids oozed from broken jars into small rivulets on the tiles and he tracked pickle juice to the back rooms. In the master bedroom, he removed and emptied the dresser drawers, pulled clothing from their hangers and emptied boxes from the closet shelf onto the mess.

Nothing unusual.

In the office, he dumped desk drawers onto the floor, rifling through their contents. He shuffled through a pile of mail on the corner table. Junk mail. Ads. Underneath it all he found an empty envelope addressed to Melody Valdez. Though it lacked a specific return address, he noted the postmark: Wichita, Kansas, four days ago.

Teo dug in his shirt pocket for a list he'd copied off the piano technician website. Twenty technicians belonged to this Wichita group. Of all the piano repair shops listed in the Midwest, Stefano Valdez had shipped Lena's piano to one in Kansas after all. Find the piano, and he'd find Valdez at the same time.

He savored the notion for a moment. This jerk had created enough trouble for him. It was payback time.

Teo pocketed the envelope and strode from the cabin. He left the front door wide open and skipped down the hill to where Felipe waited in their rented Caravan. He met the boy's questioning look with a wry smile and slid behind the wheel. "Kansas, Felipe. We're going to Wichita, Kansas."

⊷⟞⟝⊶

Melody managed to slip out of headquarters at 10:15. She settled Nico into his infant seat and they headed through debris-lined paths to the town's temporary postal office. When she lifted Nico to enter the trailer, she caught a whiff that told her he needed a change. She pawed through the diaper bag, but found no diapers.

"How did I manage to get away with no fresh diapers?" She shook her head in disgust. Had she been that distracted by the short text message from Stefano?

With no reliable place in Reedsport to get diapers, she'd have to return to the cabin. She collected the mail for Global Relief, tucked it beneath Nico's car seat, and strapped him in. He squirmed and pouted. His lower lip trembled, a precursor to his familiar wail.

"Gotta go home for diapers, kiddo," Mel said. "Mommy didn't have her head on straight this morning. Sorry." She tweaked his chin as she settled behind the steering wheel. He burbled tiny bubbles in the drool on his lips.

Mel parked at the cabin and left the engine running. "Be right back, Babe." She blew Nico a kiss as she dashed to the house. Halfway there, she halted, her mouth agape. The front door swung open. Glass shards from a broken window lay scattered across the concrete stoop and over the ceramic flower pots at the entrance.

She caught her breath and tiptoed forward to peer inside. Trembling, she stepped into the front room and her vision blurred with tears. The place was a mess. She grabbed the doorframe to steady herself and tripped over the door sill. She scrambled up and rushed to the idling pickup truck. She reached through the open window for her phone. Nico fussed in his car seat.

"It's okay, Babe. Mama has to..." What? What exactly did she have to do? What had happened here? Why here? Why now? "Mom—" she wailed in a voice that scared Nico. He released a wail and she joined him as she lifted her phone and dialed.

43

IZZY EVALUATED STEFANO'S progress on the piano daily, impressed that he'd remained sober since Roberto's phone call. He managed to repair the fractured stretcher bar, filled jagged edges in the cabinet veneer, and sanded the old finish off the soundboard. With long spruce shims filling the sound-board cracks, Izzy planed them even with the board while he removed the old bridge pins. They leaned over the soundboard together to double-check the work when Izzy's phone jangled with Melody's ringtone. "Hey there." she answered her call. "Mel?"

Stefano lowered the scraper.

Mel's voice screamed into the shop, "Mom—somebody broke into the cabin!"

"Mel, would you say that again? It sounded like you said—"

"Somebody broke into the cabin."

"When?"

"This morning."

"Take a deep breath, Sweetie," Izzy said as panic welled in her heart. "Are you at the cabin? It's ten in the morning there."

"I ran home to get more diapers, and—and—" Her words came in a rush.

"Melody, get out of there," Stefano blurted out.

"Stefano? You're there?"

"Sí, my love."

After a silent moment, Melody spoke again, her voice soft and plaintive.

"I took a few minutes to run home," she muttered. "And the front door glass—it's broken. The door wide open. Every-thing's a mess—food all over the kitchen. Drawers dumped."

"Have you called for help?" Izzy asked.

"I called you."

"Call the sheriff. Right now. Then call me back. Do it." Izzy disconnected the call. Chills washed over her body in waves. First, a stalker and now a break-in. Her gaze flew around the room and settled on Stefano's eyes.

He stared at her, eyes narrowed, mouth twisted, fists clenched. "I gotta go to Oregon."

Kurt stepped into the shop. "Hey, I'm hungry. Ready for lunch?" His light-hearted banter ceased. "What?" Kurt said. "Something wrong?"

"It's Mel," she said. "Somebody broke into the cabin."

Mel's ringtone split the air again.

Izzy answered on the first chime. "Did you reach them?"

"Yes, Mom. They're short-handed and overextended. A little break-in isn't top priority right now."

"Can you find another place for a few days? Check into a hotel."

"There are no hotels."

"You have to go." Stefano stressed each syllable.

"Could you stay in town at the headquarters? Or with another staff member?" Izzy said.

Nico's little voice wailed in the background. "Hush, little one. It's okay. Mommy's here." Mel's attempts to sooth him fell short and he screamed louder.

"Nico is with you?" Stefano's voice boomed.

"Of course."

He said, "Mel—find another place to stay."

Izzy said. "Stefano's right. We're both worried about you."

"That would make three of us," Kurt said.

"Dad? You're there too?"

"It's lunchtime."

"Have you sensed your stalker today?" Izzy said.

"A stalker?" Stefano yelled. "Mel, listen. The Diaz family my sister married into is bad news. And we found out Teofilo Diaz is looking for me. He wouldn't hesitate to hurt you to get back at me."

"How could he possibly know I'm in Oregon?"

"That CNS interview. The world could see you," Izzy said.

Stefano studied Izzy, eyes narrowed. "She's right. If he knows you and I met after Francine, and he saw that interview, he went up there to find me."

"Is that guy—Teofilo—is he behind this?"

"I don't know," Kurt said. "But don't take any chances."

"Get in the truck and lock the doors right now," Stefano said. "If you see a stranger coming at you—run him down."

"You scare me," Mel said.

"Leave, Melody," Izzy repeated. "I'll end this call so you can take Nico to a safe place—relief headquarters? Let me know when you get there." She disconnected the call and silence shrouded the piano shop. She stared from Stefano's stricken face to Kurt's wrinkled brow.

Stefano broke the silence. "I gotta go to Oregon. She can't face this alone."

"I don't disagree, Stefano," Kurt said. "However, if you go, you'd be walking into a trap and with all the chaos up there, you'd be on your own."

Stefano nodded. "But this changes everything."

"Yes. But it doesn't make sense for you to run straight into harm's way," Kurt said.

"He's right, Stefano," Izzy said. "If this is Diaz, he wants to draw you out. Soon as you show up..." She left the sentence unfinished.

"Why wouldn't he come here?" Stefano said.

"He doesn't know where to find you."

"But he could find Melody?" Stefano's voice cracked.

"That damn interview," Kurt said, his voice a growl.

"Diaz assumed I'd go to Oregon to help her."

"Logical assumption."

"But Mel can't face him alone."

"I agree with you on that. I'll step up my plans for the summer's work trip and leave as soon as I record final grades."

"When would that be?

"Day after tomorrow. And, since Melody took your truck out there, I'll catch a flight. I could get there before dark Thursday."

"That's a plan," Izzy said. "Stefano, you stay here, unseen and unobserved. With Kurt in Oregon, Melody would be safe and it would buy us time to figure out what's going on."

Stefano's shoulders drooped. "Okay, Dad," he said, his mouth drawn tight. "Take care of my family."

"My family too," Kurt said and clapped his son-in-law's back.

44

TWO MORNINGS LATER Izzy drove Kurt to Eisenhower National early. He checked two bags of clothing and art supplies for his summer sojourn at the cabin. Before he headed through the security gate, she pulled him aside for a long embrace. "Please be careful," she said.

"Count on that," he said.

"Hug our girl for me. And that baby."

Kurt flashed a huge grin. "Count on that too."

He joined a line weaving through the security lanes and she watched until he cleared the check point. He turned and waved before he disappeared. On the drive home, the ominous clouds of personal and family drama made it impossible to focus on the road. How would she and Stefano manage alone through the summer?

At the piano shop, a car door slammed outside and she turned from the piano where Stefano measured the tenor bridge in preparation for a new cap. Brett Lander and his son Dirk ambled toward the shop.

"What brings you this way?" she asked.

"We needed supplies in town and Dirk wanted to stop and say hi."

"Dirk?"

The younger man smiled. She took his extended hand in welcome.

"You remember Dirk," Brett said.

"Of course. What's up, Dirk?"

"Next week is finals week at the university and Maddi wants you all to come up for her recital."

She took a deep breath. "I'd love to go," she said. "Kurt can't join us though."

Brett raised his eyebrows.

"He flew off to Oregon this morning to help Melody," Izzy said.

His eyebrows lowered again and he studied her. "A bit early for his usual departure, isn't it?"

She sighed. "Can't get anything past you, can I? Yes. He left in a hurry."

Stefano moved around the piano. "Someone broke into the cabin on Wednesday."

Izzy added, "Since Mel's alone out there, Kurt volunteered to go early to be with her."

Brett wrinkled his brow and turned his gaze on Stefano. "Isn't this your family?"

Stefano grimaced, and wiped perspiration from his forehead. "It could be Diaz. If I go, she'd be in greater danger since he's looking for me."

Brett looked at Izzy with suspicion. "Explain."

She summarized the events since Stefano returned home.

"You have thought this through," Brett continued. He nodded at Stefano. "I'd lay low for a while too."

Izzy said, "Stefano, you could move in out here. It would help us both feel safer."

"Good idea," Brett said. "I'd feel better if Izzy isn't here alone all summer."

Stefano said, "When do you want me?"

"The sooner the better."

"And about the recital next week?" Brett changed the subject.

"I'd love to attend Maddi's recital," Izzy said.

"Ride with us," Brett said.

"You and Dirk?"

"We'll go together, yes."

"When will you leave?"

"Friday about noon. Will you ride along?"

Izzy considered the invitation a moment before she nodded.

"Stefano, you're welcome to join us," Dirk said.

Stefano moved his things into Melody's old room at the Woods home that afternoon and dropped into bed, exhausted, after dinner. Kurt made it to Oregon. He repaired damage to the front door, and secured everything with new locks. Melody remained puzzled about the motive behind the break-in. Nothing seemed to be missing. Broken, but not missing.

The following Friday morning, Izzy and Stefano arrived at the Double-M Ranch and loaded into Brett's double cab Ford pickup. They headed to the highway, with Dirk's music blaring from the speakers.

On the smooth road, Dirk shut off the music. "I want to talk to you, Izzy. And Dad."

"Okay," she said. "Talk away."

"Well," he said, but hesitated. "You see, it's like this." He stumbled over the words.

Brett smiled with a quizzical look on his face but he said nothing as Dirk fumbled a few more words.

"What, Dirk?" Izzy prompted.

He looked down as he found his voice. "Well, you know I've spent every possible moment since March with Maddi."

She raised her eyebrows, and cocked her head. "I didn't know that, but I do now."

"Far too much time, in my opinion," Brett reproached him. "It affected her academic performance this semester."

She waved a hand. "Whoa, Brett. Let him talk."

"That's what I mean. You treat her like you're her dad or something. And I need to know for sure. I'm obsessed with her. If you must know, I'm in love with her. I want to propose."

"Oh my," Izzy said.

"You see my quandary. If we're related—if she's my sister or something—that would destroy me."

Brett smiled. "Relax, Dirk. You have no genetic ties to Maddi."

Dirk turned to Izzy. "Is that the truth?"

She nodded. "Absolutely."

"Then I want to know," he said, eyes narrow and voice stern, "what's her story? Why do you both protect her?"

"Why don't you ask Maddi?" she said.

"I will, but first I want to know how you and Dad are involved."

"I'll tell you what I know. Maddi was born a twin to the Campbell family in Pennsylvania, but was kidnapped from the hospital nursery before they took her home." Izzy spent the next hour describing how she met Maddi, and the events involved in her reunion with her Pennsylvania family.

"Early childhood trauma contributed to her socialization challenges. A doctor diagnosed her with Asperger's Syndrome, a form of autism."

"She doesn't seem autistic," Dirk said. "At least not what I understood was autistic."

"She's high-functioning, and she's made great strides since the reunion with her birth family. She's gifted with music, but has trouble with speech sometimes."

"The stuttering," Dirk said. "I find that endearing."

"And she senses moods and emotions with fragrances."

"'It's a lemon day'," he quoted Maddi and nodded.

"When Maddi was about eight," Izzy said, "the man who kidnapped her took steps to sell her to a child-trafficking ring. Desperate to keep him away from her daughter, her adoptive mother sent her with me. We found refuge and protection with your dad, Brett here."

Brett said, "And that's why I'm involved. This girl needed protection. She is a cherished friend, but she is not my daughter. Her official name is Laura Madeline Campbell."

"Well then," Dirk said, grinning, "if I wish to ask for her hand in marriage, I need to plan a trip to Pennsylvania." He looked at Brett. "Okay by you, Dad?"

Brett studied him until the pickup wandered into the oncoming lane. He turned back to the highway and slapped the steering wheel, tooting the horn. "It's okay by me," he said and laughed.

45

STEFANO NUDGED IZZY as they filed into the auditorium behind Brett and Dirk Lander. "That explains your suspicious nature, I suppose," he whispered.

"The story I told in the car?"

He nodded. They slid to the center of the sixth row in front of the stage. "I'd never heard it before."

"Hopefully that means there's no reason to panic," she said. "Life-or-death encounters can't happen twice to one little piano tuner, or her family. Can they?"

Stefano shook his head. *Caramba!* Nobody could be more paranoid than he was right now, worried about his little family a thousand miles away. He shouldn't have come. He couldn't concentrate on the music this evening. Why hadn't he stayed home?

The crowd in the auditorium hummed with conversation. Third on the program, Maddi shared her final concert with a dozen other seniors this evening.

"She knows we're here, doesn't she?" Izzy reached across Stefano and poked Dirk with the program.

With an impish grin, Dirk shook his head. "I led her to believe we had a conflict."

"She's not expecting us?"

"I wanted to surprise her."

"I hope that doesn't backfire," Izzy whispered to Stefano.

Two instrumental performances later, a stage hand rolled the concert Steinway to the front stage right. The singers in a vocal quartet entered from the wings and filed to selected spots. Maddi appeared a moment later, radiant in the spotlight. She hesitated, smoothed her satin gown and ran a hand through her long tresses.

"She looks confident," Izzy whispered.

A hush swept through the auditorium when Maddi caught her heel on the hem of her deep lavender evening gown and faltered. Dirk lunged forward in his seat, but Brett pulled him back. Maddi caught herself and stood tall. She stared into the audience and narrowed her eyes to scan the darkened room before perching on the piano bench.

Izzy muttered, "Keep it together, girl. You can do this."

Maddi played an introduction on the piano. A few bars later, the tenor launched in, followed by alto and bass singers. The soprano line swelled a moment later. The quartet sang four numbers, the first in English, followed by choral selections in Italian, German, and French. As the applause died away, Maddi and the vocalists filed from the spotlights. A stage hand moved the piano center stage and Maddi floated back to warm applause. She searched the auditorium again and paused, her face masked by confusion. With a slight shake of her head, she sat on the piano bench, took a deep breath, and closed her eyes. Her fingertips caressed the keytops a moment and she launched into her introductory number. She performed a historical sampling of piano music written throughout the ancient musical periods—baroque, classical, romantic, and modern.

She opened her finale and Stefano froze as she played an Ernesto Lecuona number he knew well. He'd played it himself. Lena had played it. And it was the same composition they'd arranged as a duet, the *Vals* she had mentioned in her card. Borne on music that floated over the heads of the audience, he flew back to Cuba. In his mind, he was home again, and Lena tantalized him with her eyes.

It's all in the melody.

That much was certain. He heard nothing else. After Maddi finished, after the applause died, after the lights came up for intermission, he still heard the melodic strains and nothing else.

༺༒༻

Dirk excused himself and headed backstage. As the lights dimmed again, he showed up with Maddi on his arm, her face aglow with happiness. She took a seat between Izzy and Dirk for the second half.

"You're radiant this evening," Izzy whispered to her.

Maddi beamed. She leaned close to Izzy's ear and whispered, "I knew you were here. Dirk anyway. My heart sings."

Izzy squeezed her hand and leaned over until their foreheads touched. "How did you know that?"

"I knew it. I did. He's here. Here—here. Dirk—Dirk—Dirk. He didn't want me to know. Didn't. Want. That. A surprise. H-h-he wanted to surprise me."

"Yes, he did."

"But I knew. The chocolate told me."

Of course. Chocolate.

Izzy's gaze met hers and they giggled like school girls with a secret. Dirk's presence infused Maddi with excitement, confidence—and chocolate.

"Let's go for drinks," Dirk suggested after the evening's performances. "We have a favorite club, don't we Maddi?"

They stood to go but Stefano remained seated, his face blank, eyes staring at the microphone on center stage.

"Stefano?" Izzy said and nudged his shoulder. "Come with us?"

He turned to look at her, confused.

"We're going for drinks. Come along?"

"I shouldn't drink."

"They'll have virgin options. Come on. Let's celebrate."

He pulled to his feet and dragged behind the rest as they headed to the parking lot.

"What's up with him?" Brett asked Izzy.

"I'm not sure. It's like he saw a ghost."

At the pub, they found an empty table along the back wall. Brett pulled out a chair for Izzy. Dirk pulled Maddi into a long, passionate embrace.

"I could die-die-die," she crooned. "Drowned in a chocolate sea. Happe-e-e. I've been hugged before but my-oh-my-oh-my in all my life, not like this. Never like this. Chocolate dripping. I taste it."

"Weren't you surprised to see me? Not even a little bit?" Dirk said.

She pushed away a few inches and looked straight into his eyes, a smile on her face. "Tricky. But you can't hide from me. Can't hide, Dirk. Chocolate, you know."

He laughed. "You amaze me."

"And you," she paused for a few seconds, eyes rolled back, mind searching. Her gaze met his again and she continued. "You are chocolate."

Izzy tugged Stefano's arm downward until his knees buckled and he sat in the adjacent chair. "You okay?" She leaned toward him and peered into his eyes.

"I'm fine," he answered automatically and with empty words.

"What's wrong, Stefano? You've been distant since Maddi's piano recital."

"I shouldn't have come." He shook his head, refusing to meet her gaze. She stared at him until he explained with a sigh, "It was the Lecuona number. It's the one Lena mentioned in that infernal postcard. I can't get it out of my head."

46

STEFANO SANK ONTO a chair across from Maddi. She radiated joy, basking in the afterglow of a flawless recital. He remembered the highs after a public performance and for the first time in a long time he missed feeling a crowd's admiration. Public performances buoyed you up for days in an adrenaline rush. He longed to feel that complete contentment as he leaned against his beautiful sister and soaked up her sunshine.

A wistful smile softened his features. Maddi reminded him of his sister. Lena used to bubble with exuberance before and after their performances. He felt a protective tenderness toward this young woman. They shared a familial intimacy through music, and even more so with pianos.

With no warning, her glance flashed to meet his and she scrutinized him. Her gaze unhinged him. "Sorry. I didn't mean to stare."

She waved away his apology.

He rushed to explain. "I was overcome by your music. Your performance—exquisite."

Maddi's cheeks bloomed. "Th-th-thanks."

"That Lecuona was my favorite. Could I borrow your score?"

Maddi's mouth dropped open a tiny bit. She nodded, reached into her bag, and pulled out a well-worn book of Ernesto Lecuona's compositions and Stefano accepted it with shaky hands.

They ordered drinks, Stefano careful to avoid anything with alcoholic content. His mind raced with possibilities that took seed when Maddi handed him the music. With an effort he pulled his mind back to the table conversation.

"One thing would make this day perfect," Maddi said with a sigh.

"What would that be?" Dirk asked.

"If my family could have been here. Mama and the Campbells."

The air inside the pub chilled ten degrees in as many seconds.

"What kept your Pennsylvania family away?" Brett asked.

"Th-they were busy. You know. Meggie had events this weekend."

Dirk tipped Maddi's chin toward him to gaze into her eyes. "Here's something that might make your day better," he said, breaking his own long silence.

Maddi stared at him. She shook her head. "What? You're here. Izzy and Brett are here. Stefano asked for my m-m-music even. That makes it pretty d-d-darn good."

"Hard to beat a faultless performance," Dirk said. "But..." He pulled his hand away from hers and reached beneath the table to paw through his front pocket and presented an upholstered ring box to Maddi in his open palm. "This," he said. "Take it."

Her mouth opened in disbelief as she reached for the box. She lifted it from his palm and he said, "Maddi Campbell, I am in love with you. Would you marry me?"

For an instant, she stared at him in silence before her face broke into unrestrained top-of-the-world joy and she shrieked. "Yes-yes-yes-yes. Dirk. I love you so-so-so much. No-no-nobody else. Nobody's ever been chocolate to me."

47

IZZY AND STEFANO picked up her Prius at the Double M and arrived home at one in the morning. She turned onto the circle driveway lit by the solar powered yard light. Dim light from a timer-controlled lamp filtered around the living room window. The driveway light beamed across the concrete pad as she activated the door opener and drove into the garage. She clicked the kitchen door open and they tiptoed into the stillness.

Stefano turned on the music room light, opened the keyboard on Izzy's Steinway piano, and flipped through Maddi's Lecuona book. He stopped at the *Vals* Lena mentioned in her note and played through the melody, one key at a time.

Her brow wrinkled, Izzy asked, "You got something?"

He shook his head. "I've got a brain fog right now."

She shook her head. "I'm delirious with fatigue too. Shall we tackle this in the morning?"

In spite of his exhaustion, Stefano couldn't sleep. Maddi's recital music filled his mind and he went over and over the *Vals*. At last he gave up and shuffled through the darkness to the music room. He sat at the keys and played the *Vals,* over and over again. He thought he'd go mad by morning if he wasn't mad already.

¤•¤

Teofilo parked his new Lexus in a shady spot reserved for visitors to the Malder Brothers Corporate headquarters. He turned to the child beside him and snapped his fingers to get the boy's attention. When Felipe turned his head, Teo pointed at the bridge between the child's eyes, turned his hand, and gestured to his own eyes in a wordless command. They stared at each other for a long moment. "Stay here. Not a sound. Understand?"

The boy nodded and Teo shut and locked the car door. He knocked on the security window and pointed to his watch when the guard glanced up. The interior guard clicked a button on the speaker and said, "Identification, please." A drawer slid out beneath the window. Teo withdrew the Kansas driver's license he'd acquired and tossed it into the drawer.

The guard pulled it in. "Teofilo Diaz," he read aloud and glanced at his computer screen. "Are you armed?"

"What kind of guard would I be without a weapon?" he asked, sarcasm in his voice.

"You're not hired yet," the gate guard said. "Place your weapon in the drawer. Protocol, you know."

With a dramatic sigh, Teo removed his gun holster and tossed it in the drawer. The guard retrieved it and the electronic lock on the entrance thumped. Teo pushed the door open and strode inside.

"Take a seat," the reception guard said. Teo sat in a straight-back chair and studied the room, the high-tech state-of-the-art security cameras, and the double-locking entry doors. He steeled himself. This job would be perfect cover, if he could pass the brothers' test. They must have a lot at stake, secluded away from Wichita like this. He'd heard about Dennis and Clarence Malder. These world-renowned businessmen invested fortunes in every conceivable market and banked more money than the entire country of Cuba, including Havana's thriving black market. With uncanny market intuition, the Malder brothers wielded unmatched power in the states, somewhat like two other brothers who ran Cuba for decades. They required heavy security also, and Teo knew his experience with the Castro regime had secured him an interview with the Malder brothers. If he played his angle right, he'd have a job here, in the region, less than a hundred miles from Lena's brother. He would find Stefano Valdez, and when he did, he'd find that piano.

The interior door opened. A uniformed woman stepped into the lobby. "Teofilo Diaz?"

He nodded.

"Follow me please."

He tailed the woman, matching her brisk pace. She ushered him to a Cadillac and they drove along the manicured brick driveway past a sculptured garden to a parking garage attached to the Malder mansion. She took him inside and down a short hallway to an opulent office. Massive twin desks with ebony surfaces sat at opposite ends with a businessman seated at each. A cluster of over-stuffed chairs ringed the center.

"Teofilo Diaz," the woman announced.

One of the men stepped forward, hand extended. "Welcome, Mr. Diaz. I am Clarence Malder."

Teo shook his hand.

Clarence nodded toward the second man. "My brother, Dennis." The second brother approached from the far desk, his hand extended. Teo shook it as well.

"Please make yourself comfortable." Clarence offered a cushy chair in the conference circle. "May I offer you coffee?"

Teo nodded.

"Chelle, refreshments please," he said to the woman.

The Malder brothers sat on either side of Teo. "Dennis and I reviewed your application," Clarence said. "If you are as skilled as reported, you are just what we need."

"What he's saying, Mr. Diaz—may we call you Teofilo?" Dennis interjected.

"Teo, please."

Dennis nodded. "Teo, we'd like to offer you immediate employment for a three-month trial period. We'll review your performance then and if you've proven yourself worthy, we'd extend a permanent contract, benefits included."

Clarence added, "And our benefits are excellent."

"How so?" Teo asked.

"We'll discuss that in three months," Clarence said. "Are you ready to work?"

"More than ready," Teo said and smiled. "But I need a day to find an apartment."

"We offer living quarters for staff here on the grounds. Our personal employees live in the cabins to the north. We provide grocery stores, entertainment, tennis courts, a swimming pool, and a private school for employee children. Might these accommodations interest you?" Clarence said.

"Without a doubt," Teo said. "My boy is with me."

"Yes, we know. Our educational facilities and staff are exemplary. Please take the day tomorrow to move into the cottage Chelle will show you." Clarence stood and with a nod to the uniformed woman, he dismissed Teo.

Chelle ushered Teo to a uniform closet. She helped him find khakis in his size, complete with the Malder Industries insignia. She drove him to the Malder Village and provided keys to a brick two-bedroom home on the far west side. At the entrance gate, he received clearance to drive his Lexus inside, along with appropriate papers for both of them. After retrieving his Glock, he checked the ammo and strapped the holster over his shoulders.

The guard hit the electric lock and the outside door clanked as its lock disengaged. Teo stepped onto the sidewalk outside, as a rumble that seemed to have no source and no direction grew from a barely perceptible growl to an all-pervasive thunder. He drew his weapon, and steadied it as he swung in an arc to survey the surroundings. A hanging plant inside the chain link fence swung and the fence rattled against its posts. The concrete under his combat boots shook. He continued his arc, in practiced vigilance.

The noise subsided ninety seconds later. The speaker at the security window clicked on. Laughter issued from inside the building.

"Hey man, you've got to relax," the guard said. "You jump like that at every little tremor, you'll be a nervous wreck inside of a year."

"A tremor. Right." Teo stashed his weapon in its holster.

"As in earthquake. Another friendly little Kansas earthquake. They're harmless. Can't stop them by shooting." He howled with laughter.

"Right." Teo's nostrils flared. That man had it coming, soon as he had a chance. Nobody laughed at Teofilo Diaz and got away with it. He turned his back on the insolent guard and strode to the Lexus. "Felipe, we're moving onto this compound. We'll sleep in our own beds tomorrow night."

48

THE PILLOW-TOP MATTRESS never felt better. Izzy slept until early sunlight lit the room. She dragged herself from bed and stumbled to Stefano's room. His bed, though tousled, stood empty. She cocked her head but heard nothing, no shuffling footsteps, no rustling papers, nothing. She raced from room to empty room, her chagrin growing. In the kitchen, the rich fragrance of brewing coffee reassured her.

She poured two mugs of coffee and headed out the door with them. Still in his pajamas, Stefano worked in the piano shop. He'd pulled Elsie's keys from the storage rack along the shop's west wall and flipped the frame over on the workbench. The Lecuona waltz music lay open across the bass keys, and he glanced back and forth from the music to the keys.

"Good morning," she greeted him.

He stood and looked at her, his face radiating excitement. "Morning, Mom," he said. In a rush, he apologized for his casual attire, and explained. "Lena spoke to me last night."

"Oh?"

"She challenged me to play this waltz with her, like the old days in our mother's music room when her fingers flew over Elsie's aging ivories and melodic rhythms issued from the belly of the old gal. Then it hit me. The letters follow the melody. I couldn't wait and I didn't want to wake you." He'd stop entered the shop, dawn's glow on the eastern horizon.

She peered across the keys. "What have you got?"

"Not much. It's hard to identify a particular key when they're upside down." His arm swept along a strip of painter's tape stretched across the fronts where he'd identified each key by letter name and octave number. "I labeled them all, just like you taught me, Mom."

Upside down and backwards, the identification of any key required pointed concentration. The first 8th note of the melody was C, an octave above middle C. An entire column of letters was listed on the bottom side of that particular key. The letter at the top was M. He jotted it down on a notepad. The next eighth note was B flat, 4th octave, the first letter on it an I. Over the next few minutes, Stefano identified the next few letters. C A R O H E R M A N O S T E F A N O.

"It's a letter to me. 'My Dear Brother Stefano'." He blinked to clear his vision and swiped the back of his hand across his eyes.

"You'll not get anywhere fast if you weep over the keys."

"But I found it. I found the code. Lena wrote a letter to me on the keys, through the *Vals*."

"Let me help you," she said. "I could read the music and you could find the keys."

"Here's where I left off." Stefano pointed to a note in the third measure.

"Next note, Db5," she said.

Stefano nodded. "The letter is I." He added an "I" to his list.

"F5." Izzy said.

"Letter F."

❧❧

The list grew. Stefano placed spaces and punctuation but the message took shape. When they finished, he translated to English.

> *My dear brother Stefano, if you read this, you have deciphered Lecuona. I am likely dead, killed by the Diaz men. I need you to know these things.*
>
> *When you disappeared after the storm, I believed you were dead. I was distraught. If I had but found you then. Enrique Diaz found me instead and brought me home. In my grief I agreed to marry him, the biggest mistake of my life.*
>
> *I had a child, Stefano. His name is Felipe. He gives joy to my broken heart. But the Diaz men took him from me, and allow one visit a month. I am desperate.*

This is no life to live. I worry for my Felipe. I have a plan but it's filled with utmost risk. If something should happen to me, I entrust his welfare to you, my dear brother.

> *Lena*

Stefano stared at the words he'd jotted down on the note-pad.

Felipe. Lena's son. My nephew.

Izzy moved around behind him and rubbed his shoulders. She wrapped her arms around his chest and laid her cheek next to his.

After a moment, she invited him inside for breakfast. He nodded and they headed to the kitchen. At the table, he stared out the kitchen window while she whipped up breakfast.

"You okay?" she asked as she spooned scrambled eggs onto his plate.

"A boy, Izzy," he said, his gaze still fixed on a distant spot outside the window. "She had a child and I never knew."

Izzy squeezed his limp hand. "You know now."

"Why didn't she tell me sooner?"

⋘⋙

Izzy called Kurt later that morning and described the message under the keys.

Kurt was astounded too. "Lena had a son?"

"Yes. Felipe."

"How did Stefano take the news?"

"He's been pretty quiet. I'm sure he took it hard."

"Where is he now?"

"He went back to the shop to work on Elsie."

Kurt expressed the anxiety she felt. "Watch him, Izzy."

"Last time I checked, he was focused on the bass bridge to the point of madness."

"Like I said—watch him."

They disconnected. She hustled out to the shop where Stefano leaned over Elsie's rim. He rubbed a pencil across a paper attached to the old bass bridge. The resulting map would serve to locate new holes for the rebuilt bridge.

When she greeted him, he jumped and jabbed the pencil through the thin paper. "*Caramba*—Look at this—it's ruined."

"Breathe, Stefano. It's not a big deal. We keep plenty of newsprint."

"I gotta make up lost time."

"Stefano, take it easy."

He dropped the pencil onto the bare soundboard and looked into Izzy's eyes. "I saw a boy, riding around in that Audi..." His voice trailed off, but he retained eye contact with her.

She squeezed his hand, unsure what to say.

"Felipe..." he said. "He might as well be on the moon."

49

FELIPE DIAZ JUMPED when Uncle Teo's private cell phone jangled. Teo took a look at the caller ID and motioned the boy out of the room in their cabin that served as his office.

"And shut the door," he ordered.

The boy shuffled into his own bedroom. Though small, it held high tech equipment any boy would crave. Felipe found a remote and clicked on the television mounted in the corner opposite his doorway. He turned up the volume, but had no interest in this American crap. He tossed the remote onto the bed, stepped back into the hall and clicked the door shut. With the stealth his uncle had trained into him, he crept to the office door, cocked his ear toward the door jam, and listened. What business would his uncle discuss that he was not welcome to hear?

The discussion was all in Spanish. *No problema.* Felipe was born speaking *Español.* The caller must be someone back in Havana who wondered why Uncle Teo was taking so long to complete his business in the states.

Felipe wondered that himself. When would they go home again? Why did Teo insist he stay hidden himself? Didn't he want people to know he was here?

Then why not send me home? I didn't want to come anyway.

Teo's voice rose in volume. "Pipe down. I've tracked the sonofabitch to Kansas, for God's sake. Yes, Kansas. Valdez shipped that piano to a piano repair shop around here somewhere."

Valdez. That was the name of the man they'd chased all over the country, the one Teo said killed his uncle. A very bad man.

Why wouldn't he tell me about this?

"Yes. We're in Wichita. Get this," his uncle said. "The idiot married the girl who rescued him after Francine. I found her in Oregon, helping clean up after that tidal wave. Mail in her trash led me to Wichita. My gut tells me I'll find the piano around here somewhere and when I do, I'll find Valdez. I'll have our merchandise back and he'll get what's due to him for meddling in Diaz business."

Anxiety gnawed at Felipe's stomach. He curled his hands into fists and clenched his teeth together. If he was supposed to learn how to run things, why didn't his uncle talk to him?

There was a pause in the conversation. Fearful that his temper outbreak had alerted Teo to his eavesdropping, Felipe pressed his ear to the door. Teo's voice erupted once again. "I know it's been weeks, dammit. Drop it, Torres. I'm running this operation and if I work it right, this place—the Malder brothers' operation—will be a nice addition to our business."

Addition to the business? Felipe snorted. *Right, Uncle Teo. As if...*

"I'm working on that. They hired me for my experience in Havana—"

There was an abrupt halt in the discourse before Teo erupted. "Dammit—I know I don't need a job. You want me back there and I will return when I'm good and ready. This position has its advantages. It's good cover for both Felipe and me. I have the authority of the Malder Corporation behind anything I do, not to mention their bank accounts. And the brothers trust me. Those fake ID papers you drew up for me worked well. These guys are loaded. They run the state, buying the politicians. Hell, they run the entire country.... Relax. This will play into my plan."

Felipe stumbled away from the closed door. There was much he didn't know. Much Teo hadn't told him. How could he learn the business if Uncle Teo never told him anything?

Felipe returned to his room. He'd heard enough to feed his anger. He dropped onto the bed and changed channels on the television, but couldn't concentrate. The door opened and his uncle entered, a stern look shrouding his face.

"Felipe." Teofilo's voice held reproach.

Felipe squinted at Teo's scowl, dropped his eyes, and ground his teeth together.

"Answer me, boy," Teo spoke louder.

"*Sí, Señor,*" Felipe spoke in a monotone, emotionless.

"You listened to my phone call didn't you?"

Felipe considered his options. He could lie. But Teo always knew. Somehow he knew. He resigned himself to the coming scene, took a deep breath and nodded once. The blow came at once. Teo's fist lifted the boy from his bed and Felipe smacked the wall, with a report like a blowout on a speeding automobile.

"Want to tell me why?" Teo continued the interrogation.

Felipe righted himself and struggled to his feet. He swayed a little and regained his balance. He stared at the floor, miserable and mute.

"Why?" Teo's voice rose in volume.

"Because I want to know too."

"What do you want to know?"

"When we'll go home."

"We'll go home when I'm good and ready to go, and not a moment sooner."

"If you wish me to learn how to run things, why won't you tell me what you told that man?"

"You're in training," Teo said, his voice a growl. "Right now, you need to learn to follow orders. That's your job. And you're not doing too well with it."

Felipe glared at his uncle, hate in his eyes.

Teo reared back. Felipe braced himself for another blow. It didn't come. Instead his uncle laughed. Felipe stared at him, unable to discover the mirth his uncle found in the situation.

Through his chuckles, Teo said, "You're angry, little man. You're so angry at me you'd kill me if you could, right?"

Felipe's jaw dropped open.

"That's good. It's good for you to learn how to manage your anger, but never forget its source. You'll make a fine general one day. Tough it out, boy." Teo cuffed his nephew on the ear and left the room, still laughing.

Felipe sank onto the bed. He missed his mama more at that moment than ever before. Inconsolable, he curled into a ball against the wall. He wanted Mama to wrap him in a big hug, to sing with him, to tease him with her smiling eyes. These things he would never know again.

50

IZZY REACHED ACROSS the soundboard and picked up the torn paper. She folded it in half, slid it into a trash bin, and pulled a fresh sheet from a stack of blank newsprint.

Stefano stared at the exposed and unfinished bridge on Elsie Lenore's soundboard.

"Are you thinking what I'm thinking, Stefano?" she said at last.

"The password?"

She nodded. "Let's go."

In the office, Izzy handed the mini SD card to him. He activated the computer and slipped it into the card reader. The screen opened on the familiar password prompt. "Try Felipe Diaz," she said.

"Okay. F-E-L-I-P-E-D-I-A-Z. Nothing."

"Initials?" she said.

"F.D. Still nothing. F-D-V. Tradition in the Cuban name system would give him Valdez as a second surname."

"Didn't work." Izzy said. "What about simply F-e-l-i-p-e?"

Stefano typed the letters of his nephew's given name. The screen blanked out and a menu popped up with four folders. Three bore the labels "Felipe," "Stefano," and "Elsie Lenore." One file had no name.

"You did it," Izzy said. "You broke the code.

≈૭ૐ

Stefano clicked on the unlabeled folder and it opened to the content list. He opened a photograph of a dark room with half a dozen men around a table, Teofilo Diaz at the head. The next photo showed a contract written in Spanish. In rapid succession, he clicked through the rest of the photos—smoke-filled meetings, individual paper documents, contracts, Teofilo

Diaz leaning over the table with menacing looks toward his younger brothers. "Diaz needs this chip," Stefano said in a low voice.

He clicked open the file labeled "Elsie Lenore." More photo icons filled the screen. The first one he opened showed a piano diagram with arrows pointing to boxes penciled at locations along the piano's rim and leg. "What do you suppose those arrows mean?"

"Something there? Should we take a look?" Izzy said.

"I want to check the other folders first."

The named files worried him. He longed to open them, but at the same time, he felt overwhelmed with a dread that he couldn't explain, or even justify. Of course, they would impart information from his sister. But what? Hadn't she already told him about her son? Her miserable life? What more would there be?

He allowed the cursor to linger over the file labeled Stefano.

Izzy patted his shoulder. "I'll give you space," she whispered.

He didn't hear her, nor did he open the file. Instead he slid the cursor to the "Felipe" file and clicked it open to find photos of Lena throughout her life. The collection opened with scenes that showed her holding a baby and playing with a toddler. He had never seen any of them, but he recognized the old family photos from her childhood—Lena on stage, playing with her brother on the family piano, and family portraits through the years. He viewed all the photos and went back to the one labeled with his name. It stared at him from the screen, cajoling—begging—daring him to open it.

He couldn't stand it. He pushed away from the desktop computer and headed to the kitchen for coffee but detoured to the music room. He sat at the keys, flexed his fingers, and for an hour, he played music from his past until he came to the *Vals* that had opened the door into Lena's life. A few bars into the waltz and he was ready. He headed back to the office.

He clicked a key on the computer, and opened Felipe's file again. He gazed with longing at the images of his sister, and advanced through the family shots, one after another. The boy Felipe resembled his own boyhood photos, but he had Lena's dimples. Each scene jabbed him in the gut like darts thrown from the past. The moments of frozen time, the love, the joy, the closeness of his Cuban family—he couldn't get enough. Cycling through the photos over and over, though agonizing and painful, offered atonement for the guilt he felt about Lena.

With a great flourish of his arm, he clicked out of the family photos. The file labeled with his name stared back from the computer screen, taunting, beckoning. The cursor hovered over the file for a moment. When at last he clicked it open, a video clip loaded onto the computer's media player. Stefano gripped the chair and steeled himself.

The scene opened on a comfortable sitting room with an empty green chair. Lena walked into the camera's view, turned, and straightened her shirt. She sat on the green arm chair and gazed into the screen, red eyes rimmed by her face aged with worry searched the camera lens. Her body sagged with unhealed emotional wounds but her lips turned up in a longing smile. As she looked into the camera, tenderness radiated from her eyes.

Stefano wiped his face with his palms. They came away wet. He reached toward Lena, touching the image of her face with a tremulous hand.

On the screen Lena held up her hand, as if she had anticipated his gesture. She closed her fingers around a grasp which was invisible to her, and she said, "*Hola,* Stefano."

51

LENA'S MESSAGE

I pretend you are with me—right behind the camera. I wish it was so, dear brother. I miss you. Right now, on this day, I would like nothing as much as to throw myself in your strong, gentle embrace. In a way, that's what I am doing, I suppose. This is my life, my story—my letter in a corked bottle that I cast into a stormy sea. I send my love. I ask for your help—not for myself, but for the sake of my young son, Felipe.

If you see this message, then you uncorked the bottle and you surely may sense the dire urgency my message reflects. There is much to tell you and I have but a few minutes alone before someone might discover me. Let me explain. That storm—the hurricane that separated us in New Orleans—I had no idea the changes it would bring to my life. When the wind died down, I looked for you—I don't know how long. Many days. I didn't sleep. Didn't eat. I could think of nothing but finding you. In despair, at last I gave you up for lost. I thought my life was over. Without you and without our dear Mama, what did I have left?

Exhausted, hopeless, and more alone than I'd ever been in my life, I couldn't bear it. That's when Enrique Diaz found me. He wooed me with his charm, his authority and confidence. It was all false. I know that now. But at the time, he seemed like a God-sent angel. He brought me back to Havana—brought me home. And together we picked up the pieces of my life.

Hardly six months passed and Enrique convinced me to marry him. My school girl sweetheart, Raoul—you remember—was furious at my connections to the Diaz family. He shunned me for it. But I didn't listen. You could have talked sense into me, but you were not here.

Fool that I am, I agreed to marry Enrique. And life turned into a living hell for me. No longer was he courteous, nor con-

siderate or flattering. I belonged solely to him, his ornament—a trophy he paraded to parties and meetings. He brought Mama's Elsie Lenore to the Diaz mansion. He bade me to play. I was an ornament on his arm and entertainment for his guests—all the businessmen who looked at me drooling.

I want you to know, Stefano, I carried my head high. I struggled, but he did not break my spirit. I am, after all, a Valdez. You would be proud. When I learned you had survived and that you'd been rescued and made a home in the states, my heart rejoiced. I was happy for you. But I felt shame and didn't want you to know how foolish I'd been. Then I heard you were looking for me, and my heart leaped with joy and hope. Enrique refused to let me respond to your inquiries. I was forbidden to contact you or anyone else from my past life. He ripped me from everything I held dear.

Then I had a child, a son. Little Felipe brought joy to my heavy heart and gave my life purpose once again. How I longed for him to meet you, to know an honorable man, a loving and gentle man. Felipe became my life. Every waking moment, I sang to him, played with him, talked to him and taught him. And I played Mama's Elsie Lenore. I played my heart out, wishing that through the music Felipe might connect to all that was good and just and beautiful in this world.

As if he couldn't stand to see me happy, Enrique broke my heart again. He stole Felipe from me, his mother. When my son was four years old, the Diaz brothers removed him from my care.

"He should learn what it means to be a Diaz," they told me.

At first, they allowed Felipe to spend two days a month with me. Oh—our reunions. You should have seen that little boy's face light up. We hugged like we'd never let go and we struggled to catch up, to keep up, to remember our love.

One visitation day Enrique showed up without Felipe. He said the child had become too spoiled during his days with me. After that, he was allowed visits only on special occasions, like holiday parties. Never again could we spend time alone together.

My life returned to a dismal existence. Enrique expected me to perform. I was his ornament again, his trophy, his slave. I had no life. No joy. Oh, I continued to play Elsie Lenore, and I put my whole heart into the music. Classics and Cuban jazz. I played with gusto, and imagined that Felipe listened with his ear to the wall. I hoped Felipe could hear the music in his quarters and he'd remember how much his mother loved him.

And then one day, I met him in the hallway. He walked with Teo, the eldest Diaz brother. I'm sure my face lit up when I saw him—I had eyes for nothing else. But Felipe did not smile at me. No.

Instead he puckered his young lips. And he spat on my dress. Stefano—he spat at me.

That day my world fell apart. Joy died in my heart and I knew it would never return. I wanted to die.

Enrique is insufferable. His demands in our bed chambers border on the grotesque. I feel trapped. There's no escape for me, save one. Felipe—my son—is dead to me. I grieve for him as we grieved for our mother but this much harder because Felipe is a child. I cherish memories of a precious boy who no longer lives.

There was a pause in Lena's oratory. Tears filled Stefano's eyes as he watched her cross her arms in front of her chest and grip her own shoulders. She rocked back and forth, her eyes closed, cheeks damp. When she opened her eyes, she sighed and stared into the camera lens and spoke in a whisper.

Stefano, my brother, I say this truly. I welcome death. If not my own, then Enrique's. Know this: I care not to live. But as I die, I will serve chaos to the Diaz clan, with the help of God almighty. And I will start with Enrique.

Do you remember, dear brother, when you told me how the old masters—the technicians who kept the school pianos thriving—do you remember telling me how they dusted the keybed and action parts with arsenic powder? You told me that arsenic is a poison and would kill termites, moths, and rodents. Do you remember?

I looked it up and read about arsenic and how it can make someone ill, even kill a person. And I remembered how you, Brother, could pull apart the piano to work on the hammers.

I stole a tool. A screwdriver. I removed the key's slip and blocks to look under the keys. I had watched you do the same about a hundred times. And I checked Elsie's keys. The white powder is there. I sift it from the dust and serve it to Enrique, a little every evening in his after-dinner drinks. Day after day, it builds up in his bones. I will kill him, I swear it. If he doesn't kill me first.

If he does, that is of little consequence. My life ended when he took Felipe from me.

I continue to perform. I play for little Felipe, remembering him, loving him. We used to feel lifted by the music. Maybe deep inside, a part of him will remember that.

Enrique insists that I continue to get dolled up. Still an ornament. He insists that I perform for parties and private gatherings. His business dealings are secret and almost terrifying. But one good thing about being an ornament is that people forget you're there when they are busy. After the entertainment, I sit in the corner, waiting for more demands.

And they carry on their dealings. I'm sure they have no concept that I listen. I slip my phone out of my pocket. And with its camera I take photos. Teofilo, Julio, and Enrique Diaz and their business partners are in many of the photos. Some men are not even Cuban, but their discussions are brutal. I'm sure they're evil.

The secret photos are in the unnamed file. The business meetings, a few contracts they left on the table when the meetings disbanded, and piano diagrams. Last week Enrique made talk about a tour of the US Gulf States—and taking me and Elsie Lenore along. For cover, I suppose. I don't know.

If there's a God, and if Mama is watching over me, perhaps I can alert you to Elsie's location. Perhaps you can rescue Ma-

ma's piano. Perhaps you'll find this message—my letter in a bottle, set adrift on a sea of Cuban piano music.

Stefano, if you are listening, there is a God after all. Know that I love you, dear brother. Know that I pin all my hopes on our family connection. Felipe is lost to me since I am but a woman, of no consequence to his father. But you... you are a man, my brother. You are Felipe's uncle as surely as Julio and Teo claim that title.

If I succeed at poisoning Enrique, Felipe is left to his uncles. If there's any chance to redeem my son, it will rest with you. Help me. Help Felipe. You hold my hope to save the child of my heart.

Please. Brother. I—

On the screen, Lena cocked her head.

They're back. I have to go. Stefano, always remember how much I love you, and if you have a chance tell Felipe I loved him more than life itself.

She rose and dashed to the camera. The screen went blank.

❧

With his fingertips, Stefano brushed the computer screen where his sister's image had been. A gentle tap on the office door startled him and he swiveled the chair around, dazed.

Izzy peeked inside the room and searched his stricken face. "Everything okay?"

Without meeting her anxious gaze, he blurted out, "I have to go back for my nephew."

She bit her lips. "You can't do that," she said.

He nodded toward the computer. "I have no choice. Watch this. You'll see." He bolted for the door and ran from the house.

52

IN THE PIANO shop, Stefano stared at the unfinished bridges on Elsie Lenore. Lena's video message made perfect sense. All the mystery and coding—it wasn't about her or their mother's piano after all. It was about Felipe, her son. When her options evaporated in Havana, she reached out to the one person she knew would listen. Her brother. And he understood.

He knew what had spurred his sister's desperate plan to murder the father of their child. He knew how she managed to do it. Thanks to the piano diagrams in the unnamed file, he knew why they had brought Elsie to the states. It made perfect sense. Teofilo Diaz had followed his brothers to New Orleans for the piano. He must be desperate to retrieve whatever the piano diagrams referred to.

Stefano assumed Diaz wanted the information his sister hid in the keys also. But did he even know about it? Had Lena managed to keep her purpose secret, relying on her brother's intimate knowledge of both the Lecuona *Vals* and Elsie Lenore? He didn't doubt she could do that. She was brilliant. If the arrows referenced something important Diaz was intent to recover, both of them had used Elsie Lenore to conceal and transport something.

A vision of her face entered his mind, nodding and encouraging, as if her spirit knew he'd broken the code and opened the file. She expected him to follow through. But how? He needed more information. He needed a plan to discover what more the piano could tell him.

Those diagrams.

If he could discover what Teofilo Diaz needed to find, he could use it to trap Diaz. With him out of the way, Stefano would concentrate on rescuing Lena's son. He dropped to his knees and crawled underneath the Steinway. He fingered one marked location along the Steinway's inner rim, probing every fraction of an inch. He ran his fingers along the bottom surface of the rim, slipped them upwards, and felt the inner surface.

Nada.

His fingers felt nothing out of place.

◈◈

Izzy couldn't stand it. She had been overwhelmed by Lena's video message. How much more would it have affected Stefano?

Legato, Isabel. Calm yourself.

She told herself this was Stefano's challenge, but her mother's heart worried. The child he'd learned about was his and Melody's sole nephew. How would he deal with this? Nobody needed him to flee to Cuba again. He couldn't do that. He just couldn't. She wouldn't let him. But it was not her place to decide. She could lend a sympathetic ear, and ask questions, but the decisions had to be his.

She found him in the shop, on his back under the piano. She knelt and peered beneath the soundboard. He ran his fingers along the support beams, one hand on each side.

"Find anything?" she asked.

He shook his head.

She tapped his knee. "I watched the video," she said. "Let's talk."

He scooted from below the piano, stood, and brushed dust from his jeans. "You understand, right? I have to find Felipe."

She nodded. "I understand. Have you considered how to do that?"

"No. I just know I have to for Lena. For my mom. For my family. Felipe is family."

"Won't you enlist help before you take off for Cuba this time?"

He nodded. "I doubt I could do much without a plan. At least I know he's there."

"We haven't heard much about Teofilo Diaz lately," she said. "What if he returned to Cuba, hoping he'll lure you back? You'd be in trouble."

"I can't go back the way I went before. I need official travel papers. I don't want to hide anything. I need to let Mel know about it, and I need to keep in touch with my Kansas family. After all, when I find Felipe, he will be part of our family here."

"Papers take time, don't they?"

"I'll use the time to gather information. I want to go prepared with as much as I can find from people I know in Havana, and from Elsie."

53

STEFANO SLIPPED INTO a routine with his work on Elsie. He worked from dawn until dusk, driven by the notion that he was behind a phantom schedule. With long hours he made steady progress on the rebuilding project. He examined the cabinetry on the old Steinway frequently, but always came up empty. The piano sketches Lena included in the secret files seemed meaningless.

Early one July afternoon, he leaned over Elsie Lenore and tapped a chisel handle with a small hammer. A slice of wood curled from the new maple bridge. When it met the angled notch, he shifted position and tapped against the root of the shaved wood. The curl dropped onto the spruce soundboard. Stefano brushed it into a pile of shavings, ran his fingertip over the fresh cut, and nodded approval at the smooth new notch. Positioning the chisel's cutting edge at the next mark, he tapped again with the hammer.

The shop door swung open with a familiar creak. He sensed someone enter the shop but his concentration didn't waver until the next maple curl lay on the soundboard. He stretched up, eased the tension in his shoulders with a few circles, and turned to face his visitors with a smile.

He raised his eyebrows and nodded a welcome to Brett, Maddi, and Dirk. "*Hola, Amigos.* If you seek Izzy, she's out on her day's service route."

Brett Lander extended his hand. "No. We wish to speak to you."

Stefano offered a firm handshake. "Me?"

"We wanted to discuss the wedding," Maddi said.

"With me?" He didn't hide his surprise.

Dirk said, "Would you play piano for our wedding?"

Stefano pondered the request. "You want me as a wedding musician? I'm afraid I'm out of practice."

"B-b-but you could work s-s-something up, right?" Maddi said.

"Depends. When's the wedding?"

"We're leaning toward autumn," Dirk said, "when the leaves turn in mid-October."

"Leaves? What do leaves have to do with your wedding?"

"We want an outdoor c-c-ceremony."

"Ah. And where would this happen?"

"Not sure yet," Dirk said.

"Maybe at B-b-botanica, in Wichita," Maddi said.

Brett added, "How about the Bartlett Arboretum?"

"And do these places furnish a piano?"

"Couldn't you bring one?" Dirk said.

"You want me to perform and provide the piano?"

"What about th-th-this one you're rebuilding?" Maddi said.

"You want me to haul Elsie Lenore to an outdoor venue for your wedding? In October? What if it rains? Or snows?"

"We'll figure it out. W-w-will it be ready?" Maddi blushed and dropped her gaze. When she looked back at him, she smiled. "Will you—will you do it? Play for our wedding?"

Stefano shook his head. "I can't make that kind of commitment. My priority is my family and I have no idea where I'll be this fall."

"Are you planning to head to Oregon?" Brett asked.

"I might go back to Havana." He explained the situation with his nephew.

❧❧

Returning home from the day's service calls, Izzy's mind wandered as she turned up the volume on the Beethoven symphony. Her thoughts roamed to Maddi and Dirk.

Chocolate.

Their relationship had escalated fast. Was Maddi making a mistake? In her own youth, she and Kurt believed they could together conquer whatever the world tossed at them in a shared destiny. They were young and so naïve.

Maddi had met Dirk a few short months ago. There was naïveté displayed there too.

Married life required hard work—harder than tuning pianos. She hoped Maddi and Dirk realized that. She hoped Melody and Stefano could see that also and would soon patch up the wounds in their relationship.

When she rolled onto the driveway, Maddi's little Focus sat parked by the overhead doors to the piano shop. Maddi, Dirk, Brett, and Stefano ambled toward the house.

Rallentando, Isabel.

Something was up. She parked her Prius and hurried to join them. Maddi offered a hug and the others acknowledged her with nods.

"What brings you all here on this fine afternoon?" Izzy asked.

"Maddi and Dirk asked me to play for their wedding," Stefano said.

"What a wonderful idea. When is it going to be?"

"October, we think," Dirk said.

"Gives you plenty of time to prepare, Stefano," she said.

"I don't think I can commit to that," Stefano said. "I may be in Havana by then."

"You turned them down?"

With a miserable nod, he shot Izzy a knowing look and returned to the shop.

"I'm g-g-glad to see you too, Izzy," Maddi said. "I was wondering if you'd help me shop for a dress."

"A wedding dress?"

Maddi and Dirk both nodded.

"I don't know how much help I can be with that," Izzy objected. "But I'll do my best. It would be an honor."

Brett tapped her on her shoulder. "What's all this about Stefano returning to Havana?"

"Didn't he explain?"

"Not yet. Want to fill me in?"

"Brett—we're trying not to bother you. You are retired from the Bureau, you know."

"I may be retired, but I'm not dead. I care, Izzy. If there's ever any way I could help you, all you have to do is ask."

She sighed. "I know."

He brushed her knuckles with his fingertips. "I still want to make it all up to you."

"Brett, we're fine. We're good and we don't need you to put a wedge between us again. Kurt's fine. I'm fine."

"Stefano fine?"

Her silence held volumes of information.

"Izzy?"

"Okay. We cracked the code on his sister's data device and he found a message she had recorded for him. She explained everything. It's all about her son, Felipe. She was desperate to help her son."

"She had a son?"

"Yes."

"Can you share the files?"

"They are on the computer. I actually would like to get your professional take on the whole thing."

"Will you show the three of us?"

At her nod, Brett turned to his son and Maddi, "You two up for a slide show?"

54

STEFANO BRUSHED ACROSS the fresh notches on the tenor bridge with his fingertips and picked up the hammer and chisel. He shook his head to clear the fog from his mind, rounded the tail of the Steinway, and tilted his head to study his recent work from the other direction. He rubbed a thumb across his eyelids, took a deep breath, and gripped the hammer with his right hand. He positioned the chisel blade to bisect the row of three holes on the bridge.

Enfocate, Valdez.

He set his jaw and raised the hammer. The instant he tapped the chisel's handle, her voice echoed in his mind.

Stefano—

He jerked his hand aside and dropped the tools. The hammer clanged on the shop floor. The chisel nicked the keybed.

Lena.

Her voice resounded in his mind again. *Felipe—can you help him?*

If only there was a way.

If there is, I know you will find it.

He ran a hand through his disheveled hair and stared at Elsie Lenore but he saw Lena's face, drawn tight with stress, her eyes beseeching his help. He backed away from the piano and collided with the workbench holding hammers and dampers from the piano's action.

He spoke in silence to her ghost image. *You are persistent.*

In his imagination, she offered an understanding smile and said *I am desperate.*

He tipped the keyframe up and studied the coded letters beneath the keys. He fingered the notch on C88 which had concealed the miniature SD card and spoke aloud. "Clever, Lena. Secret message in a piano-shaped bottle."

Meant for you, my brother.

"This Teofilo, your brother-in-law—he's looking for Elsie Lenore?"

Lena's image nodded.

"Did he know about your coded messages?"

The image in his mind remained mute.

"I've looked and looked for hidden objects and—nothing." He knelt and ran his fingertips along the inner rim of the piano again.

Caramba—there was something there.

This time his fingertips located a couple of wooden plugs that filled recessed holes in the rim. "These aren't standard." He reached for a screwdriver, tapped the narrow blade against a plug, and worked it free. Seconds later, another wooden plug rolled beside the first on the concrete floor. He activated the flashlight in his mobile phone to peer inside the cylindrical hole, but saw nothing. He poked the screw driver shaft into the hole and tapped it.

With a snap, a small door swung down on a scissor-like hinge and a plastic bag of white crystals slipped from a hidden cavity to the floor. He searched the rim for similar twin plugs, located three more, and tapped the levers that released the doors. One other chamber contained a similar package of white crystals but the other two were empty.

The significance of the packages hit him with the force of a gale in a prairie thunderstorm. "This is what he's looking for."

Lena's image nodded at him. The look in her eyes seemed to say, *"What took you so long, mi hermano?"*

He continued. "And he's looking for me."

A smile bloomed on her ethereal face as she raised her eyebrows in expectation.

"What if?" He paused.

She tipped her head, inviting more.

"What if I offer both of us to him at a time and in a place I choose?" He wrinkled his brow as he considered the possibilities. "It might work," he said and bolted for the door.

Felipe sat cross-legged on the kitchen floor and stared out the apartment's double-wide glass door to a common area devoted to recreational activities. Matching glass doors on other apartments looked on the space where children could play basketball, tetherball, soccer, or swim. He watched neighbor children splash in the pool on this hot summer afternoon. He longed to jump in, to cool off, and to toss the red-and-white beach ball.

He raised his knees, wrapped his arms around them, and sighed. Resting his chin on his knees, he tried to conjure a few scenes from Havana—from home, but the details fogged. He recalled sitting on the porch watching other boys play there, much like he watched the other children swim today. The dark-skinned, scruffy Cuban boys in his memory played a ball game on the street below their house. He'd not been allowed to play with them either.

55

STEFANO BURST INTO the office. Maddi sat on the desk chair with Brett, Dirk, and Izzy leaning over her shoulders, intent on the photos from Lena's secret files. They turned when he entered, and Maddi swiveled the chair to face him.

"I've got it." Stefano launched his explanation. "Diaz followed me to the states, right?"

Brett nodded. They all stared at him.

"He wants me, right?"

"Yes," Izzy said.

"And if not me, then he's after the stuff hidden in the piano." He thrust the bag of white crystals at Brett. "I found this hidden in the piano case, behind a spring-loaded trap door. I feel it in my gut that he's not going to leave without this stuff. He's still around, biding his time, waiting until he can spring on us like a panther."

Brett raised the bag shoulder high, allowing everyone a view.

Stefano continued, in a rush, "Why not let it leak that I'll be playing piano at your wedding? If I can stay hidden until then, we'll force him to show up at the wedding. We'd lure him out, and nab him when he shows up. After he's locked up, I'm free to look for Felipe."

"Wait—wait—wait, here," Dirk said. He released Maddi from his embrace and crossed his arms over his chest. "You want to use our wedding to bait this Cuban crime lord?"

Maddi's face glowed. "It's brilliant, Dirk. B-b-brilliant."

"No, we don't." Dirk shook his head.

Silent to this point, Brett spoke up. "It might work if he is still in the states. I'd need to know what this stuff is, but if it's contraband, I know people who would be interested." He nodded toward Stefano. "Good idea."

Dirk looked at Maddi. Her gaze bored into his eyes. "You really want to do this, Maddi?"

She looked into his eyes. "Yes. I do. Please."

"But it's our wedding."

Stefano said, "If I'm your wedding musician, and you choose a venue Diaz could infiltrate, we could lure him into a trap."

Dirk still wasn't convinced. "Wouldn't guests notice if the attendants all wear police uniforms?"

Brett laughed. "Plain clothes. Undercover. And at an outdoor ceremony, agents could patrol the perimeter. Diaz would be apprehended with no notice at the altar whatsoever."

"Mom—Dee, you remember her—would be furious if anything went wrong. She'd write us both off as insane."

Maddi looked around the room. "We will help. Right, Dirk?"

"Tell me why we need to use our wedding in any way other than a grand celebration of our future happiness."

"Because," Maddi said, "it's the right thing to do. To help F-f-felipe."

Dirk studied her face a moment. "Okay then," he said. "If you're sure."

Maddi threw her arms around him. "Thank you," she whispered.

❧❧

Stefano and Izzy wandered back to the shop after the trio from the Double M Ranch departed. He picked up his chisel, positioned it on the bridge and gave it a tap. He grinned as he ran the tip of his thumb across the new notch and gave a nod. "*Bueno*," he said. "What do you think?"

She reached across the rim to feel the notches in the maple. She checked the edge which bisected the line of triple holes drilled for bridge pins. "Looks good, Stefano. As soon as you've completed the notches, we can install the pins."

He beamed.

"You'll have your hands full, re-building the piano and re-hearsing for a wedding."

"*Sí*. I need a practice piano. Got any ideas?"

"Feel free to rehearse on my piano anytime. Shall we take a closer look at the other marked locations?"

"Like the legs?"

Izzy pulled a plywood box from a wall shelf, opened the clasp on its hinged front, and removed a hydraulic jack. She positioned the box and the jack below the keybed and pumped until the piano leg lifted off the floor. Stefano loosened a slotted screw head and knocked aside an elliptical key holding the leg in place. Izzy tapped inward on the leg and the locking plates released with a snap. The leg toppled into his arms.

"The arrows indicated something under this plate," Stefano said. He removed the screws holding the plate to the upper surface of the leg and pried it off to reveal a deep cylindrical hole.

Izzy rolled her eyes. "Not again," she said.

Stefano reached into the leg and withdrew three Cuban cigars wrapped in plastic. "They smuggled drugs and cigars in Elsie Lenore. This piano is key to everything, isn't it?"

The following week Stefano rebuilt Elsie's legs. He filled the spaces along the beams and turned over the cigars and more contraband samples to Brett. Shop work agreed with him, when his mind didn't wander to Oregon with Mel, or to Cuba with Felipe. Izzy stopped in one afternoon to watch the installation of bridge pins. He laid down his hammer and the pliers he used to grip the pins, and shook out the cramps that plagued his joints.

"Take your time," she said.

"I'm worried I'll hit the wrong pin. Got to go easy," he said. "*Enfocate, Stefano,*" he added, speaking to himself.

They worked together on the long, dense blank of pinblock plywood. Stefano cut it to fit the iron plate. Izzy worked with him to shave the edges, mating the new block to the piano. With the new tuning pin block mortised into the piano's case, they lowered the refinished cast iron piano plate into position and bolted it in place. Stefano drilled holes for the tuning pins with a moveable drill press and Elsie was primed and ready for new strings.

Each evening, Stefano sat at the Steinway keyboard in Izzy's music room. His hands flew over the keys. He ran arpeggios defining a romantic Latino dance. With closed eyes he let his fingers find old familiar chords. At one point he heard dissonance in Izzy's instrument. He stopped, ran a short phrase again, and stopped again to listen.

The phone.

He'd heard his phone's ringtone behind the piano music. He flicked open his phone to find Mel's name and face on his caller ID. Heart racing, he fumbled with the controls, anxious to answer her call before it disconnected. "*¿Hola?* Hello? Mel?"

"Hi, Stefano." He could hear hesitance in her voice. "Did I wake you?"

"No, no. What time is it?" He glanced at the wall clock. "Geesh. It is late. I hope I haven't kept your mom awake."

"What?"

"I'm practicing. Piano. You know. For Maddi's wedding."

"Yes, I heard." Mel's voice softened. "I'm glad you're doing that, Stefano."

"*Sí, mi flor.* I'm glad too. I hope to do three things with this gig. First, I will honor my family's music tradition, for Mama and Lena. Second, I will open a path to my nephew. And third... I hope to bring you and Nicolas back to me."

"Mom says it's dangerous. That guy—Diaz."

"*Sí*, Melody. Please stay there with our boy until he is in custody. This is bad stuff. I don't want you in harm's way."

"I can't return until the relief efforts wind down anyway."

"You haven't had any further confrontations, have you?"

"No, the stalker is gone."

"The wedding will be in October. Much as I would like to see you, I wish you'd stay there until it's safe. I did stupid things, terrible things—drinking until I didn't know the time of day for weeks on end. I want to make that up to you."

"You were out of your mind with grief. But you're back, Stefano. And we'll be back soon enough too."

"I can't wait to meet my little Nico."

"Is there a chance to save your nephew Felipe?"

"Half a chance, anyway. First step is to get Diaz out of the picture."

"I want to know your thoughts about Felipe's future. Should we open our home to him?"

Stefano didn't answer for a moment. "I like what you said. Our home. You'd adopt my sister's boy?"

"Yes, I would. I have a son too, and there's nothing I wouldn't do for him. I understand now. Lena was desperate and out of options. I will stand by our sister. Felipe is family."

56

IZZY KEPT UP with service calls through July and August. She checked in with both Maddi and Mel on a daily basis and fell asleep every night to Stefano's serenade. Kurt returned from Oregon in mid-August. Melody remained to wrap up the relief work. To Izzy's surprise, Stefano had discouraged her from returning before Maddi and Dirk's wedding. "Anything goes wrong, and Diaz'll be out for blood. It would be easy for him to target my family. I want her safe," he said.

"Since you put it that way, I can't disagree."

≈≈≈

Sitting cross-legged on the floor at the kitchen's sliding glass door, Felipe gazed longingly at the children splashing in the private outdoor swimming pool. The apartment's front door opened. He strained to see who had entered, lost his balance, and toppled over. Teo entered the kitchen to find him sprawled on the floor, propped on an elbow.

"Why are you on the floor?" Teo said in his typical gruff manner. "Get up."

He scrambled to his feet, and stood at attention.

Teo ran a firm hand across the boy's shoulders and backside, brushing off imaginary dirt. When satisfied, he stood back and announced, "We have an appointment. Come with me."

Felipe hesitated a moment too long.

Teo whipped around, fire in his eyes. "Felipe, follow me." There was an angry undertone in his voice, an unmistakable warning.

Felipe stepped toward his uncle, his gaze captured by Teo's flaming eyes. He cleared his throat and said, "Please, Uncle Teo. I'd like to know where we're going."

"Your job, Felipe, is to obey orders without question."

"Forgive me, Uncle. If I have an appointment, I'd like to know with whom."

Teo glared at the boy long and hard before a spark of mirth crossed his face. His lips crinkled in a lop-sided smile. "Cheeky boy. You are a Diaz. Definitely a Diaz. We're going to the school building in this compound. You will meet your teacher."

Felipe reared back. "School—but aren't we going home soon?"

"We will. But not yet. And since you're a child, and school is mandated for American children, you will attend the school."

"I don't speak their language. I don't understand them. How can I learn?"

"It's your job to learn. The more you know about people—especially Americans—the more efficient your future leadership will be."

Felipe turned to look again at the swimming pool. "You want me to make friends?"

"Not friends. But watch them. Observe. Learn to speak English. Soon enough our time here will end. What you learn at this school will bring lifelong benefits. I don't mean math and science. I mean your secret observations."

"I am a spy?"

Teo nodded. "My spy. Come."

Felipe tailed his uncle's brisk walk from the residence circle to the business square. They entered a brick building set apart from the rest, pine trees and lilac bushes clustered at each corner. Inside, closed doors lined a hallway. A welcoming light beamed into the hall from an open door near the far end. Teo pushed Felipe into the open room. A thirty-something woman with short auburn hair looked up from her desk and smiled.

She spoke to him in Spanish. "You must be Felipe. I look forward to having you join my class this term."

Felipe stared at her, unsmiling, a small reproduction of his large uncle.

Teofilo asked a few pertinent questions about the curriculum, her expectations, and the other students. The teacher answered each question, a warm expression on her face. Teo asked about discipline. She responded that she used a reward system for good work and courteous behavior.

In English she said, "Let me show you around." She led the way around the room and pointed out the latest technological innovations for education, the student activity areas, and the cubby boxes for each student's supplies. Felipe imagined himself in the room with other children and a knot grew inside his belly.

The teacher led the way to the play areas outside for recreational breaks and physical education. They toured tennis courts, the soccer field, and a track set among lush green trees in a manicured lawn.

"Let me show you our auditorium. We use it for drama and music productions." She led them back inside to a double door and they entered a darkened room. "One minute. I'll get the lights."

Felipe discovered they stood on a small stage, complete with spotlights overhead and heavy stage curtains. A small upright Yamaha piano stood across from him.

"Students produce shows for the compound's employees a couple times each semester," the teacher said. Her voice came as a small noise in the background. A rush like a fierce wind filled Felipe's mind and he stumbled toward the piano. The wind in his mind transformed into music. Somewhere in his hidden memories, he knew piano music.

He pushed the fallboard open to expose the stark white and black keys.

"Felipe, come back here." Teo's voice sounded somewhere in the distance.

The music in his mind swelled and he remembered a black-haired woman smiling at him as she played a grand piano in the sitting room of their Havana home.

"It's okay. Let him look," the teacher said.

He reached for the keys and pressed one, and another, jumping at the clear tones he produced.

"Is he musically inclined? We could arrange a few lessons," the teacher said.

"I don't want him learning that namby-pamby shit."

"He was drawn to the piano when he saw it today. You saw it too. You should foster his interest. I'm sure the Malders would bring in a piano teacher if you asked. Felipe may have talent."

"I forbid it. That's not his destiny." Teo marched across the stage and clamped his fingers around Felipe's upper arm. "Time to go."

57

A WEEK AFTER Kurt's return, Izzy concluded a service call in nearby Winfield. She tossed the temperament strip into her tool bag and headed home. She found Stefano in the shop, installing the long copper-wrapped bass strings. He wound a segment of new steel wire onto a shiny new tuning pin and hammered it into the prepared hole.

"Need a hand?" Izzy asked.

Without waiting for an answer, she slid around the mahogany rim to the piano's tail, pulled out the next string, and slipped the loop onto the hitch pin. He wound the steel end of the string onto the next shiny steel pin and pounded it into the pre-drilled hole in the pinblock. He winked at her. "Thanks, Mom. It gets irksome to run back and forth all the time."

"I've enjoyed your evening serenades," she said. "If your rehearsals are any indication, the wedding music will be unmatched."

"*Gracias*," he said. "Maddi and Dirk favor several native Cuban dances."

"Have they finalized their selection?"

"Almost."

"It's a busy time. Maddi asked me to go along tomorrow to shop for a dress."

"That's an important task. I remember Mel's wedding preparations. A bride needs to find the right dress for her wedding."

"I'm hardly qualified to pass judgement."

"You'll do fine, Mom."

"I'm still relieved that Maddi will check with a few others in a video conference while we shop. At least it won't all be on my shoulders."

❧

Felipe stared out the glass doors, mesmerized by the sunset. Clouds flamed in every shade of red and orange. He could almost hear exultant musical chords as the brilliance flared, the discovery of the school piano captivating his heart. Teo slapped the office desk and whooped. He summoned the boy, and Felipe turned listlessly toward the office.

"Look here," Teo waved at the computer screen. "You wanted to know when we'll be able to head home. Here it is."

Felipe slid behind Teo's shoulder and stared at the screen.

"See?" Teo prompted him.

Of course he didn't see. The words were in English.

Teo glared at him. "Right. You've got a ways to go before you take the reins of any part of our company. It's an engagement announcement." He translated the news from the city's online social section.

"Paul and Bridget Campbell, Philadelphia, Pennsylvania, announce the engagement and approaching marriage of their daughter Madeline to Dirk Lander, son of Brett Lander, Wellington, and Deanne Robinson, Bend, Oregon. Miss Campbell is a graduate of KSU in Manhattan. Mr. Lander works as a ranch hand at the Double M Ranch in Cowley County.

"An October 17 wedding is planned at the Bartlett Arboretum in Belle Plaine. Music for the occasion will be provided by a friend, pianist Stefano Valdez."

He whipped around. "That's our man. Let me check something." With a few clicks, he brought up wedding shops in the city. With skills he'd learned in training classes at Malder Industries, he hacked into their appointment calendars. "This bride-to-be has an appointment at David's Bridal shop in the morning. You want to learn our business? You will come with me to find her."

That evening, Teo fitted a leather gun holster to Felipe's slender shoulders. He slid a 9mm Glock into it and snapped the strap to hold it in place. "You'll need these," he said and clipped a set of ear protectors around Felipe's neck. "Let's go," Teo said.

"Please, Uncle, where are we going?"

"Time you learned skills of our profession."

He dragged Felipe to the security team's target practice and handed him extra practice rounds for two weapons with gruff instructions. "Stick close and hand me more ammo when I say. Come."

They climbed a rope ladder to a hunter's blind. Teo stretched flat on his belly, steadied his binoculars, and leaned forward onto his elbows. Felipe wiggled beside him.

"What are you doing?" Felipe whispered.

"Assessing. Where might a target take cover? Is he alone or are there additional targets? Assassins work with intent, not passion. Watch and learn." He clicked his tongue, popping each model with an imaginary round. Felipe strained to see what Teo stared at. The older man nodded toward the sunset glow and Felipe squinted into the evening's dim light. Several flat human outlines stood among the cedars. Teo held out his hand. "Ammo," he said. Felipe handed him a magazine.

Teo nodded. "Give the brothers credit. This target range is designed for elite marksmen. Top of the line. Cream of the crop." He grinned at the boy. "And I'll be damned if I'm not one of them."

Teo inserted the clip in his own Glock. In one fluid, calculated move, he fired at a distant target and Felipe jumped. A puff of dust danced against the fading light. "That's yours, Valdez." Teo rolled to the edge and dropped to the ground. He crouched low, aimed, and fired again. The second target slammed to the ground. He glanced over his shoulder at Felipe and with a jerk of his neck, ordered the boy to follow. Felipe crawled to the ladder and climbed down.

His uncle dashed to a tree ten yards away, braced himself and fired at a third target. "*Adios, amigo.*"

He crouched and rolled, coming to rest with his aim straight for target four. He chortled with approval as the fourth target slammed to the dirt like the others. "Bye-bye baby."

Teo sprinted low to the ground to the top of a low rise and dove to his belly. Felipe trotted after him, lugging the pack with extra ammunition. Teo fired. The half-hidden target waved behind a small sapling as the round nicked it, but it didn't fall.

Teo yelled. He jumped to his feet and fired round after round into the obstinate target. His second bullet felled the model, but he didn't stop. He continued to advance, firing into the flattened target until the magazine ran dry.

"Serves you right, jerk," he said. He straightened his posture, took a deep breath and returned to Felipe. "Reset the targets."

Felipe dropped the bag and ran to each steel target to reset them, while Teo sauntered back to the blind. "Want to give it a go?" he asked when Felipe returned.

"You mean shoot?"

"That's the idea, kid."

Should he? Or shouldn't he? Was Teo offering him a choice? Or would this turn into another lesson in following orders without question? Did he want to shoot the human figures? He squinted at a target under the cedars, barely visible in the dusk. Would Teo be angry if he said no? He could hear his uncle's mocking laughter when he missed the target but how could he hit something he couldn't see?

Felipe hesitated a moment too long. "Enough, anyway," Teo said. "You're not ready, are you? Let's eat. I'm famished."

Uncle Teo holstered his gun and took the bag from Felipe and they returned to the residential circle.

58

MADDI COULD NOT conceal her excitement as they headed to her appointment at David's Bridal in the city.

"Let me guess," Izzy said, grinning. "It's a lemon day?"

Maddi nodded. "Lemon, for sure." She had made sure the store offered Wi-Fi to allow a conference call for dress advice with Melody in Oregon, her mother and twin sister in Pennsylvania, and her aunt Heidi in New York. Maddi beamed as the sales attendant assisted her to try on a gown. A clip here, a hidden pin there, and the fit adjusted to her slender figure. In each new dress, she twirled in front tri-fold ceiling-to-floor mirrors while Izzy held the phone, allowing the camera to share each option with her satellite advisory team.

The distant observers reviewed each dress. Izzy thought they all looked good on Maddi. As the morning progressed, she noticed subtle changes in Maddi's mood the others missed. The bride's smile diminished with each fitting. Her shoulders drooped a little lower. Oblivious to Maddi's melancholy, the sales attendant helped her step out of the sixth and last planned dress. While she donned her street clothes, Izzy chatted wedding trivia with the women on the video call. The shop attendant re-hung the dresses and smoothed them. She placed each one on a peg designed for the final inspection and greeted Maddi with a wide smile when she emerged from the dressing room.

"How about the Parisian gown?" the attendant asked. "It was stunning on you."

Maddi gave a little nod and turned up her lips in a forced smile. "They are all beautiful," she said in a soft voice.

Her mother's voice piped up from the phone. "Maddi, that last one—wow—exquisite."

Maddi stared at the dresses. Her eyes roved from one to the next, from the floor to the bust and shoulder design. "I don't know. I just don't know."

"I liked the third one," Meggie voted.

"Mel?" Izzy prompted her daughter's comments.

"Maddi looks beautiful in all of them," Mel said. "It's her choice that counts."

"She's right," Izzy said. Bridget and Meggie echoed the sentiment.

"But I can't decide. C-c-can I have time?" Maddi asked.

"Of course," the sales rep said. "Call me when you make a decision."

They made their way toward the front door. Izzy's phone beeped with a text message from Heidi. She, too, had noticed Maddi's mood swing. "I'll send you a photo of the gown our mother wore at her wedding," Heidi noted. "It was also Nola's wedding gown. Let me know if I should ship it to the ranch."

As they left the store, Maddi's tension leaped upward and Izzy felt it.

Sforzando. Why is she frightened?

Maddi pushed Izzy's shoulder and urged her toward the parking lot. "Hurry, Izzy," she whispered with unmistakable panic in her words.

Izzy glanced backwards at a tall, dark-skinned man in a khaki uniform. A Malder Industries logo blazed across his shirt pocket. A boy in similar garb, though minus the logo, ambled at his side. The boy's gaze cycled from the man, to the store, to Maddi, to Izzy. The man's rude gaze roved along Maddi's slender form until it settled on her eyes. His lips twitched in a vulgar sneer.

Maddi grabbed Izzy's hand and pulled her to the car.

"L—l—lock the doors," Maddi said, once they landed inside. "That guy—did you smell him?"

"I—no—smell?"

"Like r-r-rotting flesh. Dead animals. Let's go. We have to g-g-go. Now."

Izzy started the car and they sped from the parking lot. Maddi glanced over her shoulder. When they stopped at a red traffic light, she shrieked. "They're following us."

Izzy checked the mirrors.

"See him?" Maddi said.

"No."

"Three cars behind us. Dark blue car with smoky windows."

Izzy adjusted the mirrors for a clearer view. "I see," she said. "We'll watch the Lexus."

The driver behind her Prius bleeped his horn when the light changed. She drove across Rock Road into another parking lot. The Lexus followed. She circled onto the Kellogg access road. The Lexus remained behind them.

"Accelerando, Isabel," she said and floored the accelerator. "Maddi, can you call Dirk? Or Brett?"

They raced up the ramp onto the freeway. The Lexus followed. She drove west to the mid-town bypass, exited Kellogg, and swerved onto the ramp with the Lexus still two cars behind. At the last second, she switched lanes to merge onto the north-bound Interstate 135. He followed without a hitch.

Maddi whined, a sound peculiar to her that Izzy had not heard in years.

"Stay calm, Maddi. I need your eyes," she said. "Any luck raising the Landers?"

"N-n-neither answered."

"Try Kurt. Or Stefano." She accelerated to their top speed.

The Lexus pulled into the adjacent lane and crept beside them.

"Why's he following us?" Maddi wheezed through her wail.

"I'm not sure."

"What should I do?" Maddi wailed. "Nobody answers their phones."

"I need you to stay calm. Please. He's right beside us."

"Should I call the police?"

Izzy considered that option for a few seconds and felt hollow inside. When had local police ever listened to her? "If the guy is in uniform as a security guard, the police may not help us much. We'll try to lose him."

They drove in parallel paths past the next off-ramp, the Lexus edging closer to the lane division, squeezing the Prius toward the shoulder. Unable to see through the darkened glass, Izzy imagined the driver laughing at their plight. Rage welled inside her. "No you don't," she shouted.

She braked hard, darting onto the 13th Street ramp. The Lexus missed it. The Prius coasted to a stop at the end of the ramp. Izzy took a deep breath to calm her shaking hands, drove across on the green light and entered the freeway again. She accelerated to a moderate speed, drifting with traffic in the exit lane until they rolled off the freeway onto 21st Street. The Lexus had disappeared.

"Did we lose him?" Izzy asked.

"We'd sure be easy to identify with the p-p-piano signs stuck on the doors. Can you take them off?"

"Do you see him anywhere? I'll take them off."

While Izzy drove east to the university, Maddi looked in all directions and reported no sign of their stalker. Izzy swung onto a campus drive and found a parking spot in a crowded student lot. She raced around the Prius, yanking the magnetic piano signs off the doors, tossed them onto the back seat, and dove into the driver's seat again. They returned to 21st Street in time to watch the Lexus roll to a stop at the stoplight that admitted them into city traffic.

"Damn," Izzy said. "Did he recognize our car?"

Maddi answered with a soft whimper. Izzy turned south on Rock Road and caught a glimpse of the same blue Lexus, way back in the line-up. It crept into the turn lane and headed south behind them again.

"Why won't he leave us alone?" Maddi asked.

Izzy shook her head. "Let's see if we can lose them in Towne East." She drove into the huge parking area north of the shopping mall and wound through parked cars. The Lexus crept along behind them. On the west side, Izzy zipped into a prime spot. She and Maddi raced to the west entrance. Inside they watched the Lexus roll by their parked car. It cruised through the row, came back in the adjacent row, and parked in a spot forty yards away from their car.

"They're getting out," Izzy said.

They dashed to the nearest escalator and rode it up to the second level. Their stalkers ambled through the shop aisles, splitting up at the escalator. The boy rode up while the man headed into the center corridor. Izzy grabbed Maddi's hand and they rushed toward the north end. They circled the island offering fast foods. They raced to the far side and came face-to-face with the somber khaki-clad boy, fifteen yards away. He raised his hand as if summoning her to approach him.

Izzy whirled and raced the opposite direction, pulling Maddi behind her. They headed into the Dillards store and slipped into the women's apparel area. Peering through the racks of dresses, she watched their stalkers reunite in the main corridor. The boy said something to the man, and they turned toward the food court. Izzy led Maddi through toward an exit and they raced to the Prius.

59

FELIPE'S MIND RACED. He wasn't sure why Teo insisted they follow those two women. How did they pose a threat to the Malders? Or to them? Music always comforted him when life presented conundrums. Perhaps it would help now.

They had searched the stores in that mall until Teo gave up, angry that two women had slipped from his grasp. Back at the Malder compound, Felipe wandered to the school building and slipped into the dark stage area. He pulled the flashlight Teo had given him from his pocket and swung the beam around until he found a light switch. Once lit, he crossed the stage, opened the piano and played a few keys. He searched his memory for a lost melody, improvised several melodic combinations, and built a song from his lost childhood. He heard nothing beyond the phantom melody in his mind as the afternoon slipped away.

His trance broke when Teo stomped down the hall. Felipe could not mistake his uncle's footfalls. Nor could he mistake the angry voice which followed. Uncle Teo shouted at the teacher. "Where is Felipe?"

The woman murmured, a pleasant, reassuring sound. But Teo didn't buy it.

Felipe turned to the keys again, his cheeks red, heart racing. In desperation, he searched his mind for the melody, but it had disappeared. Struggling to ignore the angry exchange from the hallway, he played a few notes.

The stage door creaked as it opened a crack. "See?" she said. "It's okay. He's fine."

"There's no time for this."

"Sh-sh," the teacher said.

Felipe played a few keys. The piano notes sounded sour. He couldn't drown out his uncle's voice.

"Don't shush me, woman. I need the boy and I need him now."

Teo thrust the door open and reared backward, fuming. "What is this?" His words erupted in a sinister whisper.

The teacher said, "Relax. Your son seems mesmerized by the piano."

"Who gave you permission to teach him this shit?"

"I'm not teaching. He was drawn to it. You saw him—a bolt to a magnet. I'm sure the Malders would hire a piano teacher if you asked. I think he's talented."

"I will not—" Teo stopped his tirade in mid-sentence.

Felipe held his breath, waiting for the anger, but it didn't come. When Teo spoke again, he was a different man. "Lessons, you say?"

Felipe renewed his efforts at the keyboard, his forehead creased as his right hand jumped from one key to another. *Damn Teo anyway. Why'd he come here today?* He let out an anguished cry and slammed his palm across a few keys, hitting them over and over.

The teacher rushed to him, speaking soft reassurance. Teo followed her without a sound. Felipe's eyes met his and a flicker of defiance crossed the child's face before he dropped his hands to his thighs and stared at the floor.

"Felipe," Teo said, with slow deliberation. "Your teacher insists you'd benefit from music lessons. Would you like that?"

Felipe brought his head up and straightened his back.

"Would you like to learn, Felipe?" the teacher asked in a tender voice. "It's okay. Let me know."

Felipe nodded once. He looked at the floor, not once meeting Teo's gaze.

"All right," Teo said. He placed his massive palm across the boy's shoulders. "If he's to take lessons, we should call a piano tuner."

"Well, yes," the teacher agreed.

"Let me recommend someone."

"The Malders employ a fine technician."

Teo stared at the woman, his nostrils flaring. He answered with ice in his voice. "If you want my cooperation, you will let me choose the tuner and the instructor."

The teacher's mouth dropped open. She nodded without a word.

Teo scribbled information on a scrap of paper and handed it to the teacher. "Time to go, Felipe."

60

DUST SWIRLED AROUND the Prius as Izzy braked to a stop in her driveway, like the fog of panic churning in her mind. *Forzando.* She'd be checking her mirror for a dark Lexus for the rest of her life.

Latino music wafted from the open windows of her piano shop. She slammed her car door and hurried inside. Stefano glanced up from the workbench where he tested a handful of Elsie's action hammers. "I was beginning to think that you and Maddi drowned in the dresses." His light banter ceased, killed by the look in her eyes. "What?"

She shook her head slightly. "Stefano, we were followed."

He dropped his jaw and stared at her.

"This creep terrorized us three full hours. Finally gave him the slip in the big shopping mall."

"Do you think it was Diaz?"

"If it was, he must have found the engagement announcement. Can we look at Lena's pictures again?"

Stefano pulled up the files at the office computer. He opened the nameless file and Izzy leaned over his shoulder, staring at faces as he clicked through the images. Her heart raced faster at each scene. In one shot the eldest Diaz brother leaned across a table toward four scowling men, shooting a threat toward his youngest brother with menace in his expression. Izzy laid her hand over Stefano's knuckles and whispered, "Stop. That's him. That's the man we encountered outside the bridal shop."

Stefano exhaled deeply. "Teofilo Diaz. He took the bait then." He swiveled the chair around and stared into her eyes.

"He's in Wichita," she said. "He followed us to the midtown bypass and back to Towne East." Her voice broke. "He tried to run us off the road."

The office telephone rang and the caller ID showed an unknown Wichita number. Izzy and Stefano stared wordlessly at each other while the phone rang.

"You going to answer that?" Stefano said. He coughed.

Izzy took a deep breath, lifted the phone, and forced pleasantness into her voice. "Good afternoon. Woods Piano Service."

A woman returned the greeting. She asked to arrange a service call for a piano at a private school in the north part of the city. Izzy checked the calendar and mentioned a couple of dates. The new client chose a Friday in late September. She gave the street address and Izzy wrote it down. "You'll need to enter through the security gate off Thirteenth Street," the caller said. "Give me a call when you pull up to the check point and I'll approve your admittance."

"This number on my caller ID?" Izzy asked.

The woman confirmed the phone number, and Izzy expressed thanks, and disconnected the call.

Gated entry. Security checkpoint. North Wichita.

"What school is this, Stefano?"

He pulled up Google maps on the computer screen and typed in the address. A big empty square popped into view. He zoomed the view outward. "It gets weirder," he said.

Izzy gasped. "Malder Industries. This Teofilo—he wore a uniform with the Malder logo on it this morning."

"He works there?"

"He's got to be behind this tuning request."

"How would he even know your name?"

Drat. Frizzy Izzy. She closed her eyes and knocked her forehead with her palm. "He pulled the number off my magnetic signs. They were on the Prius during the dress appointment. How could I be that stupid?"

"Izzy, you better cancel that appointment."

"There's something strange about it. Why would he even want to mess with a tuning appointment at this private school?"

"It's obvious. He needs to find those packets that we pulled out of Elsie."

"You think he wants to follow me here?"

Stefano shrugged. "You gave him the slip once. He won't let it happen twice."

She took a deep breath and backed out of the office. Stefano followed her to the music room. Izzy leafed through the pages of Maddi's Lecuona piano book. "What if there's something more, Stefano? Diaz wasn't alone today." She tossed the music onto the piano bench and whirled to face him. "Show me Lena's family photos." She tugged his hand and they returned to the office.

Stefano brought up the file of family photos. As he cycled through the collection, Izzy studied the faces with a contagious intensity.

"What is it?" he asked.

"This morning there was a young man, maybe eleven or twelve, with Diaz. Stefano, I think it was Felipe."

"How could that be?"

"These photos show him much younger, but I'm almost certain. It was him. Your nephew isn't in Cuba at all. He's in Wichita."

Stefano's nostrils flared. He ran his hands through his hair. "That changes everything. Izzy, don't tune that piano."

"But didn't Lena describe how she used to play for Felipe? What if he is somehow connected to this request? Not the older Diaz, but Felipe? What if Lena was able to reach him with the music and this request is for him?"

"If that is the case," Stefano said with deliberation, "I still don't think you should keep that appointment. Give it to me. Let me tune the piano at the Malder School."

PART III: PRESTO FURIOSO

61

APPLAUSE ERUPTED FROM the waiting audience as the curtains rose. From his backstage location, Stefano Valdez nodded approval at the grand pianos in the spotlights. Elsie Lenore nestled against the nine-foot concert grand, their piano curves spooning like lovers, lids removed, and strings glinting in rays splayed out from the keyboards.

He squinted into the wings across the expansive stage. Lena hovered in the shadows, as yet unseen by the audience. Her hair cascaded across her shoulders in magnificent ebony ringlets. She returned his gaze, a sparkle in her eyes.

This was their dream, on tour at last, their talents presented in the grandest venues. Having practiced together since childhood, they could sense each other's moves and respond in perfect synchronization that never failed to bring down the house.

The passion—the skill—the music. It was all on display for the world to see.

An expectant hush blanketed the crowd as Lena stepped into the light, her brow lifted in a question. He raised a thumb.

Accompanied by thunderous applause, he proceeded with assurance to the waiting Steinway. At the bench he flipped up the tails of his tux and sat at the keys. He closed his eyes and raised both arms with dramatic flair.

Enfocate, Valdez. Time to concentrate.

When he opened his eyes, a nod from Lena brought his hands onto the keys with resounding introductory chords. He lost track of the crowd. He lost sense of Mel and his son. His fingers flew over the keys and the music which mesmerized every heart in the hall.

They played a number and paused, allowing ample applause time before the second selection, their favorite Lecuona arrangement. The instant his fingers met the keys, Lena yelled. His fingers stumbled on the keys and he glanced up.

Her black eyes blazed into his and she screamed, "Run, Stefano!"

He struggled against restraining bonds, his chest heaving with panicked breaths. After what seemed an eternity, he yanked the quilt off his shoulders and sat up in the darkness. In a daze, he stood and groped through the blackness for something solid. His fingers bumped a lamp. He steadied it, flicked the switch, and flooded the room with light.

A dream. He'd dreamed the whole scene. Drenched in a cold sweat, he swung his feet to the floor and stood in the darkness.

It took a moment before his mind cleared and a related urgency slammed his consciousness. "Elsie," he said aloud. If Diaz gleaned Izzy's business phone number from her magnetic car signs, he would find the shop.

Stefano raced the short distance down the hall to the master bedroom and pounded on the door.

"Stefano?" Izzy's voice quaked as she woke from a deep slumber.

"Sorry to wake you, Izzy, but I had a dream. Diaz could find us easily, and when he does, he'll find Elsie."

"What are you saying?"

"We need to move her."

"Move? Where would we take her?" She opened the bedroom door, tugging a bathrobe onto her shoulders.

"Somewhere safe. Somewhere I could complete the rebuild with no worries that Diaz will burst through the door."

"Where would that be?"

"No idea. I'm open to suggestions."

Bleary eyed, Kurt leaned over his wife and squeezed her shoulder. "What about the little shop behind my artist's cooperative in Winfield? It's vacant at the moment."

"When do you want to move Elsie?" Izzy asked.

"As soon as possible."

"Could we wait for daylight?" Kurt said, winking a droopy eye.

62

TEO PULLED THE Lexus off the narrow pavement at the top of the hill and stopped, his tires crunching through dry grasses. He studied the message engraved in the limestone roadcut. "The crooked made straight." Huffing in contempt, he pulled field glasses from a case on the seat beside him and sighted down the steep hill. The road dove into a narrow valley, passed over a small bridge, and disappeared in a copse of tall oaks. That piano shop should be around here somewhere, but where? Given his proclivity to look down on things, he expected to find it at the summit, right here where the crooked road was made straight a century ago, but he saw no dwellings.

Panning the roadside methodically, he looked for driveway entrances. A movement in the distance caught his attention and he focused the binoculars on a pickup truck pulling a white trailer. It turned onto the paved county road half a mile distant. Good thing the sun shone behind him. The pickup driver would not get a clear view of him, thanks to the blaze of the morning sun.

He waited a good two minutes after the truck disappeared, pulled back onto the road, and coasted down the incline, engine idling. Across the small bridge, he found what he'd been looking for, a gravel driveway leading through a late summer meadow.

Teo swung onto the drive, coursed through the meadow, rounded a hillock and entered a private yard. He swung east along a circle drive and parked between the house and a detached garage. The doors on both buildings were shut. No signs of life met his scrutiny. He tapped twice on the walk-in house door. When nobody answered, he turned toward the garage, tapped on the door, and stepped sideways to peer through a window pane. The interior appeared cluttered with equipment, work benches, and—there they were—pianos lined against the opposite wall.

He tried the door and found it locked. Teo stepped backward and slammed his heel above the door knob. It held fast. He kicked again with no better luck.

Returning to the window, he hammered the glass with the grip of his Glock. It shattered. He knocked out fragments with the handle and crawled through the window. He searched the shop twice but found nothing more than a large empty space in the shop's interior. He cursed. *That trailer.* They'd moved it, only moments ago in the trailer. Why hadn't he followed that trailer when he saw it leave?

Never mind. They couldn't be taking it far. He would find it again.

He marched to the door and flipped off the deadbolt. The instant he opened the door, a shrill alarm sounded. *Dammit.* He dashed to the Lexus and raced off the premises.

On the outskirts of the neighboring town of Winfield, Izzy's phone shrieked, an alert that the security system alarm at home had been activated. She showed the screen to Stefano. "Shop west entrance" flashed repeatedly.

"*Caramba!*" he said.

"You were right, Stefano."

"What do we do?"

"Let the sheriff check it out. They'll get this alert also."

Kurt said, "We won't go back until we get assurance that all's well."

"But he knows where we live," Izzy said in a piercing whisper.

"He's after the piano, remember?" Kurt said.

"And me," Stefano said. "He'll find me too."

"What will he do when he doesn't find the piano?" Izzy said. "That's what worries me."

"We need to move fast to free Felipe," Stefano said. "When's that tuning appointment?"

"Friday, next week. That's the day I plan to meet Maddi's clan at the airport. Two birds, you know? One trip to Wichita."

"Do they know I'm doing the piano tuning?" Stefano said.

"Not yet."

"I want to involve Brett. Would he be willing to talk to me?"

"Willing?" Izzy said, rolling her eyes. "He's a race horse waiting for the starting gun. Yes, he'd talk to you. Call him."

≈≈

Half an hour later, Elsie stood in a rear corner of the vacant shop, shielded from view by a room divider. Izzy and Kurt taped newsprint to the window while Stefano attached the piano's pedal lyre.

"I know a couple of art students who could paint this window with autumn leaves," Kurt said, rubbing a three-inch strip of tape over the paper seam.

"That would make people wonder," Izzy said.

"At least nobody could see inside."

"Just don't want students talking," Stefano said.

Kurt waved away his concern. "All they care about is painting. And the hottest weekend gossip on campus. Who's seeing who? Who ran out on who? Who's out for blood? Who's out for love? They won't even notice a piano in this empty store."

"Have you called the Fultons?" Izzy asked.

"Yes. They said bring it on out."

"To hide the trailer?" Stefano said.

Kurt nodded. "They have a barn on their property up by the lake with plenty of room for the trailer."

"No need to draw attention to our piano transport when we get the 'all clear' from the sheriff," Izzy said.

"We'll need it here next anyway, on Maddi's wedding day." Kurt whistled the opening of Wagner's "Bridal Chorus."

Stefano laughed. "Get out of here. That's not even on the list."

Five minutes after Kurt and Izzy left with the trailer, Stefano jumped at a bold knock on the locked door. *Couldn't be, could it?*

He tiptoed to the window and parted a seam in the newsprint. Brett Lander stood outside, his fist raised to knock again. Stefano unlocked the door, pulled Brett inside, and locked the door again.

"You expecting someone else?" Brett asked.

"No. Glad it's you. You didn't waste any time. Izzy thought you'd consider helping us. She told me to call you for advice."

"She did, did she? Where is Izzy?"

"She and Kurt are hiding the trailer."

Brett raised his eyebrows. Stefano drew him behind the divider and played an arpeggio across the span of Elsie's keys.

"Hiding the piano too, I see," Brett said. "I heard about the scene in Wichita after Maddi's dress appointment."

"Izzy identified Diaz from Lena's photos. And her car sported the piano signs yesterday. She received a request to tune the piano at the private Malder School."

"Did she accept it?"

"Yes."

"If Diaz found her business number, he could find her business."

"That's why we moved."

"Good thinking, Stefano. When's the appointment?"

"A week from Friday. I won't let her go, though. I want to tune that piano. A boy accompanied Diaz yesterday. Izzy's sure it's Felipe, Lena's son. My nephew lives with Diaz in Wichita. I need your advice, Brett. Will you help?"

"I will. For you. For Izzy. And for the boy. Maddi's intuitions have always been dead right and the vibes she got from this man... scum of the earth."

"Felipe faces grave danger. What do I do?"

"Give me a day to look into the Malder complex. Early next week, let's scout out its perimeter."

63

FELIPE HAD NO idea why Uncle Teo changed his mind about the piano lessons. He felt happy about it, however. The piano teacher not only knew music, she spoke fluent Spanish. It almost made the extended tour away from home bearable. Almost. Given a choice, Felipe would prefer to return to the land of his birth, but even the first music lesson lit a spark in him. He felt important. He didn't know why, but the music spoke to his heart and fanned a determination to prove to Teo that he was no longer a child. The Monday after they had stalked the bride, Teo summoned Felipe to the study.

"How are your music lessons?" Teo asked.

Felipe tried to deduce Teo's angle. What would the right answer be? The one that would appease his uncle. But that was unpredictable.

"Well?" Teo said, his voice tainted with gruffness this time.

"Fine. I think," Felipe answered.

Teo nodded. He leaned back in his chair and pressed the tips of his fingers together, bridging his hands. "Don't get too used to them," he said, a smirk on his face.

"What do you mean?" Felipe asked, his voice filled with wariness.

"Sit down. Say nothing. If you want to be part of the decisions in our family, listen up." His uncle pulled his mobile phone from his pocket, his personal phone. He hit a key and the phone dialed a long sequence of numbers. When a man answered, Teo turned on the speaker phone, glared at Felipe and touched his lips in a grim reminder to remain quiet. He turned on the charm and smiled into the device on the desk.

Claude Torres replied. "It's bad and bound to get worse here, Diaz."

"I'm sure you'll handle it."

"You need to get back."

Teo's voice rose in volume. "I plan to stay until the wedding."

"Wedding?"

"Not mine, dimwit. Valdez is slated to play piano for this wedding," Teo said.

"For God's sake, Diaz, it's been six months. You need to get back here at once."

Teo's voice erupted. "I know. It's been seven months, dammit. The wedding is in October. That's when it all comes down."

Felipe sat straighter. *October.* And September was half gone.

Teo continued, "I have a lead on the repair shop where Valdez shipped that piano. Once I retrieve the samples, I'll take care of him."

"And all that happens in October, after all this tim? Right."

"The October wedding for sure."

"I'll believe it when I see your face."

"*Adiós,* Torres." Teo concluded the phone conversation and turned to Felipe. "You understand?"

Felipe met his gaze and nodded. "After you find Valdez—"

"No more piano lessons."

"Uncle, I don't understand why you allowed my lessons in the first place."

"To appease your teacher. And it's cover. Important to appear normal. And if I miscalculated, we'll use the piano tuner. She will be here next week."

Stefano slid the Steinway action onto the portable action table. He adjusted the bass string target height and depressed the lowest key. He pulled the action toward him a fraction of an inch and the bass hammers hit the wooden string target dead center. Holding a measuring jig under the faux string, he played a few keys and tweaked the jack connection a little on those he judged to need refinement.

When his phone jangled, he glanced at its screen to find Melody grinning at him. He tossed his tools aside and accepted the video request, a wide smile across his face. They connected and he crooned, "Hey, Beautiful."

Melody returned his smile. "Look who's here," she said. Eight-month-old Nico sat propped on her knee. Stefano made faces at his son, who first stared, then chortled an infectious infant laugh. Stefano laughed with delight.

"How's Elsie Lenore coming along?" Mel said.

"Almost there." Stefano reversed the phone's view to show Melody the piano action. "Isn't it gorgeous? Brand, spanking new hammers and wips, repaired ivories. Such uniformity. Such precision."

Melody laughed. "Looks amazing, Stefano."

"It is. Wait 'til you see it all together. The tone—so rich. I'm in awe."

"You've been playing her?"

"Not yet. I need to finish the fine regulation. Then we'll see." He returned the phone's screen to his face, "My arms ache to hold you and Nico."

Her voice filled with tenderness. "I love you, Stefano."

64

BRETT STOPPED BY the shrouded store two mornings later and Stefano climbed into the pickup beside him for their reconnaissance trip to Wichita. "Got your phone?" Brett asked.

"*Sí.*"

Neither spoke during the forty-minute drive. Stefano fiddled with the radio receiver but couldn't settle on a station. As they rolled off the bypass on the east side of Wichita, he clicked the radio off. They passed a shopping center with a pond and fountain at its center.

Brett braked to a stop at the next red light. "I'll drop you at the southeast corner."

"And I will walk to the next stop light and head north."

"Act normal."

"I'll try. My heart's in my throat."

"Take a deep breath. If you see any breaks, note the location. Keep your eyes moving. Make a mental note of any visible security devices and snap a casual picture on your phone, if you deem it safe."

"And you?"

"I'll cruise through the adjacent housing district. I have an override code on the admission gate. Pick you up at the northwest corner. Fifteen minutes. Twenty, tops." He braked to a stop.

Stefano settled a cap on his head, gripped his phone, and opened the door. He nodded to Brett and watched as the pickup rejoined traffic. He shrugged his shoulders and stepped forward. The narrow grassy strip along the busy street lined an eight-foot tall masonry fence, broken every twenty yards by attractive wrought iron splices. He settled into a brisk pace along the cement walkway which wound from one side to the other in gentle curves. The design invited a casual stroll, but he preferred a simple straight sidewalk. He

held his phone in his left hand and clicked surreptitious photos at every break in the wall without faltering.

❧

Teo stared at the monitor screen in Malder security headquarters. A loathing for Stefano Valdez coursed through his veins,
fueled by anger and unfettered by logic. How did that man
continue to stay one step ahead of him?

"Dude, look at this guy," his partner said with a snort of
contempt.

Teo glared at the other guard.

"This creep," the guard explained. "He's walking our exterior, snapping pics on his phone, pretending nobody watches.
Take a look."

Dammit, Teo thought. He had better things to do. He
needed alternate plans to locate the infernal piano.

"Suspicious behavior if you ask me. Look at this vagrant."

With a grunt, Teo spun his chair to the screen his partner
had pegged. A solitary pedestrian strolled off the camera. Seconds later, he strolled onto the adjacent view. Teo's heart
thumped. *That face.*

He straightened and stomped his boots on the concrete
floor. Leaning close, he scrutinized the face on the screen. *No
doubt about it.* "Valdez," he said, his voice a growl.

The guard raised his eyebrows. "You recognize him?"

Teo bounded to his feet and grabbed keys to a company
Lincoln Navigator. "I'll check him out," he said with no further
explanation, and stomped outside.

❧

Stefano turned north at the stoplight and hiked along the wall
lining this street. The meandering sidewalk disappeared at the
corner and he stepped up his pace. His heart thumped as
cars raced by on the busy four-lane boulevard. Horns blared.
Engines raced. He crossed a gateway, secured by a shut iron

gate, and paused a few seconds to snap a set of pictures before he hustled northward.

Fifty yards before he reached the railroad right-of-way which marked the corner of the Malder property, a vehicle slowed behind him. The driver tooted two beeps on the horn. Stefano glanced over his shoulder. He exchanged nods with Brett and jogged the remaining distance to the railroad dike where Brett half-pulled from traffic onto the raised right-of-way. Stefano yanked open the door, leaped inside the truck, and swung the door shut as the pickup rolled back into traffic.

Back on the bypass, Stefano removed his cap and wiped perspiration from his brow. "See anything promising?"

Brett shook his head. "Not on the residential side."

"Something tells me these people won't allow substitutions."

"Something tells me you're right," Brett said.

"How will I pull this off?" Stefano spoke his thoughts aloud.

"You'll need help."

"*Sí,*" Stefano said. "Lots of it."

৵৵

Teo drummed his fingers on the steering wheel. Would the gate ever open? As soon as it offered a lane wide enough for the Navigator, he nosed to the street and wedged the SUV into a small gap. The approaching car's driver laid on the horn and blared a rude objection into the morning air. Teo rolled down his window and waved his finger at the angry driver as he sped west.

He approached the site where the camera had caught the pedestrian and slowed, studying the walk in front of him. Trapped at the corner light behind three cars, he could not see the exterior of the compound on the west side. When he turned north, he narrowed his eyes and stared along the grassy border.

No pedestrian. He scrutinized the wall breaks as he cruised along the route.

Zip. Nada.

Where did the cur go? At the railroad dike, he glanced east. Still no Valdez. He swung through a shopping center and retraced the route. Nothing. Had Valdez crossed the street at the stop light then? He peered west at the stop light intersection, to no avail.

Teo drove the compound boundary three more times before he returned to the compound. He raced the Navigator through the gate, burned rubber on the concrete drive as he slid to a halt, and slammed the door to headquarters as he entered.

"Missed him, did you?" The other guard taunted him.

Teo's eyes flamed as he glared at the insolent guard. "Won't happen again," he said.

65

IZZY TUCKED HER tuning lever and mutes into her tool bag and closed the lid on her client's piano in east Winfield. She headed to the front door. A ping from her cell phone announced the arrival of a message from Stefano. "Meet me at the gallery ASAP."

About time.

He'd been reluctant to reveal anything about his walk around the Malder compound up to now. She backed the Prius down the driveway slope onto the street.

Accelerando, Isabel.

She slipped into the gallery and found Brett in the middle of the room, contemplating a large photograph of a prairie scene that hung among other enlargements. He looked up when she opened the door and flashed one of his smiles. His blue eyes twinkled and her heart melted.

He spoke first. "Is that tuning still set for tomorrow?"

"Yes."

"They still expect you?"

"I haven't changed anything. But I have a bad feeling about it. Stefano should not go in there alone."

"Let's go talk to the others. Maddi and Dirk met him to go over wedding plans."

"In the shop?"

Brett nodded and raised an arm to usher her next door. They slipped into the small shop. Short phrases of piano music and laughter floated from behind the room divider, but her mind fixated on tomorrow's appointment at the Malder compound. Would Stefano be allowed to take her place? Would he find Felipe and be able to transport his nephew away? What would he face while she met Maddi's Aunt Heidi and her grandmother, Dollsae Pack, at the airport across town? What sinister motive prompted Teofilo Diaz to arrange the tuning? Would Stefano even get out of there alive?

Applause erupted from the piano corner. Jolted out of her trepidation, she slipped behind the divider, with a forced smile on her face.

"We all need to talk," Brett said. "Big day tomorrow."

Stefano nodded and wiped sweat from his forehead. The smile brought by Maddi and Dirk's enthusiastic applause wilted and his eyes lost their light.

"Assuming all goes well," Brett said, "we'll need to prove Felipe's relationship to Stefano in order for his immigration papers to gain approval. We can do that. We have Lena's video plea, and the boy's DNA should confirm a family connection to Stefano, but that will take time."

"How long?" Stefano asked.

"At least a couple weeks. Until then, he's at risk of deportation and it may be impossible to get him back."

None of them responded.

"We need to find a place to shelter Felipe until the paperwork is complete," Brett said.

Stefano's voice wavered. "What do you mean?"

Brett's gaze bored into Stefano's. "How's Melody?"

Stefano leaned backwards, staring at Brett. At last he answered, "She's fine. We're in the process of reconciliation, if that's what you mean."

"If our plan works, we could use Melody's presence on the west coast to our advantage."

"Explain," Izzy said.

"If she's agreeable, we could transport Felipe to her care until we can prove the blood connection to Stefano."

"That sounds too risky," Stefano said. "I don't want my family harmed."

"This whole operation carries risk," Brett said. "Look, you asked for my help. I suggest you contact her to find out if that's possible. Otherwise we'd be forced to turn him over to immigration officials, and lose him. Would Melody be willing to help?"

"I want to know," Izzy said with urgency, "what we do about tomorrow?"

"You'll have to c-c-cancel," Maddi said. "You c-c-can't go in there alone, Izzy."

"Nor can Stefano," Izzy said.

"I won't," Stefano said. "If we work things right, we could use the tuning appointment to gain entry to the compound and connect with Felipe."

Panic flooded Izzy's mind. "Tomorrow?"

"No," Brett said. "You should reschedule."

"To when?"

The room filled with a heavy silence before Stefano spoke. "How about the morning of October 17?"

"No way," Dirk said.

"That's our wedding d-d-day," Maddi whispered.

"You can't mean that, Stefano. Not the wedding. How will you manage to be in both places at once?"

"I will need your help. I will need help from all of you," Stefano said. "If you will keep that appointment, Izzy, there's half a chance. Think about it. Diaz follows me to the Arboretum that morning. You'd have time to tune the piano while I get set up on location."

"You want me to find Felipe?" The knot in her middle tightened.

Brett said, "I'd go along and do that while you work. Perfect cover."

"Brett will find Felipe and take him to safety," Stefano said.

"And leave you alone and exposed? No way. That's too risky."

"Did you forget the agents?" Brett said. "Stefano will not be alone."

"Who would expect Felipe to disappear during your appointment?" Stefano said. "After Diaz is apprehended, bring Felipe to me at the wedding. What could go wrong?"

"Everything. You need support at the Arboretum."

"It's my best option," Stefano said. "Won't you help?"

"I w-w-will," Maddi said. She nudged Dirk.

After a moment, he sighed and nodded.

"Izzy, reschedule the tuning," Brett said.

"I can't do that."

"Yes, you can," Stefano said.

Brett turned her to face him. "You and I will use your work schedule to gain access to the compound. Stefano and Kurt will set up the piano at the Arboretum early that morning. We'll leak that information to Diaz and he'll vacate the compound before we arrive."

"Do you plan to hitch a ride in my trunk?"

Brett considered the possibility. "Great idea. It might work."

"If it doesn't?"

"We'll figure something out." He lifted her chin with a tender flick of his index finger and leaned closer. "Will you call the compound?"

She sighed. How could anyone resist this man's charm? Against the protests raging in her mind, she said, "I will. 8:30, October 17. Consider it done."

66

FELIPE STARED AT the words on the page of the chapter book. *T-r-a-v-e-l. Tr-a-vl. Travel.* What did the word mean? *I don't understand. I can't do this.* He pushed the book across the school desk and rubbed his eyes. He could not read this English. Everyone in the school knew it too. The other students no longer tried to speak to him. When they laughed, they laughed at him.

He opened the book again and stared at the letters on the page. His frustration peaked at the moment a door slammed in the hall. Someone stomped down the hall. Felipe's classmates exchanged looks. When Teo burst into the room, a murmur passed through the class. In sync his classmates swung their collective attention to Felipe. He was in trouble but he didn't know why.

"Goddamnit," Uncle Teo swore. "You said the appointment was scheduled today."

Irritated, the teacher waved away his concerns stepped toward the hallway. "Mr. Diaz, I must ask you to leave."

"I'm not leaving without answers."

Without concealing her irritation, she urged him to be quiet.

"Don't shush me, woman," he said.

"We're in a timed reading activity. I insist that you not disturb the students."

Teo ignored her. "Where's the piano tuner?" His voice bellowed, undamped by her request.

The teacher took a step backward and said in a steel-cold voice, "Something came up. She canceled."

Teo snorted. "She say why?"

"Family emergency. Mr. Diaz, things happen. You need to relax."

Teo searched the faces in the room until he found Felipe. "I dislike changes," he said by way of explanation. His eyes shot an accusation toward the boy.

As if it's my fault? Felipe pressed his hand into the open book and looked at the page again.

"You're in for a hard life," the teacher said.

"Did the piano tuner happen to reschedule the tuning?"

"Yes, she did."

"Mind telling me when?"

The teacher narrowed her eyes and studied Teo under a wrinkled brow. "Why do you need to know?"

Teo took a deep breath. His demeanor changed and he spoke with courtesy. "I want to meet her and ask a few questions to help Felipe. Cubans are famous for their music, you know. He should have the piano properly prepped."

Snickers from the other students brought fire to Felipe's cheeks. *Lying bastard.*

"I see," she said. "This after you forbade his lessons."

Teo shrugged off her sarcasm. "The boy has talent. He deserves a chance. The appointment?"

She considered a moment before responding. "She rescheduled for the morning of October seventeenth. It's a Saturday. No interruptions."

"October 17th?"

"Yes."

"You're sure about that?"

"Positive."

Felipe could not recall a time Teo had been speechless. His uncle contemplated the information for what seemed to Felipe an eternity. Then he nodded and left.

✌✌

The plane from New York arrived thirty minutes late. Izzy helped Maddi's Aunt Heidi and Grandmother Dollsae collect their luggage and they headed straight for the Double M. Maddi threw the front door open to welcome them. Heidi and Dollsae burst inside, their arms spread to invite hugs. Maddi squeezed both of them. She turned to Izzy. "Could you tune Mama's piano while you're here?"

"I have nothing else to do today," Izzy said.

Maddi tugged her guests toward the kitchen. "Come, meet Dirk."

Izzy retrieved her tool bag from the car and dropped it beside the polished grand piano in the front room.

Halfway through the tuning, Heidi entered the room. "What will we do about the wedding dress?" she whispered with urgency.

"She's ready to hit second-hand stores."

"I can't believe Nola discarded our mother's dress. Is it stored here somewhere?"

"There's a storage closet over the stairwell. Why don't you check there?"

"Show me where," she said.

Izzy led the way to a narrow closet in the attic and Heidi became entranced by the stored memorabilia. "Look at these," she said. "I can see Nola in this outfit."

Heidi thumbed through the garment bags. She pulled the last one from the closet rack and backed out. "If this is what I think it is...," she said and winked. She unzipped the bag a few inches and caught her breath. "Call Maddi."

"What?" Maddi asked when Izzy summoned her.

"Got a surprise for you," she said.

"In the piano?"

"No, upstairs. Come up here."

Maddi, Dirk, and Dollsae hurried up the narrow stairway and Heidi met them on the landing in front of the closet, her arms tucked behind her back and a big grin spread across her face. Impatient to discover the surprise, Maddi peered around Heidi's shoulder.

"Whoa, girl," Heidi said. "We need to do this right. You turn around and close your eyes. I'll let you know when to look."

Maddi pouted.

Heidi swept her away with a gentle backhand wave. The bride-to-be acquiesced and turned around. Heidi unzipped the bag and it fell to the floor. She smoothed the fabric, raised the garment, and turned toward Maddi. "Okay," she said in a voice overcome with sentimentality.

Maddi whipped around and gasped at the floor-length lace-covered ivory gown. "Is that?" she whispered.

Heidi nodded. "Nola wore this at her wedding." Heidi glanced at Dollsae with raised eyebrows and the petite woman nodded her agreement.

"Mama?" Maddi said, blinking away tears.

"Yes, Maddi. This was Nola's dress, and our mother's before that. It's antique."

Maddi clutched the lace-covered satin to her chest. Her jaws worked, but she said not a word. She drew in a ragged sob breath and managed to say, "If I wear this dress, it will be like Mama holds me through the ceremony."

"Nola would be pleased," Heidi said.

67

TWO WEEKS PASSED in a flurry. Heidi and Dollsae insisted they would prepare the rehearsal dinner, set for the evening of October 16 at the art gallery. Heidi offered to bake a three-tiered wedding cake. Dollsae applied her tailoring skills to alterations on the antique wedding gown.

Maddi and Izzy met the Campbell clan at the airport on Wednesday before the big day. While Brett treated Dirk to a father-son outing dinner before the wedding, Maddi modeled the heirloom gown.

Bridget blinked back tears. She smoothed the hair from Maddi's cheeks. "You're beautiful, Madeline," Bridget said.

"You don't mind, do you, Mother? Aunt Heidi found this dress in the attic. We think it belonged to my... N... Nola's."

"And now it's yours. As it should be," Bridget said.

Stefano tuned and re-tuned Elsie Lenore and tweaked a few adjustments on the action. He talked to Melody and Nico daily. Kurt confirmed there would be Wi-Fi available so they could view the ceremony from Oregon.

Dirk met his mother's airplane at Eisenhower National Airport on Thursday evening and Friday afternoon everyone convened at the Bartlett Arboretum for a rehearsal. Afterward, they headed to the art gallery in Winfield for the dinner Heidi and Dollsae had prepared.

Surrounded by artwork produced by talented local artists, and seated between Kurt and Brett at the table, Izzy felt strange. The two most significant men in her life flanked her place at dinner. She said little, but caught conversation snippets from various dinner guests. Dee nudged Brett and said, "Maddi seems nice. Is she the girl who was with you on that raft ride a few years ago?"

He gave a nod. "The very one."

"She blossomed. The child I recall was withdrawn."

254 | Ann Christine Fell

"Her life took a turn for the better."

"In Pennsylvania?"

"Yes."

"You are employed by her parents?"

"I'm their ranch manager."

"How convenient." Dee's voice carried a sneer.

"What do you mean by that?"

"That you could hire Dirk when he came looking for you."

Brett said, "Dirk is a fine man. You raised him well."

"No thanks to you." Her comment was almost inaudible, mixed with the jovial topics around the table.

"Give me a break, Dee," Brett said, his voice filled with resentment. "You might have mentioned we had a son."

"What? Then you'd have dropped everything to play daddy to him? I knew you better than that. We'd never have seen you and that would have been harder for him. Besides, I didn't even know how to find you, remember? Whenever you wanted to disappear, you just... vanished."

"I don't know, Dee. You could be right. On the other hand, I know how shocked I was when he showed up here a few months ago. I missed out on his entire childhood."

"Brett, don't start with me. You weren't interested in a commitment." She stressed her words with a finger pointing at his chest in accusation.

He turned to her, clasped her bobbing finger, and pushed it down. "We will never know, will we? But that's behind us. Look, I don't want to argue. I meant what I said as a compliment. Dirk is an outstanding young man. That's to your credit and I thank you. Can we move forward?"

She studied him a moment before she extricated her hand from his and lifted her fork to her mouth. "Yes. Let's move forward. Our son is getting married. Let's party."

◈

As dinner drew to a close, Dirk stood and clinked his fork against his wine glass. "Hey, everyone," Dirk announced, "Our wedding will be unforgettable for many reasons. One is our musician, Stefano Valdez, friend of my bride." He nodded at Stefano and raised his hand in an invitation to stand.

The guests applauded. Stefano bowed low, with a flourish.

Dirk continued the speech. "And part of what makes Stefano's music unique is the Steinway baby grand he rebuilt in time for this occasion."

More applause.

"Stefano, is she ready?" Dirk prompted.

"She is," Stefano said. "If you please, follow me."

The guests filed from the dining area and tagged after Stefano's energetic gait out the back door and into the little shop behind the gallery. They gathered around Lena's Steinway, its lid propped open in invitation. Stefano swept an arm toward the waiting piano. "With great pleasure I introduce Elsie Lenore, my family's fine piano."

He sat on the bench, flexed his fingers and launched into a Lecuona waltz that mesmerized each listener. The vitality and finesse in his performance brought tears to Izzy's eyes. When Stefano finished, a profound silence filled the little shop. Several breathless moments passed before Kurt clapped his hands and jogged the rest into a resounding applause.

The wedding party swarmed around Stefano, clapping his back with accolades. He found Izzy's eyes through the throng and beamed. Tomorrow's wedding would be unparalleled with passion. Izzy harbored no doubt.

68

AS THE ACCLAMATIONS faded, Dirk faced Maddi and tipped her chin back. Her eyes met his and they gazed at each other with tenderness. She wilted into his arms and he leaned in for a passionate kiss.

"Just think," he said, "This time tomorrow, we'll be forever family."

"Forever," she echoed, and tilted her head back for another kiss.

"Are you nervous?" he asked when they came up for air.

"N-n-nervous? Yes. I'm nervous, but n-n-not about us."

"What then?"

"I'm worried about little F-f-felipe. He'll be confused. Help me reassure him that everything is fine."

"I still wish we could just get married and rescue the boy another day."

"This is the best plan. You know that."

"No, I don't. Did anyone consider an alternate plan?"

"Dirk, don't be that way." Maddi pressed her lips into a pout.

He stole another kiss and erased her pout. "What about that pianist? He's awesome, isn't he?"

Maddi nodded. "I hope he doesn't get hurt tomorrow."

"I hope nobody gets hurt." He ushered Maddi to the shop's door.

"But we'll still be married, right?" she said.

"Yes, my dear, we will."

"Then it will be fine in the end."

"In the end." Dirk echoed her thoughts as they left.

Kurt and Stefano followed the wedding couple outside with the other guests close behind them.

Brett turned to Izzy before he left. "Big day tomorrow."

"In more ways than one," Izzy said. "Wish we could rehearse everything else."

Brett chuckled. "That would be nice, wouldn't it? Meet you at the Walmart parking lot?"

"What time?"

"Seven sounds about right."

"Seven it is."

He pulled an intricate device from his shirt pocket. "Here. Take this."

"Looks technical. What is it?"

"A microscopic recorder. I'll carry a duplicate. We might need them if Plan A goes awry."

"I wouldn't know what to do with it."

"I'll talk you through it." He grinned and reached for her. She gave him an awkward hug.

"Try to sleep tonight," he said in farewell.

Tomorrow would indeed be a big day.

❧❧

Teo sat at the computer, typing and reading, typing and reading. Felipe pulled frozen meat pies from the freezer and warmed them in the microwave oven. He slid one pie beside the computer monitor for his uncle. Teo grunted.

Felipe returned to the sofa where he watched a movie on the big television screen. At half past nine, Teo called him to the office.

Teo leaned back in the chair and beckoned the boy to approach. "Look here," Teo said, showing him arboretum photos. "The place is closed to the public all day. No morning hours."

Felipe stared, uninterested.

Teo slammed the desk with his fist. The empty pie plate hurtled to the floor and Felipe jumped.

"Pay attention," Teo said. "You hear me?"

The boy nodded.

"Tomorrow will be a big day for us. We will return to Havana soon. I'll jump a train before you're up tomorrow."

"We will take a train?" Felipe asked.

Teo snorted with derision. "Think about it. No. We won't be taking a train. I will hitch a ride on a train. Valdez and I have an appointment with destiny tomorrow. Here." He tapped the computer screen. "At this park. He'll arrive sometime in the morning, and I'll be the welcome committee. Got that?"

"*Sí*, Uncle Teo."

"I should return here by midmorning. But in the event that I'm delayed, you're in charge here."

"Me? In charge?" Felipe couldn't hide his astonishment.

Teo swore.

Felipe's cheeks burned. He didn't know what to say that would placate the angry man.

"I don't mean the entire compound. I mean in charge of our private, secret plan."

Felipe said nothing. He looked toward his shoes.

"You with me now?"

The boy chose his words with care. "What do you want me to do?"

"There's a woman coming to tune your school's piano tomorrow. If I'm not back by nine-thirty, you hustle over to the school and detain her until I arrive."

"How?"

"Cripes. 'How' he asks. I don't know how. Do it. Talk to her. Ask questions. Lots of them. Do not let her leave before I get back. Understand?"

He nodded. He wasn't sure what he'd do, but he dared not show his confusion to Teo.

69

ON HIGH ALERT all night, Felipe relied on tactics his uncle had drilled into him. "Fall asleep and die," he told himself. His heart beat fast as he listened to Teo's footfalls. His uncle paced the length of their two-bedroom cottage, back and forth, back and forth. When the pacing stopped, Felipe slipped from his bed and opened his bedroom door a crack to peek out. Dressed in running clothing, Teo left the cabin. Felipe parted his window blinds and watched his uncle jog away. When Teo reached the edge of the circle illuminated by the pole light, he broke into a dead run. Felipe checked his watch. One forty-four. Seven minutes of ominous silence later, he checked his watch again. He almost wished Uncle Teo still paced through the house again. The silence lulled him into a fitful doze.

He jerked awake when the cabin door opened and Teo re-entered the cabin. Two-sixteen. Sweat glistened on Teo's forehead as he passed the bedroom door. Water sprayed in the shower. When Felipe glimpsed his uncle again Teo wore hunter's camouflage clothing. He stopped at the kitchen table to check the pocket contents and donned a brown leather jacket. When he left the cabin again, Felipe relaxed. He knew he would not see his uncle before the day's events had concluded. At two-thirty with seven hours left before he was to drop in on the piano tuner, he crawled into bed and fell into a deep sleep.

✍✍✍

Stefano rubbed his eyes and checked the clock on the dresser across the room. He stood up, stretched, and splashed water on his face in the bathroom. He stopped in the kitchen to put on a pot of coffee. Izzy and Kurt met him there and they sipped on the coffee while reviewing the morning plan.

"Got your wedding attire?" Kurt asked. "I'll go hitch up the trailer." He hugged Izzy and headed out the door.

Stefano met him at the truck with his clothes bag and they drove to the little shop in Winfield. He ran through the entire chromatic scale on Elsie, and smiled at the rich tones that met his refined ear. He removed the music desk, wrapped it in a padded quilt, and clamped the fallboard shut to guard against it swinging during the road trip.

Dropping to the floor with a screwdriver and a mallet, he loosened and removed the pedal lyre. Kurt pulled a mover's skid from a wall shelf. Together, they removed the leg beneath the bass keys and lowered Elsie's straight side onto the padded skid board. Stefano clamped the lid shut and they removed the remaining two legs, wrapped the piano in moving quilts, and strapped her tight to the moving skid. Elsie Lenore was ready for her journey.

They rolled Elsie up the ramp into the trailer, jacked the skid off the wheels, and settled her to the floor. Kurt tied the piano to rails lining the wall while Stefano loaded the parts he'd removed.

"That it?" Kurt asked.

"Let me get my tools," Stefano said.

"One more thing," Kurt said. He opened a shop cabinet and removed two vests. "Brett left these for us last night. Let's put them on now."

"What are they?"

"Kevlar vests."

"He thinks of everything, doesn't he?"

"He's done this before. I hope he found one that fits Izzy too."

৵৵৵

A train rolled through Belle Plaine in the hour before dawn. The train whistle blew as it neared the town's center, and again as it approached an intersection with a state highway on the west side. When it rolled through the barricaded intersection, Teo shot from a train car and rolled into the ditch.

Once the train passed and the whistle signaled its approach at the next crossing, he uncoiled and froze in a crouch. A moment later he ran up the slope shrouded in blackness, keeping low to the ground. He crossed the paved road, jumped a low perimeter fence and disappeared inside the Bartlett Arboretum.

༄༅

Izzy rolled into the Walmart parking lot at the appointed hour and parked her Prius. Glancing around, she shook her head. No sign of Brett.

Figures.

She clicked open her phone to see if she'd missed a message. Nothing.

Where is he?

She downloaded a few emails. Two identical black Camry sedans rolled to either side of her. *What's this?*

A chill raced down her spine.

Brett stepped from the car to her right and tapped on the window. She rolled it down and he reached across the seat with the Camry key.

"I don't understand," she said.

"Simple. This is your company car today," Brett said. "Help me move your equipment over. I'll ride along in the trunk and exit once you're settled inside the school."

"How will you do that?"

He waved a duplicate key inside the palm of his other hand. "Trust me," he said, and winked.

"Why two cars?"

"Joe's our back-up. He'll wait across from the west compound driveway to assist once we have Felipe. Time's wastin'. Let's move."

She switched her service gear to the black Camry. Brett aligned the cases along the sides and reserved the center space. He pulled a jacket from the back and held it open for her. "Put this on," he said.

She backed into the coat, adjusting her shoulders to its fit. "It's tight."

"It's supposed to be. Keep it on please." He turned her to face him and let his hands linger on her shoulders. "I don't want anything to happen to you." He tweaked the tip of her nose.

Izzy nodded. "It's one of *those* jackets."

"One more thing. New earrings for you today."

He brushed her frizzled curls aside and wound two gold-colored devices behind her ears, clipping tiny spheres to her ear lobes.

"Brett, you shouldn't have," she said in mocking accusation. "What are these?"

"Just a way we can keep in touch. I will hear your conversations and you can hear me."

"I don't much relish surprises."

"Me either. Let's roll." He curled into the spot reserved for him.

70

IZZY STOPPED AT the compound's entry gate a few minutes after eight o'clock and rolled down the Camry's window. The stern guard in the booth eyed her. She handed him a business card and introduced herself. "Isabel Woods, Registered Piano Technician. I was instructed to call the school teacher to gain access to the school's piano. She asked to have it tuned."

Without a word, he checked the computer's calendar and nodded. "Yes," he said, glaring at her. "She's off grounds this morning. I'll call for an escort." He waved toward a small parking lot behind her. "You may leave your car there. A company car will take you from the gate."

It took a few seconds for Izzy to understand what he meant. "Wait, you mean I have to leave my car here?"

"That's what I said."

"I have all my tools and supplies. What if I need something from the car?"

"You may transfer your equipment to the escort vehicle."

Crap.

She made an attempt to dissuade the guard. "It would be simpler to let me drive my vehicle in."

"Security protocol," he said. "I can't allow that." He pointed toward the empty parking lot. "Park there."

She forced her mouth to turn up in something that she hoped resembled a smile. Heart racing, she shifted into reverse and backed into a turn-around spur. Brett's voice whispered in her ears, "Plan B. Park as close as you can to the trees on the far side. Face west."

Tuning a piano is a fishing expedition. You cast downstream to test the stability and fit of a few sample tuning pins. After testing the waters, you decide what the best tactic to complete the job. Setting the trap for a wanted person is much the same. First, gather information about what you face. Test the waters. Stock your bag for any and all circumstances and proceed with caution. Assuming the central Malder Corporation compound would never allow a substandard piano onto the grounds, she checked her basic tuning kit to make sure it held everything for a standard tuning. With several rubber mutes, a roll of hand tools, her iPad, and her favorite tuning lever in her tool bag, she headed to the gatehouse.

The security escort ushered her to the piano and left after instructing her to call when finished. Alone in the school building, she opened the Yamaha console piano's lid and removed the music desk. After running through the entire eighty-eight key scale, she checked the piano's pitch. In the center it was a little low, but nothing unusual. She checked the pedal operation before removing the practice pedal rail with its thick felt strip attached. With the tuning pins exposed, she inserted long felt strips to silence all but one string per key. As she finished the prep work, Brett's voice sounded in her ears. "I'm out. Heading to the back-up Camry. Can you hear me?"

She whispered, "Yes. Can you hear me?"

"Loud and clear," he said. "You have that device I gave you last night?"

"Yes."

"You'll have to install it in the security system wiring."

"Brett, I have no idea—"

"I'll step you through it," he said. "Keep your phone with you and send me photos."

He described the plan and she panicked. "What if I mess up?"

"You won't, Izzy," he said. "I know you can handle it. Take a deep breath or two. Calm your nerves. I'll be waiting."

71

THE CLOCK RADIO on Felipe's dresser blared with obnoxious talk and laughter at seven-thirty. He jumped, springing from his covers to stand alert. It took a moment before he recalled that he was alone. The alarm never rang. Why today?

Of course. Uncle Teo.

When would his uncle ever trust him? Felipe grabbed the radio and yanked its cord from the wall outlet. He raised his hand and smashed the device onto the floor.

He headed to the kitchen, grabbed leftovers from the refrigerator, and dragged a chair onto the back deck. Watching the Malder compound awaken, he took his time eating.

Teo would expect him to wash the empty bowl. *I'll wait until later, thank you very much.*

With his uncle gone, he could do as he wished, at least to a point. He headed to the bathroom and found a note taped to the mirror.

Orders, of course. Uncle couldn't let him be.

He reviewed the written commands. Nothing there he hadn't been told in person. Did Teo believe he wouldn't remember? Felipe ripped the paper in half and scrunched it into a ball. He tossed the wads into the toilet and flushed them away.

Today, I'm the boss. I'm the spy.

He checked his watch. Seven-fifty-three.

He entered Teo's office and approached the computer. After a moment's hesitation, he touched the button which woke the computer. He imagined Teo tucking the computer into a pint-sized bed, drawing a cover decorated with pixels up to its non-existent chin and laughed. Waking the computer.

"Buenos dias, computadora."

Where was the photo Teo had showed him, an aerial view of the Bartlett Arboretum? He clicked open a file labeled pictures and advanced through images of people, buildings, doors, and rooms inside that showed furniture and window locations.

He decided the photos must be related to the clandestine Havana project, the one he was to act as a spy for today. He came to a photo of lush trees at the arboretum and stopped. Uncle Teo would be there now. Had he found that other guy, the wedding pianist? If not, where would he wait?

If he was Teo, he'd climb a tree and watch from above. Nobody ever looked up. It would be a safe place to hide and wait. Which tree? He zeroed in on a tall ash near the open area flanked by pathways and a few roofs. Where would the wedding be, anyway?

Felipe closed his eyes and imagined himself in Teo's shoes, his mission to locate and eliminate a family adversary. He dozed again.

❧❧

With practiced skill, Kurt backed the piano trailer to a ramp at the rear of the tree house stage. Stefano trotted to its rear and opened the doors. He extended and secured the trailer ramps while Kurt untied the piano from the wall. They jacked the moving skid off the trailer floor and slipped a wheeled cart under it.

Without speaking, they rolled Elsie away from the wall and along the ramps. Once on the stage, they secured the skid, attached the legs to the piano, and tipped it onto the casters. While Kurt removed the padded quilts and the skid, Stefano reattached the pedal lyre and slid the music desk into place.

He played a short section of the wedding processional and nodded. "A little tweaking before the wedding. She'll be ready."

❧❧

Izzy recorded five minutes of her normal tuning process on her iPad. She set it to play back the continuous plinking and twanging. A casual listener would hear someone taking great pains to tune the mid-section on the compound's Yamaha piano.

Should be fine.

She grabbed her phone and the tool roll, and slipped Brett's device into a pocket on her jacket. "Ready," she said in a barely audible voice.

"Out the door to your right. You will find yourself on the back side of the school building. Prop the door open." Brett's voice spoke in her ears.

She leaned into the emergency exit door. It didn't move. "The door won't open. Could it be locked from the outside?"

"Against fire codes. Push harder."

She leaned into the metal door again. It creaked. With a swift kick to the base she managed to dislodge the door. It creaked open far enough she could squeeze out. "Hope nobody heard that," she whispered. "I'm out."

"Turn left. On the corner. Look for a metal box mounted chest high on the bricks."

Landscaping bushes flanked the exterior wall. She found a dry twig and left it in the doorway gap before squeezing along the brick wall. The bushes rustled as she moved. Dry leaves on the ground crackled with each footfall. She made steady but slow progress to the corner where—sure enough— a metal box was attached to the bricks.

"Got it," she said.

"Take the cover off," Brett said.

Noting the slotted bolts which secured the cover to the box, she knelt in the bushes and spread her tool roll on the ground. She selected a screwdriver and wriggled upward along the brick wall. Six bolts later, the cover tipped outward. It scraped metal as it tilted. She dropped the screwdriver and reached to catch the lid but it slipped through her grasp, crashed through the bush, and landed on her foot.

Her toes throbbed. "Yeouch." She whispered in a subdued yell. She knelt to prop the cover against the wall and before she could stand again, she heard a sound she dreaded, the rhythmic plodding of feet slapping the ground.

"Someone's coming," she said and flattened herself against the wall behind the bush.

72

ELSIE LENORE STOOD on the stage, her lid propped wide open in invitation, new steel strings reflecting the bright morning sky. Stefano stepped back, awed by the warm glow from her polished satin mahogany case.

"I'll move the trailer to the back lot," Kurt said. "Need anything from the truck?"

"Let me get my tool case," Stefano said. "I want to work with this old girl. Get her warmed up."

He retrieved his field bag and set it behind the piano. "Guess we should leave our wedding clothes in the dressing room."

"I'll handle that. You tend to Elsie. After I unhitch the trailer, I'll head to a deli in Wichita. Izzy wants me to pick up lunch for the wedding party."

Stefano nodded. He sat on Elsie's bench, flexing his fingers. He extended his arms to the keyboard ends, adjusted the bench to his preference, and struck the first chord of the processional. Kurt smiled as he turned to go. The resonance emanating from Elsie Lenore's belly bloomed with a rich tone that bonded with the wind song in the autumn trees.

Oblivious to Kurt's departure, Stefano launched the vivacious contra-dance Maddi had selected as prelude music. He pulled the accompaniment for a vocal solo from the bench and rehearsed it also. A tender waltz followed. Stefano retrieved his tuning lever and a rubber mute from his tool case. With deliberation, he played the tenor notes. A couple notes wavered from pure, clean tones. He plucked the strings on the questionable notes to identify the offending string in the trio, set his tuning lever on the appropriate pins and tweaked them.

A gunshot split the still morning air. Stefano dove to the floor beneath Elsie, his heart racing. After a minute, when nothing further occurred, he crept out and hauled himself up. Peering over the piano's rim, he scanned the area, the rows of empty seats, the trellis adorned with autumn leaves and sunflowers. Nothing. There was not another soul in the arboretum. His gaze switched to the piano and he discovered the string he'd just tuned had broken.

Damn. Broke a string.

He reached into his tool bag for a digital micrometer to measure the bass string's core wire. *Size 15. I need my stringing kit.* "Kurt," he said aloud. He whipped out his phone and dialed his father-in-law. "You still here?" he asked when Kurt answered.

"Just leaving. Why?"

"I need the stringing kit in the back seat. Got a broken bass string."

"I'll be right there," Kurt said.

❧❧

The footsteps approached the school building on a walking path and passed by without a pause, leaves rustling with each footfall. Izzy rose to peer over the bush. A man in shorts and a t-shirt jogged along the tree line and disappeared.

"You okay?" Brett whispered in her ear.

"Yes. Jogger out for a morning run."

"Can you study the wiring now?"

She stood and wriggled upward through the bush, lost her balance, and stumbled backward into the bush. She recovered her stance and craned her neck to view the box.

"What do you see?" Brett asked.

"Wires tangled together—all different colors."

"Send me a photo."

She activated the camera on her phone, zeroed in on the wiring, and snapped a photo. With two clicks and a swipe on the screen, she sent the photo to Brett in a message.

"Set your phone for a video call. I'll talk you through it," he said.

When she established the video feed, he asked, "Do you have any pliers?"

She replied in the affirmative.

"See the orange colored wire on the right?"

"Yes," she whispered.

"Work about three inches away from the neighboring wire. Careful."

She slipped the phone into her pocket to free her hands. "You want me to cut the orange wire?" she asked.

"Not yet. We will cut it at the right time, but no sooner. If we sever it too soon, all hell breaks loose."

73

THE ALARM ON the kitchen oven blared waking Felipe at the computer. He didn't move. When the shrieking continued, he stood and trudged into the kitchen. A note left by his Uncle Teo was propped against the control panel on the oven.

"Stop the piano tuner, Felipe."

He silenced the timer with a punch that was harder than it needed to be. Uncle Teo had to control his every move even from a distance.

Felipe slipped on his shoes and pulled a jacket onto his arms. He left the cabin and shuffled toward the school, in no particular hurry.

✌✍

"All hell, huh?" Izzy said. "Thanks for the warning. This good enough?"

She aimed the camera lens at her handiwork.

"Looks good. Scrape the insulation off two half-inch segments an inch or two apart. Do not—I repeat—do not cut the wire. Just the orange insulation."

"I can't stop the shaking in my hands."

"Take a deep breath. You'll do fine."

She pulled an Exacto knife from her tool roll and peeled back two pieces of insulation.

"Now twist the device I gave you into the bare sections."

"I can handle that. I twist wires all day long." With the pliers, she twisted the wire ends of protruding from the device onto the orange wire.

"It's time to activate the device."

"How?"

"There's a switch on the side. Move the arrows together."

"Okay. Now what?"

"We wait three minutes. Then you will cut the orange wire between the two exposed segments and get back to the piano."

"What does this device do?"

"It records the feed from the security camera on the west drive. Once you cut the wire, it will play back these last three minutes in a continuous loop, allowing me to open the gate and enter the grounds undetected."

"You timing it?"

"Yes. Gather your things."

She set the box cover at her knees and returned the knife to her kit.

"Now." Brett's voice conveyed unmistakable urgency. "Cut the wire."

She cut the wire with her pliers, replaced the cover, and slipped back inside the building. Pausing a moment to listen at the door, she heard nothing unusual. All hell was contained.

So far, so good.

She entered the building and pulled the door closed.

∼✑✐∼

Kurt drove to the parking area behind the small stage and Stefano selected the size 15 string roll from his kit.

"Anything else?" Kurt asked.

"Hope not. This should take care of the splice, and I'm back in business."

"I'll head out to that deli then. Have you seen the agents?"

"Nobody here that I can tell."

"Diaz?"

Stefano shook his head.

"Wonder if they nabbed him already."

"Wouldn't that be nice?"

Kurt raised a hand and Stefano returned to Elsie Lenore. He spliced the broken string, tuned it to pitch, and tweaked a few high note triple-string unisons to complete the prep work. Seated at the keyboard, he played the waltz again with his eyes closed to allow clean listening. Halfway through Lena's favorite waltz he stopped. He could see her in his imagination as she swayed on the piano bench and the melody bonded with her soul.

Stefano bowed his head. He sighed. "For you, Lena," he said and sat straight, renewing his efforts at the keyboard.

He concluded his warm-up with the vivacious selection Maddi and Dirk chose for their recessional. Striking the opening chord with panache, he ran through the entire composition with flawless elegance. He sat back, palms on his knees. How was Izzy getting along at the Malder school? What if Diaz delayed his departure until she arrived? He sure hadn't made an appearance here. Was it possible that Diaz had been apprehended already?

He patted the music desk and rose to his feet. Elsie Lenore was ready. He hoped he wouldn't let her down.

74

IS THIS HOW a spy is supposed to walk? Felipe recalled hearing about silent steps, using stealth to surprise your target. The shuffle he'd adopted was not silent. His shoes scraped the walkway. He paused and straightened his shoulders, pulled his hands from his pockets freed his arms to swing. He took a few steps. What was it about indigenous people? Forest-wary? Big game hunters? The way you placed your feet on the ground. Backwards. Not heel-to-toe, but toe-to-heel.

Toe-to-heel. Toe-to-heel. A few silent steps later, he glanced around to see if anyone watched him. Nothing. One black car rolled along the driveway toward the business compound, but there was nobody else in sight. Felipe stepped off the path and came to a stop behind a large evergreen bush. He peeked through the branches toward the buildings, and watched the car stop beside his hiding place. He considered peeling out at a run, but decided against it.

As he turned to cut across the grass toward the school, a car door slammed behind him.

"Felipe," a strange voice said.

He stopped and faced the strange man. *He knows who I am.*

In perfect Spanish with Cuban inflections the man explained that his uncle had sent for him.

Felipe eyed the man, unsmiling. "Are we going home now?"

"*Sí,*" the man answered. "You're going home, son. Come with me, *por favor.*"

≪ひ≫

Izzy supposed there existed as many different ways to approach a tuning as there were to approach life. What mattered were the results. But if you overlook even one small segment on any of the two-hundred-plus wires, the whole thing goes awry.

Life can also sour on a small note too fast.

She settled into her usual rhythms on the Yamaha, tuning the strings over the bass bridge to the calculated pitch before she tackled all the center strings on the tri-chord steel unisons, half an octave at a time. She removed mutes and pulled in the outside strings, testing octaves and other musical intervals throughout the process. If a key sounded off, she tuned it again.

Like life. Never give up.

There was no word from Brett as she worked. Had the plan worked? What did Stefano and Kurt encounter at the arboretum? How was Brett managing outside? If anything went wrong for him, her options would be limited or nonexistent alone here in the Malder Corporation compound.

As she pulled the felt from between the first un-damped treble strings, Brett's voice sounded in her ears. "Got him. Wrap it up and join us."

⋙⋘

Stefano left the platform, collecting his tool kit as he left. He bounded down the rear stairs and strode along the path toward a train caboose remodeled into a meeting house. His heart buoyed by the piano music in his mind, he almost felt Lena's touch on his shoulder. If the dead inhabited the Earth, she'd be happy to hear Elsie Lenore sing again.

With a muffled thud, a man wearing a hunting outfit landed on the path in front of him. The sneer that spread across the hunter's face could belong to no one but his nemesis.

Stefano dropped his tools and extended his arms, flexing his knees to run. A malicious laugh rumbled from Diaz and Stefano felt his heart thump in his throat. This was the plan. He was supposed to lure Diaz away from Felipe.

But—where is everybody?

"Hola, Valdez." Diaz spoke. There was no welcome in his voice. "I've been waiting a long time for this day." He pulled a gun from his beltline. Aiming at Stefano, he waved the barrel along the bark-covered path. "Move."

Stefano hesitated. His mind raced in a search for options.

Diaz firmed his aim. "Move," he said again.

Stefano straightened and stepped onto the path, his arms still extended at shoulder height. Diaz fell in behind him, nudging him between his shoulder blades with the barrel of his Glock.

75

IZZY COMPLETED THE tuning, replaced the stray pieces of the piano case, and stored her equipment in the tool bag. She called security for a ride to her car and swore to herself that she'd never return.

The escort car rolled to the front steps. Its driver neither glanced her way, nor stepped from his car. She opened the back door, slung her bag to the floor board, and draped her feet over the case as she sat down. At the gate she gave a little wave to the gate guard and hurried across the lot to the Camry.

Its twin waited in the Natural Grocers parking lot. She pulled to a stop beside the second Camry. Brett departed the back seat of the matching car and held the door open. A grim-faced boy in a child-sized uniform stepped to the pavement.

Brett seated him behind Izzy and crawled beside the boy in the back seat. "*Felipe, mi amiga Isabel Woods,*" he said. "Izzy, this is Felipe."

∾∾

Something didn't feel right. Felipe couldn't pinpoint what it was but something wasn't right. The woman driving the matching car made no pretense about being Cuban. She spoke English. Perfect American English. She and his escort seemed to know each other well. How was this couple going to bring him home again?

The strange woman looked at the clock on the car's dashboard. "Any word from the others?"

Brett looked at the screen on his mobile phone. "Not yet." As the matching car left the lot, he said. "Joe will join the team on location and let us know."

"I need to run inside for a moment." The woman trotted to the store, leaving Felipe alone in the back seat with his escort.

"Who is she?" Felipe ventured a question.

"Most folks call her Izzy," the man answered.

"How is she going to get me home?"

"You'll see."

"I want to know now. Where did she come from?"

The man reached for his arm and Felipe leaned away from him. He jerked the door handle upward, but discovered it was locked.

"Easy, son," the man said. "We'll wait for her right here."

"I am not your son."

The man sighed. "No, you're not."

"Who is she really?"

"Izzy tunes pianos."

Felipe's head exploded with alarm. He whipped his head to glare at his escort, eyes flaring. "She tuned my school's piano."

The man nodded.

"I was supposed to meet her and question her."

"And you have met her. You'll have plenty of time to ask questions."

Felipe grilled the man. "Does she speak Spanish?"

"A bit."

"How can I question her if she isn't fluent?"

The man shrugged.

"Where are we going?"

"To a wedding."

"Where?"

"It's an outdoor wedding about an hour away from here."

Felipe hissed and spat out a word. "Arboretum."

Again, the man nodded.

"You lied to me."

"No. I said I would take you to your uncle."

A fire grew in Felipe's belly. He was heading to the scene where Uncle Teo planned to intercept and take out that Valdez guy. He knew it. He could feel it in his gut. Teo's instructions had been clear. He hadn't followed the plan and he was in big trouble.

❧

Diaz guided Stefano to a path concealed by trees and brush. They disappeared into vegetation and followed a small stream toward the arboretum's boundary. Minutes later they arrived at a limestone bench above a still pond. Several stone steps descended to the water's edge in a rectangular, stone-framed cove. Diaz pushed Stefano to his knees, aiming point blank at his head.

Stefano closed his eyes and braced himself. He breathed a silent apology to Maddi. What would his absence do to the wedding? A pang of guilt hit him. Lena had counted on him to intervene for Felipe.

Minutes passed. How long he knelt he didn't know.

Why am I still alive?

A ridge in the limestone patio dug into his knees. Why hadn't Diaz already pulled the trigger? He opened his eyes and cast a glance toward his captor. Diaz sat on the bench, consulting his mobile phone.

Stefano coughed. "What are you waiting for, man?" His voice rasped with agitation.

Diaz scoffed. "You in a hurry, Valdez? Deal with it."

"Come on. Get it over with."

"I will fire when the next train passes. Nobody will hear anything over the train."

"That could take a while."

"Noon. Next train due here at noon." Diaz raised his eyebrows. "You have twenty minutes to live, Valdez."

76

DIAZ NUDGED STEFANO'S rump with his boot. "How did you give me the slip in Havana?"

Stefano shook his head. "Got lucky."

"Someone helped you."

"No. I had no help."

"Who helped you?"

"Nobody. And I wouldn't tell you anyway."

"You will give me names."

"You think I'm going to give you somebody's name?"

"I'll drag them out of you."

"Tell you what, Diaz. Let me play the wedding. I'll meet you here afterward and tell you everything you want to know then."

Diaz scoffed and raised the gun.

"Suit yourself. You'll never know," Stefano said. "If you let me go back, nobody would miss me for hours. Kill me now and the feds will crawl over this place within minutes."

"You do not give orders."

"Just suggestions. You're the one with the gun."

"I will find your conspirators with or without your help."

❧❧

Settling behind the driver's wheel, Izzy glanced at Brett. He shook his head, a terse movement that she would have missed if she hadn't been alert. *No news yet.*

"Let's take the scenic route," she said in a cheerful voice. She drove a circuitous route to allow Joe ample time to connect with the rest of the team and send a report. After an hour, Brett's phone pinged with a message. "All's quiet in Belle Plaine," he said.

"It's time we showed up then," she said, turning south on a highway that paralleled the turnpike. She parked the Camry in the empty lot across from the main arboretum entrance. Brett disembarked and rounded the car to open Felipe's door. With a firm grip, he pulled the boy to his feet and guided the boy with a hand resting on the back of the boy's neck. The boy shuffled forward and stared at the path. He'd not uttered one word during the journey from Wichita. In fact, Izzy hadn't heard him speak at all.

She fell into step beside Felipe. "The morning light pops out the colors," she said when his eyes darted her way. "How do you like autumn in the plains, Felipe?"

He said nothing, but wriggled his shoulders to dislodge the hand on his neck. Brett's fingers tightened in response. Izzy sighed.

The morning sunshine warmed the crisp autumn morning. She breathed the fresh air, basking in the moment's stillness. The day's pace would accelerate soon enough but for now, she cherished the peaceful garden.

They wound along a path across a picturesque bridge toward the caboose headquarters. On the wrap-around deck, Heidi and Dollsae engaged Bridget in animated conversation. Maddi glowed after her salon appointment. The bride saw their approach and her face lit with a welcoming smile. She skipped down the deck stairs, to meet them.

⋙⋘

Hidden in the shadows with Stefano, Teo scanned the activity in the arboretum. Muted voices floated from the path but Stefano focused his gaze on the stones he knelt on until Diaz hissed behind him. Stefano glanced at his captor. Rigid with anger, Teo glowered at the bridge over the headwaters of the pond. He swore again and gritted his teeth, his jaw muscles rippling, nostrils flaring. The voices receded and Diaz booted Stefano in the small of his back.

Stefano sprawled on the leaf-strewn rocks. He stifled a yell and rolled to his side.

Teo glared at him. "Why's Felipe here?"

Stefano struggled to his knees. "Felipe?"

"That's what this is all about."

"Who's Felipe?"

Teo bent over Stefano and slugged him. His shoulders slammed into the concrete bench.

A stunning young woman with flowing blond hair flitted toward Felipe as he and the two adults approached the caboose. The woman named Izzy grinned. "Look at you—you are radiant."

The young woman gave a nod to welcome the man and the woman, but she stopped in front of Felipe and bent forward until her eyes leveled with his. She reached for his hands and squeezed them. Her touch was soft and warm.

Hesitant, Felipe met her gaze.

She spoke in Spanish. "*Hola*, Felip-p-pe. I'm Maddi and I'm glad you're here. Welcome to my wedding." She squeezed his hands again and whispered. "Felipe, it will be okay. You'll see."

He instantly liked her. Her murmuring voice calmed his angst. She welcomed him, smiling at him. Of all the people he could see in this park, he sensed she understood. She knew what he felt.

She knew.

He stepped beside Maddi and they continued to the repurposed train caboose. Golden, orange, and red leaves floated through the morning air, sprinkling the crowd at the caboose with color. Felipe searched the crowd. At the base of the steps, he planted his feet in the bark-covered path and refused to go further. He swung to face the man he'd met outside his cottage. "Where's my uncle Teo?"

77

STEFANO STRUGGLED UP from his prone position and sat on his upturned heels, his fingers splayed across his thighs. He stole a glance toward Diaz who stared through the trees toward someone Stefano couldn't see. He heard voices in the distance. Was that Izzy?

Diaz faced him and his voice rumbled. "You behind this, Valdez?"

"Behind what?" Stefano said.

Diaz booted him between the shoulder blades. "Get up."

Stefano stood and peered through the trees. Izzy and Brett accompanied a dark-haired boy along the path. His heart leaped. They had Felipe. No matter what happened to him now, Lena's son would have a chance. In the distance, the bride dashed to meet them and leaned over to talk with Felipe.

"You planned this," Diaz said.

"No." Stefano contradicted him. "Lena put us up to this."

"You lie. She's cold in the grave."

"She sent a message—a plea for help. All she ever wanted was the safety of her son, a boy you and I both call nephew."

"He calls you murderer," Diaz scoffed. "You got a message from the bitch? Impossible."

Stefano called on every ounce of inner strength to remain calm. "It's true. Lena begged us to save Felipe. I would not know he existed without her plea for help."

∾

Izzy leaned close to Brett's ear and whispered, "You told him Diaz would be here?"

Brett raised his eyebrows and shrugged, extending his hands, palms up. But he said nothing.

Guilty.

Brett must have encountered the boy while she tuned and lied about Teofilo Diaz sending for him. How would Felipe react to this this betrayal? What fuse had Brett ignited?

Exclamations rose from Maddi's family as Dirk and his mother bustled into the caboose. Maddi squealed and stepped toward him, but her sister stopped her. "Oh no, you don't," Meghan said. "Not before the wedding."

Dirk grinned and shook his head across the room.

Izzy didn't see Stefano, but the reports from all the advance agents had been positive. Nobody had seen or heard from Teofilo Diaz. Stefano could be prepping Elsie Lenore. He could be changing in the dressing rooms. He might have accompanied Kurt to pick up food at the delicatessen but a few minutes later Kurt arrived alone. She mouthed her question across the crowded room. "*Stefano?*"

Kurt shook his head.

A pang of anxiety hit her. She slipped out of the busy caboose to check the ceremony stage. No Stefano. No Stefano on the trails either. Izzy circled the caboose. No Stefano.

She returned to the caboose and caught Brett's gaze across the room where he stood beside Felipe. She shook her head. His raised brows beckoned her over.

She slid beside him. "It's Stefano. He's missing," she whispered.

Felipe's eyes flashed to meet hers and he coughed, spraying cookie crumbs over her bodice. A knowing look filled his face and he laughed, not a laugh of jollity, a laugh she'd never expect from a boy his age. There was something about it, something sinister, almost evil. Felipe was gloating.

❦

Diaz stared at Stefano through narrowed eyes. "How? How did she send you a message?"

"Through our old family friend, Elsie Lenore."

"Your accomplice?"

"You could say that," Stefano said.

"Is Elsie the woman escorting Felipe?"

"It was what Lena called our mother's piano. Elsie is the piano you've been looking for."

Diaz scoffed. "That crumpled piano held a message for you." His boot met Stefano's shoulder blades. "Sure it did."

Stefano closed his eyes, wincing at the blow, but he contained the scream that begged release.

"Get up, Valdez. Look at me when I talk to you."

He struggled to a stand and looked up into eyes that sparked fury. "The piano carried several messages," he said, drawing out the words. "You know this. And I do also."

"Who else? Name those who helped you. Who else knows the piano served as courier?"

"Go to hell," Stefano said.

Diaz looked beyond Stefano and narrowed his gaze. "Damn."

Stefano turned to see what drew the attention away from him. Izzy and Brett disappeared behind a tree with the boy he would never meet. Diaz raised his handgun, braced his arm, and took careful aim at their backs.

Stefano's mouth went dry and his heart rate shot upward.

"Pow." Diaz said and lifted the gun barrel skyward in a mock recoil.

In the distance a train whistled its approach. Diaz consulted his phone. "Eleven fifty-six, Valdez. I need names."

"Like I said," Stefano said, "I will tell you after the wedding but not before."

"Where did you dispose of Lena's piano?"

"Dispose?"

"I need the merchandise that belongs to my family."

"I see. It's no longer yours, Diaz. And I didn't trash the piano as you presume. I rebuilt her. Elsie Lenore waits to sing for this wedding on the Treehouse stage." He nodded toward the open meadow across the pond where empty chairs awaited wedding guests.

The train whistled again, louder and closer.

Diaz pulled a set of binoculars from a pocket in his pants and scrutinized the stage. "Impossible," he said. "That's not

Lena's piano. Julio told me what he did, looking for the merchandise."

"But it is," Stefano said. "She was a real mess when she came to me, but I put her back together, better than new." The clatter of an oncoming freight train drowned his words and its whistle blew from a block away.

Diaz faced Stefano and braced his stance with bent knees. He stood motionless as the train arrived.

Stefano's heart raced. This was it, the moment Diaz had been waiting for. The train cars rattled past. Why didn't he shoot?

The train rolled away and the clanging bell at the highway ceased. The clacking wheels against the rails receded in the distance. Stefano was still alive. He stared at Diaz, confused.

"Plan changed," Diaz said.

78

BRETT RETREATED TO a corner to alert the agents. He checked with them every few minutes to monitor the ongoing search for Stefano. Each time, he caught Izzy's eyes and shook his head.

Nothing.

Stefano had vanished. How could this happen with agents stationed at every gate? Others patrolled the exterior on all sides. But there was no sign of him, or Diaz.

The wedding party split up, heading to separate dressing rooms. Nobody else noticed Stefano's absence.

On the phone again, Brett met her questioning glance and shook his head. Izzy glanced at her corduroy slacks and autumn orange sweater. It would have to do. Her dress clothes hung on garment hooks in Kurt's truck, but she would not take time to change.

That did it. She had to do something to find Stefano. She slipped out the west door, tagging after the bride's party. When they entered a service building, she ran the other way.

≼≽

"Move," Diaz commanded. He prodded Stefano's chest and pointed in a direction to his rear. Stefano turned and stepped forward.

I'm still alive. Where would his captor take him next?

"Move," Diaz repeated, malice in his voice. He pushed Stefano forward, fist between his shoulder blades.

Stefano stumbled along the path. They traced the perimeter until they approached the east gate. Diaz held him back to search for movement in the trees. When he judged it safe to cross without being detected, they passed the gate and entered a sunken garden. Due east of the Treehouse stage, Diaz waved his gun toward the tented meadow where a few wedding guests wandered along the rows of chairs. He looked at Diaz.

"Okay, Valdez," Diaz said. "They've got my nephew and my piano. I want both back."

Stefano said nothing, certain beyond a doubt he would not like the new plan any better than the old.

"Play the wedding, Valdez. I'm watching you. Say nothing. Do nothing to alert anyone to my presence. If you even smile at the groom, or belch out of place, I'll turn the bride's white gown red with her blood."

For a long moment their eyes locked. They glowered at each other, reciprocated loathing in their frozen stares.

"I'm not bluffing." Diaz said. "Not one word. Not one smile. Not one raised eyebrow. You get in there, play the wedding and meet me at that boat launch as soon as the guests leave. Understand?"

Stefano nodded and turned to go.

"And Valdez," Diaz added, "if you cross me, not only will this bride die, I know where your bride lives."

❧❧

Izzy raced to the Treehouse Stage, empty as before. Darting down the bark-covered path, she headed toward the main gate. Wedding guests ambled along the path, exclaiming about the beautiful fall day and the vivid autumn leaves under a clear blue sky.

She slipped out the entry gate and dashed across the street to search the parked cars. Nothing. Back inside the arboretum, she trotted through dormant flowering bushes to the pond's edge. Circling south, she scanned the shoreline and the trees shading the west side, crossed another bridge, and dashed toward the Storybook path.

As she left the crowd, she saw him. Stefano half-stumbled and half-trotted from the brush-filled waterway toward the caboose.

"Stefano!" she yelled. He ignored her and ran faster.

She cut across the forested area, desperate to catch him, calling his name.

He neither slowed, nor looked her way. They arrived at the caboose together.

"Stefano," she said, urgency in her voice, "I've been worried."

His eyes flitted to hers, connecting for a split second. She'd have missed it if she wasn't watching. He gave one tiny shudder and kept moving. He said nothing.

Agitato.

Stefano's behavior was beyond bizarre.

"He's here, isn't he?" Izzy said under her breath as they met on the path. "Is he watching us?"

A tiny nod from Stefano told her all she would know. She moved away from him, without a pause. Stefano retrieved his tuxedo and slipped out the east door, a strained smile frozen on his face.

79

STEFANO MOUNTED THE stage, adjusted his lapels and strode to the open piano. The scenario burned into his awareness. Sun sparkled through the autumn leaves stirred by a gentle breeze. Ushers seated the guests. The wedding party lingered under the boughs behind the stage. He glanced at Maddi, radiant in her gown. She beamed at him and nodded.

He spread his arms the length of Elsie's music desk, caressing the satin finish on her rich mahogany highlights. He lost a moment, thinking back to a time his mother had coaxed magnificent melodies from Elsie. And then Lena sat at the keys.

He cast a silent supplication to the previous keyboardists. "Give me strength, Mama," he prayed in silence. "Guide my fingers, dear Lena, for Felipe."

With grim determination, he straightened and flexed his fingers. They trembled. How could he pull this off? Stefano shuffled music, and delayed his introduction in a futile attempt to build confidence. Nothing seemed to help. Unable to control the tremors, his arms shook from the elbows down.

He closed his eyes. When he opened them, sat on the bench, flexed his fingers, and reached for a chord. Where was it? He couldn't find it. Though he'd played the prelude music hundreds of times over the last weeks, he couldn't even remember the first chord.

Stumbling over the keys, discordant notes crashed from his fingers. He dropped his hands to his knees and stared at the piano. In his mind, she stared back at him.

Damn it.

This was supposed to be his moment. Without question, it was Elsie's magnificent return to life. She deserved better than this. But he had poured his heart into Elsie Lenore for months and he had nothing left to give. At the moment he needed it most, he'd lost his nerve.

Enfocate, Valdez.

He refused to shrink from this. For his family, he must do this. If this was to be his last hour, he vowed he would make it count. For Maddi and Dirk, for Lena, for Felipe, for Melody and Nico, he would pour his soul into Elsie Lenore and live through her and the music. Like the pianist in Lena's favorite poem, passion would flow from his fingers and his feet today, before his hands and lips were stilled.

Stefano brought his fingers to his lips, kissed them, and reached for the keys. When he struck the opening chords this time, Elsie Lenore swelled to life.

❧

Watching from the sidelines, Izzy winced when Stefano played a sour opening. Folks in the audience glanced at him and whispered among themselves.

At her elbow Brett said, "What's with him?"

"He's seen Diaz," she said. "We're being watched."

"Where?" Brett whispered.

She shrugged. "He's here, watching from a hidden place."

Stefano renewed his efforts and garnered attention this time with his passion. He seemed oblivious to anything outside the piano keys and Izzy marveled at his will and the skill with which he performed.

Kurt sidled to her other side. "Awesome," he said.

An usher tapped Brett's shoulder. As father of the groom, he had a special seat. "Can Felipe sit with you two?" Brett whispered.

Kurt said, "Sure." Throwing an arm over Felipe's shoulders, he drew the boy to his side and they turned to an attendant who ushered them toward seats in the middle.

❧

Felipe stared at the piano player. That man should not be here. Where was Teo? Had this Valdez fellow, this murderer of his uncle Julio, somehow bested Uncle Teo too? When the discordant introduction blared, Felipe gloated. This fellow made a fool of himself. He was nothing like Felipe's mother. The man who had picked him up at the compound—a kidnapper for sure—spoke in the piano tuner's ear. She said something back. He couldn't quite hear or understand. They both stared toward the stage with concern etched on their faces.

The piano player struck another introduction. This time, the melodies stirred a passion in his heart. A man took his kidnapper away and he remained with the piano tuner and her companion. Felipe scrutinized the pianist on stage. The familiar music awakened a vision of his mother's face. How dare this man, this murderer, take his mother's music?

An usher prodded him forward. Felipe stumbled along the aisle between rows of white folding chairs, sandwiched between that piano tuner and the man nobody bothered to introduce. And his mother's music washed over him in a flood of memories.

80

THE PASTOR WINKED at the bride before he mounted the platform steps with the groom and his attendant. The music changed and Maddi clasped her father's arm and they moved onto the path. A young woman with the features similar to the bride arranged ruffles on her wedding gown and they processed up the path, lace floating around the bride at each graceful step. At the stage the groom reached for her hand and helped her up the three steps to the platform. With perfect timing, the pianist concluded the music.

Felipe glared at the pianist on the small stage. Every chord and phrase sent lightning through him. He tensed the muscles along his spine and upper torso and sat rigid as a stone between the woman and the man he did not know. His temples burned with unquenchable fire.

How dare he play Mama's music?

Yet somewhere deep in his heart, tenderness flickered. He hung on the music and felt devastated when it stopped. He wanted more. But he wanted the melody to flow from mama's fingers, not from this man—this imposter—this murderer.

That's who he was, right? Uncle Teo jumped a freight train to confront this piano player, up there in his fancy tuxedo.

Where's Uncle Teo?

Why was this imposter still playing the piano? Had something gone wrong? Did Teo even get here as he'd planned? Had he boarded the wrong train? He could be in a different state by now. He would be pissed to find no Felipe when he returned.

Teo was not prone to miscalculations, Felipe reminded himself.

What then? Had this piano player turned on Uncle Teo? Impossible. He could not have beaten Teofilo Diaz in any kind of a duel. He didn't have what it took.

❧❦

Intent on the ceremony, Izzy watched Maddi and Dirk face the pastor, with Meggie to her left and Dirk's best man to his right.

"Welcome friends," the pastor said. "We are gathered here today in witness the marriage vows between Madeline Laura Campbell and Dirk Robert Lander."

The pastor described the love between the bride and groom. On behalf of the groom, he asked her parents for permission to proceed. Across the aisle, Heidi caught Izzy's eye and wiped a tear from her own. With a closed fist she thumped her chest over her heart. Izzy nodded. Her heart overflowed as well. If only Nola could have been here.

The pastor prompted Maddi to recite her vows. She faced Dirk and reached for his hands, took a breath, and said without the slightest stumble, "I, Madeline, take you, Dirk, to be my husband."

Dirk replied in his luscious baritone voice, "I, Dirk, take you, Madeline to be my wife."

They continued in sync, offering the same promises to each other in the same moment. "I promise to always be your biggest fan and partner in your adventures. I promise to create and support a family with you, in a home filled with laughter, patience, understanding, and love. I will love you whatever may come. Through the good times and the bad, I will always be there. As I have given you my hand to hold, so I give you my life to keep."

❧❦

I, Melody, take you, Stefano. Stefano heard the voice of his wife echoing the words Maddi spoke.

And I, Stefano, take you, Melody—forever and ever.

He closed his eyes and saw Melody's face. Mel, all business and authority, directing volunteers as they searched for disaster victims. Mel's angelic face framed in her wedding veil.

My angel.

Mel, laughing as he stumbled into their small home, carrying her across the threshold.

Mel's eyes sparking flames as her rage surrounding his planned trip to the Breeze erupted.

Melody. Mi flor.

Would he even see her again? Hold her again? Cuddle their infant son? If Diaz carried out his plan, he would not.

As the bride and groom spoke their vows across the stage, the words wrenched his heart. *Forever, Mel. I'm yours in life. And in death.*

A scraping noise came to him and Stefano jolted back into the moment. Wedding guests stared at him from the meadow. Had he said something aloud?

Maddi and Dirk stepped aside and a beautiful young woman mounted the stage steps. She moved into the cove of Elsie Lenore's case and glanced at Stefano over her shoulder.

The solo!

How long had he been daydreaming? Stefano sat straight, arranged a sheet on the music desk and played the introduction for the wedding vocalist.

81

IZZY SQUIRMED IN her seat. Itching to run to Stefano's side, she forced herself to remain seated. *Legato, Izzy. Can't do that.*

Beside her Felipe stared at Stefano. He opened and closed his fists, his teeth grinding. She draped her arm around his stiff shoulders but he shrugged it off and pulled away.

The vocalist sang of everlasting love and the couple sifted two small vases filled with contrasting colors of sand into one vessel, a symbol of new life in the promise of their future together. Maddi and Dirk exchanged rings. At a nod from the pastor, Dirk folded her veil back and kissed her trembling lips. The crowd erupted in thunderous applause for the couple, forever joined in a brand new family. Stefano struck the chords of the jubilant recessional music and the couple stepped off the stage.

Izzy sighed, lost in memories. The frightened waif they took into their lives years before had just been married. The couple looked happy and content.

Maddi and Dirk floated down the path through rows of chairs toward a feast laid out on long tables under the trees. Ushers dismissed the guests, row by row. People followed the bride and groom to the reception area. When their row got the nod, Izzy tugged Kurt's hand and they stepped aside, working toward the stage along the edge of the meadow. With a touch on the boy's shoulders, Kurt pushed Felipe ahead.

The recessional music continued until all the guests left. When Stefano struck the last chord, a handful of other guests joined Kurt's and Izzy's enthusiastic applause but Felipe refused. Stefano looked at them and his mouth turned up in a smile, but when his gaze locked with hers a shadow clouded his face and his smile disappeared. He averted his eyes and would not look at her again. He stood and lowered the lid on the piano.

"Come, Felipe." Kurt propelled the boy toward the stage.

❦

Why is this strange man pushing me to the stage?

Felipe planted his feet on the path, locked his knees, and braced himself. The man gripped him harder. No—he would not go up there. Nobody could make him. He would not go. This whole scenario was a lie. Teo had not sent for him. The man who kidnapped him from the compound was not a friend. It was all lies.

Lies—lies—lies. Why did everyone lie to him?

The stranger behind him leaned into his back and spoke in a congenial manner from behind. "What's wrong?" The soft voice puzzled him.

Felipe twisted under the man's grip and darted to the side, down a row of chairs. The man grabbed his elbow before he could get away. Fingers closed around his wrist and the man dragged him toward the stage.

The piano tuner woman got upset. "Kurt," she said, "Don't force it. Go easy on him."

Felipe leaned away from that man, the Kurt, and locked his knees again, digging his heels into the mowed grass. Kurt turned and spoke to him, face to face. "You should meet your Uncle Stefano."

Without warning the ground wobbled beneath his feet. Felipe yelled, and flexed his knees to absorb the tremors.

Teo. It had to be Teo.

How could one man shake the entire meadow? Was it an explosive? People in the reception line shouted and several voices yelled something about an earthquake. Felipe snorted. *Right. Temblor de tierra. No. Temblor de Teo.*

Recalling their Oregon experience, he remembered what tremors felt like, and it wasn't this. This was Teo's plan. The shaking beneath his feet was a cue Teo devised to test his response and his loyalty. He was to stop that pianist imposter.

He twisted a hundred-eighty in the opposite direction, bounded for the stage, and flung himself at the tuxedoed man beside the piano. "*Asesino!* Murderer!" Felipe yelled. He pummeled Stefano's chest with stone-like fists. Julio's killer pushed him away and he kicked the man's thighs with all his strength. The man yelled and bent over, shielding his head with his arms. Felipe tore the man's cummerbund and scratched his neck and cheeks until his fingernails drew blood.

❧

Stefano shielded his face from the enraged boy.

Lena—I didn't want this. Your son hates me. Damn that Diaz for poisoning his mind.

Felipe's eyes blazed and his attack intensified.

Stefano lowered his arms and reached toward the flailing fists. "Stop, Felipe," he said in Spanish. "I want to help you."

The boy yelled and rained blows across Stefano's head and shoulders. Stefano folded his arms across his chest, each hand clasping the other in a herculean effort to refrain from retaliation. Let the boy slug him. He deserved this beating.

❧

Kurt and Izzy dashed onto the stage.

"Hey," Kurt said, "He's your mother's brother." He squeezed between the boy and Stefano.

Felipe's screamed a high-pitched chilling shriek and unleashed a tirade of swings onto Stefano's chest and arms.

Stefano sank to his knees, but did not raise a hand to fight back. The earth rumbled again and Elsie Lenore rolled toward the back edge of the platform.

82

THE PLATFORM SHOOK and the piano rolled but Felipe continued his assault on the tuxedoed man. Other people leapt to the stage. The piano tuner dashed toward the piano and grabbed its rim, bracing against its weight. The bulk of the instrument arced against her and halted. The Kurt man stood over the murdering pianist, his arms fending off Felipe's blows. That other man, the kidnapper in the compound, bounded onto the stage and grabbed him from behind. He pulled Felipe back, disentangling the boy from the pianist. "That's enough, Felipe," he said in Spanish. "Calm down."

Felipe struggled in his iron grasp, but the man wrapped his arms tighter.

It was no use. He was no match for the kidnapper.

"Let's go," the man said and backed toward the edge of the stage, half carrying the boy. The earth tremors waned and Felipe felt the energy drain from him. He dropped his arms. Subdued in the man's lock grip, he shuffled away, looking over his shoulder to stare at Stefano with undisguised hatred.

&\'\?&

Stefano winced at the unnerving look in Felipe's eyes.

Kurt said, "Hey, man, I'm sorry. I should have known better." He offered Stefano a hand.

Stefano declined his help and stood on his own. "It's okay. We couldn't know." He turned to Izzy and said in a lusterless voice, "Quick thinking, Mom. Any damage?"

Izzy scanned the piano's interior and lowered the lid. "No harm done."

"We better chock the legs against another tremor," Kurt said. He jumped to the ground for pebbles while Stefano helped Izzy roll the piano to the middle of the platform.

Kurt handed up a few flattened stones and Stefano arranged them around the leg casters. When he stood, Izzy reached to brush a leaf from his lapel. "Good thing the ceremony is over," she said. "Your vest is soiled."

Stefano ran his hands over his chest and checked the cummerbund and each pocket on the trousers. "*Sí.* I can imagine the lies Diaz fed him."

Diaz. The ceremony is over. No more time.

To protect everyone in attendance, he had to leave. Now. "He ripped my tux. I need to change. Go on to the party. I'll catch up with you later."

≈৬৫≈

The tuxedo damage was an excuse. Stefano was hiding something. Izzy knew it. He wouldn't look at her and seemed anxious to get away from them. Kurt held out a hand to shake Stefano's. Stefano bowed his head lower, and gave a halfhearted shake. She touched his other arm, running her fingers along his forearm, willing his eyes to look into hers, to reach out for help. "Great performance," she said.

"Thanks," he said, without looking up.

His fingers twined with hers for a second, and they rubbed palms. He pressed hard into her palm, turned away, and darted toward the utility building where the men changed. She closed her fingers around a small piece of paper.

Sforzando—what's this?

She dared not look at it. Not here. Not now. Kurt put his arm around her shoulders and directed her toward the crowd at the reception area. The uproar over the earth tremors had calmed down. Wedding guests swarmed around the newlyweds to offer congratulations. Others congregated at the refreshment tables. Izzy fell into step beside Kurt and headed toward the refreshments, an ominous premonition looming about the paper in her hand. They joined the reception line behind Brett and Felipe, sullen but quiet. She felt desperate to check that paper, but if Stefano had been threatened—and if

Diaz watched every move he made—she didn't want to provide any reason for a sniper to act.

At last Izzy stood in front of Maddi. Radiant, but speech-less, the bride's face spoke for her. Izzy offered a genuine smile and stepped forward to hug her. Her arms wrapped around the bride and she uncurled her fingers, Stefano's note caught in a vise-like grip with her thumb.

Sometime during the wedding ceremony, he'd managed to scrawl two words, "Boat launch."

83

IZZY SHIVERED AND stiffened. Maddi pushed Izzy away and looked into eyes glazed with apprehension. The radiance on the bride's face vanished.

"Wh-wh-what?" she said.

Izzy shook her head and forced a smile. "Nothing."

"You okay?" Maddi whispered.

"I'm fine," Izzy said. She squeezed the bride's hand and lifted it to admire the rings sparkling on her finger.

"Stefano?" Maddi asked.

"I better check on him." Another quick hug and Izzy slipped away.

One thought repeated in her mind. *Boat launch.* What does that mean? Was there a boat launch nearby? She slipped away from the crowd and headed through the empty meadow toward the changing rooms. A glance at Elsie Lenore as she passed the stage assured her the piano remained safe. Stefano stepped out of the utility building, looking scruffy in his work jeans and sweatshirt. Izzy waved, but either he didn't see her or he preferred to avoid contact.

He turned and walked north. Her mind raced. Was there a boat launch to the north? She recalled a set of sunken steps hidden in the trees lining the northern fence line. It might have served as a boat dock at one point in time.

Stefano didn't walk a straight path to that corner. He passed beneath a cypress tree and a shadowy figure dropped from a branch, a cat pouncing on a mouse. Decked out in a hunter's camouflage fatigues, he'd been invisible until he dropped to the ground.

Diaz.

Izzy dropped to a crouch behind the stage and peeked over the platform. The hunter prodded Stefano with his gun. Stefano stumbled and continued north on the path. Diaz fell in behind him and they disappeared into the thick brush along the storybook path.

Where are all the agents?

How much time was left before disaster broke? She flicked open her phone and pulled up Brett's number. He didn't answer. Had the crowd distracted him enough that he missed the call? Was Felipe providing further disruption? If someone didn't do something, nobody would ever see Stefano again. She had to do something. She had to cripple whatever plan Diaz designed, or die in the attempt.

Boat launch.

That was her only clue.

Stefano counted on her. She leapt to her feet, darted toward the secluded corner, and stumbled over a leather bag, hidden in shrubs beside the rear access to the stage.

Stefano's tools.

She slung the bag across her shoulders and sprinted for the arboretum's main bridge. Beyond that, the path split and the smaller fork led to the structure she hoped would be Stefano's boat launch. She arrived at the sunken stone steps winded but desperate. There was little time—minutes, maybe only seconds. Could she climb a tree and drop onto Diaz as he passed beneath? The nearest tree was covered with bark smooth enough she'd never keep her grip. Could she hide behind that tree, jump out and club him with Stefano's tuning lever? She stepped behind the tree, dropped the tool bag, and pawed through its contents.

Agitato.

No tuning lever. Had she dropped it in the mad race across the arboretum? She dug in the bag again and pulled out a spool of medium gauge piano wire. This would be a surprise.

It's a surprise to me already. Presto now, Isabel. You've done this a thousand times.

She unwound several feet of the wire and knotted a small loop in the free end with a pair of vise-grips from Stefano's bag. A four-inch thick cypress knee provided an anchor for the coil she slipped around it. She strung the wire across the path, measured two extra feet at the open end, and cut the wire. She dashed to the cypress knee and fed the cut end through the loop in the knot, tossed the tools and extra wire into Stefano's open bag, and returned to the water's edge. Weighting the free end under a stone, she kicked leaves over the wire on the path. The whole procedure took less than a minute.

Time's running out.

Shivers raced along her forearms as she eyed the unbroken surface of the pond. Fallen leaves crunched as someone approached the stone steps. She set her jaw and dropped to a crouch. With a deep breath, she leaned back and slid her feet over the rock edge. The instant chill sent a shock wave through her entire frame, but she snaked forward into shallow water. Propped on one elbow, she lifted the stone securing the extra length of piano wire and coiled it around her hand. She slid onto her belly in the muck, clung to the edge, and peeked over the rock shoreline.

Stefano rounded the last bend and shuffled up a low rise toward the stone boat landing. Diaz followed with the barrel of his handgun nudging Stefano's spine.

84

IZZY HELD HER breath. Her heart pounded against her breast bone and her cheeks burned in spite of the water's chill. Could she do this?

You have to. Deliberamente, Isabel.

Would Diaz see the wire strewn through the fallen leaves? Would he spot Stefano's tool bag behind the cypress tree? What if Stefano tripped on the wire? Things could go very wrong, very fast.

Steady, Frizzy Izzy. Deep, cleansing breath.

Stefano stepped over the wire.

Thank you, God. Focus.

She tightened her grip on the loop of wire.

Easy now. Wait...

She exhaled and drew in a lungful of air. He stepped behind the wire. A low rumble emanated from the rocks surrounding the boat launch and the water's surface shimmered with vibrations. Diaz hesitated. She froze.

Another earthquake. Disaster.

He snorted and shook his head, prodding Stefano. He stepped forward. She raised her arm and yanked. The wire rose through the leaves, ankle-high to Diaz. She braced against the rocks.

Diaz tripped and his arms splayed outward. As he struggled for balance the gun fired and flew into the air. Both men yelled. Diaz threw himself at Stefano and they rolled down the slope together, arms and legs flailing in a whirlwind of fallen leaves. Water showered the rock steps when they hit the surface of the pond. Izzy threw her arms up to divert the stream and the pond churned with bodies. She lunged for the wet rocks the instant the men emerged, Diaz with an arm clamped around Stefano's chest and a knife blade to his throat. Diaz dragged Stefano erect. They swung in a circle, the knife point scribing a dot of blood that coursed down Stefano's neck with the dripping pond water. Diaz scanned the shoreline. When his black eyes bored straight into hers, she froze.

❧❧

Spewing water from his mouth and nose, Stefano gasped for air. Water rippled in another aftershock from the earlier fracking-related earth tremor, and he rolled into the water with Diaz He wrestled with Diaz, and struggled to stand but tripped and swallowed a mouthful of rank water. Seconds later, Teofilo Diaz hauled him to a stand, arms in a locked around his chest, and a blade at his throat.

Diaz swung him around, a complete circle, until they faced the path they'd followed and there was Izzy, crouching against the boulders at the water's edge.

His heart thumped. *Sí—she understood his note.*

Diaz growled behind his ear and the blade inched deeper into his neck. Izzy leaped from the pond and scrambled onto the rocks. On her knees, she swept her hands through the leaves littering the mossy limestone. Diaz shoved Stefano forward, and swung his leg toward Izzy. With one swipe against her legs, he dropped her back into the water. She screamed and sprang upward. Water sprayed in all directions. Diaz kicked again but she jumped his ankle and clambered from the water. Diaz bellowed. He tightened his steel grip around Stefano's chest.

The ground shook again. The pond filled with waves from another aftershock. Birds ceased their songs in the low thunder of an earthquake. Water sloshed and Izzy screamed.

His head tilted backward into his captor's chest, Stefano faced Izzy. The blade sliced through his skin below his jawbone. A trickle of blood mingled with water streaming from his face. Stefano yelled.

Izzy shouted and stepped toward them.

Diaz spoke in Stefano's ear. "Names, Valdez. Tell me the names of your Havana accomplices."

"Go to hell."

"Is she one of them?" Diaz pressed the knife tip harder into his neck. The blood trickled between his collar bones.

Izzy called his name.

"Names." Diaz said, his voice a bear's growl.

"You wish."

A deeper cut. The blood streamed faster down his neck.

"Who helped you? How did you get back to the states?"

Stefano closed his eyes and set his jaw.

Diaz continued his hammering questions. "How'd they get Felipe this morning? Talk, Valdez."

In the distance a train whistle signaled the approach of another freight train.

❧❧❧

Felipe watched the bride thank a wedding guest for the autumn bouquets. "They are beautiful, G-g-grandma Dollsae," she said. The woman, who stood no taller than Felipe, hugged her. Felipe rolled his eyes. Sentimentalism turned his stomach.

A rumble announced the arrival of more earth tremors. The ground shook beneath their feet.

The groom leaned into his bride's ear and said, "You shake my world."

Felipe snorted.

In the distance a man yelled and a shot split the morning air.

Uncle Teo.

The people around him paused their conversation. The bride scanned the crowd. Her expression changed. Her eyes registered shock now. In the distance, a woman screamed. This was another order for Felipe to acknowledge and he knew it would be his last chance. Teo had no tolerance for disobedience.

He yelled and twisted from the grip on his arm. He tore from the reception area and raced toward the far corner where the disturbance originated. Behind him, people shouted. Tension buzzed but he kept running. At the bridge, he glanced over his shoulder. Those two men, the piano tuner's Kurt and his morning abductor, tore along the pond's shore toward him. Behind them, the bride and groom jogged along. She held her wedding dress to her chest and stumbled along while her new husband jogged beside her, pulling the lace folds from entangling her legs.

～♧～

Diaz pressed the knife into Stefano's throat. "Now, Valdez. Names."

Stefano opened his mouth and gasped for air. "Go to hell."

"You certainly will."

The aftershock ebbed and ceased but a commotion from the wedding party rose as people raced toward them.

"Go ahead, Diaz. Kill me and you'll never get out of this alive."

Diaz swore.

Behind them, Felipe splashed into the water. Diaz swung in a half circle. A grin spread across his face and he spoke to the boy in Spanish. Felipe stopped. His expression changed and he splashed past his two uncles and clambered to the rocks behind them.

"He's looking for the gun, Izzy!" Stefano yelled.

85

THE BOY TORE up the stone steps and dropped to his knees beside the path. With her feet, Izzy swept fallen leaves aside, working toward the cypress tree. The last thing they needed at was a surly child with a gun. She raced to locate the weapon. Felipe pawed through piles of fallen leaves tangled in native vines. He swung his arms in wide arcs as he crawled up the low hill.

Where had the gun fallen? What trajectory did it trace after Diaz tripped? He'd held it in his right hand, hadn't he? Or was he left-handed? She backed through the accumulated autumn debris toward the cypress knee and swept leaves from the path as she retreated but she found no weapon.

Felipe scrambled through a rock garden between the path and the boundary fence, fifteen feet away. Izzy crawled toward him, clearing debris with both hands. With a jubilant shriek, the boy stood with his uncle's gun in his hands. He turned it over and glanced at the men still in the brackish water. Diaz issued an authoritative command and Felipe aimed at her. She froze. Balanced on fingertips, a knee, and the ball of her left foot, she stared at him, pulse racing.

Diaz yelled a string of instructions at Felipe in Spanish. Stefano yelled. The approaching train whistled its arrival at the edge of Belle Plaine.

❧

Felipe fingered the trigger. The gun felt cold. Heavy and cold. What steps did Uncle Teo use at target practice? First, assess the situation. Easy. He held the gun. How many times had he watched Teo fire this weapon? He traced the curve on the trigger with his index finger and stared along the barrel toward that piano tuner lady. He could pop her off right now. That would teach them all. And when he was done with her, maybe he'd shoot Uncle Teo with the next bullet. He closed one eye and lined up the sights on top of the slide.

He heard a buzz of strained voices as the crowd approached. Felipe swept his gaze across the scene. Everybody looked at him. Someone stepped in his direction. That man—the one who picked him up at the compound. He stared at Felipe with an intensity that mesmerized the boy. Felipe stared back and swung the gun toward the man.

"Easy now, Felipe," the man said in Spanish, "Let's put the gun down and nobody gets hurt."

In the background, Teo yelled opposing instructions. "Shoot the bastard. Coward. You are not my nephew if you can't stand up to this."

In a flash, Felipe understood he controlled this scene. These powerful men wanted him to do something different, but he was the boss. He held the gun and he felt powerful. It was a good feeling. His face wrinkled into a gloating grin. He relished the feeling and wanted it to last forever.

Teo yelled a warning, "Behind you—fool—you lost your focus."

Footsteps approached from behind and he turned to face Kurt. The piano tuner's husband lifted his arm skyward at the moment Felipe pulled the trigger and the round flew into thinning autumn leaves above their heads.

Diaz directed a tirade of accusations at him at the moment the second man, his morning kidnapper, wrapped his arms around him. Kurt pried the gun from his fingers and Felipe no longer held power over the day's events.

Uncle Teo spewed a string of profanity toward him. "Idiot—you failed to act. Do you know who these people are?"

Felipe glared toward his uncle. "You've met this fool in my arms," Teo said. "You know who he is. He murdered your uncle Julio, your mother and father as well."

The man in Teo's arms protested in a strained voice. "Don't listen to him, Felipe. It's a lie."

In silence Felipe struggled against the arms holding him.

Uncle Teo continued. "These people mean only to harm you. The man at your elbow is no friend to you. He's devious. Watch him."

Felipe howled a blood-curdling scream and clamped his teeth on the arm that held him. The man yelled and pulled his arms away. Felipe turned to face him and pounded the man's chest. "Traitor—you lied to me—traitor. Traitor!"

Kurt stepped forward, lifted Felipe, and pulled him away from the kidnapper. He screamed and kicked with what he hoped was lethal. His legs met nothing and he howled. The bride rushed to him. Her flushed beauty filled his vision. "Hush, Felipe. Hush," she said in the language he could understand. "Listen to me. I know what it's like. I know you are confused and terrified. "

The boy shrieked louder.

"Listen," Maddi said, "Please listen. I know because I've been there. I lived through what you're facing. I KNOW, Felipe." She repeated. "I KNOW. Please believe me when I say this man who holds you—he's a good man. The woman on her knees—she's a good woman. They saved my life once, and they will save you. But you must quit fighting. Please, Felipe, if you ever loved your mama, believe me. Relax. I won't let anything happen to you."

She reached for his hand. Felipe stopped struggling. Maddi leaned toward him until their foreheads touched. She pressed his lips with her beautiful fingers. "*Gracias*, sweet Felipe. *Gracias*."

The approaching train whistled its arrival at the town's center.

86

"I WAS RIGHT, wasn't I, Valdez?" Diaz said. "You had to have help to pull this off and the people you would name face me at this moment. All of them."

Stefano said nothing.

Diaz directed accusations toward Brett. "You there—you are responsible for whatever happens today."

"Not so," Brett said. "The decisions have all been yours."

"You'll soon discover that you don't want me as an adversary. I never leave things unfinished."

"Free your hostage," Brett said, "or you'll soon find yourself buried so deep in a federal prison you'll never see daylight."

Diaz laughed. "I have connections that will rub your face in your own shit."

No longer a mere trickle, a rivulet of blood coursed down his neck. Anyone who stepped forward to end the stand-off could prompt Diaz to sever his carotid artery. Diaz swung his attention from one to another of the observers on the shoreline, ignoring his hostage.

Maybe he forgot that I'm alive.

Stefano hadn't moved a muscle since he'd been silenced by the knife point. His mind raced to come up with something that might alter the situation to his advantage—anything to throw Diaz off balance and save his life at the same time.

My life, Izzy's life, Brett's life. Felipe's life. Melody's life.

One strategic decision might save everyone. Or seal their doom. The decision belonged to him.

Focus, Valdez.

Standing waist-deep in the water, his back pressed against the belly of Teofilo Diaz, his sodden clothing weighed him down. Then it dawned on him. The tuning lever was in a pocket of his jacket. And the other pocket held a length of extra piano wire.

His hands swinging free, they trailed through the water each time Diaz redirected his focus, from Felipe and Brett at the southeast, to Izzy on the eastern bank, to the team of unnamed men circling closer from all directions. Without a twitch in his forearm, Stefano allowed his hands to drift toward his pockets.

Diaz issued threats to all who dared approach. A dozen curious wedding guests stood behind Maddi and Dirk. Stefano closed his hand around the tuning lever.

The train arrived at the crossing outside the arboretum boundary. Its whistle shrilled through the air. Train engines rumbled and wheels clacked along the rails, drowning yelled threats. Ripples crossed the water, jiggled this time by the passing freight train.

Stefano swung the tuning lever out of his pocket. He arched away from Diaz and drove the handle of the lever into his stomach. Diaz howled in pain at the blow to his solar plexus. He released Stefano and bent over gripping his gut. Stefano pivoted. He swung a leg behind Diaz's knees and yanked. The man fell backward into the water.

Stefano leaped behind him, stretching the piano wire between his hands. He wrapped it twice around the Cuban's neck in a lightning move his pianist's hands managed with ease and he pulled it tight. Diaz roared, arching backward into his chest. Stefano braced his splayed feet against the mud-covered rocks on the pond's floor and pulled the wire tighter. Diaz clawed at his forearms with rigid fingers and released a stream of profanity in Spanish.

"Enough, Diaz," Stefano said.

Teo clawed at his hands. When that produced no effect, he yanked on the wire. He pushed against his neck and worked his fingers against the wire loops, in a futile attempt to relieve the pressure against his windpipe.

"Stop struggling and I'll let you breathe," Stefano said.

A half dozen suited agents posing as wedding guests splashed into the pond. Diaz went limp in his arms. Stefano allowed the wire to slide through his fingers and relaxed the loop around the man's neck. Hands grabbed him from behind. Voices murmured reassurances. "You're good, Stefano," Brett called. "It's over. Let him go."

With immense relief, Stefano stumbled for the shore. Six hands pulled him from the water. "Call an ambulance," somebody said as he sank to the ground. Still in the pond, agents wrestled Diaz to his knees and secured him with handcuffs. They prodded him to his feet and led him to the steps.

Diaz struggled, but it was futile. He threw a last hate-filled glance toward Stefano and spat at his chest. He met Felipe's eyes and ranted in Spanish.

An agent took the weapon from Brett. The boy stood hand-in-hand with the bride, twenty feet away. Felipe stared after Uncle Teo without a word.

"Be strong, Felipe," Diaz yelled.

"Shut up," one of the agents muttered.

Diaz ignored the agent. "Remember Uncle Julio. Avenge your father. I will come for you. Be strong. I will be back."

Felipe stared after his uncle, his face blank. Maddi leaned toward him and wrapped her arm around his shoulders. He looked down and his shoulders sagged, his fight gone

87

RELIEVED WHEN BRETT took charge, Izzy threw a blanket around Stefano's sodden shoulders and waited with him while the rest returned to the reception area. Twelve minutes later, an ambulance arrived, siren announcing its approach. Stefano squirmed.

The emergency medical technicians hustled to the stone bench by the pond with a gurney and Stefano objected, "I'm fine."

Izzy shook her head and rolled her eyes. "You will let them check your injuries," she said sternly.

"Only if they let me walk. I don't need that." He nodded at the gurney and stood, drawing the blanket tighter.

The nearest EMT tugged the blanket off and replaced it with a warm, dry towel. "This way," she said and took his elbow.

Izzy wandered back to the wedding location. Now in her travel outfit, Maddi almost had Felipe smiling with her light-hearted banter. At least he appeared relaxed under her umbrella of concern.

Dirk, Brett, and Kurt had loaded Elsie Lenore into the trailer. Heidi and Dollsae had cleaned up the reception area. When Izzy approached, Brett beckoned her to the stage.

"Felipe should stay with you and Kurt tonight. I'll bring documents to clear his travel before you leave in the morning."

"Stefano?" she asked.

Brett shook his head. "I'll see that he gets home, but I think it will take time before those two can be together."

⁂

Back in his own home late that night, courtesy of Brett, Stefano rubbed his eyes and swung his legs over the edge of the bed he'd shared with Melody for the last decade. The trauma to his neck had been minimal compared to his psychological angst, and he'd arrived home shaken, but with nothing more than a hospital bandage to cover his knife wound. He switched on the lamp. The bulb threw a golden half-circle onto the floor that felt alien to the chill in his heart. The warmth of its glow taunted him. Why couldn't he sleep? It couldn't be Mel's absence. She'd been missing for months.

The look in Felipe's eyes.

That look haunted him. What poison had Diaz injected in the boy's mind? How could he repair the damage? It shouldn't be left to Mel. Was it even wise to send a hostile boy to her? If things took a dive, what recourse would she have?

He had to convince Felipe he was a good man and there was little time to do that. Lena was the key to building their future together, as a family. She loved them both. Stefano dug an old Android tablet from the closet and headed to the small corner room that served as his and Melody's office. He booted up the computer and opened a copied set of Lena's family photos. One-by-one he opened and reviewed the images and assembled them into a Valdez family slide show. An online search for recordings in the public domain produced a familiar Cuban contradance and he set the show to piano music. The eastern sky glowed with dawn's light before he transferred the slide show to the tablet.

❧❧

Stefano drove to the Woods family's rural home early in the morning to help unload Elsie Lenore. Mel's parents were already bustling in preparation for the long drive to Oregon. Izzy opened the overhead shop door while Kurt backed the trailer toward it.

"Are you sure you don't want to deliver Elsie to your little bungalow?" she asked.

He shook his head. "No room. I'm looking for a bigger place."

They set Elsie up in the shop and cleaned the trailer. Kurt backed it to the other studio and Stefano and Kurt loaded two commissioned granite sculptures bound for a bank in Eugene, Oregon.

∽∾

Felipe lingered in the piano room, gingerly touching the keys on the piano lady's Steinway. He wandered outside with a melodic phrase running through his mind and watched the activity from a secluded spot under the house eaves. He'd slept fitfully in Mel's old room through the night. He understood he was to go west today, with that piano tuner lady and her Kurt. This plan felt rushed and uneasiness crept into his heart.

The trailer rolled to the circle drive, ready for departure. The Kurt driver grinned and winked, but Felipe averted his gaze and made no response. And there was that pianist, Valdez. Where had he come from? He glared at the man.

A car horn announced the arrival of the newlywed couple after their wedding night at a Casino Hotel on tribal land in Oklahoma. The bride's eyes sparkled with excitement and she burst from the car. She went straight to Felipe, clasped his hands, and touched his forehead with her own.

"We're both traveling today," she said. "I wish you a safe journey. I'll see you in a few weeks."

The piano player stepped to her side, a small tablet in his hands, and Felipe recoiled. He pulled away, but Maddi tightened her grip on his hands. "Felipe, Stefano is a good man. He is a victim, like you. Give him a chance."

Felipe looked from Maddi to Stefano. Stefano held the tablet toward him. "*Por favor,* take it," he said.

Felipe refused.

"I put pictures on it. They will help you understand."

Felipe bristled and made no move to accept the gift. In private, he sniggered at the bandage on the man's neck.

"You'll find pictures your mother sent me of you and her," the pianist said. "Also photos of me with her, long ago. I loved your mother, Felipe. We grew up together, brother and sister." He met Maddi's gaze. When she held out her hand, he presented the tablet to her and backed away.

A farmer's pickup rolled to a stop behind the newlyweds' car. Felipe flared his nostrils when that Lander man—the lying traitor—slid from the driver's seat. "Had to come see you off," Lander said with a sweeping gesture.

Felipe shrank away. Maddi pulled him to the double cab Dodge Ram and opened the back door. She gave him a nudge and he climbed inside. She reached into embrace the surly boy and tucked the tablet in the seat beside him. "You need to see the photos," she said and winked. "When you're ready."

Maddi and her new husband returned to their car and waved Kurt swung behind the steering wheel and rolled down the windows. The piano tuner lady climbed into the front seat and said, "Thanks for everything, Brett."

The Lander man craned his neck, winked at Felipe in the back seat, and handed a sealed envelope to the piano tuner. "This should provide a temporary reprieve if you have to answer questions. I'll hound INS to expedite Felipe's paperwork."

Kurt shifted into gear and followed Dirk and Maddi down the driveway. At the county road, the honeymooners turned left and the pickup carrying Felipe to his new life turned right.

FELIPE STARED OUT the window, immobile and silent. In town they stopped for fuel and the piano tuner dashed inside for drinks and snacks. Felipe dared a glance at the tablet on the seat beside him. With a hesitant touch, he laid it on his legs and the screen glowed with life. He found his name on a folder and touched it. Piano music floated from the tablet and the screen opened on a photo of his mother. Smiling, she held him in her arms and the adoring toddler grinned at her. Felipe swiped the screen and another photo slid into view. It was his mother again, bouncing a baby which he recognized as himself, years ago. Photos from his life cycled past until an image of his youthful mother at a piano floated across the screen. Bright stage lights lit her elegant gown and at her left sat a young man, someone he knew was not his father. He looked closer and recognized that wedding pianist, the man Uncle Teo labeled an enemy. Yet Mama looked relaxed and comfortable in his presence, the way he remembered her when his father had been absent.

The journey resumed and Felipe grew mesmerized by the family history in the photos. There were plenty of shots of that man as a youth, laughing with his young mother. They looked ecstatic.

Her brother? He was her brother?

Everyone insisted this man was his uncle. Could Teo be wrong about him? Felipe proceeded through photos of the two siblings as children, photos where an older woman he didn't recognize fawned over them. *Grandmama?*

A grandmother. That would be nice. He looked up and stared at the woman in the front seat. Frizzy curls tickled her cheeks. She was taking him to see her own grandson. What kind of grandmother would she be for that boy? If that wedding pianist was indeed his mother's brother, he was an uncle to Felipe. That baby was his cousin.

He considered that a few moments. Cousin Nicolas. Aunt Melody. He headed west to meet those people. Felipe listened to the light banter between the man and the woman in the front seat and he relaxed. Maybe this wouldn't be too bad. Maybe he already belonged to another family and they were... nice.

Bueno.

The contradance accompaniment to the slide show slowed and swelled. A collage of images flew in from every angle to create a bouquet of faces. One showed his mother Lena beaming at him. Another corner held the photo of the grandmother doting on two young musicians. A third photo showed Stefano with his bride and the two adults who sat in the front seat at this moment driving him west to Oregon. The last photo to settle into place was a photo of Aunt Melody and the infant Nicolas.

It was a family collage for Felipe's future. He stared at the faces. They all looked happy and nice and loving and generous. And they were his family?

Give them a chance.

The beautiful bride had urged him to do that before they parted.

It might be worth a try.

◈◈

Stefano's phone jingled as the travelers drove out the driveway. Melody requested a video call.

"Good morning," she said with a smile. "How are things?"

"They're off," Stefano reported. He reversed the phone's camera to show the receding cars.

"How did the night go?"

He swung the phone's camera back to his face. "Felipe was calm this morning—not jolly, but not ranting either. I gave him a set of the family photos and he took it."

"Good thinking," Mel said. "Don't worry. He'll come around."

Brett waved and caught his gaze. Stefano waved as he drove round the circle drive and headed down the driveway. Contented coos and gurgles drew Stefano's attention back to Mel. "Who you got there?" he asked, grinning.

"Hey, Nico, wave to Daddy." Mel showed the baby's face.

Stefano waved, pursing his lips. His son stared a moment, then chortled with an unmistakable giggle.

"I wish I was in that truck heading west," he said.

"I wish so too."

"It won't be long, and all this will be behind us. We'll be together again, one happy family."

"Very soon," she said. "Where did you put the piano?"

"She's set up in your mom's shop again."

"It's a beautiful instrument, Stefano. You did yourself proud."

He turned toward the shop. "Elsie will adorn our new home. I'm looking already."

"Don't get anything before I can help in the search. What will it be, a couple more weeks?"

"With a little luck. Brett's got his people on the paperwork. I wouldn't dream of choosing a home without you." Stefano entered the shop and switched the camera to show Mel the morning light reflected on the rich satin finish.

"Stefano, Elsie Lenore simply glows. Play something for me."

"What? Right now?"

"Of course. You got something better to do? Play our song."

"You want our song?" He grinned. "You got our song."

He set the phone on the music rack, propped Elsie Lenore's lid open and perched on the bench. Stefano Valdez raised his arms, brought his fingers to the keys, and played his heart out for the woman he would always love.

And Elsie Lenore sang.

~ ACKNOWLEDGEMENTS ~

Sometimes the universe defies imagination and understanding. *Sonata of Elsie Lenore* offered me prime examples of this. My support team—the village which raised Elsie—includes names and connections that transcend time and space and I extend humble gratitude to all friends who helped launch this book. This includes you—readers too numerous to name—who urged me to write another piano adventure. I hope this tale pleases you.

Thanks to the artistic vision of Onalee Nicklin for the cover design, and to Ryan Fell for its conversion to a book cover. Thanks to Debora Lewis for her formatting skills. My deepest gratitude goes to my team of expert readers and editors: Barry McGuire, Mary Bonczkowski, Mike Fell, Kathy Hampson Baker, Sandra Whiteside Taylor, Errin Moore, Chaz West, Paul Bishop, Mary Coley. Special thanks to Rand Simmons and Tracy Million Simmons for their technical advice. Thanks to Melba Maechtlen and Robbie Banks of the Walnut Valley Music Teachers Association for their enthusiastic support, and to Cowley College in Arkansas City, Kansas.

Thanks to Mike Brown and Janet Dagenais Brown for permission to include the beautiful poem of Julia Dagenais. And I would be remiss to omit mention of my belated gratitude to Ralph Dagenais for extending the same permission, with regret that he didn't live to see the completed project.

My life was changed by a trip to Cuba and my heart goes out to the beautiful and long-suffering people of that island nation, with great admiration for their resilience and passion for life. A special nod goes to David Pérez Martinez and his family for friendship which transcends national boundaries and encompasses generations.

Most of all, thanks to my family for their patience and encouragement during this long process. I would be nowhere without you.

ALSO BY ANN CHRISTINE FELL

SUNDROP SONATA
A Novel of Suspense

IN THE SHADOW OF THE WIND
A Story of Love, Loss, and Finding Life Again

Made in the USA
Columbia, SC
27 January 2020